BREAKING
THE
BANK

BREAKING
THE
BANK

YONA ZELDIS McDONOUGH

DOWNTOWN PRESS
New York   London   Toronto   Sydney

DOWNTOWN PRESS

Downtown Press
A Division of Simon & Schuster, Inc.
1230 Avenue of the Americas
New York, NY 10020

First Downtown Press trade paperback edition September 2009

DOWNTOWN PRESS and colophon are trademarks of Simon & Schuster, Inc.

For information about special discounts for bulk purchases,
please contact Simon & Schuster Special Sales at 1-866-506-1949
or business@simonandschuster.com.

The Simon & Schuster Speakers Bureau can bring authors to your
live event. For more information or to book an event contact the
Simon & Schuster Speakers Bureau at 1-866-248-3049 or visit our
website at www.simonspeakers.com.

Designed by Renata Di Biase

Manufactured in the United States of America

10 9 8 7 6 5 4 3 2 1

Library of Congress Cataloging-in-Publication Data

McDonough, Yona Zeldis.
   Breaking the bank / Yona Zeldis McDonough.—1st Downtown Press trade paperback ed.
      p. cm.
   1. Single mothers—New York (State)—New York—Fiction. 2. Life change events—
Fiction. 3. Brooklyn (New York, N.Y.)—Fiction. I. Title.
   PS3613.C39B74 2009
   813'.6—dc22   2008051085

ISBN 978-1-4391-0253-4
ISBN 978-1-4391-2699-8 (ebook)

For Sally Schloss,
who believed in the magic from the very start

ACKNOWLEDGMENTS

For the abundantly generous ways in which they listened, shaped, and counseled, I would like to thank: Pamela Brandt, Anne Burt, Catherine DuBois Fincke, Bonnie Friedman, Patricia Grossman, Amy Koppleman, Eric Marcus, Constance Marks, Gina Nahai, Jane O'Connor, Kyle Reeves, Kathy Sagan, Pamela Redmond Satran, Sue Shapiro, Adrienne Sharp, Ken Silver, Nina Solomon, Marian Thurm, and David Zeldis. Special thanks, too, to my smart, funny, and deeply devoted editor, Abby Zidle, her assistant, Danielle Poiesz, and my incomparable agent, Judith Ehrlich.

Money doesn't talk, it swears.

—*Bob Dylan*

Money talks, all right. It says good-bye.

—*Richard Russo*

BREAKING
THE
BANK

ONE

M IA SAUL WAS late—again. She raced down the stairs of the subway station, an overstuffed canvas bag of produce hauled from the greenmarket thumping uncomfortably against her hip. Just as she reached the platform, which, despite the pleasant coolness of the September day, still held the wretched August heat, not one but two trains—the N express and the R local—pulled out simultaneously. Mia watched the retreating red lights and wanted to cry. This was the third time in a week she would be late picking up her daughter, Eden, from afterschool, the third time she would have to contend with the teacher, who would no doubt charge her the fee no matter how profuse her apology, the third time she would have to face her sullen child, standing outside the double doors of the gym and dragging the toe of her new forty-dollar Converse high-tops across the pavement in furious, stabbing lines.

However, instead of crying, Mia pulled an apple from the bag and, after giving it a surreptitious wipe on the front of her shirt, took a big, noisy bite. A woman standing nearby turned to look, and Mia, embarrassed, stepped away, making sure that her next bite was not so loud. She hadn't eaten lunch, and she was ravenous. She consumed the apple in tiny, fastidious mouthfuls, not only because she wanted to be quiet, but also to make the fruit last. The organic Macouns, the pear cider, the goat cheese, and the tangy cheddar in her bag were really too expensive for her budget these days, but were purchased in the hopes of getting Eden to eat. Eden's eating was just one more thing Mia had to worry about. As of June, Eden had stopped eating meat or poultry of any kind, and just last week she announced that fish was off her list, too.

Rather than engage in yet one more battle, Mia had chosen to pursue a tack of enticement and temptation. She figured she had to try—for all she knew, next month Eden would eschew dairy products, too.

Finally, an R train rumbled in and Mia worked her way through the throng so that she was right in front of the double doors when they slid open. Good thing, too—some of the people waiting behind her didn't get to board before the doors closed and the train began its journey to Brooklyn. Twenty-five minutes later, Mia was bounding up the staircase at the Union Street station.

It was ten past six when Mia turned the corner onto First Street. As she anticipated, Eden was waiting outside with a lone teacher who was checking her watch, probably not for the first time, either. But the thing Mia did not, could not, anticipate was the fact that Eden's hair, or rather half of it, had been hacked off, as if by an inept scalper who had suddenly lost his nerve. On the left was the braid that Mia remembered her daughter plaiting this morning; on the right, an angry bristle, scarcely more than an inch long.

"Who did that to you?" Mia burst out. "I'll have them expelled." She put the bag down, panting with an ugly combination of exertion, stress, and shock.

"Eden's teacher tried calling—" began the woman whose name Mia could not recall.

"So why didn't you reach me?" But even as she spat the words, Mia remembered that she had turned off her cell phone during an editorial meeting and neglected to turn it back on later.

"I know they left messages," the woman continued. "At least two." She glanced over to Eden, who had so far not said anything. "Why don't I let Eden tell you what happened." She turned to Eden and waited. Still nothing. "Eden," she began again, in a cloyingly sweet voice. "Eden, we're waiting."

"No one *did it* to me," said Eden, sounding too jaded for someone who had only recently entered the double digits. "I did it myself."

"You cut half your hair off? Why?" All of Mia's righteous, maternal indignation evaporated in an instant, leaving her drained and reeling.

"It was in art class. We were doing self-portraits, and they were all so boring. I wanted mine to be different. Interesting."

"So you had to cut your hair?"

"Well, you wouldn't let me get a nose ring." She waited a beat and then asked, "Would you?"

The teacher, whose name simply would not coalesce in Mia's mind, cleared her throat discreetly before speaking.

"We thought that it might be a good idea for the two of you to see Ms. Jaglow. You can call tomorrow to make an appointment..."

Ms. Jaglow was the school psychologist. Although it was only the end of September, Mia had already met with Eden's teacher, the principal, and the learning specialist whose job it was to diagnose kids who had what were euphemistically called "special needs." *Special, my ass,* thought Mia, the first time she had heard the term applied to funny, brilliant, and, she had to admit, increasingly weird Eden. *They don't mean special. They mean nuts.*

"Yes, of course, I'll call her first thing in the morning," Mia said now, deciding that what she needed to do was get Eden home, away from this woman, to have whatever conversation they were going to have in private.

"Good; I'll tell her she can expect to hear from you," said the teacher, who glanced at her watch a final time. Mia knew that this meant she would be charged the late fee for the day, but she was too upset and too exhausted to plead. She touched Eden on the shoulder; Eden readjusted her backpack slightly and they began the short walk home.

Mia sent several covert, searching looks Eden's way, but Eden steadfastly ignored her and kept her eyes straight ahead. Mia felt tears begin a nasty, hot trail down her cheeks, and she turned her face away. She wished she could talk to Lloyd about all this. Lloyd was her best friend/lover/soul mate/husband. And now ex. He was big—six feet four, size fourteen shoes. Big hands, big jaw, big nose arching proudly over a big, handsome face. Oh, and big dick, too, though it mattered way more to him than to her. They had been together since college; Mia thought that they would be together forever. Wrong. The signs had been there for a while; she had just been idiotically slow about reading them.

Lloyd made documentaries about *premodern workers in a postmodern world*. He followed postmen, hospital orderlies, and grave diggers throughout their days, finding the hidden poetry in the mundane. He made a film about a man who owned a shoe-repair place tucked in an arcade at the Thirty-fourth Street subway station, another about the woman who sold empanadas on a street corner in Spanish Harlem.

His last project had been about the Asian women who worked in the nail salons all over the city. Bits and pieces of their stories came glinting into his conversation: one had come from Vietnam at the age of twelve; another had perfected the painting of minuscule lilies on individual nails. Mia had not been paying attention, or she would have noticed that one name, Suim, kept cropping up. Suim this. Suim that.

Lloyd left her for Suim—blubbering noisily as he said good-bye— maintaining he couldn't help himself, he loved Suim *beyond words, beyond measure*, and that if he stayed with Mia, he'd be living a lie. Instead, he had chosen to live in Queens with Suim, and he actually thought Mia should be happy for him because he had found this unexpected gift, this enduring, monumental, deathless love, when he was still young enough to appreciate it. That was Lloyd all right, so thoroughly enamored of the worthiness of his own desires. So authentic, so passionate in his own adoring eyes. So goddamn big.

Once a week he came to pick up Eden, and though he could be generous, even lavish with her during these visits, he was spotty about child support, claiming that he didn't have the money, he'd get the money, please, please, please, could she not make everything about the money? Eden returned from these weekends with tales of the fancy restaurant in Manhattan where they had eaten crepes oozing with chocolate and apricot jam, or clasping a bag from Barneys—Barneys! A place Mia wouldn't even walk past, much less actually shop in—filled with fanciful, impractical clothes. Mia felt sick when she thought about the black hand-knit sweater with the marabou collar that Eden adored—and lost the very first time she wore it. Or the long, pleated silk skirt, winking with tiny mirrors, that was useless at school, on the playground, or just about anywhere else that Eden actually went.

"Take her to Target and give me the rest for groceries!" she begged Lloyd when he dropped Eden off, this time with a stuffed toy giraffe that was taller than she was.

"There's no magic at Target, Mia," Lloyd said; his condescension dripped like honey.

"She needs new underwear, not magic," Mia said.

"Were you always so humdrum?" asked Lloyd.

Humdrum pays the bills, she wanted to say. But when they quarreled, Eden would get very quiet and start twisting a piece of her own skin—elbow, cheek, thigh—until it turned pink and eventually blue, so with great effort, Mia controlled herself.

Then quite abruptly, Lloyd decided to pick up and travel with Suim to Asia; he would not say how long he planned to be gone. At first, he was good about staying in touch, showering Eden with postcards, with gifts: a red lacquer box, an expensive-looking doll with a parasol, an enormous fan. But after a couple of months, nothing—not a word, not a forwarding address. Eden was alternately furious and weepy; Mia was sure part of her daughter's behavior was linked to Lloyd's disappearance, and she planned to mention this to the psychologist tomorrow.

MIA RUMMAGED IN her bag for her key. Their building was right on Fourth Avenue, a cheerless corridor filled with auto-body shops, car washes, and discount beverage warehouses. Traffic whizzed by all day and night; the multilane thoroughfare was bisected by narrow, weed-infested islands littered with broken glass, flattened beer cans, and used condoms. But Fourth Avenue was changing and the rising hulks of big new buildings—co-ops, condos—were crowding the sidewalks, grab-bing at the sky. These behemoths boasted pools and gyms, parking garages and doormen. None of this would help Mia and Eden; in fact, apartment buildings like theirs would soon fall prey to the renovators or the wrecking ball. Then Mia and Eden would be priced out of even this marginal neighborhood.

The building itself—red brick, lighter brick trim, heavy glass doors enhanced by decorative black iron scrolls—was not without a certain faded elegance. Once inside the lobby, though, the desolation and de-terioration were evident: the terrazzo floors were cracked and the Art Deco bas-reliefs on the walls were stained and peeling. One wall was overpowered by peel-and-stick mirrored tiles that were glued, inexplica-bly, to two-thirds of its surface, and the space was filled with a varying assortment of cast-off furniture that seemed to change monthly: a red velvet sofa spilling its upholstered guts, a scarred coffee table of some obsidian-like substance, a pair of office chairs in cracked turquoise vinyl.

Because the elevator had been broken for weeks, Mia and Eden climbed the stairs to the fourth floor. They passed the apartment of their across-the-hall neighbor, Manny, a tough Hispanic guy of about twenty-five. Mia did not know his last name; on his buzzer were the words *Cloud Nine.* He had decorated the had-to-cost-a-thousand-dollars steel door he'd installed with puffy, spray-painted clouds in shades of pink, baby blue, and yellow. People showed up at all hours of the night looking for him; Mia knew this because if he did not answer, they rang her bell instead.

"Where *is* he?" they implored. "I gotta see him *now.*" Mia was sorry for these lost souls, but there was nothing she could do.

Directly next door lived Mr. Ortiz, a widower with a pair of fat, white, soiled-looking Pomeranians. Even Eden, confirmed dog lover that she was, could not abide the obese, wheezing creatures and shrank back whenever she saw them. Mr. Ortiz walked stiffly and with difficulty. Ever since the problem with the elevator began, he had taken to opening his door and letting the dogs do their business in the hallway, much to the annoyance of the other tenants, especially Manny.

"Your dog shits here again and I break his snout," he snarled one day in Mia and Eden's hearing. "You get that, Ortiz?"

"I am so sorry, Señor Manny," said Mr. Ortiz. His gnarled hands were clasped, and his furrowed forehead shone. "My knees—" He gestured in their direction. "Terrible, terrible. I can't make it down the stairs." The dogs, sensing his distress, circled anxiously. "They're all I have."

"Well, pretty soon you're not gonna have them. I'm tired of living with the stench." He stared into the face of one of the dogs, which had come close to where he stood.

"What are you looking at?" he said. In response, the dog uncoiled its long pink tongue to lick his shoe.

"Jesus H. Christ, Ortiz," said Manny. "Keep that mutt away from me." He yanked on the steel door, which emitted a percussive sound as it crashed shut.

Fortunately, Manny, Mr. Ortiz, and the dogs were not in evidence today. Eden dumped her backpack on the floor just inside their apartment door, pried off her sneakers, and headed for the tiny alcove off the kitchen that constituted her bedroom.

"Hey, where do you think you're going?" called Mia to her retreating back.

"Later, Mom," she said in that irritating, condescending tone she had lately begun to adopt.

"Not later. Now." Mia's voice was louder and sharper than she meant. But then, this kid could really take it out of her. Eden stopped, and Mia pressed her advantage. "I want an explanation."

"For what?" Eden turned to face her.

"What do you mean, for what? Your hair, Eden."

"I told you already: I was bored."

"That's not an answer, that's—" Mia began, but then the sound of voices—one angry, the other pleading—in the hallway stopped her midsentence. Even though she knew she shouldn't, she went to the door to listen. Eden was right behind her.

"I thought I told you to keep those goddamn dogs out of the hallway. Enough is enough. I just *stepped* in it, man. Do you get it? *I stepped in your dog's shit!*" Manny's voice was loud enough to be heard even without Mia's opening the door.

"Señor Manny, I am so, so sorry," Mr. Ortiz said. "I was just going into the apartment for a paper towel; I was coming right back—"

"I warned you, Ortiz," interrupted Manny. "I warned you more than once. Now the warnings are over, man. Over."

"Señor Manny, no, please, please no!" Mr. Ortiz said. "I'll clean your shoe myself, I promise. Here, just give it to me and I'll be happy to—"

There was a sudden, excruciating yelp and then the sound of the steel door slamming. Mia and Eden looked at each other and then, very cautiously, Mia opened her own door a crack. Mr. Ortiz was bent over the body of one of the dogs; its small, white head bloomed with blood. The other dog whimpered pitifully. Quickly, Mia closed the door.

What to do? Go out and confront Manny? Comfort Mr. Ortiz? Call the ASPCA? Before she could figure out a plan, she looked at Eden, in whose eyes tears were pooled, and everything else stopped for a second.

"Did he kill it?" Eden asked in a small voice.

"I don't know," Mia said, encircling Eden's shoulders with her arm. Close up, Eden's hacked hair looked like feathers. Mia wished she could burrow her face in it, but Eden had recently become skittish about displays of affection, so Mia reluctantly kept her distance. Mia no longer had the interest or energy to discuss Eden's hair. There would be plenty of time for that tomorrow, when she called the teacher and the psychologist.

"I hope not," Eden said. The tears leaked rather than fell, giving her small, intelligent face a glazed and syrupy look. "I mean, I did hate them and all, but . . ."

"But you didn't want to see one of them hurt."

"Or dead," Eden said in the flat voice that scared Mia more than anything else about her child.

"Or dead," Mia repeated softly. Eden stared at her for a moment and then drifted off in the direction of the television set. Mia watched her departing back, not sure whether to continue the conversation or let it go for now. She was still shaken; maybe calling the ASPCA would be the best idea. But first, shouldn't she go to see Mr. Ortiz? Maybe the dog would be all right if she could help him get it to a vet. Her mind darted back and forth between competing options as she stepped into the kitchen; only then did she realize she had left the canvas bag and all the food it contained on the sidewalk in front of Eden's school.

"Shit!" she said loudly. "Shit, shit, SHIT!"

"I'm listening to all this," called Eden in a singsong voice.

Mia stopped cursing and walked into the other room.

"I left our food outside," she said. "In front of the gym," she added, as if that were somehow important.

"Uh-huh." Eden was rapt in front of the television; despite the fact that she had read *Of Mice and Men* three times and was now onto *The Red Pony,* she still could be entranced by the most vapid of cartoons.

"I'm going to go back and see if I can find it."

"Whatever." Mia ran a hand, experimentally, it seemed, over the shorn part of her head.

"I'll be back as soon as I can. You know my cell number, right?"

"Right," said Eden. "Your cell. Sure."

"Love you." Even though she knew Eden wouldn't like it, she swooped down for a quick kiss on the back of her daughter's neck. Eden's fingers rose to the spot and rubbed, as if to erase the imprint of Mia's lips. It hurt, that small unconscious gesture, more than she wanted to acknowledge. But she said nothing, because really, what could she say?

WHEN MIA OPENED the door, she saw no sign of Mr. Ortiz or either of the dogs, though the offending smear was still there, along with a smaller but more menacing puddle of blood. Drops of blood painted an ominous trail back to the door of Mr. Ortiz's apartment. She went back inside and returned to the hallway with a wad of paper towels and a spray bottle of Fantastic. The larger problem of Mr. Ortiz's dog would have to wait until she got back; right now, she had to see if she could find that damn food that she couldn't afford to buy in the first place and certainly couldn't afford to lose.

She trotted the few blocks to the school. Maybe it would still be there. It was possible; it hadn't been all that long. But when she reached the spot, the only thing on the sidewalk was a Popsicle stick with a sticky orange residue at one end. A shaggy brown dog leaned over for an experimental lick; his owner pulled him away. Mia thought of Mr. Ortiz again, and her heart constricted. She would call the ASPCA as soon as she got home; she would bang on Manny's door and berate him herself; she would—Mia stopped, suddenly depleted. It was all too much—her kid, her ex, her job, her life. There was nothing left over for fighting Mr. Ortiz's battles. It was a shabby, unpleasant truth, but there it was.

She began walking again, and her thoughts turned to the more immediate crisis. The food that she planned to offer to Eden for supper was gone, and in her wallet there was only thirty-six cents. It had been twenty-nine dollars and thirty-six cents this morning, when she left her apartment. The trip to the greenmarket had depleted that by twenty-five.

Then she had seen the guy—pallid, bony face, glasses held together at the bridge of his nose with a bit of masking tape—sitting on the sidewalk, coffee cup nestled between his knees.

"Please help me get something to eat," he said in a monotone. "Please help me get something to eat."

No one stopped to give him anything. No one even looked. One more guy begging on the street elicited no reaction, not a coin, not a word, not a glance. In the past, Mia would have been one of the crowd, just hurrying by in an effort to make it through her own day. But lately, guys like this one had begun to exert an effect on her, a sort of gravitational pull into their own particular orbits. What would it feel like to be sitting on that sidewalk, asking for money, and have no one stop? It would be as if you had been suddenly rendered invisible to everyone else, invisible in plain sight.

The thought stung her, causing her to stop and dig around in her bag for her wallet. She quickly checked what was inside. She could get a sandwich. If she skipped buying a drink, four bucks would cover it. That left thirty-six cents, mostly in pennies. Not much, she knew. Still, it was better than nothing. Better than acting as if he weren't even there. She walked over to where he sat, deposited the money in his cup—it was empty—and kept walking. She didn't watch him look in the cup, look at all those pennies and the one lone dime. But she could feel him doing it even without seeing it. The feeling was not good. Then she heard a voice behind her and she paused.

"Oh wow!" said the voice, bristling with sarcasm. "Oh wow, I can buy something really delicious to eat with all *that* money!"

Mia knew that she shouldn't have been standing there, that she should start moving, now, quickly, to get away. But something kept her rooted to the spot. He was beside her in seconds.

"Thanks for the *pennies*," he almost shouted. "Thanks a *lot*." He tossed them into the open lip of her bag. He was a good shot; only one coin landed on the sidewalk. Mia's cheeks felt scorched as she knelt to retrieve it. She didn't look up, but even from her crouched position, she could see him stride back to his spot and resume his vigil with the once-again-empty coffee cup.

Then she stood, and even though she was terrified of what she was about to do next, she knew that she would feel even worse if she did not make the trek back to where he sat. He did not look up, but stared down at the cup.

"I'm sorry," she said. Her face was still hot, and she was shaking a little. "I didn't mean to offend you."

He didn't say anything.

"I know it wasn't very much. But I wanted to give you something. I wanted you to know—" Her voice betrayed her here, breaking a bit as she spoke.

"To know what?" he asked. He still sounded angry, but now the hostility was curbed by something else. Curiosity maybe.

"To know that I saw you. All those people were going by, and no one stopped, no one gave you a thing, no one even noticed you were there. It was like you *weren't* there. But I saw you. I saw you, and I wanted you to know that I saw you. That's why I had to give you something."

"Pennies," he said quietly. "You gave me *pennies.*" His voice was no longer angry, though; he just sounded worn out and sad.

"I know," she said. "And I'm very sorry." There was a sob gathering in her throat, but she wasn't going to let it out. Instead, she looked down at the four dollar bills—the last four dollar bills from her wallet—that were crunched in her moist palm. "Here," she said, giving him the money. "Take it."

He stared at the bills and then up into her face. "Why are you giving me this?"

"Why not?"

"Are you sure?" he said. He sounded suspicious and held the bills by their edges, as if they were not truly his.

"I'm sure. Just get yourself something to eat." The sob had subsided, but the heat in her cheeks was still there, an uncomfortable flush. "Get yourself lunch."

Fingers closed around his prize, he sprang nimbly to his feet. Mia watched him lope off and waved back, weakly at first, and then with gathering energy, when he turned to look back at her.

SO NOW, STANDING there on the sidewalk contemplating the lost groceries, she was well aware of just how much—or, more aptly, how little—money she had left. She had no credit cards, having some time ago snipped them up and tossed them away; temptation was worse than penury, she had decided.

But she could go to the bank. Yes, that was a good plan; she would run up to the bank on Fifth Avenue, and then stop at the market on the corner of Carroll. True, it was more expensive, but it was getting late and she had to feed Eden. She would buy edamame, strawberries, organic frozen yogurt—all food her daughter was likely to eat. The issue of Eden's eating had come to dominate much of Mia's thinking these days: would she eat, what would she eat, had she eaten enough, how could she tempt her to eat again. It was like having a picky toddler all over again, and it was grinding her down.

THE BANK, COMPLETED only months ago, was all chrome shine and gleam. Mia pushed open the heavy glass doors and headed for the row of cash machines against the wall. She quickly inserted her card and followed the prompts by pushing the necessary buttons. GET CASH, she commanded the machine. There was a brief dimming of the screen, which Mia thought was strange, but it was followed by the familiar whirring sound, and then the bills were spit from a slot. She took the money without counting it, checking the receipt first to see how dangerously low her balance had dipped.

The constant, grating anxiety about money was new, the result of the divorce and the nearly simultaneous loss of her longtime job as a children's book editor. Now that her unemployment checks had run out, she had been freelancing, temping, and even filling in for her friend Julie as a waitress some nights—doing whatever she had to do to keep herself, and Eden, afloat.

Mia checked the balance again; she had enough to pay the rent, which was due at the week's end, but not much more. Lloyd owed her money, of course, but since he had flown the coop, it was going to be impossible to collect it. Still, she should call her lawyer. Right now, though, she was going to go to the store so she could make a meal for her child.

She stuffed the bills into her wallet. The wad seemed unusually thick, so she began to count. One, two, three, four, five, six—but wait. There were more twenties than there should have been. She had taken out one hundred dollars, so why all the bills? Had the machine spewed out tens instead?

Mia checked again. No, they were all twenties. Only more of them than there should be. She looked again at the receipt. One hundred dollars was deducted from her account. Just to make sure, she stepped back to the cash machine to check her balance.

An odd thing happened when she did—the screen paled, and for a second, it seemed to shimmer. A prelude to the machine shutting down or malfunctioning in some way? But no. She was able to check her balance and saw that the information on the screen matched the information on the printed slip.

Slowly, Mia counted the bills again. Ten twenties, two hundred dollars. A bank error in her favor, sure. Would they catch it tomorrow, next week, or in a month? And if so, was someone going to get in trouble, maybe lose a job? She looked again at the machine, the panel of squarish buttons, the hyper-blue of the screen. If the machine made the mistake, then no one could be blamed. She decided not to debate this with herself any longer. It was just good luck, and she certainly needed some of that. Tucking the bills and the receipt carefully into her wallet, Mia headed back out through the double doors and into the street again. She bought the food she had planned; since Eden was famished by the time Mia returned, she ate everything without comment or complaint.

THE NEXT DAY, Mia didn't have time to think about the extra money. She spent twenty minutes trying to arrange Eden's hacked hair into some semblance of an actual style, but eventually had to give up and admit defeat. This meant that she was late dropping her off to school and late heading into the publishing firm where she was filling in for someone on medical leave. Once she arrived, the day took off, non-stop. There were the calls from both the psychologist—clueless—and the teacher—hostile—to contend with. There was a long drawn-out meeting at which she was expected, God help her, to participate. The company had made a mint on the Mommy Mousie series, books so treacly and asinine that Mia wondered daily if their appeal was not pure camp. *Mommy Mousie and Her Six Baby Mousies*, a major hit, was followed by *Mommy Mousie Minds Her Manners* and *Mommy Mousie Makes a Milk Shake.*

Today they were discussing the next books in the series and whether the alliterative titles ought to continue. One hot young editor wearing rhinestone eyeglasses and a miniskirt over a pair of olive drab leggings was intent on keeping the "melodious M's," whereas one of the older editors, all rumpled shirt and well-worn khakis, was in favor of branching out. To Mia, the discussion was immaterial: the stories were smarmy, the drawings inept and charmless. Her mind wandered; it was a strain to look interested.

Finally, it was five o' clock, and even though many of her coworkers stayed later, Mia gathered her things together and raced out. It was only when she passed the greenmarket that she slowed. Given her little windfall, she decided to replace yesterday's lost groceries. She bought cheese, apples, cider, and, since she was feeling flush, organic cashew butter, pumpkin spread, and some onion rolls that, as it turned out, Eden loved. While they were eating, Mia found herself scrutinizing Eden's hair. Did it look a little better today, or was Mia just getting used to it? Or maybe it was the effect of those extra twenties in her wallet—everything seemed a tad rosier.

The next week Mia received her bank statement in the mail. She tore it open, scanned the page with avid, searching eyes. No indication of the bank's accidental largesse. Mia pored over the statement, looking for clues to what might have happened. There was none. She folded the statement in thirds and tucked it in a drawer.

On Saturday, while Eden was embarked on a marathon playdate— Brooklyn Museum, Rollerblading in Prospect Park, movie at the Pavilion—Mia found herself walking past the bank. She didn't actually need any cash, but she felt herself drawn through the doors anyway. Once inside, facing the row of machines, she stopped. Did anyone else know what had happened last time? And that she was stupidly hoping and wishing that it might happen again? Could there be a look on her face? An odor she emitted? The other patrons of the bank came and went quickly, transacting their business, tucking away their cash, talking on their cell phones, admonishing their children. No one noticed her at all.

Nervously, she approached a machine, the same one she used last time. She inserted the card, punched in the commands to receive one hundred dollars, and waited. There it was again—that paling and darkening of the screen. Then came the humming that preceded the ejection of the money, the printed receipt. She grabbed the receipt first. A debit of one hundred dollars, just like before. She reached for the wad of bills. It felt thick in her hands, and she counted hastily. Ten bills. But they were not twenties, not this time. Instead, she was holding ten one-hundred-dollar bills. Mia closed her eyes, thinking that she was imagining the number, seeing what she wanted to see, not what was in fact there. When she opened them, the one remained fixed in the corner of the bill, solidly buttressed by the twin zeroes. One thousand dollars. She was overcome with a sensation of heat and cold simultaneously: her scalp grew hot and itchy, as if it were shrinking perceptibly, while her armpits were suddenly drenched with sweat. One. Thousand. Dollars. A thousand dollars. A cool grand.

TWO

MIA THOUGHT ABOUT the money all the time now: while she was readying Eden for school; girding her loins for another round with Mommy Mousie; riding on the crowded subway; trudging through the aisles at the supermarket; nagging Eden to do her homework; lying in bed late at night, waiting for sleep to come and release her from the day.

How could such a thing have happened, not once but twice? That the bank could make such an error, two separate times, seemed barely within the realm of credibility, but the subsequent failure to rectify or even acknowledge such errors was on another plane entirely. She waffled back and forth about what to do next: Tell someone there about what happened and offer to return the money? Consider herself lucky to have hit the jackpot on those two occasions and leave well enough alone? Go back to the bank to see if the magic would work yet again? She tossed all the options in her mind as if she were juggling balls in the air.

Mia wished she could talk to someone about this. Her first impulse was to call Julie, to whom she ritually confided everything. Julie was the person she called when Lloyd told her he was leaving; it was Julie who listened as she poured out her worry about her daughter, about her growing disillusionment with her brother. But even as her mind articulated the desire, Mia knew she was not going to do anything of the kind. To talk about it to anyone else would pin it down, qualify it in some way she was not ready for.

She hid the money in a box high up on a shelf in the apartment's single closet. In the box were the ivory *peau de soie* shoes Mia had worn on the day she married Lloyd. The dress, the ring, the preserved bouquet of gardenias she had given away, sold, trashed. But she had loved the shoes with their delicately curved heels and their low, sexy vamp and was unable to part with them. She rolled up the bills and tucked half inside the left shoe, half in the right. Although she had used a few, and would no doubt use more, she didn't want to keep the money in her wallet. Better to have it high up, so that every time she wanted it, she would have to go through the ritual of dragging a chair over to the closet, climbing up, rooting around for the box.

MIA HAD HAD the benefit of a comfortable if not affluent upbringing in a large prewar building on Ninety-ninth Street and Amsterdam Avenue. The address was far from swanky; the Upper West Side, in those years, was not yet the upscale, monied enclave it would become. The neighborhood was replete with bookstores and bagel places, butcher shops and dry cleaners. Mia was fitted for her first bra at the Town Shop; her mother bought produce at Fairway, herring and lox at Barney Greengrass, coffee at Zabar's. The streets were populated by men with beards, turtlenecks, and wide-wale cords; the local women wore silver jewelry, Birkenstock sandals, and "ethnic" clothing: Mexican shawls, printed cotton skirts from Africa, ponchos from Guatemala. The kids, like Mia and her brother, Stuart, went to private schools but not those rarefied, East Side places like Chapin or Spence. West Side kids were enrolled at Ethical Culture, Horace Mann, or Fieldston.

Mia's father taught astronomy at Columbia University and spent a good deal of time up on the roof of their building with a small phalanx of telescopes. Sometimes Mia and Stuart would go up there with him, but they were generally too impatient to see whatever it was their father was trying to focus on with the long, vaguely riflelike lens. When he was downstairs in the apartment, he was, despite his distraction, a mostly indulgent, even tender parent. He sang lyrics from Gilbert and Sullivan operettas; he walked ten blocks to buy a pint of Mia's favorite

Louis Sherry pistachio ice cream. On the nights her mother was out, he spent the evening playing Monopoly with them; dinner was Twinkies or Devil Dogs accompanied by Cheez Doodles and washed down by a whole gallon of milk.

Their mother, Betty, also taught—in the Political Science Department—and was a tireless signer of petitions, an organizer of movements, a veritable nucleus of progressive causes, concerns, and agendas. She was also an occasional painter and covered the walls of their apartment with her large-scale canvases, mostly fuzzy blobs of color on which she worked in a fevered, joyful frenzy for days at a time, ignoring most of her other responsibilities until the wellspring of creativity had, for the moment, run dry. Stuart and Mia were united in their disdain for these paintings as they were united in so many things back then, and one of their favorite games was devising what they deemed impossibly clever titles for them.

"Big Blotch About to Devour Little Blotch," said Stuart as they viewed their mother's latest effort, still wet and propped against the dining room wall. It depicted a huge squarish shape the color of a rotted eggplant that was butted up against a smaller shape of a similar color. Mia stood back so she could let the feel of the thing, atrocious as it was, enfold her.

"How about *Grape Gone Wild?*" she countered.

"It has definite possibilities," Stuart said. "I like it."

But to Mia's surprise and grief, the cement that held her family together seemed to crumble when her father died. Mia's mother decided to take early retirement and sell the apartment. Suddenly unmoored from her home and her work, she took several extended trips out west, married a local, Hank Heyman, and settled into a cream-colored bungalow near Santa Fe. At first Mia and Stuart had a lot of fun with Hank's name—"Hey, man"—but they did have to acknowledge that Hank, a short, athletic guy in his seventies who sported a stunning pair of eagle tattoos on either bicep, did make Betty happy. Abandoning all her paintings, along with almost everything else in their old apartment, she had invented herself anew in the relentlessly scorching and sun-baked landscape. She took up gardening, and now presided over a yard filled with a dozen varieties of cacti and succulents, tumorlike forms covered in long, lethal-looking needles. Mia had tried to enlist Stuart's contempt for their mother's new hobby, but Stuart had, inexplicably, become Betty's biggest booster.

"Don't you find them, oh, I don't know, a little *threatening*?" she had asked him in a phone conversation not long after she had returned from a visit to their mother's. "*Vagina dentata* and all that?"

"I think you're being too hard on her," Stuart had said. "They actually look kind of cool to me. And I'm glad she's rebounded from Dad's death so well, you know?"

"Rebounded. Right," Mia said, miffed that Stuart was no longer her partner in crime, even in a matter as inconsequential as this. He had grown so tolerant; she missed the judgmental, scathing Stuart of her youth.

MIA HAD, IN recent months, contemplated asking Stuart for a loan. He could certainly afford it. He was a corporate lawyer and lived with his corporate lawyer wife, Gail, in Greenwich, Connecticut. They both made serious money and owned a big, pretentious house with a big, pretentious swimming pool, to which Mia and Eden had been invited exactly once. Gail's repeated attempts at in vitro fertilization—many thousands of dollars a pop, none of it reimbursed by health insur-ance, of course—eventually resulted in two sets of twins, a quartet of wan, fair-haired girls called Marguerite, Cassandra, India, and Skyler. In their coordinated hand-smocked dresses and velvet hair bands, they smiled frozenly out of the annual holiday card Gail sent to her two hundred and fifty closest friends and business associates. Mia knew that Gail wanted her precious, pampered daughters to have as little to do with their weird, child-of-divorce cousin, Eden, as possible.

"She's terribly precocious, isn't she?" Gail had said during that ill-fated visit. "Precocious," in Gail's lexicon, was code for "perverted little sex-obsessed tramp." Her comment had been prompted by Eden's having drawn purple pubic hair and cherry-colored nipples on Cassandra's Barbie doll. Never mind that when presented with Eden's handiwork, Cassandra had shown more animation than she had all day; the child was so without affect that Mia had secretly wondered whether she might be borderline autistic.

Mia disliked her sister-in-law, a relentlessly organized achiever with streaked blond hair, waxed eyebrows, and a gumball-sized diamond engagement ring at which Mia had seen her gaze, rapt and besotted, as if into the face of her newborn child. Gail, Stu had confessed, was a person who actually scheduled sex with him into her iPhone.

"And the reason you put up with this is . . . ?" Mia asked when he told her at one of their infrequent lunches near his Park Avenue law firm.

"We have a very powerful . . . connection," he said. Mia thought he looked embarrassed; he took a nervous sip of his imported bottled water.

"You mean sexual?"

"Yeah. Sexual."

He turned pink with the disclosure. Mia had trouble believing his sudden modesty—this was the brother who used to make elaborate charts rating and ranking the various body parts of the girls he wanted to screw.

"What, she's so great?"

"Not great." He put down the water glass with a muffled but still emphatic thump. "Incredible."

Mia, both jealous and unconvinced, said nothing.

Stuart's defection to the corporate ethos and his marriage to the über-corporate Gail was an ongoing loss for Mia. Stu was only fifteen months her senior, and they had been inseparable throughout childhood and adolescence. Stu was the one who had shepherded her through all the major teenage rites of passage like cutting school, smoking pot, and drinking. The first boy she'd ever slept with, Josh Horowitz, was Stu's best friend, and as soon as Josh's breathing had slowed sufficiently to roll away from her, she had gotten up and found a phone so she could call her brother to tell him about it. When Stu went off to Oberlin, Mia spent the first couple of months without him in a kind of quiet mourning, but she pulled herself together and managed to follow him there the next fall. His decision to go to law school was initially puzzling, but it had not interrupted their continued closeness; when he came home, they still holed up in his room the way they always had, sharing a bottle of Heineken or a joint.

Now it felt like there was a chasm between them. Stu still called her, though always from his cell phone or from work, never from home. But their lives had diverged, leaving Mia circling kind of forlornly at the perimeter of his existence. She knew he would give her money if he could, because he was and had always been a generous guy. But now that he had to answer to Gail, things were not so simple. And Mia couldn't bear Gail's knowing how hard up she was. Gail had already made it clear that she thought Mia was a loser; asking Stuart for money would only confirm that belief.

Stu's birthday was approaching, and Mia was trying to decide what to get him. Not that there was much he couldn't get for himself—Mia had seen the bespoke suits, the Thomas Pink shirts, the T. Anthony accessories that filled his closets—but still, she wanted to find something that alluded to their special bond, something Gail would not have thought to buy. And now she even had some money with which to do it. The secret stash of bills from the ATM was burning a hole in her wedding shoes; she was in a position to spend, even splurge a little.

One thing that Mia was absolutely sure she wanted to do, though, was take Eden for a real haircut. On Saturday afternoon they walked over to Goldilocks, a local hair salon presided over by Simone, an obese woman with creamy skin, beautiful auburn hair, and an unapologetic attitude about her weight that Mia found immensely heartening. No muumuus or shifts for Simone. And no black, either. She wore her plus-sized jeans tight and studded with rhinestones, her tops clingy and vibrantly hued—red, turquoise, and violet.

When they walked into the shop, Simone took a quick look at Eden and said, "Halloween come early this year?" Eden's response was a joyful snort. Mia had not heard her child laugh like that in so long, she could have kissed Simone with gratitude. After settling Eden in a chair and shampooing her with something smelling of mango and mint, Simone deftly proceeded to crop the rest of Eden's ruined hair into something both waiflike and adorable. *Peter Pan*, thought Mia. *Jean Seberg.* She paid and, owing to her little windfall from the bank, handed Simone a hefty tip. Eden was supremely happy with her new look; on the way back home, she took her mother's hand and began swinging it as they walked.

"That was so fun." Eden said.

"Uh-huh," Mia replied, squelching the impulse to correct and say, *so much fun.*

"Almost as much fun as going out with Daddy." Eden unconsciously corrected her grammatical error.

Mia was quiet; she knew better than to pounce on that bait. *See,* she addressed an imaginary audience, *I'm being good, I'm not a bash-the-ex-in-front-of-the-kid bitch.*

"You have fun with Daddy." It was a statement, neutral and safe.

"Lots of fun."

"What did you like best? Of all the places he's taken you?"

"Barneys," answered Eden without a second's hesitation. "Would you take me there sometime?"

Mia squeezed her daughter's hand but did not reply. Her heart was slamming around too furiously in her chest for that. Barneys again. This was Lloyd's fault, of course. Impractical, selfish, self-indulgent Lloyd, stoking appetites in Eden that there was no way Mia could appease.

"Well, can we go?"

"We'll see," said Mia, offering the universal maternal equivocation. "We'll just have to see."

WHEN THEY GOT home, Mia waited until Eden was otherwise occupied—cartoons again—before she attempted another visit to *the machine;* in her mind, she could see the italics. Whatever magic, black or otherwise, the thing possessed was not something she wanted her daughter to witness, even in the most passive of ways. What if there was some Faustian bargain at work here? Endless supplies of cash in exchange for Eden's health or, God forbid, life? She knew it was crazy, but then a machine giving out money that was neither requested nor recorded was pretty crazy, too.

In fact, the whole thing made her so skittish that she actually donned a disguise of sorts. She located a big square silk scarf buried in a drawer and tied it under her chin, very Grace Kelly. To this, she added dark glasses and vivid red lipstick, a shade she had not worn in so long that it qualified as part of the costume.

"Hey, is Halloween early this year?" Eden said, parroting Simone.

"Very funny," said Mia, grabbing her bag. "If we're going to Barneys, I'll need to freshen my look a little. So I'm experimenting."

"Whatever," said Eden, clicking the buttons on the television. The remote went missing ages ago, and Mia had not yet replaced it.

WHEN MIA OPENED the door, she saw Mr. Ortiz and one of the Pomeranians. The absence of the other dog was somehow weighty, a thing alive.

"Hello, Mr. Ortiz," she said. Guilt, sadness, worry, shame shuffled rapidly through her brain like a deck of cards.

He squinted in her direction; clearly, he did not know who she was. Then, recognition settled on his face, and he smiled.

"Señora Saul," he said, inclining his head. "Nice to see you." The dog minced along the hallway, squatted, and piddled. Mr. Ortiz bent, with difficulty, to clean the mess with a rag, but waved off Mia's offer to help. Mia waited a moment, and then when he went back into his apartment, she left. She was still thinking about him when she arrived at the bank a few minutes later. But thinking about him and doing something for him were two different things. Mia knew herself to be deficient, but could not shoulder the burdens of Mr. Ortiz's life. Not now.

She looked at the row of machines. Several of them were free, but *the machine* was being used by an elderly woman who carried a big umbrella and wore a faded black raincoat, though there was not a cloud in the sky. With an uncertain hand, she punched in the numbers so slowly she might have been underwater. Mia fidgeted impatiently. Should she wait? Wouldn't it look suspicious, when there were other machines available? The woman did not appear to notice Mia; however, she must have made a mistake because Mia heard her say "Jesus Christ," quite audibly. The elderly woman consulted a slip of paper in her hand and started punching numbers again, this time at an even more excruciatingly slow pace.

Mia abruptly turned and walked back outside. She was so nervous she was shaking. *Get a grip,* she scolded herself. She retied the scarf, adjusted the sunglasses, and checked her reflection in the bank's highly shined window. She was not used to wearing such thick, heavy lipstick, and her lips felt oily and slick. Then she headed up Garfield Place toward Sixth Avenue, turned the corner, and walked back down on Carroll Street. When she zeroed in on the bank again, the woman was gone and *the machine* was waiting for Mia, almost beckoning her to enter.

Mia had to remove the sunglasses in order to see the screen, but she positioned them on her head, ready to yank down if the need arose. She punched in the password, requested the one hundred dollars, and waited to see what would happen. Again, there was that mystifying change in the screen's color—first it went light, a silvery bluish color, and then it darkened to sapphire. Then, in the center of the screen, she saw a tiny dot of pure white light. Small as it was, it seemed to glow with an unusual intensity. But before Mia could begin to figure out what it was, it had disappeared, the screen imperceptibly resuming its ordinary hue as the bills issued from the slot. She reached, and ten one-hundred-dollar bills fanned out in her hands with all the glorious promise of a royal flush. Immediately, she collapsed them into a single unit and checked the receipt. There was a debit of one hundred dollars, nothing more.

THE FOLLOWING DAY, Mia and Eden took the R train to Barneys. Mia felt insecure enough to have borrowed clothes—a pair of fashionably ripped jeans, a velvet jacket, black patent leather ankle boots— from Julie for the excursion. But Eden, with her newly short hair and artfully scuffed black high-tops, seemed to feel only a pleasant burbling of excitement, serenely certain of the delights this trip would offer.

As they approached the store, they stopped to look at the windows, which were populated by several pure white mannequins possessing neither faces nor hair; their legs came to softly modulated points where their feet ought to have been. One wore a tweed jacket with a series of exquisite seams running up the sides; another, a short skirt of supple, fawn suede; a third, a mud-colored coat with a belt that looped and tied fetchingly around the waist. All the colors were lifted from a muted, woodland palette: stone, mushroom, moss, bark. The only exceptions were the white of the mannequins themselves and the burst of brilliant, gold-foil leaves—big, stylized, like Matisse cutouts—that rained down on the figures.

Once they were inside, Mia had to stop. She was overwhelmed with stimuli and didn't know where to look first in this rarefied confection of a store. Gem-encrusted sunglasses? Bags from Prada and Kate Spade? A cashmere scarf thick as a blanket? Eden, though, knew precisely how to navigate. She led her mother to a display of handmade jewelry that appeared to have been constructed from Lifesavers, and then downstairs, to the Annick Goutal counter, where, to Mia's amazement, the young woman busily arranging and rearranging the bottles of perfumes actually recognized her daughter.

"Eden!" she fairly squealed. "You came back!"

"I told you I would," said Eden, smiling as she fingered a heavy, faceted bottle of something heady, redolent of jasmine, of magnolia, of whatever petals cost a thousand dollars a pound. Then she set the bottle down and turned to Mia. "Courtney, this is my mom."

Mia nodded at Courtney, but was really agog at Eden, who was taking her warm reception quite in stride.

"Here, this one is new," said Courtney. Eden offered a wrist, which Courtney sprayed lavishly. Closing her eyes, Eden sniffed.

"It smells fruity. Like peach. Or an apricot."

Mia could not stop looking at Eden. Since when had she become so poised with adults, especially ones she barely knew? Was this the same child who was sullen with her teachers, mute with the school psychologist? And calling the perfume fruity—how sophisticated was *that* for someone her age? After Courtney sent them off with a cache of samples in tiny, gold-tipped tubes, Eden led Mia back up to the main floor, to a large tank of exotic fish, where she pointed out a yellow-and-blue striped creature that was as big as a pie plate and another, whose filmy, ruffled fins looked as if they were made of organza. By the time they reached the escalator, Mia was actually starting to relax. So far this had been fun, and it had not cost a red cent. There were four crisp hundreds purloined from the secret stash fairly pulsating in her bag, and she was primed to spend them.

The children's department was on the seventh floor. Eden got to the top of the escalator first and darted off, a little ahead of Mia. She clearly knew her way around, and Mia watched her flit past the racks, pulling out the garments that interested her, a merry little bird in a garden of her own improvising.

"Eden? Is that you?" A saleswoman with brilliant red hair and lizard cowboy boots approached. Eden looked up.

"Hi, Victoria."

Again, Mia was stunned. Was Eden on a first-name basis with all the sales help here?

"And this"—Victoria turned to Mia—"must be your *mother.*" She said it like being Eden's mother was some kind of prize. Which, of course, it was, but Mia was not used to other people seeing it that way. Victoria looked at Eden, whose arms were laden with clothes, and she hurried over to take them from her. "I'll just put these in a dressing room for you," she said, bustling off.

While Mia settled herself on a folding chair, provided by the solicitous Victoria, Eden tried on clothes—a denim jacket lined in hot pink satin, a dropped-waist, pale green dress—with feverish energy. Victoria came over from time to time to offer comments or advice, but mostly, Mia and Eden were left alone, to mull over the options—and their varying, dizzying costs—by themselves. Is this what went on when Lloyd brought her here? Mia could not imagine her enormous ex squished onto this diminutive seat, sitting passively while Eden flung garments all over the dressing room floor. No, Lloyd probably strode around the place as if he owned it, sprinkling his wit and his brilliant aperçus like pixie dust, charming the saleswomen, hogging all the oxygen. And why the royal treatment? Lloyd must have spent a fortune here. Mia fumed, thinking of the delayed child support checks and imagining a secret stash of expensive clothing that Lloyd must have kept somewhere in Queens. She was just getting herself all worked up about Lloyd—again—when Victoria reappeared, cradling something soft and blue in her arms.

"I thought you might want to see this," Victoria said. "It just came in."

"This" was a coat made of the softest, most exquisite material imaginable—the skin of a newborn lamb, no, of an *unborn* lamb, fetal skin, that was what it was, Mia thought as she tentatively reached out to touch it. High-waisted, with covered buttons, the coat flared out toward the hem, full and swingy. It looked like it belonged to a czarina, circa 1900. Mia could practically see the snowflakes sparkling on the coat's shoulders as the czarina stepped into an elaborate sleigh pulled by white horses—then she blinked, and she was back at Barneys, unable even to conjure a price for this coat. However, Eden, with her aversion to meat, would not even be interested in such a thing, would she? Wrong.

"Can I try it?" she asked. Her face had opened like a rose in June.

Mia was about to say "I don't think so" when the price tag for the coat fluttered into view. One hundred and twenty-five dollars. How could it be? Was it defective? Stolen? Cursed in some invisible but most definitely lethal way? One hundred and twenty-five was reasonable. One hundred and twenty-five was doable. One hundred and twenty-five was just a little more than what Mia might have spent if she ordered Eden a coat—and Eden needed a coat—from the Land's End catalog that was somewhere on the floor under her bed.

"I think it's your color," Victoria purred, helping Eden into it.

"Wow, it feels great," said Eden, running her small hands with their painted—black—nails along the sides of her body.

"And it's warm, too," added Victoria, leading Eden to a full-length mirror. "You won't even know it's winter out there."

Mia was still puzzling over the price when she spied the rack from which the coat must have been taken. While Eden and Victoria were engaged in admiring Eden's appearance, Mia inspected the garment label sewn inside one of the coats. *One hundred percent polyester. Cold wash; delicate dry.* No wonder it was so cheap—it was a magnificent, glorious fake. Mia strolled over to where Eden was preening.

"What do you say we get it?" she asked.

"Could we?"

"We could." Mia thought about the bills and smiled a small, guilty smile.

"Wow, oh wow, oh wow!" said Eden, slapping Mia a high five and then breaking into a goofy little circling motion with arms that looked like she was stirring a large pot; she called it her victory dance.

"Good choice, Eden," said Victoria approvingly. She waited for Eden to unbutton the coat, and then sashayed over to the register. The lizard boots made a little *tap, tap* sound on the polished floor as she went.

When Mia paid, she almost expected the bills to emit a strange glow or smell, alerting Victoria to their possibly illicit nature. Nothing of the kind happened; Victoria took the money, made the change, and handed Eden the black shopping bag with its discreet, silvery lettering. There were hugs—well, for Eden anyway—and a promise to return. And then they were on the escalator again, heading down. Eden clutched the shopping bag in both arms, as if not trusting the handles. But just before they spun through the revolving door, Eden stopped.

"We didn't get anything for you," she said.

"That's all right. This was your day," Mia answered.

"But it's not a shopping spree if you're not shopping, too."

"I didn't know this was a shopping spree." They were blocking the door, and Mia motioned for Eden to step out of the way.

"Of *course* it's a shopping spree," said Eden, sounding magnanimous and condescending in equal measure. "So you have to get something, too. What do you want?"

What did she want? Mia was stumped. And even if she had known, she didn't think she would find it at Barneys.

"Sweetie, I don't think there's anything for me here," she began. But when she saw the disappointment seep across Eden's face, she added, "Maybe somewhere else, though. Let's keep looking."

They began ambling downtown and west and, because Eden said she was hungry, decided to stop at a small noodle shop whose entire clientele consisted of Asian businessmen with cushioned laptop cases, skinny ties, and glasses. They ordered vegetable dumplings and two kinds of noodles. Eden liked the chopsticks—which she handled with some dexterity—and Mia suspected their novelty encouraged her to eat. Whatever the reason, Mia was happy. Maybe she should home-school Eden. Then they could have field trips to Barneys to study the fish, followed by geography lessons in which they sampled cuisines from around the world. Very educational. And so much less stressful than Eden's present situation. Of course Mia wouldn't be able to work any longer, but she didn't care; she wouldn't miss Mommy Mousie for a New York minute. Not even for a New York nanosecond.

"This has been the best day ever," Eden announced when they were back outside.

Better than the time you went with your father? Mia wanted to ask. But didn't. She did, however, sense that it would be permissible to drape her arm casually across Eden's shoulders. She only half listened as Eden chattered, really just wanting to feel the subtle architecture of Eden's small bones, to inhale the familiar girl-child scent of her as they walked.

"Mom." Eden slowed and pulled her arm. "Look at this."

"This" did not turn out to be anything so remarkable: a small, easily ignored jewelry store wedged in between a deli and a florist. The faded sign read MOFCHUM AND SONS. ESTATE JEWELRY. Through the grimy window, which had probably not been cleaned in a decade, Mia saw watches and chains, bracelets and pins, all heaped together with little or no apparent care. It was exactly the sort of shop that Lloyd would have loved and wanted to make a documentary about; she could see him striding in, surveying the scene, taking over. All the more reason for Mia to avoid it.

"Let's go in," Eden said. "This might be the place."

"The place?"

"Where we find something for you."

Mia had hoped Eden had forgotten about the idea of Mia's buying something for herself. Wrong. Reluctantly, she followed Eden inside. Behind the counter sat a slope-shouldered man with a broad, freckled forehead. His watery green eyes looked Mia and Eden over, though he didn't say anything, just nodded in their direction.

"This is *so* pretty," said Eden, gesturing to a cameo brooch pinned to a piece of black velvet. "Look at her face—it's, like, perfect. How did they do that?" Mia leaned over to see. The girl's tiny features were expertly carved, and a tendril of hair escaped from her chignon, grazing her smoothly rendered cheek. The thing was no bigger than a domino.

"That's one of the best pieces in the shop," said the man behind the counter. His voice was reedy, as if he didn't use it often. "You have a good eye."

"I know," Eden said serenely. "People have said that to me before."

"Are you looking for cameos? Because I've got others." He began to look around, his head stretching on his neck like a large turtle. Mia didn't know how he could locate anything in all the mess. The displays—if you could grace them with such a word—were no better than those in the window, everything crammed and jumbled. But Eden seemed entranced—touching this, exclaiming over that.

"All this stuff is really old, right?" she asked.

"Absolutely," said the man. "And every piece has a story."

"Really? Tell me about this one." Eden pointed to another pin. Eight little gold birds sitting on a golden branch. Several sparkling chips—red, blue, green—were set into their tails.

"Oh, now that. Well, that piece was made in Canada, yes, it was. And an older gentleman bought it for his granddaughter, who must have been, let me see . . ." He looked at Eden, clearly trying to assess her age. "Eleven. Yes, that was it. Eleven."

"I'm almost eleven," Eden said proudly.

"Well, this little girl's name was Alice, and she . . ."

Mia stopped listening. She was trying to figure out a way to extricate herself without actually having to buy something. Eden's impulse was undeniably sweet and even laudable, but the last thing Mia needed now was a piece of jewelry when she was worried about her rent, electric bills, and Eden's impending orthodontia. Then she saw it. A flat gold locket, maybe two inches across, suspended from a braided gold chain. It was perfectly round and sported no embellishment of any kind. Simple, but elegant. Rich, but restrained. The kind of thing that looked like it would be passed down, woman to girl, for generations. She had to touch it, to try it on.

"Now those earrings—the stones are topaz, by the way—were worn by a famous actress on the Broadway stage . . ." the man was saying to an increasingly enchanted Eden.

The locket seemed to settle into the perfect spot on Mia's neck. It was heavy enough to feel substantial but light enough to be worn every day. Peering down, she clicked open the cunningly hidden clasp at the bottom. A pair of time-bleached photographs, a tow-headed boy and girl, squinted back at her. Someone's darlings. She closed it again. Under her fingers, the gold tablet felt smooth and almost edible; she had an urge to take it in her mouth. What would gold taste like anyway?

"Ah, you found it!" He turned his gaze to Mia. "Keats's locket."

"Keats? Who's he?" asked Eden.

"An English poet who lived a long time ago."

"Did he own that necklace?"

The man smiled. "Not likely. I just call it that because it seems like something he would have liked. Something he might have given to Fanny." He directed this comment to Mia.

"Fanny?" Eden asked.

"His beloved," the man answered. "But he died young and didn't get to marry her." When he saw the look on Eden's face, he continued. "Fanny would have cherished that locket; she would have worn it every day of her life, to remember him when he was gone."

"That's so sad," said Eden, seeming to forget that this was all an invention.

The man nodded. "She might have put a little picture of him inside. Not a photograph, of course. But a tiny drawing. Or a lock of his hair."

"Hair? Eeew! That's so creepy!" said Eden. But she was clearly delighted by these morbid details.

The man bent over and began hunting for something now; he lifted yellowed newspapers and moved aside crumpled paper bags. "Here," he said, offering Mia a hand mirror with a beveled edge; the glass was speckled with dust, and a jagged crack ran down its center.

"Bad luck?" she said, but she was teasing; her bad luck had happened already, and it had had nothing to do with a mirror.

"You have to buy that," Eden declared.

Mia hesitated. The locket felt so good around her neck. Like it belonged there. But it wasn't as if she really needed it. Then she looked at Eden, whose expression had turned oddly serious.

"Maybe I do," she said finally. "How much is it?"

"Two hundred and fifty."

Two hundred and fifty was very reasonable for this locket. In fact, given the high price of gold, it was a steal. Still, that same two hundred and fifty dollars could have gone toward so many other things. But Mia wanted the locket. Wanted it in a way she had not wanted anything in a long time. At least any material thing.

"I could do a little better if you were seriously interested. Say two hundred?"

Mia looked at the man, presumably the Mofchum—or one of

them—indicated on the sign. She saw the dispirited slope of his shoulders, the defeated look of his mottled forehead. How long had it been since he'd made a sale? How long could a little dump like this, the kind of little dump that made New York so quirky and so interesting, stay afloat?

"Two hundred," she repeated, and peeled the bills into his hands.

"I'm glad it's going to you," he said. "You're its rightful owner." Mia must have looked puzzled because he said, "Every piece has its rightful owner. It may take years for the two of you to find each other. But usually you do."

Mia declined a bag; she had already decided she wasn't going to take the thing off. Before she left, he pressed his card—graying, with worn, bent corners—into her hand. GERALD MOFCHUM. FINE JEWELRY. BUY AND SELL.

"Come back and see me again," he said. "And bring your daughter." He turned to Eden. "I've got something for you, too." He fumbled through one of the display cases until he found what he was looking for—a link bracelet that jingled with a cluster of gold-tone charms. "Let me tell you about this . . ." he said. It was another ten minutes before they left the shop and emerged onto the street.

"See?" Eden said. "I told you that was the right place." She shook her wrist and the charms on her bracelet tinkled.

"You were right."

"Where's the locket? I want to touch it."

Mia leaned forward so Eden could reach.

"Who are they?" Her fingers had found the clasp, and she snapped the locket open, revealing the two blond children.

"I don't know," said Mia. "But someone must have loved them very much."

"Are you going to leave them in there?"

"No, I'll keep them somewhere safe. But I want a picture of you in there."

Eden thought about that for a moment and then asked, "What about the other side?"

"I haven't figured that out yet," Mia said.

Eden looked like she was going to say something else, but a raindrop landed on her head with a small plop and she looked up instead. Mia followed her gaze. Clouds that had been hovering for much of the day had begun to gather and darken. She wondered whether it would be worth buying an umbrella. As soon as rain threatened in the city, the streets seemed to spawn guys hawking cheap, folding versions with spokes that turned inside out in the slightest wind. The insistent cries of the vendors—UM-brella, UM-brella—were one of those distinctive New York melodies.

Looking around for one such vendor now, Mia saw instead a small black woman wearing a green plastic trash bag over her clothes. She was sitting with her back against a building, her legs tucked under her like a cat. A cardboard box sat in front of her.

As Mia and Eden approached, Mia could see that the woman had actually done a decent job of adapting the bag into a garment; there were holes cut for her arms, and she tied a sash of some kind around her waist. The cardboard box with its neatly lettered message—PLEASE HELP—held a few coins and a single crumpled dollar bill.

When she and Eden reached the woman, the sky suddenly opened and it began to pour. Quickly, the woman grabbed the box and scooted it underneath her, using the bottom of the bag as a kind of tent. Then she pulled the neckline of the bag up and over the back of her head. All this was done in mere seconds, as if she had done it many times before. Watching, Mia felt as if she were coming apart, a stuffed toy with sawdust leaking in a slow, snail-like trail behind her. She quickly ushered Eden under an awning, where they stood, shaking off the rain.

"My Barneys bag is wet," said Eden, rubbing the drops away with her forearm; again, the charm bracelet jingled.

"It should be okay until we get home."

"I wanted to keep it. I'm collecting shopping bags."

"You are?" This was news to Mia.

"Well, I'm starting today. This is going to be the first one. And now it's ruined."

"Not ruined," said Mia. "We'll leave it out to dry when we get home, and I'll press it flat under some books. It will be fine." All the while Mia was mouthing this soothing parental patois, she was watching the woman wearing the garbage bag. She huddled under it, managing to keep reasonably dry. It would have been easy enough for her to get up and try to find shelter elsewhere. Or maybe not. Maybe her feet hurt or she knew that there was a good chance she'd be asked to move. She didn't look unhappy though. She looked resigned, adjusting the bag more securely over her head, wiping water from her cheek.

Mia thought of the last few hours: wandering through Barneys, ogling, fondling, getting, spending. Then the stop at the jewelry store. More ogling. More spending. Around her neck Mia now wore a golden locket; in her bag was the card that Gerald Mofchum had given her. *Buy and Sell.* But there were other transactions, weren't there? What about *Give and Receive?* She flashed onto the bills, bills that were not technically hers yet had somehow found their way into her hands and her wallet.

"Stay right here," she instructed Eden.

"Where are you going?"

"Over there." She pointed to where the woman in the bag sat.

"Why?"

"I have to do something."

"Tell me," Eden said, a familiar whine creeping into her voice.

"I'll tell you everything in just a minute, sweetie," Mia said patiently, now quite sure of what she had to do.

She stepped from the awning into the rain, which had tapered off a bit, and toward the woman. She thought of Mr. Ortiz and his dog, the guy on the street with his coffee cup. The shame of that exchange was breathing in her ear now, propelling her forward. Wanting to help someone wasn't enough. You either helped. Or you failed.

The woman looked up. Her eyes were large and brown; the lid of one of them drooped a little, making it seem as if she were winking, a slow, private gesture.

"Here," said Mia. In her hand were three twenties. "These are for you."

THREE

MIA WAS ROUSED the following morning by the bleating of her cell phone. She groped around the floor near her bed until she found it, sitting on top of the copy of *Swann's Way* she had been moving around her bedroom for months, without summoning the energy to open and read.

"Hello?" Her voice was sleep-cracked and raspy, which she hated; it always put her at a disadvantage. What time was it anyway?

"Mia honey?"

"Mom. Hi." Mia leaned back into the pillow, trying to keep her voice low. Sometime in the middle of the night, Eden had had a bad dream and had climbed into bed with her. She was still there, burrowed into the blanket on one side of the mattress, and Mia didn't want to wake her.

"You sound congested. Do you have a cold?"

"No. No cold."

"Then what? I didn't wake you, did I?"

"Of course not. I've been up for ages," Mia fibbed. Back when she and Stu were still teenagers and living at home, Betty had made it clear that sleeping late was for losers, deadbeats, slackers. She herself took great pride in the fact that she rose between five and five thirty every morning. *I'll sleep when I'm dead*, she would announce proudly.

"That's good," her mother said. "I'm sure you're busy."

"Oh, that I am," Mia said. "Busy as a bee."

"But not too busy to pay us a visit," said her mother.

"A visit?" How was she going to afford a trip out west?

"I was actually hoping you'd come for Thanksgiving."

"Thanksgiving is not until the end of November," Mia said.

"If you want to get a good deal on the airfare, you have to book early."

Mia knew her mother was right about this, so she approached the subject from a different angle.

"What about Stu?" she asked. "Did you invite him, too?"

"Well, I think he and Gail were planning to go to her family. But if I tell him you and Eden are coming this year, it might change his mind."

"Really?" asked Mia. Her mother didn't just live in a different state now; she lived on a different planet. Didn't she know that Gail would no sooner spend a holiday weekend in New Mexico with Mia and Eden than she would board the New York City–bound train from Greenwich stark naked and singing "Amazing Grace"?

"Yes, it would be so wonderful to see all of you. Hank wants to do the cooking; did you know he's a fabulous cook?"

"So you've said." Mia had her doubts about this; her mother had always displayed a cheerful and marked indifference to food. Stuart used to say that it wasn't Betty's ear that was tin; it was her palate.

"He's found all these regionally inspired recipes. Fire-roasted turkey. Sausage, sage, and chipotle stuffing."

None of which Eden will eat, Mia thought. *But why bring that up now?*

"I can talk to him about it if you'd like," Mia offered.

"Would you? That would be so nice. He thinks the world of you, Mia honey. I just love that the two of you are still so close."

"Yeah, that's us all right. Couldn't be closer."

They talked for a few more minutes before saying good-bye. Eden rolled over, flung an arm out in Mia's direction, but remained asleep. They had stayed up late the night before making popcorn and brownies, which they ate while watching *Saturday Night Fever* on late-night TV. Even all these years later, the sight of John Travolta with his blow-dried black hair and eyes as cool and blue as a Siberian husky's stirred something in Mia. Regrettably, Travolta had of late lost his avid, lupine look and had instead puffed out like a blowfish. He'd become a Scientologist, too. *Johnny baby,* she wished she could ask, *where did you go?* As if he—or any of the other men she'd wanted to ask, ex, brother, father—could have told her.

Lying in bed, Mia mulled over her mother's request and knew that, irritated as it would make her, she would call her brother and extend the invitation. Though if this plan did actually materialize, she didn't know how she would pay for the plane tickets or, worse, tell her mother that she wasn't able to. Betty was not an ungenerous soul, but she was certainly not rolling in dough the way Stuart was. And her mother did not believe that any money she did give to Mia would be used well. *You're extravagant,* Betty had said, more than once. *You're worrying about rent and you take her to Barneys?*

STILL HOLDING THE phone, Mia rummaged around for her clock, which had, as it turned out, gotten kicked under the bed. It was a bit dusty, and she tried to muffle the resulting sneeze. Eden stirred, but slept on. It was past ten. Mia debated waking her; if she didn't, she would never be able to get her to go to sleep that night and tomorrow morning would be a fresh hell.

She was just about to do it when the phone bleated again. It was probably her mother, calling with something she'd forgotten to say during their initial conversation. Calls from Betty usually took place in several installments; when Mia clicked back on, she didn't even bother to read the number on the screen. But it was not her mother on the line. It was Lloyd.

"Hey," he said in that rich, resonant baritone of his that always got to her, even now, after everything he had done. "How's it going?"

"How's it going?" she echoed. "What do you mean, *How's it going?* Where have you been all this time? What about Eden? Did you just forget about her?" Mia tried to keep her voice down. But Eden must have had a Daddy radar that worked even when she was asleep, because she briefly lifted her head from the pillow and gave Mia a baleful look.

"I know I should have called sooner, but you have no idea how crazy things have been. But I'm calling now, aren't I? Let me talk to Eden."

"Well, isn't that just dandy! How about all that time when she didn't hear a word from you, not a single word——"

"Who's that?" Eden sat up.

"Is she right there? I know she's there. Let me talk to her."

"Is that Daddy?" asked Eden at practically the same moment. When Mia didn't answer, Eden reached for the phone. "It *is* Daddy, I know it is. I want to talk to him!"

Mia handed the phone to Eden and then, so she was not tempted to eavesdrop, got out of bed. The apartment was cold, and she found a sweater to pull on over her T-shirt and sweats. But she couldn't locate her flip-flops or even a pair of socks, so she padded into the kitchen barefoot. It was still a mess from the night before—bowl sloshing in the sink, dots of batter blobbed all over. The brownies were on the counter, and Mia broke off a piece to munch on while she made coffee. She could hear Eden, still in bed, giggling. Snatches of conversation drifted in her direction.

"And then that stupid teacher——"

"Mom and I went to——"

"So the boy who sits behind me——"

"I miss you; when are you coming?"

Was it an accident that Mia overheard that last sentence in its entirety, or had Eden's voice gotten louder, for emphasis? She stood, still barefoot, still chilly, in the kitchen, looking out the window as she sipped her coffee. It was not much of a view—a glimpse of the tiny backyards on Garfield Place—but it was better than the constant stream of cars and trucks that barreled down Fourth Avenue. And there was something so uselessly, heartbreakingly hopeful about the way people made use of even the smallest of outdoor spaces, cramming them with grills, picnic tables, aboveground pools, sandboxes, flower pots, metal chairs, a collapsed beach ball, a rusted red tricycle.

"Mom." Eden appeared behind her, breaking into her reverie. "Daddy wants to talk to you. Here." She gave Mia the phone, pulled off a big piece of brownie, and disappeared before Mia could say, *No, wait, you haven't had breakfast.*

"She sounds good," Lloyd said.

"You think? That's because you haven't been talking to her teacher or anyone else at her school."

"Do you want me to? Because I will, you know. Just give me the names and numbers. I'm there. I am *so* there."

While Mia debated whether a conversation between Lloyd and Eden's teacher would be a good or a bad thing, she heard someone in the background say something about a latte.

"Where are you anyway? Since when are they serving lattes in Sri Lanka?"

"Who said I'm in Sri Lanka?"

"Seoul then."

"Wrong again." These words were followed by a silence.

"So are you going to tell me where, exactly, you are?"

"L.A. And I'll be in New York next week."

"L.A.? What are you doing in L.A.?"

"I had to see some people here. There's been interest in some of my stuff. They flew me in for a meeting."

"Oh," she said. "Great." Was it? She was trying to process all this information—Lloyd in L.A., Lloyd in New York, Lloyd with a potential Hollywood deal—when she realized he was still talking to her.

". . . So I'll be there at the end of next week. Thursday, maybe Friday. I can let you know when it's firmed up. I want to see Eden. Of course."

"You can take her for the weekend. She'll be thrilled; in case you haven't guessed, she's missed you. Where will you be staying anyway?"

"That's what I wanted to talk to you about."

"Oh? You won't be in the apartment in Queens?" She could not bring herself to say Suim's name.

"There is no apartment in Queens."

"Why not?"

"Suim had to give it up. Long story."

"I'm sure." Mia prayed that she wouldn't have to hear it.

"Anyway, I don't want to go into that now. The point is, I need somewhere to stay." Pause. "I hoped it could be with you."

"Stay with me! You and Suim want to stay with me?"

"Suim can't make this trip. I'm flying solo."

"I don't know, Lloyd. I don't think I want you here."

"What's the big deal? I'll sleep on the couch."

"I don't have a couch. I have a love seat. And you're too tall to fit."

"So I'll sleep on the floor. Or in the bathtub."

"I've only got a shower. It would be kind of hard to sleep standing up—unless you're an ox. And I don't even have a real bedroom; there's only a flimsy partition in the living room—"

"Jesus, Mia," he interrupted. "Why are you giving me such a hard time?"

"Why am *I* giving *you* such a hard time? Let me see: Could it be because you left me, left our kid, and took up with an underage Asian call girl you found under a rock? And because you owe me, big time, for child support?"

"I have every intention of giving you a check when I get there. And as for Suim, that kind of racist talk really demeans you, Mia. I hope Eden isn't listening."

"Fuck you, Lloyd Prescott!" Mia shouted, totally losing it now.

"You are not, I repeat *not*, sleeping on the floor, love seat, fire escape, or any part of my apartment you haven't yet mentioned. So just forget about that idea."

"Oh," said Lloyd in an infuriatingly wounded tone. "If you really feel that way . . . I just thought it would be nice for Eden—"

"You didn't tell her, did you?" Mia asked. "That you were going to stay here?"

"Well, yes, as a matter of fact, I did."

Mia had an impulse to hurl the phone out of the kitchen window, but what good would that do? She would be the one out a phone. Lloyd would still be Lloyd. And she would still have to deal with him.

"That was manipulative, Lloyd. Machiavellian, in fact."

"I don't see it that way. Not at all."

"You wouldn't, would you?"

There was a pause during which Lloyd mumbled something to someone, a waiter no doubt, about his beloved latte. Then: "So it will be okay then? For me to stay?"

"Not really. But obviously you're going to do it, whether it's okay or not."

"Think of Eden," he said.

"Is that a joke?" But Lloyd had already clicked off, leaving Mia with the phone still in her hand. She snapped it shut and went in search of her child.

"Breakfast," she said when she found her, spread out on the floor in front of the television.

"I heard you yelling at Daddy," Eden said, not looking at her. Her fingers moved across her thigh, looking for a place to start twisting and bruising.

"Well, sometimes people yell, honey."

"Are you going to let him stay here next week?" Eden said in a small, quivery voice.

"It would mean a lot to you, wouldn't it?"

Eden seemed to think this question was an insult to her intelligence, because she turned back to the TV, uttering a sound that was a cross between a snort and a sigh.

"He can stay here." She waited, expecting something in the way of excitement, enthusiasm, or gratitude. Instead, Eden just kept her head turned toward the television. Mia saw the tears snaking down her profile but resisted the impulse to comfort her because she knew comfort was not what Eden would welcome or even tolerate.

Instead, she returned to the kitchen, where she made eggs and toast for Eden. She called Julie while she cooked.

"I cannot believe you are letting him stay with you," Julie said when Mia had told her the story.

"It's for Eden's sake."

"You're about to qualify for sainthood then."

"No. Just motherhood. Hold on," Mia said. She wanted to make a fruit smoothie, but since the blender had no lid, she needed both hands to hold a plate over the top. "There. I'm back."

"Is he bringing her with him?" Julie asked.

"Suim? Not this time. Thank God," answered Mia. Julie was quiet so Mia prodded. "Why? Do I have to put her up, too?"

"It's not that. I just don't want you to get any ideas."

"Ideas?"

"You know. Ideas about jumping his bones while he's there."

"Julie! Are you crazy?"

"No. I just have an ex. Two, actually. So I know how these things happen."

"Well, they aren't happening here, I can promise you that."

"Okay . . ." Julie said slowly. "I still don't think he should stay with you."

"That makes two of us. But I've already said yes."

* * *

MIA ARRANGED THE food on a tray and brought it in to Eden. The kitchen was too small for a table, so they ate their meals in the apartment's largest room, many of them in front of the television set. Eden ignored the toast, picked at the eggs, blew bubbles in the smoothie, and then said she was through.

Mia looked sadly at the uneaten food. Not a good day. She took a bite of the eggs. They were cold, but she finished them anyway. Eden was still in her pajamas, transfixed by the television and hugging the stuffed cow Lloyd had bought for her when she turned four. The cow, named Petunia, was grimy and bald in patches, but Eden worshipped her as she would a fetish, and would consent to neither washing nor replacing her.

Mia's phone sounded again; it was Caitlin's mother, inviting Eden to the playground.

"Can I go?" Eden asked.

"If you finish your homework first," Mia said.

"Homework!" Eden tossed Petunia up in the air and nimbly caught her on the descent. "I hate homework."

"Me, too," Mia said.

"Do I have to do it?"

"No. But then you have to go into school tomorrow and tell your teacher why it isn't done."

Eden thought about this for a second before getting up, hunting for her backpack, and then, when she found it, yanking the books out so that they all collided in a heap on the floor. It was another hour before she finished her two pages of math and her chapter of social studies, but finally they were out the door and on their way.

Walking to the playground, Mia and Eden passed right by the bank. Even the exterior of the building seemed to her electrically charged; Mia was sure she could feel a buzz as she walked by. But she turned her head away and wouldn't look at the place, at least not while she was with Eden. Instead, she watched her daughter pet a big, friendly black

Lab who wagged his tail so eagerly at their approach that he was impossible to resist. The dog made Mia think of Mr. Ortiz and his lone surviving animal. She had not seen him in a few days, and the hallway, she now realized, had been clean. How had it come to pass that she now worried when she did *not* encounter dog shit on the way to her apartment?

She was thinking about this when Eden tugged on her sleeve and said, simply, "Look."

A man was standing on the corner, holding out a filthy baseball cap to collect money. He was very thin and missing several teeth. Also, he stank so badly that Mia wanted to cross the street to escape the odor. Instead, she dug into her purse for a dollar.

"Can I give it to him?" asked Eden.

Mia hesitated and then said, "All right." Compared with what she had given that woman in Manhattan yesterday, this was nothing. But she had given the woman bills from the secret stash; they felt to her somewhat unreal. Today, she carried none of those bills. The money she had was unequivocally hers, worked for, worried over, counted, and recounted numerous times. She could not be quite so free with it.

The man, however, seemed to find the single bill a gift of astonishing grace and goodwill.

"Why, thank you, little lady," he said to Eden. "Thank you so much." He bowed slightly, and in so doing, swayed a bit on his feet. Alarmed, Mia thought she might have to pick him up if he toppled, but he didn't.

"He smelled really bad," Eden said in a low voice when they were out of earshot.

"Uh-huh."

"That's because he lives on the street and doesn't have any place to take a shower, right?"

"Right."

"That lady yesterday . . ."

"What about her?"

"She lives on the street, too, doesn't she? But she didn't smell bad."

"No, she didn't."

"Why, Mom?"

"Why didn't she smell bad?"

"No. Why does she, I mean, why does *anyone* have to live on the street? I don't get it."

"You know, I'm not sure I do, either," said Mia.

"Can't the mayor or the president find a place for at least some of those people to live? How about at the White House? It's big enough." Eden had gone to Washington on a school trip, and she couldn't stop talking about the White House, which to her was on par with the Taj Mahal or Versailles.

Before Mia could reply, she heard Eden's name being called, loudly, from a few feet away. It was Caitlin, and Eden ran to meet her. Mia followed behind. After she said good-bye to her daughter and made plans for picking her up a few hours later, Mia headed home. She was free for a while, though of course she had plenty to do, like start cleaning up the apartment before Lloyd descended on her; he always ragged on her for being a slob, and she just didn't want to hear it this time around. Plus, she had some work she could get a jump on. Mommy Mousie was, mercifully, squeaking away on someone else's desk at the moment, and Mia had been given a new project. It was called *All That Trash: The Real Story of Your Garbage*, and she loved it. Who knew that every ton of recycled paper could save seventeen trees, save seven thousand gallons of water, and eliminate three cubic yards of landfill space? Or that for every ton of waste we generate, another twenty tons were generated to produce the products we used? And that in spite of recycling, the per capita discard rate in 1996 was 25 percent higher than it was in 1960?

Mia devoured this data and had been peppering her conversations with such tidbits, tossing them out to her brother and mother, to Julie and to Eden, who was initially interested but who then asked her to *please* stop talking about garbage. Settling down with the manuscript for a solid couple of hours suddenly seemed more important than cleaning up for Lloyd. So the place would be messy; he was the one who manipulated his way into staying over. If he didn't like it, he could go somewhere else.

As she reached the corner of Garfield and Fifth, she saw—and smelled—the guy who was standing there a little while ago. He was still in the same spot, but he was wearing the baseball cap now, and had substituted a cardboard coffee cup for the change he was collecting. *You already gave him money,* Mia thought. *You don't have to give him anything else.* But this rationale did not seem to satisfy her, and instead, she impulsively ducked into the bank, marched over to the machine, *her machine,* and slipped her card into the designated slot. She requested one hundred dollars and waited. *It won't happen again,* she admonished herself.

The screen color repeated its weird mutation from light to dark, and again there was the dot of light at the center. Wasn't it bigger this time though? Yes, she was sure it was. Before it had been a pencil point; now it was the size of a popcorn kernel. She felt herself drawn into its light before it vanished, to be replaced by the familiar screen. When the whirring noise stopped, she reached for the bills.

They were hundreds; she could see that in an instant. But there were a lot of them—more than last time certainly. She quickly hunched over, as if she'd been sucker punched, to count. One, two, three— her fingers skittered through the pile. There were twenty in all. Two thousand dollars. She stared at the screen, as if it contained a clue she might have missed. Nothing.

SHE HAD THE sensation again, the one of simultaneous heat and cold. Somehow, some way, this was all going to catch up with her. But for now, the debit read only one hundred dollars, while she had twenty times that in her hands. She felt rich, or at least a reasonable facsimile thereof. Still hunched, she squirreled the bills away in the waistband of her jeans, all except a single hundred, which she neatly folded, so that it was concealed in her palm. Then she strode out of the bank, straight toward the stench and the man. She gave the folded bill a tiny squeeze before placing it in his coffee cup.

"Why, thank you, little lady," he said, echoing his earlier words to Eden. "Thank you so kindly." Again the small bow, and this time, an actual click of his heels in their dirty, laceless sneakers. Maybe, like Dorothy, he was hoping to find his way home.

He doesn't even know how much it is, Mia thought, smiling and walking away. *He doesn't have a clue.* She imagined him sifting through the change and the crumpled ones in the cup and coming upon the hundred; her own smile grew larger, until it felt like it was taking over her entire face.

BACK IN THE empty apartment, Mia looked again at the mystery money. She still could not get over it, the weird and unaccountable fact of a bank machine that spit out money with no memory and no record. The bills were fresh and new, as if hers were the first hands to touch them. She stared for a few more seconds before tucking them away in the shoes and sitting down with the manuscript and her red editing pencil.

Garbage, she realized, was the natural consequence of money. The more money you had, the more garbage, the *better* garbage, you could produce. Lobster shells and artichoke leaves, empty champagne bottles by the score, the rinds of rich imported cheeses. Bags, tissue paper, and ribbons from exclusive shops in Paris, London, New York, Rio, Tokyo; elegant, robin's-egg-blue boxes from Tiffany's that held gold rings, collars of diamonds. This was not just any garbage—it was expensive, tasteful, high-class garbage. Would that man on the street be able to produce such garbage? Would she? Not now, of course, but given enough money, anyone could. Money and garbage, garbage and money. There was a relationship between the two, one worth pursuing.

As she read, she wondered if the author, one Howard W. Shapiro, was going to address this issue anywhere in the text. Garbage as an indicator of class, of social rank and status. If he didn't, she was going to suggest it. The more she thought about this idea, the better she liked it. Garbage was more than what you threw away; garbage was, in some ways, what defined you. The miraculously accumulating pile of bills in the shoe box and the plastic bags full of modest trash that she deposited in the battered cans downstairs were different but connected parts of her existence, interwoven strands from the same dense cloth. Tightening her grip on her pencil, Mia settled down to read.

FOUR

MIA WAS ON a cleaning jag. Even though she had told herself she wouldn't bother, she decided she was too proud to have Lloyd come here and think she had let everything go. So on her lunch break, she shopped for supplies: mop, rubber gloves, various biodegradable potions guaranteed not to poison the water table. She lugged everything home and, after she had given Eden dinner and—more or less—successfully presided over the nightly homework battle, devised her plan of attack.

To her surprise, Eden wanted to help, and did a respectable job scouring the minuscule bathroom sink—the sort found at a gas station—and the shower walls. She polished the bathroom mirror and wiped down the tiles surrounding it.

"I think Daddy will really like it here." Eden crumpled the used paper towels into a ball, which she attempted to pitch into the wastebasket. She missed but, to Mia's amazement, got up and threw the wadded-up towels away without being prompted.

"I hope he'll have a good visit," Mia said carefully.

"Maybe he'll have such a good visit that he'll want to stay."

"I don't know about that." Mia flopped down on the love seat, dust rag in hand. "He's got a lot of work he's doing right now, remember? And he said it was just for the weekend. He's going back to California on Monday."

"He could change his mind," Eden said.

"He could," Mia said, trying to be gentle. "But I don't think he will."

"You don't know everything, Mom," Eden huffed.

Mia agreed with her there.

＊　＊　＊

AFTER EDEN WAS in bed, Mia resumed her cleaning. She lugged two large bags of trash to the door and debated taking them out then or waiting until the morning. While she stood there deliberating, she heard voices in the hall. Voices, and what sounded like a scuffle. Her heart began a nasty acceleration. Who was there? Should she check? She remained inside, ear pressed to the door.

"Fuck, you hurt me, man." The voice was loud.

"You pushed me first, asshole."

"Shut up, would you? Just shut the fuck up."

"I'm trying him again. He said he'd be here."

"Said, said, said. He's a fucking liar."

"You're the liar, dick brain. Manny's all right. If he said he'll be here, he'll be here."

Mia's heartbeat slowed just a little. Customers of Manny's. If she crept away quietly, maybe they would leave without ringing her buzzer. But then she heard the sound of another buzzer being pressed and the voices started again.

"You sure you don't know where he is?" said one. There was a response, but Mia couldn't hear it through the door.

"You're not lying, are you, old man?" said the other voice.

Old man. They must have rung Mr. Ortiz's buzzer. No. No, no, *no.* Mia opened the door and stepped out into the hall. As she guessed, the two visitors—both beefy and inflated-looking, a pair of Michelin tire guys in black leather jackets and black Gestapo-issue boots—were standing in front of Mr. Ortiz's open doorway. Mr. Ortiz wore a garishly patterned silk robe and a pair of ancient leather slippers with tarnished gold monograms adorning their cracked fronts. No dogs were in evidence.

"Can I help you?" Mia said. She stood up as straight as possible, and tried to look, if not tough, then authoritative. The act must have been convincing because both men swiveled around to face her.

"Yeah, if you know where Manny is," said one of the guys, smoothing back his abundant dark hair with both hands. His fingers were as thick as sausages, his nails glossy with clear polish.

"Manny? I heard him go out a while ago." This was a lie; she was too busy scrubbing the inside of the fridge to have heard anything. But it seemed imperative to behave as if she had information. As if she knew something.

"Really? What time was that?" said the other guy, whose hair was also dark, but curly, drooping over his forehead and crowding the sides of his face.

"Around nine," Mia said.

"Do you know when he'll be back?" Curlylocks asked.

"No. Sorry." As if he checked in with her, Mia thought.

"See? I told you he wasn't here," said Curlylocks to his companion. "We're just wasting our time."

"If I see him, I'll tell him you were looking for him."

"You do that," said Curlylocks. "You tell him we were *waiting.*"

He tugged on his pants and adjusted his crotch. Why did guys always do that? Mia wished she could just tell him to stop; instead, she watched as the two men turned and stomped down the stairs. She was left there, heart slowing, looking at Mr. Ortiz.

"Thank you, Señora Saul," he said to her in a low voice. "Those men"—he shook his head—"not refined. Not nice."

"Despicable," agreed Mia. "Like Manny."

"Señor Manny . . ." Mr. Ortiz began. It looked as if he were going to cry.

"Mr. Ortiz, where is your dog? I mean, the other one?"

"My Chi Chi is dead."

"Was it Manny—?"

"No. The doctor said she had a tumor. But I know better."

"What do you mean?"

"She died of a broken heart. After Jacinta died, she didn't want to live anymore. And I tell you something, Señora Saul." He looked at her with dark, watery eyes. "I know just how she felt."

Mia felt flattened by guilt. Why hadn't she called someone, done something?

"I am so sorry, Mr. Ortiz," was all she said, all she could say.

"So am I..." There was an awkward lull. "Good night, Señora Saul." He closed the door but not before Mia heard a small, ragged intake of breath, the sort of sound that was generally the prelude to lavish, inconsolable weeping.

THE NEXT MORNING at work, Mia was wading through garbage, or at least through some alarming and vivid descriptions of it, when she was interrupted by a call from Eden's teacher.

"Is she all right? Is everything okay?" Mia put the chapter on toxic waste aside.

"She's fine," said the teacher. "But I just wanted to check something with you."

"Of course," said Mia, trying to be as cooperative as possible to compensate for her many and glaring liabilities as a parent. To wit: she *still* could not remember the teacher's name, a lapse that continued to vex and humiliate her.

"Eden is not leaving school for an extended vacation, is she?"

"Not to my knowledge," Mia said, but she had a leaden sense she knew where this conversation was heading. "Why?"

"Well, today she told me that she didn't turn in the worksheet for her social studies project because she wasn't going to be here."

"Oh?" Mia started nervously doodling on the manuscript, which was absolutely verboten. What social studies project? She grabbed an eraser and rubbed so hard that she tore the paper. Damn. Now she needed to find a roll of tape, but the tape was nowhere to be found. "Did she say where she plans to be?"

"With her father. In Hollywood. She said he's being nominated for an Academy Award—"

"The Academy Awards are in February," said Mia, as if this bit of information would suddenly clarify everything and put it in its rightful place again.

"Yes, I *know* that." She sounded irritated. "But Eden is insistent that this trip is imminent. They are going to be staying in a big hotel with a fountain, a tennis court, and two, no make that three, swimming pools; she's going to have room service all day long and go shopping for a strapless dress and a tiara. A diamond tiara, I believe." The teacher paused to draw a breath. "I'd say her imagination is working overtime, wouldn't you?"

"I can explain," Mia said. "You see, her father is coming to visit, and she hasn't seen him for some time. He's a filmmaker, and he actually *is* in Hollywood right now. So some of it is true; the rest of it . . ." Mia trailed off. "The rest of it she wishes were true."

"Ms. Prescott," said the teacher.

"Saul," Mia corrected.

"Excuse me?"

"Eden's last name is Prescott; mine is Saul."

"Ms. Saul, then," the teacher continued, still in that irritated tone, "she told this story not only to me, but also to virtually the entire class during recess. When one of the boys said she was making it up, she hit him. And then she pulled the hair of a girl who said the same thing. When I tried to her stop her, she told me to . . ." The teacher stopped.

"To what?" said Mia.

"To *fuck off*." The teacher sighed, a disgusted and accusatory sigh.

It was unreasonable of Mia to hate this woman; she knew that. Eden shouldn't be hitting or cursing. The woman had a right, no, an obligation to call and tell her. Still, Mia hated the teacher all the more for her unimpeachable rectitude. She grabbed a paper clip and twisted it out of shape so that it was no longer a clip, but a wavy, metal line. This was gratifying enough for her to do again, and again, and still again, until she had assembled an entire arsenal of mutilated clips.

"Ms. Saul, we really pride ourselves here on letting the children express themselves; this is not a repressive atmosphere. But that kind of language . . ."

Is precisely the kind of language my daughter hears all too much from me, Mia thought. What she said, however, in a meek voice, was, "I totally understand."

"She's waiting to see the principal now," added the teacher.

"The principal." Mia moved the phone away from her ear for a second; she needed to regroup before she could respond.

"I just thought I should let you know."

"I'm so glad you did." This was the kind of lie she could spit out in her sleep, the one that went, *That's right, tell me that Eden is screwed up, that I'm screwed up, that we're the most screwed-up excuse for a family you've ever seen, and that I'm supposed to be appreciative, penitent, and, above all, thankful for this unerring assessment, this essential information about who we are.*

"She's going to see the psychologist after she's seen the principal," the teacher said. "That's in addition to her regular appointment later in the week."

Mia didn't remember when Eden's appointment with the psychologist was; she had blotted it out from memory, from consciousness, like the teacher's name.

"It's on Thursday," the teacher prompted. "Thursday morning."

"Thursday. Right." Mia tried to sound like she had known this all along. She wanted to get off the phone with this woman and to speak to Eden herself. "I'll try to leave work by four and pick her up from afterschool early." She eyed the manuscript on which she should have been working this very second, and did not see how leaving early would be possible.

"That would be a good idea," the teacher said. "I'm sure we'll be talking more about this, but right now, my prep period is over, so I have to go."

Thank God, Mia thought. She clicked off the phone, looked at the manuscript again before putting her head directly down on toxic waste. But she didn't stay down for long. If she was going to get out of here by four, she'd better hustle.

EDEN WAS SULKY and unrepentant when Mia tried to discuss what had happened at school.

"But that story was entirely made up," Mia said. She was still in her cleaning mode, and was gathering all the glass and plastic bottles that she hadn't actually recycled but that she hadn't thrown out, either. So far, there were quite a number of them.

"Big deal. It could be true."

"Well, *could be* is a lot different from *is*. You know that, Eden."

"My teacher is always saying 'use your imagination.' I was using mine. Why is everyone getting so mad?"

"Because you've been hitting, pulling hair, and cursing."

"They deserved it," Eden muttered.

"Eden!" Mia said sharply, setting the bag down hard. From the sound it made, she could tell she had probably broken a bottle or two. "There is no possible excuse or rationale for your behavior. It was totally out of line. I know you miss Daddy and wish you could see him more often, but—"

"It's your fault that I can't!" Eden said, raising her voice to match Mia's. "You! You did it!" She pressed her face into Petunia's grungy udders and began to cry.

"That is so untrue," Mia said. But of course she felt it was true, every incriminating, vituperative word. Even though she had not wanted a divorce—had pleaded with Lloyd to see a couples therapist, in a vain attempt to salvage their marriage—she still felt culpable and deficient because of it. She sat, stricken, watching Eden sob. What could she say to make it better?

"I don't care," Eden mumbled into Petunia's belly. "I miss him so much." She lifted her face and wiped her eyes with the back of her hand. "Every minute of every day. Every second. That's how much."

"I'm sorry, baby," said Mia. She wished she could gather her daughter into her arms the way she had been gathering the damn bottles. "I'm so sorry."

LATER, AFTER EDEN was asleep, Mia replayed the ugly scene in her mind. But going over all this was getting her nowhere. She had to push ahead to what was next, not dwell on what she couldn't change or fix. She began making a mental to-do list:

> *Stop cursing so damn much. At least out loud.*
> *Call teacher.*
> *Call principal.*
> *Call school psychologist. Make appointments with all three. Also learn names of*
> *   all three—for real.*
> *Call Stu.*
> *Work on chapter about composting in* Garbage.
> *Start compost heap on fire escape?*
> *Buy sheets and towels.*

The sheets and towels were not, like the locket, a pure indulgence. She thought of them as a kind of armor necessary for Lloyd's visit; she had no intention of letting him see the dingy pillowcases and fraying washcloths with which she uncomplainingly lived. Instead, she would buy herself a set of blush pink or pale blue sheets with a skin-caressingly high thread count. For the temporary bed that he would use while visiting, something subdued and tasteful, in ivory or oatmeal. For Eden, she would find a more whimsical pattern—frogs, fireflies, Ferris wheels—bounding or flying or spinning across the fabric. And while she would have loved a stack of thick white bath towels, plush enough to double as a pillow, she knew that such things were better left to those with maids or, at the very least, laundry rooms in the basement. Instead, she would be quite content with six new towels in more forgiving colors: chocolate brown, claret, midnight blue.

She would use cash from her secret stash for these purchases. And when she plucked the bills from the box, she would also set aside a bill, a crisp hundred, for a wholly different but equally essential purpose. Someone, she didn't yet know whom, would be waiting to receive it—a man in a wheelchair with his pant leg pinned up over his stump, a woman with matted hair and eczema-raw cheeks, a girl with a glassy, stoned look and bare feet black from the pavement. This person would accept her offering in a bag, a cap, a cup, or a creased and naked palm. He or she would have no idea why Mia had done such a thing. But Mia would know. Not just another consumer, taker, user, Mia would become a giver.

Suddenly, it was so obvious. Every time she spent money on herself, she would also give some of it away. A kind of karmic evening of the score—something good happened to her, something good happened to someone else. How simple, how elegant, a concept. The effortless symmetry of it eased her gently into sleep.

In the morning, Eden didn't want to go to school. Maybe she could transfer to another school and never have to go back to that one?

"I don't think that will work," Mia said, pouring juice and buttering a slice of bread. The toaster had died a couple of days earlier and she added *Buy toaster* to the list she had made last night. "You'll just have to march into this one and tell everyone you're sorry."

"What if I'm not?"

Mia placed the buttered bread and glass of juice down in front of her. "Then *lie*," she said. "*Pretend* you're sorry, okay? Sometimes, you just have to do that." She paused, and when there was no reply, added, "Now I've got to get ready for work." Then she turned away, leaving Eden to mull over this advice as she regarded, but did not eat, her food.

FIVE

Loyd looked good. Terrific, in fact. So terrific that it just about broke Mia's heart all over again. It was so patently unfair that he should look so healthy, relaxed, and glowing while she knew herself to be a wan and stressed wreck. He was the one who left her; why couldn't the remorse and strain have showed on his face, too?

He strode into the apartment, the one she had cleaned and scoured for days, like a traveling salesman peddling snake oil to the barefoot, overall-wearing, hayseed-chewing rubes down on the farm.

"Daddy!" cried Eden. "Daddy, Daddy, Daddy!" In honor of this visit she had donned the long, twinkling skirt he'd bought her a few months ago, along with a lacy white top from some other equally impractical shopping trip. But she did look so pretty. So pretty and so happy.

"How's my little filly?" he asked, grabbing her in his arms and whirling her around. "How's my girl?"

"Dad, I am too old to be called your little filly," she mock-scolded when he set her down again.

"You are? How did that happen? No one told me."

"Come on, you know how old I am." She was beaming. God, how she was beaming.

"Of course I do. Let's see—ten years, nine months, six days, three hours, and, let's see, about twenty minutes."

"See? Too old to be your filly."

"But not too old to be my cream puff, my cupcake, my wishing star. Not too old for that." He tousled her short hair and swooped down to kiss the top of her head. "Hey," he said, like he had just noticed. "I like the cut. Very chic."

Mia watched all this from the sidelines, like the wallflower at the high school prom. Lloyd had always been this way with Eden, and Eden had always loved it. Loved *him*. Mia used to love it, too. Now she didn't know. Of course she wanted Eden to have her father's affection, but at the sight of them together, her heart felt bitten, chewed, and spat back out again. She was relieved when Eden put on her new, blue soft-as-butter coat and they were ready to leave.

"Nice coat." Lloyd caressed the sleeve. "Where did that come from? Uncle Moneybags—uh, excuse me, Uncle Stuart?"

"No, it's from Barneys," Eden said. "Mom took me there."

"Oh, did she?" Lloyd looked over at Mia, who quickly looked away.

"Yes, and the salesladies remembered me, Dad!"

"Everyone will remember you, Eden. You wait." He smiled. "Now how about we hit the road, okay?"

"Not too late, okay?" Mia told Lloyd, uselessly, she knew.

"Oh, come on," he said. "What's late when you're out with your best girl?"

Mia resisted the impulse to argue; she would lose anyway, so what was the point? Instead, she watched while the coat was buttoned and the door slammed. They were gone. She was alone in the apartment, which was cleaner than it had been since she moved in. She even went after places toward which in the past she would have adopted a don't-look-don't-tell policy, like the tops of the kitchen cabinets and the fridge, under the kitchen sink, behind the love seat. And what for? All so she could prove something to Lloyd, something that he wouldn't even notice or care about if he did.

Mia first met Lloyd when she was a junior at Oberlin. He was actually a student at Princeton, visiting someone in her dorm for the weekend. The someone threw a party, Mia was invited, and there, in the middle of the room, holding court, was Lloyd. He was a tall, good-looking boy holding a large rabbit. Mia had been charmed. She had never met a guy who came to a party with a rabbit. A dog, sure. A snake even. But a rabbit?

"Are you a magician?" Mia had asked.

"Would it help get a date with you?"

"Maybe," she said. He was fun, she decided. Fun to look at, fun to flirt with.

"Then I'm a magician," he said. "Want me to make this rabbit vanish?"

Mia shook her head. "I like rabbits."

"Smart girl," he had said. He offered her the rabbit, and Mia took the creature in her arms. She was surprised at the feel of him—something in his body seemed to vibrate, even when he was still, and she could sense the subtle, animate movements of his ears. Holding him close to her chest was both a privilege and a comfort.

He had not even been Lloyd back then; he'd been Tim. It was only later that he decided that the ordinary name of Tim Prescott was incompatible with all his grand ambitions and started going by his middle name, Lloyd.

Oh, they had had fun back then, hadn't they? Lloyd had given the rabbit to Mia as a going-away gift. Mia called her Lucy. She was a tidy creature who ate her food neatly and, even when allowed the run of Mia's dorm room, confined her droppings to a single corner. Of course she called to thank him for the rabbit, and he called to check on how the rabbit was faring. Late in the semester, Lloyd drove out to Oberlin again, and the following spring, she hitched a ride east, with some friends, to visit him. He was from Massachusetts. Both his parents were teachers at Andover, so he'd gotten to go there for free; they had plenty of class but very little money. Mia never would have guessed about the lack of money; Lloyd always had an air of entitlement about him, and she supposed he always would. He was easy in the world, something she never entirely was. And he had passed along a bit of that ease to her, a gift as unexpected and delightful as the rabbit had been.

* * *

LLOYD HAD NOT been her only boyfriend, but he'd been her world-shaping, life-altering boyfriend, the one she'd grown up with, the one with whom she shared a past, a future, a daughter—everything. And then he'd left her. She had been angry at first, angry and disbelieving. She'd stormed and raged, made threats, threw things. Then she tried negotiation, bribes, pleading, none of which worked, of course. She became depressed, parking Eden at a friend's for days at a time while she remained in bed, staring at the ceiling, while tears leaked from the corners of her eyes, getting into her ears, her mouth, eventually soaking the pillow on which her head rested. In the end, she became resigned, and that was where she most of the time remained, except for nights like tonight, when she actually had to see Lloyd up close, deal with him again, remember every good and every infuriating thing about him.

AS MIA STARED at the immaculate apartment, she decided she couldn't stay in it one more second. Fortunately, Julie had invited her to Juicy, the bar where she was working tonight. They wouldn't be able to talk, of course. But even being in Julie's extended aura was better than sitting here alone and stewing. Mia fluffed her hair and applied a little more lipstick and then a little more on top of that. She didn't look too bad. She wasn't twenty-five anymore, but then no one was twenty-five forever. Her dress size hadn't changed in a decade, and her legs were still in decent shape. Her eyes—large, brown, long-lashed—were still her best feature. Anyway, what did it matter? She wasn't looking to get laid tonight—only mildly drunk.

She walked to Sixteenth Street and Seventh Avenue. It was not very cold, and the night was refreshing. She was wearing all black—jeans, ribbed sweater, leather jacket, and heavy black boots that were actually Prada, but which she'd scored at a stoop sale for five dollars. Black was a New York cliché, she conceded. Banal and predictable. But there was such a comfort in black. When she wore it, she felt like an urban warrior, at once impervious and chic.

Juicy was warm and welcoming; votive candles flickered on the tables and the long, polished hunk of wood that constituted the bar. There was a seasonal arrangement of pumpkins and gourds on a table by the door. Mia saw Julie, also in black, albeit of a more come-hither variety—tight black pants, low-cut black top, high-heeled black pumps—carrying an outsized tray filled with brimming glasses. She nodded to Mia and mouthed the word *Later.* Mia shrugged off her jacket and made her way to the bar.

"What can I get you?" said the bartender without looking up.

"Hi, Fred. Long time." Mia had filled in for Julie a couple of times, so she knew Fred.

He glanced up then and grinned.

"Mia, Mia, Mia," he said. He had a nice smile, with a slight chip on one of his front teeth. "Where've you been keeping yourself?"

"Oh, you know . . . the usual."

"The usual." Fred made a face. "As in, life's a bore and then you die?"

"I thought it was life's a bitch and then you marry one."

"Touché." He smiled again; the chipped tooth winked. "So what are you drinking? It's on the house."

"Thanks," she said. "Thanks so much."

"Don't mention it," said Fred. That tooth again. That sexy tooth.

"Well, what do you recommend? Your magic elixir, your secret potion?"

"Dirty martinis," Fred said without a second's hesitation. "Here . . . wait." He turned away and began pouring and stirring. Then he whipped around and handed her a glass. "Voilà!"

Mia sipped delicately at first, and then with greater enthusiasm. "Mmm, this is good," she said. "What's in here?"

"Snips and snails and puppy dogs' tails."

"No, come on, Fred, really."

"Organic vodka. Spanish olives. Fresh basil."

"Killer combo." Mia took another sip.

"Slow, okay? Those things can be lethal," said Julia as she swung by the bar for another order.

"Worrywart," said Fred.

"I'm okay, Julie," Mia said, already feeling a pleasant buzz. "I'm fine."

"You've eaten dinner, right?" Julie persisted. She placed the brimming glasses on her tray.

"I'm eating now." Mia reached into a small earthenware bowl filled with Goldfish crackers and popped one into her mouth. These things had cheese in them, didn't they? And what was this? A bowl of peanuts? She took a handful. So she had some dairy and some protein going on, too. The basil leaf and the olive in her drink could be construed as vegetables. Dinner. And look—it was free.

"Fred?" Julie turned to him. "Don't let her get too drunk, okay?"

"Aye, aye, captain," Fred said, with a mock salute.

"Fred!" She gave him an exasperated look and then she was gone.

"Don't worry, I'll take care of you," Fred said.

"You're a pal, Fred. A real pal." The salty snacks were making her thirsty; she needed a drink, and hey, would you look at that, her dirty martini was still right there in her hand, ready to do the job. "Organic vodka," she murmured, as she took another long sip.

"You say something?" Fred asked. Mia didn't answer. The bar was getting crowded, and she lost sight of him. He was pretty busy now anyway, pouring dirty martinis and what have you for all and sundry. But whenever her glass was empty, he refilled it quickly. Mia nursed her drink, and didn't even try to talk to the clot of twentysomethings whooping it up next to her. Instead, she arranged the peanuts and Goldfish in pleasing little patterns—a star, a heart, a flower—on her napkin, and when the design was completed, ate it. Every now and then Julie swooped by; on one of those occasions, she hustled Mia up from her seat and off to the ladies' room.

"But I don't need to go," Mia said.

"That doesn't matter," said Julie. "Come with me anyway."

It was cooler in the bathroom; Mia realized only then that she was hot in her high-necked sweater. Waiting for Julie to finish, she stared in the mirror, studying her flushed cheeks and tousled hair. Her lipstick had worn off, and she rummaged around in her purse to see if the tube was in there. It wasn't, but she found the perfume samples from the day at Barneys with Eden. Eden, who was right now with her father, the man Mia used to love more than anyone on the planet. How could it all have come to this? The two of them together while Mia was alone and exiled to the bathroom of a bar? Tears suddenly started to flow, an unexpected and seemingly involuntary response, as if she had been slicing onions.

"Mia?" asked Julie when she emerged from the stall. She hastily washed her hands and placed them, still wet, on Mia's shoulders. "What is it?"

"Everything," Mia blubbered. "Just everything."

"You mean Lloyd?" asked Julie, succinctly boiling down the vastness of "everything" to a single word.

"I guess." She sniffed loudly, and Julie passed her a tissue from a box on the sink.

"I know this is a tough weekend," Julie said.

Mia didn't say anything but blotted her eyes with the tissue.

"Listen," Julie said, looking down at her watch, "my shift is over in about half an hour. If you can hold on, we can go someplace quieter. How does that sound?"

"Thanks, Julie." Mia tossed out the used tissue and ran her fingers through her hair. "But I'm totally wiped out. I think I should just go home."

"Fred wanted to join us."

"Fred? Why?"

"I think he's got a little crush on you."

"Oh." Mia put her head in her hands. Fred. Had a crush. On her. She saw the smile, the chipped tooth. Suddenly it was all too much. She couldn't imagine going out, even chaperoned by Julie, with Fred or anyone else tonight. She lifted her head again. "Maybe some other time."

"How many of those martinis have you had, anyway? I'm really going to give it to him."

"It's not his fault. I'm a big girl."

"I suppose you are," Julie conceded. "You sure you don't want to wait? We don't have to go out. You can stay over at my place. Avoid the night with Lloyd altogether."

"You're a sweetie, but no. I should get back." The thought of Lloyd and Eden alone together in Mia's apartment was especially galling, as if he had neatly elbowed her out of her own life.

Julie looked like she was going to argue but then said, "Okay. If you change your mind, you can come over later."

"Thanks," Mia said, slurring the word a little. She stood, and the bathroom swayed.

"I'm calling a car service for you," Julie said. "You can't walk by yourself at this hour. And especially not when you are totally plastered."

Mia didn't protest. Julie was right. She *was* totally plastered, and the thought of her bed, freshly made up with its silky new sheets, was a siren song.

It seemed like in minutes she was climbing into the Lincoln's backseat, with its neat patchwork of duct tape, trying not to be sick from the scent of whatever God-awful air freshener the driver had sprayed all over. Why did anyone think this cloying, artificial smell was in any way pleasant or even tolerable? The car shot off into the night, and Mia pressed the button that opened the window. That was better.

Much better. Her head was even a little clearer, and she focused on the dashboard and windshield area of the car, which was like a portable shrine, with several brass-plated statuettes of Indian deities, a knot of red beads hanging from the rearview mirror, and a collage of photographs. Mia leaned forward to inspect them better. A black-haired girl in a princess costume, a boy holding a baseball bat and grinning, a baby with its mouth open and a fine thread of drool dripping from its parted lips.

"Yours?" Mia asked, indicating the pictures.

"Yes, mine," said the driver. He sounded both shy and proud.

"Sweet," said Mia. "How old?"

"The boy is nine. The girl, six. And the baby"—his voice softened—"she's eight months."

"You have a lovely family," Mia said. She looked at his balding head, his broad back, the little tuft of hair at the nape of his neck that tapered until it disappeared into his shirt collar. He was nice, this guy who clearly loved his kids and kept their pictures where he would see them always, his own personal constellation, there to light his way.

The car slowed, and Mia dug through her purse for her wallet. But then she remembered that she was carrying two twenties from the first time the machine offered its mysterious bounty. They were not in her wallet; she had taken to keeping the bills and any change they spawned separate, like milk and meat in a kosher kitchen. The fare was eight dollars; she handed the driver the twenty and said, "Keep the change," as she somehow knew she would as soon as her fingers touched the bill.

"Thank you," the driver said as he studied the bill, then sought her gaze in the rearview mirror. "Thank you so very much."

THE APARTMENT WAS dark and quiet. *Lloyd and Eden must still be out,* she thought. The momentary glow Mia had felt when she handed the driver the money faded when she thought of her ex-husband. She slipped out of her boots and jacket and padded into the bedroom. On the way, she saw that she was wrong—Lloyd was asleep on the air mattress, his big, handsome face pressed into the new pillowcase she bought just for this purpose. The blanket she borrowed from Julie was pulled up only partway; his chest was bare. Probably the rest of him, too; she had never known Lloyd to wear pajamas. She checked on Eden, who was also sound asleep amid a riotous pattern of trombones and saxophones. Petunia sat propped at the foot of the bed, alert as a guard dog. Mia watched briefly, deriving that peculiar satisfaction experienced by mothers everywhere, as her child quietly drew and expelled breath.

So they were here. Well, it was late, after all. She went into her so-called room and took off the rest of her things. Rummaging through a drawer, she pulled out a large man's shirt. The collar and cuffs were frayed, and the fabric had that particular softness achieved after years of washing, drying, starching, and ironing. It was only when she was in the bathroom, brushing her teeth, that she realized the shirt once had belonged to Lloyd. This made her weepy all over again, and she sat down on the closed lid of the toilet and cried for a while. *It's those dirty martinis,* she decided. *Dirty, dirty, dirty martinis.* For the second time that evening, Mia wiped her eyes and tried to get a grip.

The new sheets were as smooth and luxurious as she imagined, and she fell asleep almost immediately. She began to dream, a complex dream in which she was navigating mountains of garbage. She held a staff, the sort of thing seen in a fifteenth-century painting depicting a pilgrim, only the staff was made of some lightweight metal, like aluminum. But that was okay; she was happy, a happy hiker, with her twenty-first-century staff, her canteen, and her binoculars. She was as nimble-footed as a goat, as joyful as a lark . . . until she wasn't. She began to pant. The staff became a crutch. Her canteen was gone, and she was thirsty. Walking was a torment. But she kept going until she reached the biggest mountain of all, except it wasn't really a mountain, it was a wave of garbage: broken dolls, blackened banana peels, sodden diapers, and rotting heads of lettuce all rising up, threatening to rain down on her. In a panic, she woke.

Mia remained in bed, waiting for her heart to slow, but even when it did, she was unable to get comfortable again. She turned this way and that, listening to the sounds of the apartment at night: steam hissing through the pipes, a door banging shut down the hall. A muffled shout, from somewhere in the street. A car alarm, with its predictable, annoying *wee wop, wee wop.* Damn. Mia sat up in disgust. She was drunk and exhausted, but she couldn't get back to sleep.

She yanked off the covers and headed into the kitchen, for what she was not sure. Hot milk? Cold water? She stopped to look at Lloyd. He was on his side now, a position she remembered well. She used to snuggle into the attenuated comma created by his body, his long arm casually draping across her chest, claiming her, keeping her safe.

Was it this memory or the backlash of the dirty martinis that caused Mia to cross the room and slip into the air-filled bed beside him? It didn't matter. Julie's warnings echoed faintly in her brain, but she quickly shushed them. *Nothing is going to happen,* she silently argued with Julie. *You don't have to lecture me.* Carefully, she settled in, trying not to wake him. There. She drank in the sense memory of his arms, his shoulders, the familiar rise and fall of his chest. She moved, ever so slightly, and her hand grazed his bare skin—she had guessed correctly, still no pj's—and she let it stay where it was. He was no longer her husband, but he had been once. And that meant something, although she was not sure what.

Husband. Such a cozy, happy-sounding sort of word. When they first got married, she would repeat it in the privacy of her own mind, and found numerous excuses to work it into the casual exchanges she had with other people. *My husband loves that cut of beef,* she could remember saying to the butcher. *I'm looking for a sweater for my husband,* she told a salesman at Bloomingdale's. *It's his birthday next week.* But now all that was over. Instead of a husband, she had an ex. She even hated the sound of the word—just a short vowel away from *ax*—and brimming with a kind of latent violence that was an affront to her sensibility and her soul.

Tentatively, she moved closer. He was warm. He smelled good, too—a combination of some new, citrus-infused aftershave mingled with his own, inimitable odor. Here he was. Her ex. The father of her only child. In her apartment, naked. And she was right next to him.

She continued pressing, and though she thought he might have still been asleep, she felt him stir. Which, she realized, was exactly her aim. She hadn't had sex in ages; she hadn't wanted to. Right now, though, she very much wanted to have sex. And crazy as it was, she wanted to have sex with Lloyd. She knew him, and she had loved him. Maybe she still loved him, hard to know when she was always so angry with him. But even if she didn't, he was her past, and, in some perverse way, she felt like he was still hers.

"Mia?" he asked quietly. So he *was* up.

"Were you expecting someone else?"

"What are you doing?"

"I think it's pretty obvious."

He didn't say anything, but he didn't try to stop her, either. Mia felt his body responding, and his breath quickened, just the slightest bit, in her ear. This was permission enough, and she guided Lloyd into her from behind, a position they had both always liked. She shuddered when the connection was made. Had she thought it didn't matter about his having a big dick? Well, she was wrong. Wrong, wrong, wrong. She started to move against him and placed his hand between her legs, so that he could stroke her, too. She loved those big hands of his, with their skillful, knowing fingers, she always had—

But then he stopped and eased himself out of her.

"Where did you go?" she said.

BREAKING THE BANK | 75

"This is not a good idea."

"No, it's not," she agreed.

"Then why, Mia? Why do it?"

"For old time's sake?" She tried to be jaunty but failed miserably. At least she wasn't crying. Not yet anyway.

He was silent, and so was she. When the silence stretched a little longer, Mia tried willing herself to get up and off of the mattress, but it was no use. She was lonely, she was heartsick, she missed Lloyd and the life they used to have together. She was drunk, too—weepy, self-pitying drunk as opposed to angry drunk, jolly drunk, or philosophical drunk. Weepy drunk, she knew from experience, was the worst.

Then she felt him move against her again, and within minutes, they were at it in earnest. It was wet, it was hot, and it was over all too soon. Lloyd came with a small grunt, and then remained still, breathing hard. Mia didn't know what to say, so she waited; when she ventured his name, he let out a clipped, guttural snore—he had fallen asleep. Mia wished she could drift off next to him, but the thought of Eden—who might find them together the next morning and infer all sorts of happy endings that were most emphatically not going to come true—propelled her back to her own bed. The insides of her thighs were chafed and sticky, but she fell asleep anyway, almost as soon as she closed her eyes.

SIX

MIA AWOKE THE next morning awash in shame and remorse. Plus she had a monumental, sanity-obliterating headache; she couldn't even open her eyes without pain. Sex with Lloyd? What a truly terrible idea. Why had she initiated such a thing? To establish the scope and shape of her own hurt, the way she might touch an iron, to test the heat, and then snatch the finger away again? Only she hadn't snatched her finger away soon enough; she'd let it stay put and now the burn remained. The thought of facing him, in Eden's presence no less, was unendurable.

There were noises coming from the kitchen; Eden's high, excited voice blending with Lloyd's deeper one. The noises added a new dimension to her pain. She kept her eyes closed and her head very still. Soon there were smells. He was making French toast, one of his specialties. His version called for cream, nutmeg, and grated orange peel; since she had none of these ingredients in her kitchen, he must have gone shopping to procure them. Eden would eat at least three slices of this confection. She would eat anything Lloyd prepared—Mia was grateful for this, if not for much else about Lloyd—and lick the plate clean, too. She had always adored her father, but since he left, she fairly worshipped him.

Mia's stomach rumbled. She was hungry. No wonder, considering her largely liquid meal of the night before. But she couldn't rise up over the wall of pain to get out of bed and deal with Lloyd. So she remained where she was, treating her throbbing head as if it were a centuries-old Ming vase, too fragile and precious to be handled. Soon she was asleep. When she next opened her eyes, the apartment was quiet and the throbbing in her head had retreated sufficiently for her to contemplate getting up. She ventured into the kitchen, where dishes had been washed and put away. On the fridge, she found a check and a note:

*Thought I'd let you sleep in. I'll take Eden today, so you can
do whatever you need/want. We'll be back after dinner.*

She was somewhat mollified by the check, but remained roiled, first by Lloyd's presence, and then by his absence. To shake off the mood, she took a shower in the still-clean bathroom and used one of her plush new towels. Her head still hurt when she got out, but it was a mild hurt, almost a relief when compared to the earlier pain. And she discovered that she had gotten her period. Another relief. At least she wasn't pregnant.

After the shower, she found that Lloyd had left the French toast batter in a Saran Wrap–covered bowl on the counter. There was a loaf of sliced challah bread next to it, and she made herself two slices while considering how to deal with the rest of the day. She could work on *All That Trash*, which was intermittently brilliant but also uneven. She could run errands. And she could visit Julie to confess her idiotic behavior of the night before, though the conversation would no doubt be peppered very heavily with *I-told-you-sos*. But Julie, who was on occasion prone to equally idiotic behavior when it came to men, would also be sympathetic.

Armed with something like a plan, Mia dressed, brushed her teeth—with extra vigor, as if that would scour away last night's excesses—and settled down with the manuscript. She used color-coded Post-its and Sharpies; she jotted down extensive notes that she would type up at the office on Monday. While she worked, she had the enormously gratifying sense that she was doing something tangible; her red editing pencil was a trowel, a ruler, a pair of scissors.

The palpable sense of accomplishment carried her out into the day.

It was a gorgeous morning, the weather a kind of Pied Piper, calling people out of their brownstones and apartments and into the brilliant sunshine, newspapers and cups of coffee abandoned in favor of the golden day. Mia ran into Caitlin and her mother, two other girls from Eden's grade, a woman from the exercise class she used to attend, and a puffed-up, self-important guy from the Food Co-op, whom she adroitly dodged because she was delinquent in working her shifts and knew she hadn't a prayer of catching up. And then she bumped into Fred, who looked, in the crisp October air, even better than he had last night. The bar was too dark for her to have taken proper notice of quite how blue his eyes were, for instance. The sun ignited his buzz cut to an amber sheen. And then there was that tooth.

"So we meet again," she said, striving to sound playful.

"So we do," he bantered back. He scrutinized her face and added, "You look pretty good, considering."

"Considering what?"

"How looped you were when you left. Julie really chewed me out. She said it was my fault you had to go home."

"Julie worries too much. I was fine," Mia fibbed. "Just tired after a long week at work."

"I'm glad that was all it was," he said, and his blue-eyed gaze held hers for a second or two longer than was necessary.

"What else would it have been?" she said, but she had a feeling she knew what was coming next and did not want to hear it.

"I thought maybe you didn't want to go out when Julie told you I wanted to come along."

"Now why would you think that?" But Mia knew perfectly well why. She felt uncomfortable knowing it, too. Fred was a decent guy, and decent guys were hard to find. The only catch was that it seemed she had no interest in decent guys right now. Only the perfidious, reptilian ones. Like Lloyd. She burned afresh at the thought of last night. "I was really wiped out."

"Some other time then?"

"Sure."

"Like when?"

"It's hard to say. Between work and my daughter, I hardly ever come up for air."

"Why don't you call me when you're free?" Fred said, digging into the pocket of his jeans and producing a card with his name and number in crisp block lettering.

"I will," she said. "Call you." She took the card, which she had a momentary impulse to deposit in the next trash can she saw. It wasn't that she didn't like him. She actually liked him quite a bit. But she didn't feel ready for the wild ride of courtship, the crazy dips and drops. Then she looked at Fred, all buzz cut and hopeful smile. Just a date, she thought. A quiet dinner somewhere, a drink or maybe two afterward. She could deal with a date. The card fit neatly into her wallet. She *would* call. She just couldn't say when.

"See you," he said, giving her a last blue-eyed look, and then he was gone.

Mia continued down Seventh Avenue, wishing she had a pair of big Jackie O sunglasses. There were times when Park Slope felt a little too small, and this was one of them. Up ahead, she saw a group of people milling around on the corner of First Street. Maybe she should cross over, just in case there was someone else she knew and needed to avoid. But the light was against her, and she remained on course.

As she approached the cluster of people, the reason for the crowd became apparent. She saw several kittens in plastic carriers. A big sign read TAKE HOME SOME LOVE. ADOPT A PET TODAY. People were cooing over dogs, fondling cats. Good thing Eden was not here; she'd want to adopt every single mutt they had. Mia was almost past the display when the sight of a small black-and-white dog stopped her. Something about the animal's pointed ears and snout looked familiar.

"What kind of dog is that?" she asked one of the volunteers, a teenage girl with a frizzy top knot and multiple facial piercings.

"Pomeranian," the girl replied. "Isn't she cute?"

Mia would not have described the creature as cute. She was scrawny, with a terrified, slightly crazed look in her black eyes.

"Want to hold her?" the girl persisted. Without waiting for an answer, she scooped up the dog and handed her to Mia. The animal felt like she weighed about five pounds and she trembled violently. But she placed her tiny head on Mia's clavicle and looked up. Then it clicked: Mr. Ortiz had had Pomeranians, though the two overstuffed, wheezy creatures that waddled along the hallway had little in common with this waif.

Mia handed her back to the girl, who put her down again. The dog limped over to a bowl of water and took a few laps.

"What's wrong with her leg?"

"It's not her leg, it's her foot." The girl knelt and gently grasped the dog, holding up her back right paw for inspection.

Mia saw that a couple of the toe pads were missing; the sight filled her with a small but creeping sense of anxiety.

"Some sadist burned her paw with a cigarette. Can you believe it? We found her wandering around with that back paw oozing green gunk and swollen to twice its normal size. So in the end, those two toe pads had to come off. She's lucky she didn't lose the whole foot."

Mia could believe it. She glanced at the other animals. There was a squat, bushy dog wagging its bushy tail on one side of her and an enormous cat with only one eye on the other. The rejects. The ones no one wanted. The black-and-white Pom circled a few times with her limping yet oddly ladylike gait before she curled into herself and settled down.

"I want to adopt her," Mia said, the words a surprise to her own ears.

"Hey, that's great!" said the girl. "She's a little love. Wait and see." She pulled out a clipboard of forms and handed it to Mia. "Fill out the top," she instructed. "I'll find her records." She began shuffling through a big stack of papers.

Mia looked again at the Pom. There was something so wounded and pitiful in her expression that Mia didn't think she could stand to see it. But she wouldn't have to. She was going to adopt the dog, not keep her.

She would forgo Rite Aid and the library in favor of the pet store on Ninth Street. She had one of the shoe-box bills with her today; she'd been keeping a couple in her bag, just in case. She would use it for dog food, a couple of toys, whatever. She would not ask Mr. Ortiz if he wanted the dog; that was not in sync with her newly assembled plan. First she had to get the dog safely home.

The girl returned with a sheet of medical records that Mia folded and stuffed in her bag. She didn't want to know what had been done to this animal; what was the point? What mattered was what was going to happen now, not what had gone on before. At the pet store, she stocked up on several varieties of dog food, dog treats, and a new leash and harness. Then, accompanied by the limping but surprisingly agile creature, Mia headed home.

It was only when she had reached her apartment building that she addressed the question of how the dog was to be walked. The landlord seemed deaf to the repeated pleas on the part of the tenants to fix the elevator, but Mia had to find a way to make sure the dog was taken out, not allowed to roam the hallways. She was willing to do it sometimes. And Eden could help. Then there was her secret stash—she could use some of that, too. It suddenly became imperative to her to make this work.

She was so psyched by her idea that she went directly to Mr. Ortiz's apartment. She pressed the bell and waited for him to shuffle to the door.

"Señora Saul," he said. He was dressed in dark pants and a deeply yellowed white shirt. She almost never rang his bell, and she could tell he was wondering why she was doing so now. "Can I help you with something?"

"Yes, you can. And here she is." Mia held out the dog, which was cowering, naturally. Cowering seemed to be her M.O.

"You have a dog?" Mr. Ortiz reached for the creature.

"She's a rescue." Mia sidestepped the question.

"Rescue?"

"You know. She's from a shelter. If someone doesn't take her, they'll put her to sleep."

Mr. Ortiz looked at the dog and tentatively stroked her head. She moved a little closer into his embrace.

"That would be a great pity," he said slowly. He continued to stroke the dog, whose trembling did not stop but visibly diminished. Or was this Mia's imagination?

"I think so, too. So you'll take her?"

"I would like to, Señora Saul. But the stairs . . . my knees . . . Señor Manny. I really don't think I can."

"I've thought about that," Mia said excitedly. "We'll find someone to walk her. My daughter Eden will do it sometimes. And so will I." This was a rash, extravagant promise. Walking the dog late at night, early in the morning, when it rained, sleeted, snowed . . . Then she remembered the horrible sound the other dog had made in response to Manny's brutal kick and knew she was going to find a way. "Don't worry. I can take care of it."

"That is very, very kind," he said. "But I can't let you."

"Why not?"

"It wouldn't be right," he said. "It's too much trouble."

"Then the dog will be put to sleep. Killed." Mia knew this would get him.

"You are sure?"

"Who's going to adopt her with that foot?"

"I don't want her to die," he said, more to the dog than to Mia.

"Neither do I," Mia said. Impulsively, she squeezed Mr. Ortiz's shoulder. The dog seemed to cringe when she got close. "You're doing the right thing, Mr. Ortiz," she said. Then she handed him the bag of dog paraphernalia and retreated, before he could change his mind.

LATER, SHE WENT to Julie's. Shoes were everywhere: the floor, the sofa, the chairs, the table. Julie was a fanatic about footwear and had decided to use her night off to sort through every pair she owned. Mia moved aside high-heeled boots, suede clogs, and raffia slides in three colors—tangerine, lime green, and pink—in order to create a place to sit down.

"How are you?" Julie wanted to know. "Totally hungover?"

"Not anymore."

"That's good." The shoes were being arranged in groups: one for the shoemaker, another to give away, a third to put back in her closet. "Anyway, how is it going with Lloyd?" When Mia didn't answer, Julie gave her a swift, sharp look. "Okay, you better tell me about it. *All* about it."

So Mia did. When she finished, Julie tossed a black velvet ballet flat in her direction. It just missed her head. "Watch out," she said, tossing the shoe back. "You almost hit me."

"Too bad I didn't," Julie said. "It might have woken you up. How could you? Didn't I tell you not to do that? Not even to *think* of doing that? Sleeping with an ex is always a terrible idea." Julie, who had two exes, had slept with both of them.

"You were right." Mia sighed.

"So then—why?"

"Why did you?"

"I was younger."

"By about . . . let's see . . . a year?"

"Listen, it's only because I did it that I know what a disaster it is. There's no reason both of us have to go through it, is there?"

"Well, it's too late now."

"True. Now it's a matter of damage control." Julia slipped on a pair of red patent-leather spike heels with big red flowers at the toe. "Are these hot or are they tacky?" She stepped back.

"Tacky," said Mia. "Get rid of them."

"What did you say to him this morning?" Julie removed the shoes and held them almost tenderly, as if loath to let them go.

"I haven't seen him yet. He made Eden breakfast and then they disappeared."

"When you do see him, apologize in as few words as possible and then never bring it up again. It's done, over, finished."

"I don't see that it makes much difference whether I mention it again or not."

"Oh no," Julie said firmly. She finally deposited the red shoes in the discard pile, but not, Mia could see, without some regret. "You're trying to save face. And saving face is crucial."

Mia stayed for dinner: frozen burritos in the microwave, Diet Coke, and a virgin box of Mallomars. As they were saying good-bye, Julie handed her a shopping bag bulging with shoes.

"Would you drop these off at the bar on your way home?"

"What for?"

"Because I promised them to Fred. His daughter is in some local theatrical thing, and they're scrounging for costumes."

"I guess they're all playing call girls?" Mia peered into the bag; the red heels were right on top.

"Very funny. Now could you please just take them over? It's on your way."

"Will Fred be there?"

"Do you care?"

"Well," said Mia, picking up one of the red shoes and holding it in her hand. "Sort of."

"You said you weren't interested, so what's the big deal?"

"I bumped into him today. On Seventh Avenue. I don't want him to think I'm stalking him."

"If you aren't interested, he'll figure it out. So don't worry. Now would you please just go?"

Mia took the bag—it was heavy, but she wasn't going to protest any more—and started out toward the bar. The place was crowded, and she was greeted by the seal-like yelps of merriment emanating from a group seated at a large, central table. The bar was packed, too, and it was only when she was directly in front of it that she was able to see Fred, smoothly moving back and forth as he poured, mixed, stirred, and shook. Mia spied a bottle of gin and felt her stomach clench with the memory of last night's excess, but she composed her face into a reasonable facsimile of a smile when her eyes met his.

"Hey," was all he said, but Mia could tell he was glad to see her.

"Hey, yourself." She couldn't find a seat at the bar and resigned herself to standing. She set the bag on the floor close to the bar, so no one would step on it.

"Are you following me?" asked Fred. His hands were in constant motion as he spoke; Mia watched, lulled despite herself, by the way he moved them.

"It looks that way, doesn't it?"

"Uh-huh."

"Well, I'm not. This afternoon was an accident. And tonight . . ."

"You realized that I'm the guy of your dreams, and you had to come and tell me about it." He grinned and the chipped tooth winked hello.

"Not exactly. The guy of my dreams left me for a Korean manicurist and I stupidly let him stay in my apartment anyway."

"Now why would you do a thing like that?" Fred's blue eyes were bright with concern.

"Because he's the father of my kid, and he's always known how to sweet-talk me."

"Ah . . ." said Fred, but it was a wise and knowing *ah*, and hearing it somehow made Mia feel understood, even appreciated.

"Anyway, I brought something I think you wanted."

"You did? A present for me?"

"Not a present. And it's not technically for you." She hauled out the bag.

"Julie's shoes!" said Fred, looking down. "Kyra will flip."

Before Mia could respond, a waitress put in an order for drinks, and for a few minutes, Fred's back was turned while he worked. Mia studied him openly, the span of his shoulders, the ever-so-slight bounce in his step. He turned back to her again. "Thanks for bringing these." Then he looked at her more carefully and said, "I think you need a drink." Mia must have looked slightly sick at his words because he quickly added, "Don't worry—it will be something without any sting." He got busy again and handed her something in a tall glass. The liquid was ruby-colored and garnished with a sprig of mint and the thinnest half-moon of orange. Mia took an experimental sip, followed by another, longer one.

"Delicious," she said. "What's in it?"

"Pomegranate juice, ginger ale, and a hint of mango nectar. Good for whatever ails you."

"Really?"

"Really," said Fred. "Even sweet-talking exes."

"You have one, too?"

"Do I ever." Fred sighed in a deeply theatrical way. "But you don't want to know about that."

"Yes, I do," she said. And it was true. "But not tonight. Okay if I call you?"

"You have my card," he said.

"Right." She sucked the drink down through a straw. Of course she had his card—it was in her wallet. "And I'll use it, too." She tried to pay for her drink, but he refused her money. So she set the empty glass on the bar and said good night. Two leggy young women had their arms around each other's shoulders and were doing a drunken version of the cancan while their respective dates—and several other guys—looked on appreciatively. Mia resisted the impulse to pet the blonde one—she had a headful of ringlets as if she were a dog. A dog! Didn't she promise Mr. Ortiz she would walk the dog? Jesus, she was so impulsive sometimes. Most of the time, really. She had better hurry.

It had gotten colder. She walked along Seventh Avenue, arms clasped tightly around her chest. As if that would help. She couldn't decide whether she hoped that Lloyd would be awake or asleep when she got home. In either case, she was going to stay as far away from him as she could manage in six hundred square feet. She took the stairs up to her floor, and when she came to Mr. Ortiz's door, she was surprised to see that he had pulled it open and was standing there, as if he had been waiting for her. He wore his paisley robe and ruined slippers; the dog was clutched tightly in his arms.

"I'm here to walk her," said Mia, guilty for not having remembered earlier.

"No," he said. "She doesn't need to be walked." Mia must have looked puzzled, so he added, "It's really like a little miracle, Señora Saul. You won't believe it until you see it. Come." He gestured for her to follow.

Mia waited a beat before entering the apartment. She had never been in there before, and was not sure she wanted to see how Mr. Ortiz lived. But she followed him down a long hall whose walls sported a faded and dirty coat of aquamarine paint. At the end of this hallway was a room that seemed to be their destination.

"There," he said, extending his arm. "Can you believe it?"

Mia wasn't sure what he meant: the brocade sofa with its taut covering of clear, impervious vinyl, the large still life on black velvet—a massive bowl of fruit containing oranges, pineapples, and bananas that had the heft and menace of weapons—the six ornately carved chairs crammed around a small octagonal table. But somehow she sensed that none of this was what Mr. Ortiz was intent on showing her, and so she looked again and noticed the open bathroom door and the plastic box on the floor.

Mia got closer and saw that the box was filled with kitty litter, and right in the center of the kitty litter was a small, tight coil of excrement. Mia was too stunned to comment. Did he really just call her in and ask her to walk down the hall to look at this? The poor guy. He was losing it, he really was. She summoned the nerve to look at him; he was smiling beatifically. Nuts, she thought with pity. Totally nuts. Then the significance of what she was seeing hit her, and her slow-breaking smile mirrored his.

"The dog?" she asked. "Did it in there?"

"Yes!" Mr. Ortiz said, looking down on her with a kind of melting rapture. "She went right in. Knew just what to do. Now I don't have to worry about the elevator or my knees ever again."

"A dog that's litter box trained. Pretty amazing."

"Señora Saul, would you hold her for a moment? While I clean up?"

Mia took the dog. The creature was not trembling now, not even the slightest bit. She had come home, Mia thought. She had come home, and she knew it. Stiffly, Mr. Ortiz bent down and scooped at the kitty litter; a moment later he flushed the toilet. Done. Mia waited until he washed his hands and dried them on a tiny, fringed hand towel that was the same faded color of the hallway. Then she handed him back the dog. They said good-bye at the doorway to his apartment and Mia felt oddly fortified for whatever she might face in her own.

But the feeling evaporated as soon as she stepped inside to find Eden and Lloyd, asleep together on the love seat. Eden was in Lloyd's lap; Lloyd had his neck stretched back, and his head was resting against one of Mia's pillows. But when Mia attempted to slip past them, he opened his eyes and looked straight at her.

"Bed?" Mia asked softly. Lloyd didn't answer but shifted Eden's body slightly so that he was cradling her in his long arms, a limp, outsized doll, and then he stood up. Eden's eyelids fluttered and she mumbled something incomprehensible, but she didn't wake. Mia sat on the love seat, nervously picking at stray threads, until Lloyd had deposited Eden on the trombone-splattered sheets and came back into the room.

"We went to the zoo today," he volunteered.

"Prospect Park?"

"Bronx. She went crazy over the snow leopards. She wants to be a snow leopard for Halloween."

Mia was silent. How was she supposed to find a snow leopard costume anyway? Maybe Eden would change her mind by then.

"About last night . . ." Lloyd began.

"It was a mistake," Mia said quickly. "A big mistake, and I'm sorry." She hoped that this would suffice.

"I'm sorry, too," Lloyd said. "I shouldn't have gone along with it." Now that was decent of him, Mia thought. But then he spoiled it by adding, "More sorry for you, though. You aren't handling things very well."

"I'm not handling things very well?" It took all her willpower not to scream. "You *left* me, Lloyd. You left *us.* That's a lot to handle, okay? You can find it in yourself to forgive me if I sometimes don't do a very good job."

"But you've got to handle it. For Eden's sake. And for your own, too. You can't let yourself get stuck in the past. It'll wreck you, Mia."

You wrecked me, she wanted to say. But would not allow herself to. She resumed pulling threads out of the love seat with a new ferocity.

"Anyway, I'll be going tomorrow," Lloyd continued.

"Eden will miss you."

"I'll miss her, too. But I'll be back," he said.

"When?" she asked.

"It's hard for me to say right now."

"Well, it's hard for Eden not to know."

"Look, there's no point in trying to make me feel guilty."

"Why not?" she asked. "You should feel guilty. You *are* guilty."

"Guilty of what? Of not loving you anymore?"

This was like a fresh blow, and she said nothing, not trusting herself to speak.

"I still love Eden though. I love her very much," said Lloyd.

"Then try showing it."

"You don't think I show it?" Lloyd was genuinely incredulous. "Why don't you ask Eden about that? I'll bet that she'll have a different interpretation. I think she knows I love her. And I think you know that she knows."

With that, Lloyd stood and reached for the pump to inflate the air mattress, which was folded neatly on the floor. Mia stood, too. She wished she could deliver some perfect parting shot, but suddenly, all the vitriol and fight was sucked right out of her, and she was sad, just sad, without being even the least bit drunk.

In the morning, she was still in bed when she heard the sound of the apartment door opening and then closing. She waited a few minutes before getting up. In the kitchen, there was an envelope with Eden's name on it and underneath her name, a rather inept but still charming drawing of what she supposed was a snow leopard. Mia walked over to the apartment door and opened it. Lloyd was gone and the only sound she heard was a small, distinct *woof* from the Pomeranian who now lived across the hall.

SEVEN

Mia finished her work on *All That Trash*. She was confident her suggestions would make the book, already good, even more marketable. Nonfiction books rarely got the accolades in kiddie lit, and Mia understood the almost-universal preference for Harry Potter and vampire stories, though the charms of Mommy Mousie would forever remain elusive to her. Still, she hoped this one broke out and got some serious attention for the author; he deserved it.

Of more immediate concern was that her freelance job at Winthrop Lee Publishing was about to come to an end. She'd known this for some time but had not wanted to deal with it—she had been too busy dealing with Lloyd, the assorted cast of characters at Eden's school, and Mr. Ortiz's new dog, whom he'd named Mariposa. Within a week of her arrival, Mariposa developed a serious kidney infection, resulting in piteous howling and puddles of blood-clotted urine that were, thank God, confined to the litter box and elsewhere in Mr. Ortiz's apartment, not the hallway. This had necessitated trips to the vet and various medications, all of which Mia paid for with her bills from her precious stash.

"You are so kind, Señora Saul," said Mr. Ortiz. "I am forever in your debt."

Something about those words unsettled Mia; she didn't want anyone in her debt. That's not why she had helped him. But she shook off the feeling; Mr. Ortiz was only trying to thank her.

When her last day at Winthrop Lee arrived, Mia started feeling the familiar thrum and pulse of *what next*. Lloyd's check was some help, and she did have a little money socked away from her visits to *the machine*. But this, she knew, was not to be confused with a long-term plan. Or even a short-term plan. She spent the morning cleaning out her cubicle and was treated to a farewell lunch by several of her coworkers. Then there was the obligatory good-bye visit to the editor in chief, a grandmotherly woman whose brass-buttoned cardigans, lace-up shoes, and short gray hair were totally at odds with her sharp-witted and occasionally foul-mouthed outbursts at the editorial meetings over which she majestically presided. After that, Mia was a free agent once more.

She walked slowly toward the subway station, for once not in a rush. The greenmarket tempted her, but she was already carrying quite a lot, and Eden wouldn't be home that night anyway. Since it was Friday, she was going to Caitlin's for a sleepover. Mia continued south, past the entrance to the subway, until she reached the Strand Book Store, on the corner of Twelfth Street and Broadway.

Ah, the Strand! Mecca for lovers of used, old, and rare books, it had been around for decades. Her father used to bring her here with Stuart on Saturdays when they were kids. He gave them each five dollars and let them loose in the store. While he pored over titles like *The Night Sky* and *The Stars Above*, she and Stuart tried to outdo each other by finding books with pictures of naked people. Stuart's *National Geographic* volume showing bare-breasted and scanty-loincloth-covered Africans was the clear winner until Mia came up with *A Passage of Wonder: Witnessing a Child's Birth*, which showed pictures of a real, live baby emerging from a painfully stretched, hair-covered orifice. They bought the book for $1.98 and spent the subway ride home trying to yank it out of each other's hands for a better view of its many and reverently photographed images. Their father, deeply immersed in *The Edge of the Universe—And Beyond*, was oblivious to the precise nature of their purchase; not that he would have been perturbed had he known.

Mia checked her bulging canvas bag as soon as she entered the Strand

and so prowled blissfully unencumbered through the stacks of books. Here was a hefty volume on medieval tapestries that she would have loved to own. Or how about this one, devoted exclusively to patterns on eighteenth-century French dinnerware? She skimmed the pages, almost tasting the dense, deeply saturated colors: cobalt blue, apple green, the wholly unreal, enamel-like pink of a perfect sugar rose. She dipped into the poetry section, and then toured through astronomy, where she felt the momentary presence—warm, like the wind in July—of her father's ghost. Travelogues from the 1900s, novels whose reviews had intrigued her, twenty-six volumes of a child's encyclopedia published in 1937, amply illustrated in Art Deco duotones. She was not planning to buy anything for herself; she had scores of books at home, and anyway, she was a big believer in the Brooklyn Public Library system. But she didn't need to buy to be happy. The slight whiff of mildew in the air around her and the fine coating of dust gently anointing the spines and pages of all these books soothed and centered her; Mia was content just inhaling the aromatic and faintly mournful scent of the literary past.

A wide, flat book, no dust jacket, only a blue-cloth cover, attracted her eye. *The Magic of Money.* The cover alone was a curiosity. Books published today had cloth spines and cardboard covers. A fully cloth cover was obsolete, like subway tokens or milk in bottles. She picked it up. Roman coins, with their crisp-edged profiles of long-dead rulers; humble ha'pennies and farthings; a solid gold crown with a resplendent profile of Queen Victoria on the front. There were pictures of paper currency, too, the earliest notes printed in the brand-new United States, the intricately idiosyncratic bills of Western Europe before the euro homogenized everything like the monetary equivalent of Starbucks. She looked at the title page; the book had been published in 1974. The Strand's familiar neon orange sticker on the inside cover read $7.98. A veritable bargain. And the perfect birthday gift for Stuart, precisely the kind of book they would have loved and fought over in their childhood. She brought the book up to the cash register, where a by-now routinely pierced and tattooed young person took her money and handed her back the bagged book. It was a bit unwieldy when added to all the other things she was carrying, but she nonetheless managed to get everything home.

Without Eden, the evening seemed to stretch on forever. She read a chapter of Proust; she had a nap. Cooking for herself seemed like too much of a chore, so she ate an apple, a pear, a stale granola bar, and finally one of the shockingly sweet Milky Way bars she had been stockpiling for Halloween. Around nine o'clock, she opened *The Magic of Money*, which she planned to read before wrapping up for Stuart. But interesting as the book was, she couldn't concentrate. The title just started her thinking about money all over again. Her job had ended; she would have to hustle to get something else. What else was new?

She closed the book with a decisive snap. *The machine. The machine* was new. Why hadn't she thought of it sooner? Because to think about it was insane, that's why. This outpouring of unasked-for cash could not possibly continue. The bank must have found out, corrected the mistake, and was at this very second tracing the missing money directly to her. They would be coming for her soon. No, not soon. *Now.* Guilt and dread turned her heart into a sodden sneaker, pounding in a dryer, ka-thump, ka-thump, ka-*thump.*

But she was being ridiculous. There was no possible way to trace this error to her. Her receipts, her statements from the bank—and she had saved every single one—offered no evidence, not a shred. No, she had been lucky, that was all. And she might just get lucky again. Before she could change her mind, Mia got her boots and jacket and was off.

The avenue was filled with people spilling out of the restaurants, into the bars. Mia hurried, head down, not looking anyone in the eye. She was at the bank in a matter of minutes, using her bank card to gain entry past the now-locked double doors. No one else was in the vestibule; thank God for small favors. She must have looked as guilty as if she'd just bought a gun and held up the Korean market across the street.

Mia slipped the card into the slot. Immediately, the screen brightened, as if it had been flooded with sunlight. So intense was this light that Mia had to shut her eyes, and even so, she could still sense the light through her closed lids, painting their insides with wavy red squiggles and incandescent red blobs. Instinctively, she brought both hands to her face, to shield it.

But when she heard the music—violins, the trill of a flute, a harp— her hands fell to her sides and she opened her eyes once again. The screen was still unusually bright, though the intensity of the light had diminished. The usual array of instructions and options had vanished; instead, there were these words:

A gift. For you, Mia. Use it well.

The music—a harp had come into it, too; she was sure it was a harp—swelled, filling the space in her head and in her chest. Then it subsided and everything was quiet. She stood there, trying to absorb what she had just seen and heard. She didn't, contrary to cliché, feel that she was dreaming. Instead, everything had a lapidary clarity. The big, shiny squares of tile on the bank's floor, the smudged fingerprints on the plate-glass window, and the crumpled receipt that had missed the trash can were as real to her as the unexplained music and the blinding light. And the words. The words that were still there.

Stunned, she looked down and saw the single bill that waited only for her to claim it. When she did, her hand began not so much to shake as to vibrate, like a cell phone with the ringer turned down. The bill she was holding—fresh, crisp, and that particular cool, silvery, goes-with-anything green—was not a twenty or even a hundred. In her tingling, electrically charged fingers, Mia held an honest-to-God ten-thousand-dollar bill.

EIGHT

A<small>T LEAST SHE</small> *thought* it was a ten-thousand-dollar bill. How would she know? She had never seen one before. She doubted that many people had. But this was neither the place nor the time to examine it. She had to get it home where she could look at it more carefully. She was too nervous to put the thing in her pocket, so she carefully inserted the bill down the front of her jeans, letting it lodge near the top of her panties, just under her belly button. Then she raced back to her apartment, trying to hold her stomach in, so the bill wouldn't get wrinkled. Her heart was thudding like a hammer in her chest, quite possibly the precursor to a heart attack. Or maybe it *was* a heart attack and she was too stupid to know. But no, after a minute or two, the quiet of the apartment calmed her and her heart rate returned to something approaching normal. She had messages—one from Eden, calling to say good night. Another from her mother. She'd call them back.

Mia extracted the bill from her pants and set it on the kitchen counter. It certainly looked real. She rummaged through a drawer, rejecting an ice-cream scoop, chopsticks, a serrated knife, until she came up with her prize: a magnifying glass. Under the thick glass lens, the subtle, undulating weave of the paper was revealed. God, it looked convincing. There was a seal, and a serial number, and all that official-looking jazz that was on legitimate bills. She put down the magnifying glass and picked up the bill by its edges.

On the front was a portrait of someone named Salmon Chase. Who was Salmon Chase? He must have done something significant to earn such an exalted place. And what kind of a name was Salmon? Did his buddies call him Sally? Looking at his bald head, his stern, accusatory expression, she doubted it. She'd Google him right now, but her laptop was on the fritz; she had gotten by using the computer at Winthrop Lee, so it hadn't seemed imperative to get it fixed. Now she wished she had. She turned the bill over. THE UNITED STATES OF AMERICA, it read, and underneath, TEN THOUSAND DOLLARS. The number 10,000 appeared, blocky and squat, at each corner and was superimposed, in a larger, lighter typeface, across the central panel.

Mia was burning to know whether this bill was the real thing. But there was no way for her to tell, and no one she could ask. Holding the bill away from her body by a single corner, as if it might be radioactive, she walked back into the other room. *The Magic of Money* was still on the floor where she'd left it.

She pounced on the book and pawed through its pages. Sure enough, there was a brief section on paper currency in the United States. Skimming it quickly, she hit pay dirt in the third paragraph:

From the late 1920s through the late 1960s, Federal Reserve Notes were routinely traded in commerce. Their most common use was bank to bank, when large sums of money were transferred. But the advent of bank wires rendered them obsolete. In 1969, the U.S. government asked the public to redeem any remaining in circulation for smaller denominations. These rare bills will always retain their face value at banks, but they possess a much higher value to collectors.

She felt the hum of excitement growing as she continued to read.

$500, $1,000, $5,000, and $10,000 denominations were printed only in the 1928, 1934, 1934 A, 1934 B, or 1934 C series. Although all these denomination notes are highly uncommon, the 34 B and 34 C series are the most rare; no known examples have been encountered. The 1928 series were "Redeemable in Gold on demand." The 1934 A, B, and C series were the last high denomination notes printed in 1945. Finally, on July 14, 1969, the

Department of the Treasury and the Federal Reserve System announced that the high denomination notes would be discontinued immediately; they cited lack of use as the reason. All high denomination notes that are turned into banks are forwarded to the Federal Reserve and destroyed immediately.

There were a couple of pictures, too, though none of the ten-thousand-dollar note. But she was encouraged to learn that the Treasury had printed big bills at one time; while the bill she had might not be genuine, at least the possibility of its authenticity was there. She checked the series—A—and the year—1934. So it was not one of the rarest notes. But if—and this was a big if—it were real, it had to be worth something above and beyond the face value. The question was, how much? She would have to proceed very carefully here, try to figure out what to do with the damn thing. She certainly didn't want to send it to the Treasury. But she couldn't exactly spend it at the supermarket either. There must be someone who would want it, not as currency, but as the collector's item that it obviously was.

Forcing herself to stop thinking about the bill for a few minutes, she called Caitlin's apartment to say good night to Eden.

"Mom, is it okay if we watch a movie that's rated PG-13?"

"What movie?"

"I don't know yet. But Caitlin and I want to find one with that rating."

"That's no way to pick a movie."

"Why not?"

"Let me talk to Caitlin's mom."

"We asked her already. She said it's okay with her if it's okay with you."

"All right then. But nothing too bloody or scary."

"We're not interested in bloody or scary, Mom," said Eden. She had that jaded, patronizing tone that Mia found so exasperating.

"No? So what are you interested in?"

"You know—kissing. Also cursing."

"Kissing is okay," said Mia, surprising herself by thinking of Fred, not Lloyd. "But just kissing. Nothing else."

After she said good-bye to Eden, she went into her bedroom, climbed onto the chair, and put the bill in the box with her wedding shoes. It was only when she was actually in bed with the lights out that she allowed herself to think about the other part of what had happened tonight: the mysterious light, the music, and, most unbeliev-able of all, the message: *A gift. For you, Mia. Use it well.* Three lines. Eight words. What possible explanation could there be for such a thing? A bank error, if this *were* a bank error, was a random occurrence. But this was not random, not at all. The machine had known her *name.* It was communicating with her. This was beyond weird, beyond strange. But it was also, in some entirely credible way, wonderful. Mia had not felt so special or chosen in years. She shifted under the new sheets, as alert and animated as if a pint of coffee had been injected directly into her veins.

Once upon a time, she had felt chosen. By Lloyd, as a lover and wife. By her brother, as his best friend. By her parents, whose occasional be-nign neglect and respective self-absorption in no way obscured their obvious, encompassing love. There had been a gym teacher in tenth grade—a hectoring, desiccated woman who decided to punish Mia for some infraction by making her stand on her head in a far corner of the perpetually dim and foul-smelling gym. Betty had swooped (literally— she had favored a long, flowing cape and ankle-length skirts in those years) into school, magnificent as a swan defending the nest. "I didn't raise my daughter for you to abuse!" she told the teacher, cowing her into an apologetic submission that lasted at least until Mia's gradua-tion. And, years earlier, there had been the Halloween when Mia was the Queen of Hearts. Betty had painted a copy of the playing card onto two large pieces of cardboard. Mia, in a red pleated skirt, red sweater, and red shoes, had proudly displayed the likenesses of the gaudy queen looped over her shoulders. Her crown was cardboard covered in aluminum foil. Best of all was the white bakery bag, on which Betty painted a simple red heart. How Mia had loved that bag! It had lifted her out of the ordinary ranks of children, with their dreary, dun-colored bags, and made her feel uniquely prized. Somewhere along the way, though, she had lost the sense of being special, and she had not expected to find it again. Until now. She got up and went in search of the bank receipt. As usual, it showed a withdrawal of one hundred dollars.

There was something printed on the back of the receipt, an offer extended by the bank for opening a CD or money market account. *A gift for you . . .* it began. There were those words again. Astonishing. Just astonishing. She thought of the numinous screen at the bank. If the bill really was a gift, it exonerated her from any wrongdoing. How could it be wrong to take what was given—specifically, unequivocally—to her? She put the receipt with all the others before getting back into bed. Her last waking thought was of her mother—she had forgotten to call her. Mia felt the familiar spark of guilt and tried to stub it out. Too late to phone now; Betty would have to wait until tomorrow.

THE NEXT MORNING, Mia was out before nine, striding along Union Street in the brittle October air to the main branch of the Brooklyn Public Library at Grand Army Plaza. She was there when the doors opened, and so was able to nab a seat at one of the library's computers. She had only a thirty-minute window before her turn was up, so she had to work fast. But Google didn't let her down, and, in minutes, she had retrieved the names of a dozen dealers in rare coins and currencies; she also found out that Salmon Chase was the Treasury secretary under Lincoln. *Go, Salmon,* she thought as she logged off. *Sally, you sly dog.*

Back at home, she climbed onto the chair in search of the shoe box; when she found it, she half expected that the bill would be gone, or turned into a smaller denomination. But no, it was right there where she left it. She took it out of the box and tenderly carried it into the kitchen, where she set it on one of her new bathroom towels. Then she turned to the list. Four of the currency dealers were located in New York City. It was a long shot that any of them would be working on a Saturday, but why not try? Eden didn't need to be picked up until noon, so Mia had a little time. Some of the names danced across the page; others marched. One of them, Oscar Kornblatt, actually seemed to ooze. Kornblatt was not a felicitous name, she decided. She wouldn't call him. What about Tony Latazza? Or Mike Scopes? She liked those zz's in Latazza; they had a certain flair. Scopes was strong, unapologetic, honest-sounding. She tried Tony first, but the number was no longer in service, no further information available. The number for Mike Scopes rang and rang; clearly he didn't believe in answering machines. The last name on the list was Solly Phelps. She tapped in the numbers, not expecting much. But someone answered on the first ring.

"Phelps here." The voice was deep, rich, and smooth. Mia could imagine it being poured through the phone line, like molten chocolate. It was even better than Lloyd's voice, which was saying a lot.

"Solly Phelps?"

"Solly Phelps. Can I help you?"

"I found your name online," said Mia, suddenly flummoxed. Now that she was actually about to tell someone about the bill, she was frightened. Her voice emerged from her throat in an unnaturally high pitch, almost a squeak. This would not do. Solly Phelps was not going to take her seriously if she sounded like one of the characters in the Mommy Mousie series.

"Are you buying or selling?" Solly Phelps cut right to the chase.

"Well, I'm not sure . . ." Mia said. "That is, I'm thinking of selling. But I wanted to get some more information first." The bill glowed, silvery-green, against the garnet color of the towel.

"What have you got? Silver? Gold? If it's silver, I'm not really interested. Gold is good though; gold is always good."

"Actually, it's paper."

"Could be interesting. The denom?"

"Denom?"

"Denomination."

Mia stalled. She was not ready to disclose the amount yet. "It's a large . . . denom," she said, carefully trying out the word.

"Could be interesting to me. But condition is important. I'm really only looking for VF and EF."

"Sorry, I'm not following you," Mia said.

"VF is very fine; EF is extremely fine," Solly explained in that expensive-liquor-smooth voice of his. "EF shows signs of light handling only. No more than three light folds or one strong crease. VF is still attractive, but shows more wear. You know—vertical and horizontal folds. Some dirt on the paper."

"Actually, the paper is very clean. It has a kind of sheen. And it doesn't show any signs of handling at all." Mia stared at the bill. "It looks new."

"You've got an uncirculated bill? Really? What is it? A five-hundred note?"

"No. It's bigger than that."

"Hey, what is this? I don't have time for twenty questions."

Mia waited a beat. She had better just say it. Otherwise, she was going to lose him. "It's a ten," she began.

"A ten?" He cut her off. "Listen, don't waste my time."

"Ten thousand."

"A ten-thousand-dollar note? You're kidding." He was not asking, he was telling.

"No," she said. "I'm not."

"But there are almost none of those in existence anymore. And certainly none in private hands."

"Well, I've got one in mine," she said. Salmon Chase glared up at her. "I'm looking at it right now."

"How do you know it's real?" he countered.

"How do you know it isn't?"

Solly Phelps was silent. "I'd like to see it," he said finally.

"All right." She had done it, she realized. She had taken the first step. Toward what, she didn't know.

"Can you come in later today?"

"Not today. Not tomorrow either. Monday."

"Monday," confirmed Solly. "Nine o'clock all right?"

Mia thought for a second. No job to hustle to; Eden's drop-off was at eight fifteen. Enough time to hop on the train and get to Manhattan by nine.

"Nine's fine."

He gave her an address: 540 West 30th Street. Must be over by the Hudson River. Or maybe in the river.

"What did you say your name was?" Solly asked.

"I didn't say. But I will on Monday. Bye." She clicked the button and terminated the conversation. Her hands were tingling again, and her heart was starting to pound. Was this smart? Could she trust him? She considered the idea of a sidekick, an accomplice. Julie? Yes? No. It should be a guy. Stuart was a natural for the job, but though she wished she could have told her wild story to Stuart, he no longer seemed like a willing ear. He had retreated to some inaccessible, Mia-free zone that she had to fight to penetrate. And Lloyd, even had he been around, was out of the question.

Then it hit her. She knew just whom to ask. Glancing at her watch, she saw it was almost time to get Eden from Caitlin's. But first, she dug into her wallet, where Fred's card was still tucked in one of its creased leather folds. It took a minute to retrieve it from deep in the wallet's innermost recesses; she sat looking at it briefly before she reached for the phone. Fred was a good guy, that much she could acknowledge. And if she were in the market for a good guy, he might even be the one.

But if she asked Fred to accompany her, she would have to explain the nature of her errand, and how she came to be in possession of this bill. Which was something she did *not* want to do. As long as no one knew about the machine and its mysterious gift, a gift for her, it had said, the gift was hers alone, to ponder over, marvel at, use as she saw fit. Once she told someone else, everything would change, and her private little miracle would be exposed to the scrutiny—and the judgment—of everyone around her.

Mia tucked the card back in her wallet, taking the time to smooth out its upper left corner, which had gotten a little bent. Like it or not, she was on her own.

NINE

SUNDAY IT POURED. Mia didn't mind; it gave her an excuse to stay home with Eden and putter. Glorious, sunny weather brought with it a particular kind of reproach: shouldn't she be out biking/skating/flying a kite in the park with her child? The rain absolved her of all that relentless good cheer; they could stay at home, content to watch the fat raindrops hit the windows and then trickle down, to pool on the cracked, chipped sills.

After breakfast, Mia and Eden played a series of board games: Monopoly, Life, Stratego, Scrabble. Not one of these games was intact; there were pieces missing from all of them, but Eden didn't mind.

"We don't have to do what the rules say anyway." She confidently rattled two mismatched dice in her hand. "We can make our own rules, right?"

"Right," said Mia, feeling irrationally proud of her. "We sure can."

It had been hard for Eden since Lloyd left. There were two more incidents of cursing in school—this time just at other kids though, and Eden claimed they cursed at her first—and a couple of extended crying jags. One morning she just wouldn't get out of bed, and Mia, recognizing depression when she saw it, let her spend the day at home, drawing, watching TV, and leafing through her old comic books and *Mad* magazines.

Mia had documented every bump in her daughter's rocky road with the teacher, the school psychologist, the learning specialist, and the principal. Everyone had a different opinion, and everyone seemed to suggest a different course of action. She needed to be given *more respon-*

sibility yet *less pressure;* she had to be held to *a greater level of accountability* but *left to her own devices* and not *pushed too hard;* she should spend *more time on schoolwork, less time on schoolwork, avoid excessive stimulation, seek out more new learning opportunities.* What Eden really needed, in Mia's humble and admittedly not expert opinion, was to be assured of Lloyd's continued love and devotion, which, given his highly erratic life at the moment, was something Mia could not do. Lloyd's attention was like a tropical storm: heavy and drenching when it came, only to dry up and vanish with scarcely a trace.

Late in the day, the rain cleared and they took a walk up to a pizza place on Fifth Avenue. Pizza was cheap and generally something Eden would eat. Mia used one of the twenties from the secret stash to pay for a slice with broccoli and red peppers. To her amazement, Eden wanted the same thing and ate it all. Score one for Mom. Or for the magic money, which seemed to charm whatever it touched. The only dark note in the day came at bedtime, when Eden began talking about Lloyd in that longing yet manic way of hers.

"So you know that Daddy said he's going to take me to Asia with him next time, right? We're going to all these really cool places, like Japan, and Vietnam, and Korea," she said. "He's going to buy me silver chopsticks. Maybe even gold. It's going to be great. No, not great. Amazing. It's going to be amazing." She had Petunia tucked up under her chin as she spoke, and was squeezing her hard.

"He told you that?"

"The last time he was here." She sounded defiant now.

"He didn't mention it to me."

"Well, he mentioned it to *me*," said Eden. "He really and truly did." She flopped back on the bed, Petunia flopping down obligingly alongside her. "So I can go, right? Even if I have to miss, like, a ton of school?"

"I'm not sure," Mia hedged. "We'll have to discuss it." She prepared herself for another round of begging and badgering. But it did not come. Eden was uncharacteristically quiet, and in a few minutes Mia realized that she was asleep.

When her daughter's breathing had settled into an easy, somnolent rhythm, Mia was able to think about her appointment with Solly Phelps. How was she going to carry a ten-thousand-dollar bill, especially one whose condition seemed to be of the utmost importance? She rummaged around the apartment for a few minutes, managing to locate the pieces of cardboard that came with her new sheets (good thing her housekeeping was not *that* expert), a manila envelope, and a Hello Kitty backpack that just yesterday Eden informed her she no longer wanted. Mia trimmed the cardboard to fit the envelope, slipped the bill between the two pieces, slid the pieces into the envelope, and sealed the whole thing with a sponge—her mouth felt so dry she didn't have any spare saliva. The envelope then went inside a book and the book inside the backpack. If she looked ridiculous with Hello Kitty's bloated, wall-eyed face peering out from behind her, then so be it.

Although she knew that the money was not exactly hers, Mia had a hard time believing that keeping or using it was an actual crime. If the mistake had happened once or twice and had then been noticed by the bank, she would, of course, have given the money back, because someone was going to be held accountable; someone would have to pay. But this was on a completely different level, one that seemed to defy human error or even involvement. A ten-thousand-dollar bill, especially one that came with a light show, music, and a personal message, was so outside the realm of the ordinary as to be fantastical, magical, otherworldly. Who didn't notice that ten grand was missing? The only explanation that made sense to her was that it wasn't missing because it hadn't come from the bank at all.

Her father, resolute scientist that he had been, nevertheless had his less-than-scientific side. He believed, for instance, that his grandfather had appeared to him in a dream, and had given him his blessing the night before he began his doctoral program in astronomy. Since his parents were visibly disappointed that their studious, A-garnering son had not elected to join the bright-Jewish-boy triumvirate of doctor/lawyer/accountant, having his grandfather's approval had meant a lot to him. He also owned various lucky objects, though none so predictable as a four-leaf clover or a rabbit's foot. Mia remembered a flat white stone, almost perfectly circular in shape, and a black, crudely fashioned key that opened no door or lock she ever knew of. Then there was the brass gyroscope—still in its original, disintegrating cardboard box—he'd loved as a kid, along with his first penknife and a big blue marble that glowed with the intensity of a planet from a distant galaxy. Whether these objects possessed any actual magic power was immaterial. Mia and Stuart believed because their father believed—that was enough. On the day of a big exam, a tryout for a team, an audition for a play, the marble or the stone would be pressed into a moist palm. The gyroscope sat on Stuart's desk while he typed out his college applications; the key accompanied Mia on her first solo trip to Europe.

So it was conceivable—okay, not likely, not plausible, but in the end, not entirely impossible either—that she, Mia, had stumbled onto a mother lode of magic, right here in her very own backyard, so to speak. And if that were the case, then accepting the benefits that such magic might offer was not only not wrong, but was her right, her mandate even. Who was she to argue?

THE NEXT MORNING was charmed. Eden woke early, dressed without serious incident (the yellow shorts worn over thick ribbed purple tights and topped by a frayed sweatshirt might have given some other mothers pause, but not Mia), and brushed her teeth without being asked. When they were on the way out of the apartment, Mr. Ortiz opened his door and asked Mia if he could speak to her. Mia couldn't help a glance at her watch, but Mr. Ortiz seemed to be bursting with barely containable news.

"I know you are in a rush, Señora Saul," he said. Mariposa limped daintily into the hall, and Eden was happy to squat down to pet her. The dog was looking much better now: less thin, shinier fur. "But it's about Señor Manny."

Manny? What trouble was he causing now? Mia's good feeling about the morning quickly began to evaporate, a puddle in an August sun.

"No, it's not bad," he added, seeing her worried expression. "Señor Manny—he's gone away."

"Really? Are you sure?"

"The policemen came. Three of them. Just yesterday. There was a siren; it was so loud. Also Señor Manny was loud. He was yelling so much." Mr. Ortiz shook his head at the memory. "So much. They put on the—how you say it?—wrist cuffs?" He gestured by placing his own knobby wrists together.

"Handcuffs," supplied Eden, still stroking the dog but looking up with curiosity now.

"Yes, handcuffs. And he has not been back since."

"Well, that's terrific," Mia said. She didn't know how she managed to miss all this, but it was great news. She looked again at her watch. "I really want to hear more about this, Mr. Ortiz. But right now, we've got to hustle." She turned to Eden. "Let's go, honey. You don't want to be late."

"Of course, Señora Saul," Mr. Ortiz said. "You can ring my bell any time." He made a clucking noise at Mariposa, whose pointy ears rose like twin peaks on her dark head. She trotted into the apartment, and he gently closed the door.

"Is Manny going to jail?" Eden asked.

"There's a good chance that he will," said Mia as they descended the stairs. All during the walk to school, Eden wanted to talk about Manny and his progress through the New York City penal system. How big was jail? Did you have to wear striped uniforms, like in the cartoons? Would his family send him a file baked into a birthday cake? Would his leg be shackled to an iron ball?

"No, they don't do things like that anymore," Mia said.

"Too bad. He deserves it."

Mia couldn't exactly disagree, but she felt compelled to add, "He'll have to have a trial first. No one is put in jail without a trial."

"Even someone like him?"

"Even someone like him."

Eden was silent for a moment and then said, "Why are you wearing my Hello Kitty backpack, Mom? Isn't it, like, a little young for you?"

They had arrived at the school, so Mia didn't answer. Instead, she resisted the impulse to kiss Eden atop her tousled head and confined herself to a chirpy "Have a great day!" Then she headed for the subway station, where she swiped her MetroCard, cursed silently until the train arrived, and squeezed in at the last second before the doors closed.

She changed trains at the next stop. The express train was even more crowded. The backpack seemed to her transparent and ablaze with lights; people were staring at it right now; she could feel it, she was sure—she dared to raise her eyes and look around. Several of the seated passengers were reading; a couple of people had their eyes closed; someone in the corner was actually picking his nose—did he think he was invisible, for Christ's sake? A tall, hefty girl with a large beauty mark on one cheek took advantage of the train's brief emergence from the tunnel onto the Manhattan Bridge to pull out her cell phone and make a call. "Tommy?" she said in a breathy voice. "Tommy, it's me." Tommy said something on the other end of the line that made the girl press the phone closer to her face and smile.

When she saw that smile, Mia actually began to relax a little. Or rather, she shifted her worrying to another sphere entirely. Now that she was no longer convinced everyone in the subway car knew what she was carrying on her back, she allowed herself to think about what in the world she was going to tell Solly Phelps.

She had rehearsed any number of different lies in her mind. The bill had been found among the papers of an elderly, deceased uncle; the bill had been sewn into the cushions of a sofa belonging to that same uncle; the bill had been secreted between the back of a frame and a watercolor landscape she had purchased at a flea market in New Jersey. No, Maine—Maine was even farther away, harder to substantiate. But whom was she kidding? These were all, as her mother would have said, *bubbemeisers*, obviously bogus explanations that he would see through in a nanosecond.

Someone knocked against the backpack from behind, and Mia's worry gears immediately shifted again. Had the bill been somehow jostled, tampered with, touched, or, God forbid, *stolen*? She snapped her head around; it was just an old Hasidic man, with a long white beard and a black brimmed hat. His big hazel eyes were meek and harmless. "Sorry," he said. Mia nodded, heartbeat slowing only gradually. At Canal Street, the subway car emptied out, and she was able to sink gratefully into a vacated seat.

Finally, the train pulled into the station at Thirty-fourth Street. Mia practically did a grand jeté out of the doors, and strode purposefully along the platform, up the stairs, and westward. She was wearing all black again—jeans, boots, jacket, and a plush cashmere scarf Stuart had brought her as a gift from a business trip to Scotland—and she imagined the pink, white, and cherry-red backpack glowing like a beacon behind her.

The address Solly Phelps had given her was almost at the Hudson River; the wind was appreciably sharper here, and she stood for a moment before the building, watching the trash blow around the street. An empty coffee cup swirled; greasy wrappers from Burger King fluttered with an unexpected delicacy. She checked the intercom system—a series of worn brass buttons, relics of an older, more gracious New

York lined up in a neat column—before she located the one she sought. Solomon Phelps, Suite 912. She pressed it and was startled by the alacrity of the reply.

"Yes?"

"We have an appointment? Nine o'clock?" Damn, why was she making a simple statement sound like Oliver Twist asking for more?

"Come right up." His voice was even more melt-you-into-puddles than she remembered.

There was no doorman or security guard of any kind, and the small lobby was empty except for a stack of cardboard boxes piled rather precariously on top of one another in a corner. The elevator—another relic, with a lighted dial and black arrow to denote the floor—opened immediately in response to the touch of a button. The ninth floor was a warren of doors, some numbered, others not. She followed the hall in one direction and then another before finding 912. There was no bell or buzzer, so she knocked.

The door flew open, as if the wind that was blowing around outside had penetrated both elevator and corridor.

"Phelps," he said, sticking out his hand.

"Pleased to meet you." She took the proffered hand and looked up. He was huge. Not just tall, like Lloyd, but wide and solid, a veritable mountain of a man. He wore a crisp white shirt, baggy corduroy pants, a black-and-white polka-dot bow tie, and a pair of black suspenders. His hair was that kind of soft, almost shimmery white that sometimes reads as blond, and it grazed his shirt collar; his eyes—small, grayish-blue, fixed on her face—had a shrewd and unsettling look.

"Come in," he said, even though there was not much *in* to speak of. The office was cluttered with file cabinets and shelves disgorging books and stacks of papers, but also with several items of a less expected nature: a grandfather clock, a royal blue unicycle, an ornately curved wooden hat rack, and, mounted on the wall, the head of a stuffed moose whose thick, spreading antlers nearly grazed Solly's face. On the battered desk were more papers, a laptop, and a round glass bowl containing a solitary black fish swimming around and around. Mia felt almost hypnotized by the fish's lyrical circling, and she was glad when Solly broke the spell by dragging over a chair—throne-sized, claw-footed, and covered in disintegrating aubergine brocade—so that she could sit down.

"So you say you have a big bill?" Solly said, not wasting any time.

"I do."

"Well, let's have a look, shall we?" He moved aside some of the desk's clutter and unfurled a length of white paper to cover the torn, dingy blotter. There was something dignified, even grand about the gesture.

Mia sat down gingerly, and eased Hello Kitty off her back. She took out the envelope containing the bill, and when she had freed it from its various layers of protection, she placed it, faceup, on the white paper.

Solly's head swooped down like a hawk's. She saw his shrewd, small eyes widen ever so slightly; he compressed his lips, and his nostrils flared. Mia waited, but he didn't speak. Instead, he extracted a pair of latex gloves from a box in his drawer and picked up the bill. She watched while he looked at it, front and back. The same drawer yielded a sleek silver flashlight; he trained its laserlike beam over every centimeter of the paper. Then he actually raised it to his nose and, to Mia's surprise, sniffed it. Would he lick it, too? She suddenly felt hot and realized she was still wearing her jacket. She took it off and unlooped the long scarf from around her neck. Solly continued to scrutinize the bill.

"So," she said, striving for a facsimile of control she did not feel. "Do you think it's real?"

"Oh, it's real, all right," said Solomon Phelps. He set the bill back down on the white paper and gave Mia the full force of his icy silver-blue gaze. "Now I just need to know where on earth it came from."

"I can't say," Mia replied. All the possible stories she had busily concocted seemed useless at the moment.

"Can't or won't?"

"Can't," she said. "At least not right now."

"Then I'm afraid I can't help you," he said, peeling off the latex gloves and shoving them, along with the flashlight, back in the desk drawer. "A bill of this denomination would have a strong appeal to serious collectors. I have two, no, make that three, people I could call about it today. And that's without even posting it on my Web site. But in order for me to sell it, I'd have to be able to say how it came to be on the market."

She was silent. There was no explanation she could give that he would believe. Why had she thought she could deceive him with some fairy tale? He was tapping out something on the keyboard of his laptop; when he sensed her looking at him, his cold blue glance bounced up again.

"Yes?"

"I just thought there might be some way we could negotiate . . ." She knew she sounded like a fool. And a desperate fool at that. She let her words trail off.

"Haven't I made myself clear? You either want to play ball. Or you don't."

"Look, you said the bill was real. And very rare. I'm sure we could work out a deal—"

"No deal," Solly interrupted. "Not unless I know where it came from. No deal, and no conversation, either. So I'll just say thanks for stopping by, and now you can be on your merry way."

He stood up and Mia did, too. The bill remained on the desk, framed by white. Mia reached for it, hoping the gesture would cause Solly to budge, even the slightest bit. It *was* real, it *was* rare; surely he had to be interested. She tried to think of alternative strategies as she put the bill in the backpack. The black fish continued to circle lazily in its bowl, oblivious to her distress.

"What's that?" Solly said. He was suddenly standing very close— too close—to her.

"What's *what*?" She stepped back.

"That locket you're wearing."

Mia's fingers reflexively reached for it. Since buying the locket with Eden, she had not taken it off, though today the tactile pleasure of it against her skin was blunted by her sweater.

"Just something I picked up recently," she said.

"May I see?"

Reluctantly, Mia moved closer again.

"Interesting," he said, fondling it in a way that she found mildly disgusting. "Very interesting. It looks old. Victorian possibly. Or even earlier. Where did you say you got it?"

"I didn't," she said. Why was he so interested? Did he deal in jewelry, too?

"Is that also confidential information?"

"No, but I don't see what difference it makes. I'm not planning to sell it."

"Are you sure?" His eyes pinned her again, like a butterfly on a mounting board.

"Yes, very sure." Once more, she stepped away, and the gold circle slid from his fingers.

"Pity," he said coolly. "It might have been worth something to me."

"Well, it isn't for sale. So I can be on my *merry way* and not trouble you anymore."

"Oh, it was no trouble," he said. "No trouble at all. Quite to the contrary. I found this whole exchange to be . . . fascinating."

Mia did not want to respond, so she put on her jacket and scarf; it seemed imperative to hide the locket.

"You know where to find me," Solly said, escorting her to the door. "If you ever happen to change your mind."

Not likely, thought Mia, securing the scarf more tightly. She slipped the backpack containing the bill over her shoulders and was down the hall before the door was fully closed.

TEN

By November, Mia had another freelance gig—this time, at a small company producing a line of children's cookbooks. *Power Pasta* was the first title on the list; *Power Pastry* and *Power Pizza* would soon follow. Apart from the terminally cute titles—what *was* it with alliteration and kids' book titles anyway?—the books themselves were not at all bad. No insulting language that talked down to the target audience, no saccharine illustrations, just clear, step-by-step instructions and big color photographs of the ingredients and the end result. She brought home the pasta manuscript. Eden was sufficiently engaged by it to memorize the entire list in the pasta glossary and accompany Mia through the supermarket aisles, keen to find what she considered the more arcane varieties—mostaccioli, radiatore, cavatappi—which they then cooked at home.

The job had come at the perfect moment. Ever since she had left the cluttered office of Solomon Phelps, Mia had been wondering what she would do next. The cookbooks filled the gap. Of course, there was still the matter of the bill. It was real, she knew that much. It was real, and it was hers. *Use it well*, she had been told. But how? Without a market, the fabulous bill was just a piece of paper. She couldn't spend it; she couldn't sell it. She probably couldn't even give it away, though she was not about to try.

In the absence of any clear plan, she had decided to hide it under a loose floorboard that she deftly managed to pry up from her bedroom floor. How very Edgar Allan Poe, she thought, whacking the nails back into place. This thought pleased her. Just as she was finishing up, though, she whacked her thumb hard with the hammer. Almost immediately, it turned as purple as a plum and almost as big. Later, it sparked all kinds of questions from Eden—*Does it hurt? Did you cry? What were you hammering, Mom?*—but the pain wasn't too bad, and after the first week, the swelling began to subside, so she figured it would be all right. In an odd way, she relished the wounded thumb; it seemed to her proof of something—her character, her resilience, her determination to cope with whatever life lobbed her way.

THE NEXT DAY was Thanksgiving. The good news was that Betty had mercifully dropped the idea of hosting the holiday dinner at her house. The bad news was that she had strong-armed Gail and Stuart into doing it instead.

Mia and Eden woke early so that they could go to the parade that Macy's had sponsored for decades. Last year it had been so windy that one of the gargantuan balloons—Snoopy, maybe?—had knocked into a lamppost and terrorized the crowd below, but this year the danger of that happening was nearly nonexistent. The weather was mild, practically balmy. Eden had on the coat they had bought at Barneys, but she let it gape open, revealing her flounced, sleeveless dress splattered with big, tipsy-looking flowers, and fishnet tights and glitter-dusted sandals. Mia could only imagine the reception this getup would elicit from her sister-in-law.

After the parade, Mia and Eden boarded a train at Grand Central Station. The ride, under an hour, didn't give Mia enough time to steel herself. It seemed like they had just gotten on when the conductor announced, "Greenwich, next stop is Greenwich; please use all the doors." Eden, who had been dozing against Mia's arm, looked grumpy and disoriented when Mia woke her, but she rallied at the sight of Stuart, seated behind the wheel of his new, copper-colored Lexus. Eden liked her uncle, though she had no use for the anemic-looking tribe of offspring he had sired.

Mia slid into the front seat and gave him a light kiss on the cheek while Eden noisily clambered into the back, pressing buttons, stroking the dove-gray upholstery, running her fingers against the sunroof—all before Stuart could even turn around to say hello.

"So how's Mom?" Mia asked, figuring this to be a safe opening gambit.

"She's fine," Stuart said, eyes on the road ahead. "A little thinner, maybe. A lot more tan. But good."

"And Hank?"

"Hank has an amazing new tattoo," said Stuart, trying to catch Eden's gaze in the rearview mirror. Eden, however, was too busy trying to adjust the speakers in back to pay much attention.

"Really?" Mia was interested, even if Eden was not. Hank, with his tattoos and his biceps—still formidable for a guy his age—represented such a departure from her round-shouldered, bespectacled father.

"It's a scorpion. Red and black."

"Is it on his chest, Uncle Stuart?" Eden finally stopped playing with the gadgets and leaned forward. "Right above his heart?"

"Actually, it's on his left forearm. He's been wearing his shirtsleeves conspicuously rolled so everyone can see and admire it."

"I'm sure Gail must love it," Mia said, not looking at her brother, but gazing intently out the window at the passing facades of a post office, a hardware store, and a hair salon.

"She hasn't mentioned it," Stuart said defensively.

"She will," muttered Mia.

"Oh, come on, knock it off."

"What?" Mia turned to look at him then. "Knock what off?"

"I know that you can't stand her, Mia. But what am I supposed to do about it? She's my wife; you're my sister. Can't you try to get along? Just for the day?"

"Did you give this speech to her, too?" Mia asked.

"What speech? Why are you two acting all mad at each other? Who can't you stand, Mom?" Eden was agog in the backseat.

Mia took a big breath and let it out; the windshield in front of her momentarily fogged.

"Sorry," she said. "I'll try to suck it up, at least for the day, okay?"

"Thank you," said Stuart, giving her that conspiratorial smile she remembered so well from their childhood.

THE LEXUS GLIDED up to the house, a large, white-columned affair with massive windows and a slate roof. Though undeniably grand, the place had always depressed Mia; she could hardly sense Stuart's taste or presence there at all. He was like some vase or lamp—ornamental rather than essential.

Mia was still unbuckling her seat belt when the front door opened and Betty stepped outside. Stuart was right: Betty looked thinner and somehow smaller, all sinew and tendon. But she still moved quickly; nothing about her pace had slowed. Right behind her were three of Stuart's four daughters. Their pale faces looked as bloodless as ever, though Mia was willing to admit that their expressions were definitely more animated this time around. Maybe someone had been spiking their rice milk or something. One of the younger twins—Mia thought it was India but couldn't be sure—yanked the car door open wide and stared at Eden for several seconds.

"Hi!" she said finally. "My mom says you live in a bad neighborhood. Is that true?"

"India, that's not *exactly* what your mother said," admonished Betty. "Anyway, honey, let them get out of the car now, please. Grandma wants to give Eden a great big hug."

Eden hugged her grandmother enthusiastically but was more guarded with her cousins.

"Just ignore her," said Cassandra. "She's just a little tattletale anyway."

"I am not," said India, whirling around to face her sister. "And I'm telling."

"See?" crowed Cassandra. "What did I say? Tattletale, tattletale, India's a tattletale!"

"Mommy!" called India, stomping into the house. "Mom-my!"

This left Cassandra, her twin, Marguerite, and Eden standing there and staring at one another. Marguerite laughed first, just a snicker, but then the other two joined and the snicker turned to full-blown guffaws. Mia watched as Eden, flanked by her two velvet-clad, hair-band-sprouting cousins, moved off, still laughing, into the house.

"They shouldn't tease India," murmured Betty as she kissed Mia on one cheek and then the other. Mia looked over at Stuart just in time to see his shoulders rise in a small, almost imperceptible motion they used to call a "shit-eating shrug." Maybe, she thought, as she followed her mother and brother inside—past the marble-tiled foyer, the heavy crystal chandelier, the winding staircase with its painfully polished banister, and the real (Stuart had clued her in about this) Aubusson carpet—just *maybe* this day wouldn't be such a nightmare after all.

At the very least, the meal was delicious. Gail and Stuart were serious foodies both and must have been preparing for a solid week. Mia could have done with a little less exposition from Gail while they ate—did she really need to know that the turkey was soaked in a fresh-herb-imported-peppercorn brine for twenty-four hours prior to roasting, or that the fresh cranberry sauce (organic berries, locally grown) was made with the rind from a blood orange and pulverized nuggets of crystallized ginger? But this, she realized, was a small price to pay for eating the meal itself, and for watching Eden, who had somehow been transmogrified into a celebrity by her country cousins and was basking in their attention. No one ragged on her for being a vegetarian; Cassandra and Marguerite were actually impressed, Skyler hung on her every word, and even Gail listened to Eden's impassioned defense of animal rights with a thoughtful, receptive air.

After dessert, Hank had offered to drive the girls to the house of Cassandra's best friend, Jessie, who owned a horse.

"Can we go for a ride while we're there, Mom?" asked India. "Can we, please?"

"If Jessie's mother says it's all right. But you'll have to change first," Gail said. She looked at Cassandra. "You must have a pair of jeans that will fit Eden."

"Sure," said Cassandra, and together, the girls rushed off toward the stairs.

Mia tried to conceal her amazement—not only had Gail been uncharacteristically pleasant all day, she had actually suggested that Cassandra lend Eden one of her own, hallowed garments. Mia waited for her sister-in-law to ask if Eden had lice, impetigo, or possibly leprosy. But Gail started clearing the table without a word.

Mia went off in search of her bag, which she remembered leaving by the door when she came in. *The Magic of Money* was inside, and she thought this was a good moment to give it to Stuart. Then maybe she could sneak in a little snooze while the girls were with the horses. She was grateful no one suggested that she go along with them; horses, with their massive heads, fist-sized nostrils, and lethally heavy hooves, repelled and terrified her. Still, she didn't especially want to communicate her fear and disgust to Eden; she was just happy not to have to witness, firsthand, any girl-equine bonding that was about to ensue.

Now where *was* her bag anyway? She didn't see it. Perplexed, she wandered into a small room with an open door; it looked like a den, with a sofa and overstuffed chair both covered in the same tweedy fabric, and shelves that were filled with leather-bound books. Mia examined one and found that its gilt-edged pages were uncut—books for decor, not for reading. How very un-Stuart. A bowl filled with cinnamon-scented potpourri sat on a table; long-stemmed white tulips in a tall vase kept it company. Something on the wall nabbed Mia's attention, and she walked over to have a closer look. It was an oil painting, six inches at the most, depicting a bird's intricately woven nest and three tiny, moon-gray eggs. Two were perfect little ovals, but the third was cracked and empty. Search for the missing bag momentarily suspended, Mia stood there admiring the painting—so much Stuart's kind of thing and welcome evidence of his sensibility in this lavish funeral parlor of a home—when she heard voices, low but nonetheless penetrating.

"How about in here?" her mother asked.

"No, not in the dining room. Let's go into the living room." That was from Gail.

"You're going to let me talk first, right?" asked Stuart. Worry nipped at his tone.

"Where is she anyway?" asked Gail, sounding annoyed.

Mia followed the sound of the voices and came upon the three of them, all fairly reeking with guilt. Well, her mother and brother, anyway; Gail—with her bulbous blond chignon, pearl earrings, and freshly painted lips—looked impervious to guilt, or any other emotion.

"Looking for me?" Mia asked. Her bag was still nowhere to be found, but she decided it would wait. This didn't seem like the moment for gift giving after all.

"Oh, so there you are," said Gail. Her tone was silky, polished. "Let's all go sit down for a bit, shall we?"

Mia followed her obediently but was instantly flooded with suspicion. What musty old drawing room comedy did she dredge up *that* worn bit of dialogue from anyway? *Shall we?* Was she planning to curtsy, too?

"To tell you the truth, I've had a hellish week, and I was hoping I could close my eyes for twenty minutes," said Mia, trying to head Gail off at the pass. She lifted a tasseled down pillow from the couch and gave it a meaningful squeeze.

"I know you must be exhausted," Gail said. "But we really did want to have this little chat while the girls were out." Her gem-heavy fingers, with their expertly manicured nails, laced tightly together.

"Gail, you said you'd let me start—" began Stuart, but Gail's frown silenced him.

"Start *what?*" asked Mia, impatience poking through her rickety facade of manners. "Why are you all staring at me anyway? Do I have boils? Blood dripping from some orifice? You're making me very uncomfortable."

"Honey, don't get upset," said Betty. She scooted over on the couch so she was sitting closer to Mia. Mia resisted the impulse to move away; something about this whole setup was triggering all her alarms.

"You see, we want, no, we feel we *need,* to do an intervention," said Gail.

"A what?" Mia was outraged. What manner of psychobabble was this? If Eden were here, Mia would walk out of this house now. But instead she pulled the pillow onto her lap and began to tug at one of its tassels.

"Gail, you promised," Stuart said. "Now, I want you to be quiet and let me talk first."

Gail, apparently stunned, crossed her arms over her chest and actually shut up.

"You see, the thing is, Mia, we're worried about you. You and Eden."

"There's nothing to worry about," said Mia. She continued yanking on the tassel. "We're fine. It's been a little rough lately, it's true . . ." This statement called for an even more aggressive series of yanks. "That's temporary though. Strictly temporary." She knew she was lying, but she felt both exposed and cornered. If they had been alone, she might have been candid with Stuart about what she'd been going through lately. But not with Gail and their mother sitting here; didn't he know her any better than that?

"That's not what we've been hearing," Stuart said.

"Oh? It's not? Who's your source of information anyway?"

"Lloyd." Stuart had the good grace to look abashed.

"You've been talking to Lloyd?" Stuart talking to Lloyd? About her? It didn't, wouldn't add up. The sense of betrayal was blinding.

"Well, he called me. He's worried, too."

"If he's so worried about us, how come he left? Can you tell me that?"

"There's no point in going over all that again, now, is there, sweetie?" asked Betty. "That's in the past. What Lloyd wanted to focus on was Eden."

"You're defending him? After what he's done?" Mia stared at her mother. "I really can't believe this, Mom. Don't you know that Lloyd is the enemy?"

"Lloyd is still Eden's father," Betty said quietly. "Do you think he's her enemy, too?"

"Did he call you, too?" Mia knew she was being shrill but didn't care. This was not an *intervention,* whatever that was; this was a witch hunt.

"No," Betty said. "I called him."

"You *what?*"

"I know you think I shouldn't have, but Stuart and I both felt that you weren't being totally . . . forthcoming with us."

"So what did he tell you that I haven't?" Sensing that a loss of control would only add to the already considerable ammo being stockpiled against her, Mia struggled to stay calm. Or at least to seem calm, even if she was roiling within.

"He said that she was having a lot of trouble in school, and that he'd gotten two phone calls from Ms. Frobisher. They had a meeting when he was in New York."

"Ms. Frobisher?" Mia drew a blank.

"Eden's teacher," Stuart supplied; Mia could feel his pity—*she doesn't even know the name of her daughter's teacher*—and it outraged her even further.

"I've talked to her, too," Mia said. "Numerous times, in fact." Despite those conversations, the woman's name would simply not stay rooted in her brain. But did that mean she wasn't in touch with what was going on in Eden's life? That she didn't care?

"Yes, I know," Stuart said. "She told Lloyd that you're very hostile and that she thinks you may be part of the problem."

"And then there's the matter of your losing another job, and of the sociopath in your building who murdered the dog. It doesn't seem safe, honey. Not for you, and certainly not for Eden," Betty chimed in.

"I didn't *lose another job*," Mia said. She was breathing hard now, spoiling for this fight. "I was hired for a finite set of projects. They ended. I'm a freelancer, remember? And you'll be happy to know that the *sociopath* is on his way to jail."

"Before this goes any further, I think you need to calm down," Gail said. Since Stuart's brief but potent admonishment, she had not said anything, and Mia had been happy to ignore her. Until now. Feigning, lying, insincere Gail, who had been poised and ready for the kill since the moment Mia and Eden walked through the door.

"And I think you should shut up," Mia said to Gail, and to emphasize her words, she gave a final tug on the tassel, tearing it from the pillow with a swift, decisive motion. Gail, however, was so shocked that she did not appear to notice, and Mia, finding the joys of petty destruction to be significantly underrated, immediately began working on a second tassel.

"Mia!" Betty said, as if Mia were still Eden's age. "Please don't be rude. Gail is only trying to help. We all are, honey."

"You call this help? Talking about me behind my back, conspiring against me—that's supposed to help? And please stop calling me *honey* and *sweetie*. It's patronizing, and it's insulting." Something crumpled in Betty's face, as if she'd been hit, and Mia was instantly sorry for hurting her. But the three of them bearing down on her like this was just too much.

"No one is conspiring against you, Mia," said Stuart. He sat down on a chair on Mia's other side. Now she really felt hemmed in. "We just want to do what's right for Eden. And for you."

"And what would that be?"

"We're not sure . . . that's why we wanted to talk to you. Mom thought that maybe Eden should come out west and live with her for a while."

"Are you out of your mind, Stuart? What makes you think that I would let Eden do that?"

"It may not be up to you," Stuart said.

"What are you talking about?" Now Mia's anger was corrupted by fear. Was he threatening her? Stuart? Of all people? This thought was like a roller-coaster drop on a defective ride: wild and unpredictable. If she couldn't trust Stuart, she couldn't trust anyone.

"Lloyd said you came home drunk the night he was there," continued Stuart. "And he said that the incident with the dog terrified Eden. It may have even been traumatic. He also spoke to the school psychologist, and she agrees with Frobisher: they both think that Eden's home environment is highly unstable."

"So you're saying I'm not fit to raise her? Is that it?" Mia yanked off another tassel and tossed the pillow to the floor. Gail knelt to retrieve it, her expression a mixture of disbelief and horror.

"Stop making everything so global," Stuart said. "No one is saying you're not fit. We're just saying this is a rocky patch and something has to change. Maybe Eden needs to be somewhere else—*temporarily*—for that to happen."

"I will never, ever willingly agree to that," Mia said. She looked around for another pillow to destroy.

"Then you've got to work with us, give us some indication that you understand how serious the situation is, and that you're going to do something about it." The look he gave her was almost pleading, as if he expected her help in nailing her coffin shut.

"Believe me, I understand," Mia said. "I understand that you've been talking to my ex-husband, to the teacher, to the psychologist, to just about everyone in the world except me. And it hurts me, Stuart. It hurts me more than I can even tell you. But I'm not going to go there, okay? I'm not even going to address that now." She paused, willing her voice to stay steady and her eyes to stop tearing. "What I do want to ask you now is this: If you're so worried about us, why don't you and Gail just break down and give me some money? No, forget that. *Loan* me some money. Just until I can get us up and running again. That would be a real help, Stuart. A real *intervention*. After all, it's not"—she paused, looking around the room at the cascading drapes, the alabaster mantelpiece, the gilt-encrusted mirror that was the size of a small pool table—"as if you can't spare it."

"You're right—we could spare it. But we don't think that would help you," said Stuart.

"That would just make us enablers," Gail added. Her shiny lipstick had a self-righteous gleam, and she cradled the pillow as if it were a dead infant. Where did she get her nuanced psychological insight and expertise? The self-help section at Barnes & Noble? Mia wanted to slap the sanctimonious look right off her face. But she knew Gail; the woman would probably press charges. Thirty days in the slammer for slapping and pillow desecration.

"Won't you at least consider letting us have her for a while?" Betty asked. She sounded almost timid. "Hank and I would love it. Think of it as a change of scenery for her. It might be just what the doctor ordered."

"I told you—no. Eden is staying with me." But when she looked at the three of them, so convinced of their sincerity and brimming with their own good intentions, Mia felt her resolve ebbing. Yes, she felt attacked and undermined by all of them, but she had to rise above it. What was the right thing for Eden in all this? That had to be her north star, no matter how much it hurt her. She turned to

Stuart. "Well, I'll consider it, all right? But considering is not the same as agreeing."

"Okay," said Stuart. "That's something, right? Some movement, some progress." He ran his hands through his hair, and Mia noticed with an unarticulated pang that it was thinning. "I want to talk about this again. See where things stand by Christmas."

Mia didn't reply; she waited silently as Stuart and Gail moved toward the door—Gail first, with Stuart lagging slightly behind. Mia knew he was looking at her, but she wouldn't look back. Her mother, however, remained where she was; when Mia did look up, it was Betty's troubled gaze that she met.

"Are you all right?" Betty ventured. Beneath the tan, she looked old.

"No!" exploded Mia. "I am not all right!" But Mia's anger ebbed as quickly as it had frothed. Betty was—had always been—so clueless really. Mia would lash out to get a reaction, and then she would regret it. "I'm sorry, Mom," Mia added.

"I know things have been very hard for you, honey. Oops!" Betty clasped her hand to her mouth in an almost comic gesture. "Maybe Stuart and Gail didn't handle the conversation properly," Betty continued, "but their hearts are in the right place, Mia."

"Gail has no heart," Mia said.

"You know this is not just about the money," Betty said, as if Mia had not spoken. "If it were just the money, it would be easy to fix."

"Then what *is* it about?" To Mia, it was always about money when you didn't have enough.

"The choices you've been making. This implacable hatred of Lloyd—"

"Mom!" Mia burst out. "How can you sit there and say that to me?" She had gone from zero to eighty again, in a matter of seconds; just because her mother was clueless didn't mean she was harmless.

"Mia, I think that what Lloyd did was terrible and wrong, and I will never forgive him for it. Still, Eden needs him, and so you have to find a way to have him in your life that isn't eating you up inside."

BREAKING THE BANK | 129

Mia knew Betty was right, at least about this, so she said nothing. Her feelings for Lloyd were eating her up inside, chewing and grinding her to a pulp. And she wasn't helping Eden with all her out-of-control flailing. But her feelings of isolation and loss were even stronger now than they had been when she, beggar at the banquet, had walked into this house of plenty.

The noise of Hank's car pulling up and the sounds of the girls as they tumbled out onto the gravel driveway offered a brief reprieve. Mia stood, and her heel touched her bag, which had somehow gotten shoved under the couch. So that's where it was. She reached for it. Why was it so heavy? Then she remembered.

The girls burst into the room, with Stuart trailing after them.

"Mom, you should have seen that horse!" said Eden.

"He was so big!" added India.

"Here," Mia said, handing *The Magic of Money* to her brother. "Happy birthday."

ELEVEN

NINETY THOUSAND WAS a tidy little sum. Not a fortune, but a beginning. Ninety thousand was roughly what her now-verified-as-authentic ten-thousand-dollar bill was worth on the market, give or take. Mia thought of it as a down payment on a place of her own, maybe in Sunset Park, Windsor Terrace, or even Bedford Stuyvesant—one of those soi-disant emerging neighborhoods, where the prices were not as high as they were in Park Slope. At least not yet. She was angling for a place where she and Eden could settle in, feel secure. Mia envisioned a dwelling—a row house, maybe—with space enough to rent out; she was determined to provide herself and her child with income that was layoff proof, alimony proof, just-about-anything proof.

To make this happen, though, she was going to have to sell the bill. But how? Could she go back to see Solly Phelps? He had verified the bill's authenticity. He had shown interest in putting it on the market. Now she just had to come up with a viable story for how she happened to have it in her possession, a story that Solly and everyone else would buy. Piece of cake.

EVER SINCE THANKSGIVING, Mia had been in a quiet but persistent state of alarm. Her situation, seen through the damning eyes of her family, seemed even worse than she had believed it to be, and she was both furious at them for pointing it out and bewildered about how to remedy it. She had been oscillating back and forth between those two poles—rage and panic—when she discovered a blank envelope stuck in her bag. It contained a one-line note in Betty's writing and three hundred-dollar bills.

Use it well.

Those words again! They kept cropping up. And the money... what was she to make of that? She couldn't figure her mother out anymore. When Mia's father died—quite suddenly, of a coronary, his eye pressed against the lens of a telescope for what had been his final and, she prayed, glorious vision of the vast, starry skies—she had assumed that Betty would remain on Ninety-ninth Street, teaching her classes, rallying around her various causes, filling the walls of the apartment with one huge, sloppy canvas after another. Her mother had seemed to belong to the Upper West Side, and the Upper West Side had belonged to her. No new luxury apartment building, no self-interested politician, no alteration in the zoning laws had escaped the ever-humming throb of her moral indignation. Mia had grown used to her mother's preoccupation and not minded it so much; she had her father, and she had Stuart. And then there were those moments when Betty could be really and truly present: witness the humbling of the gym teacher, the white bag with its red, red heart. Yet Betty's sudden departure and subsequent reinvention of herself had left Mia feeling more forlorn than she would have expected.

WHEN MIA HAD gotten home from Greenwich, she'd found a message from Stuart on her machine. "I want to talk," he'd said. "Soon." She listened to it a few times, but she wasn't in any hurry to return the call. "Hey, Judas, how's it going?" were about the only words that came to mind. She had promised she would consider letting Eden spend some time with Betty. Well, she was considering. No need to discuss it again, was there?

She did, however, call her mother, to thank her for the money, which, though generous, nonetheless left a gritty residue of annoyance. Why the secrecy? Why hadn't she stood up for Mia when Stuart and Gail were on the warpath?

"You're overreacting," Betty said. "They were not on the warpath."

"Oh, really? So why was I maimed and bleeding by the end of the conversation?"

"Really, Mia, you are so dramatic. You always were," said Betty.

"Maybe I had good reason to be," Mia shot back. "Maybe that was my bid for attention."

"I'm sorry if you don't think I gave you enough attention," Betty said in a humbled tone. "I always tried to be a good mother to you."

"And you were," Mia hastened to assure her. The image of Betty's face—darkened by the sun, wizened, frail—suddenly swam into Mia's mind. It was the old mother-daughter push-pull: say something mean, then scurry to retract it.

She backed off, and the conversation chugged along peaceably enough for a few more minutes, until Betty mentioned bringing Eden out west during the winter school break.

"We've been over this a dozen times," said Mia, bristling again.

"It's a suggestion. Only a suggestion."

"Which I have said I would consider. So please stop mentioning it, okay?"

"There's no need to be sarcastic," Betty said testily. "You're so quick to shoot down all of Stuart's and Gail's ideas—"

"Gail is a she-devil who has bewitched my poor brother."

"Mia, honey, your attitude toward Gail is not going to improve the situation, can't you see that?"

Actually, I can't, Mia wanted to say, but she was sick of this topic, sick and tired and more than a little scared. She had no energy to argue with her mother, particularly not in the same way they had been arguing since Mia was a teenager. So she swallowed her anger in one large and dyspeptic gulp, and said nothing. Her heart felt scuffed, and it hardened against Betty, as if it were growing a protective shell. Then, succumbing to the undertow of panic that had been threatening to engulf her ever since Stuart and Gail's little *intervention*, she said, "Okay, okay. I will bring Eden to visit after Christmas and see how she likes it. Now will you and Stuart *please* get off my case?"

TEN-PLUS YEARS ago, Mia hadn't planned on getting pregnant. She and Lloyd had wanted to wait until they were a little further along in their respective careers before starting a family. He was deep into his indie-film thing, scrambling and scheming to get the funding for the documentaries that he believed ought to be made, the stories he believed needed telling. She had just been promoted to associate editor in the children's division of the small but tony publishing firm of Williams, Hatch, and Rabinisky. WHR, as it was known in the biz, had a reputation for publishing only the best, the most engaging and original of books. Working there, Mia had felt she'd found an oasis of quality in a rapidly degrading marketplace. As far as their children's list went, they had more Newbery and Caldecott winners than any three other houses combined. It was a great job, and Mia loved every single thing about it, including but not limited to her diminutive though light-flooded office in the Flatiron Building; her bosses, the revered Mr. Williams and Mr. Rabinisky (Hatch had died some years earlier); her smart and funny coworkers; the framed book jackets of WHR's classic titles that lined the halls; the bars of French lavender soap with which Nettie, the office manager, always stocked the ladies' room. And when *The Secret Journey of the Great Gray Owl*, the first book Mia had championed since her promotion, was picked as a Newbery silver medalist, Mia's star seemed to shine very brightly indeed. Oh, it was a grand situation, all right, and when she found out that the stick had turned blue, she did spend a stunned evening on the couch, feeling utterly unprepared for the maelstrom that she sensed was whirling around inside her hapless uterus.

But then she snapped out of it. Lloyd was happy; why shouldn't she be happy, too? They had wanted kids; this had been part of their game plan all along. So what if it happened a little sooner than expected? And then, right after she had found out but before she had told her boss, WHR was sold to a Dutch conglomerate, and everyone was fired on a single, soul-draining day.

Mia took the loss of her job as a sign that she was on the right path, and decided not to look for work. Instead, she grudgingly allowed herself to become the star in Lloyd's latest not-for-TV movie, which was about her pregnancy. He documented the whole thing using a handheld camcorder, shadowing Mia relentlessly during her ensuing stages of largeness. The vomiting, the swollen ankles, the tedious visits to the ob-gyn—he got it all. The culmination was the birth, at the end of which he was able to sweet-talk one of the nurses into holding the camcorder briefly so that his snipping of the umbilical cord could be preserved, like the rest of the messy, bloody business, for the ages.

Once Eden actually arrived, Mia felt as if she and Lloyd had acquired an extremely time-consuming but endlessly interesting new pet. Lloyd was great about all the day-to-day stuff with her; he handled the soiled diapers, the barfed-on clothes, the nights pierced by her hiccuppy wailing, with unusual aplomb. And gradually, Eden ceased being this unpredictable little creature, totally dominated by the intake and expulsion of various bodily fluids, and settled into being, well, herself. Despite the fatigue, the exasperation, the at times punishing twenty-four/seven-ness of being Eden's mother, Mia had never wanted to be anything else.

And now here was Lloyd—and her brother, too—saying that she was inadequate to the task, and that Eden, child not only of Mia's heart but of her soul, too, would be better off with someone else. The unfairness of this, the casual disregard for Mia's decade-long involve-

ment with Eden, was as galling as it was hurtful. Well, she wasn't going
to roll over and play dead on this one. She was going to fight back with
every weapon in her limited arsenal, and that bill, fairly smoldering beneath her bedroom floorboard, was first in her line of attack.

IN EARLY DECEMBER, Mia returned to Solly's office on West
Thirtieth Street. Her own office—at least until the cookbooks were
finished—was on West Twentieth, so it was easy enough to take a
brisk walk uptown during lunch. The temperature had dipped; Mia
retied her scarf around her neck and briefly considered buying a knit
cap from one of the vendors who stood on Broadway, rubbing their
hands in the cold. But in the end, she decided not to stop, just to keep
going until she reached the wind-blown street, even colder and more
desolate-looking than the first time she visited. She was about to hit
the buzzer when two parka-wearing guys emerged from the building,
and she slipped into the open door as they went out. She had deliber-
ately decided not to call Solly and tell him she was coming; maybe the
element of surprise would work in her favor.

Her knock on the door was sharp and confident, at least to her own
ears. And that was how she wanted to appear: Sharp. Confident. There
was a momentary silence during which Mia considered the idea that
perhaps Solly was not there. But then she heard his deep, smooth-as-
melted-chocolate voice.

"Yes?"

"Mr. Phelps? Remember me? I came to see you a few weeks ago."

Mia heard some shuffling sounds and then footsteps. And then
there was Solly, larger than life, ushering her once more into the room
which was, if possible, even more crowded than before. He wore a navy
blue jacket over gray flannel pants, and his shirt was the crisp white she
remembered from last time. His bow tie—it seemed to be a thing with
him—was scarlet.

"You again?" he said, maneuvering his bulk past a metal filing cabinet that was parked almost directly in front of the door. Mia was sure it had not been there before.

"Me again," she said. Her scarf caught on the corner of the file cabinet and she carefully tried to free it without snagging the wool.

"I've been thinking about you," said Solly, settling in at his desk. The same battered-looking chair was facing it, though the fish was gone; the glass bowl was empty and dry. "I wondered how you were progressing with that sale. I haven't seen it posted anywhere; I've checked."

"No progress," Mia said. "That's why I came back. I thought maybe you would still be interested."

"I am interested," Solly said. "Very interested. But I told you before: my interest is contingent upon information. I have to know where you got that bill before I can try to sell it." He looked at her with those cold blue eyes. Mia looked back, refusing to let herself be intimidated.

"I inherited it. From my father."

"Reasonable enough. Why couldn't you tell me that before?"

"Because there's been some contention about it in my family. My brother feels it should have gone to him. I didn't want to bring all that up before; I wanted the sale of the bill to be a private matter."

"So you wanted to sell it behind your brother's back?" Solly said.

"It's mine; I can do what I want with it."

"It says that? In your father's will?" Solly's voice was neutral, but his look was penetrating.

"Yes. The bill was left to me."

"I see." He made a bridge of his fingers and contemplated them before continuing. "When did he die?"

"My father?"

"Yes," he said. "Your father. When did he die and leave you this bill?"

"Last September," Mia said. Not true; her father had died years earlier.

"So you waited over a year to try to sell it."

"I told you: the will was contested, there was a lot of friction with my brother. But that's all resolved now."

"Yet you still want to do this on the sly."

"I prefer to think of it as discreetly."

"Semantics. Pure semantics. One person's discretion is another's dirty little secret."

"Call it what you'd like. The bill is in my possession; it's mine. And I'm asking you if you want to help me sell it."

"Did he have other notes?" Solly asked. "Was he a collector?"

"Excuse me?"

"The bill. Was that the only one? Did he collect paper currency? Did he have other denoms? Foreign notes, too? What about coins? Silver? Gold?"

"No, he didn't collect currency or coins. It was just the bill you saw. That was the only one."

"How did he come by it?"

"I don't know," Mia said. She didn't like where this conversation was going and wanted to redirect it—quickly.

"Didn't you ask?" Solly peered into the empty fish bowl, as if musing on what had become of its former occupant.

"He's dead. Under the circumstances, I couldn't really expect an answer. I don't see what any of this has to do with the sale of—"

"But what about your mother? Is she still alive? Did she know about the bill? Did she have any idea about where he had gotten it?"

"My mother doesn't have any idea of where it came from—"

"That's because she never saw the bill; she doesn't know about it because your father—may he rest in peace—never left it to you in the first place."

Mia expelled the breath she hadn't realized she'd been holding. Caught. Well, what had she expected? It was the flimsiest of stories, hastily cobbled together from equal parts of necessity and desperation.

"I came by that bill in a legitimate way," she said. "I just can't tell you how."

"And I suppose the check is in the mail, too," he said dryly. He leaned back in his chair, and waited.

"You have to help me," she pleaded.

"Help you? I'm running a business, not a charity." He gazed at her sternly. "If you want me to help you, you have to be willing to help me. Tell me where you got that bill."

"You won't believe me."

"Then we have no further business. Unless . . ." He paused, as if for effect.

"Unless what?"

"Unless you're interested in selling me that locket."

Mia didn't say anything. She had wondered whether he would bring up the locket, and because of that, she had tucked the thing under her blouse before she arrived.

"No," she said finally. "I'm not."

"Are you sure? I could make you a good offer. It might be worth your while."

"I said no."

"Well, then, I guess we're through here, aren't we? Good day, Ms. Saul."

"How do you know my name?" Mia demanded; she had given him an alias—Sarah Stein—because she hadn't wanted to reveal her identity.

"I have my ways. Just because I have a fondness for old things doesn't mean I'm not conversant with more . . . modern . . . methods."

Mia stood abruptly, knocking her chair over. To mask her alarm, she busied herself righting it; Solly made no move to assist her. But then, why should he? No reason at all. Just like there was no reason for him to believe her about the bill, no reason he should have risked his professional reputation for her. The words *Use it well* seemed more and more cryptic. How was she to use it? Why hadn't the machine given her any advice about *that*?

"I'm sorry to have wasted your time," she said. She gripped the chair tightly. "Again."

"I'd hardly say it was a waste. You're the owner of some very intriguing items . . . currency, jewelry . . . Who knows what you might turn up with next?"

Mia didn't answer; she had already said too much, much of it potentially incriminating. She was ashamed of having come here again, ashamed that she had asked for something she had no right to expect. The only dignified thing left to do was to leave, in a hurry. She didn't wait for the elevator, but walked quickly down all nine flights and out onto the street.

TWELVE

THAT NIGHT, MIA took another longish walk, this time over to Juicy. Eden was with a new friend—Luisa, an uncommonly beautiful child with big dark eyes, lashes thick as fur, and a black braid that ended at her coccyx. Luisa was a year younger than Eden, but since she lived on the floor above them, she was what Mia considered a default friend: the kid you hung out with chiefly because she was around. Not that Eden minded. Nor did Mia. Luisa was sweet, polite, and soft-voiced. And how convenient for all concerned that the girls could so easily head up and down to each other's apartment.

Mia felt cold; she wished she had stopped for that hat earlier in the day. She tied her scarf over her head, which gave her the distinct look of a nineteenth-century refugee but also offered some warmth. She was on a mission to find Julie, who had not returned any of her most recent calls. Julie's mailbox was full, so Mia couldn't even leave another message. She veered between worry and annoyance; she wanted Julie to be all right, but if she were all right, then couldn't she have managed to get in touch? Mia badly wanted to dump the story of Thanksgiving in Julie's lap; Julie loathed Gail even more than Mia did, if such a thing were possible, so she was sure to get some sympathy from her. And even, perhaps, advice. Julie was made of tougher stuff than Mia was, and she had some excellent strategies for dealing with the Gails of the world.

But when she arrived at Juicy, Julie wasn't there. Fred was, though, and he welcomed her like some long-lost landsman.

"Cold out there, huh?" he asked, stepping around from the bar, which was not yet crowded, and giving her a hug.

Mia was momentarily speechless. Since when were she and Fred on hugging terms? She replayed the feel of his arms around her, decided it wasn't bad, and allowed herself to smile.

"Very," she said, taking the scarf off her head and sitting down on a stool.

"Want something to warm you up?" asked Fred.

"Does it have a lot of bite?"

"Just a little."

"How much is a little?" She couldn't afford to get drunk, not even tipsy. She burned to think of what Lloyd had told her brother about the night she was last here. Since when had he become a charter member of the temperance committee anyway? Mia remembered the nights the two of them used to go out drinking and stagger home at three, four, five in the morning.

"Enough to take the chill off, but not enough to make you shit-faced," said Fred cheerfully.

"Promise?" asked Mia.

"Scout's honor," said Fred.

"So where's Julie?" She watched as he set about pouring, stirring, and heating. "I haven't been able to reach her."

"You mean you haven't heard?" He turned back and handed her a steaming mug.

"Heard what?"

"She's in love." He folded his arms, waiting for her reaction.

"In love?" Mia felt distinctly excluded. How was it that Julie was in love and Mia had to hear about it from Fred?

"She met a guy—I don't know, maybe three weeks, or even a month ago. He totally swept her off her feet."

"Well, she could have called me back and told me about it." Mia blew gently on the surface of the drink, not wanting to scald her tongue.

"She's not calling you because there's no service where she is now."

"What are you talking about?" Mia tasted the drink. Apple cider, a touch of brandy. A little nutmeg, a sprinkling of clove. Could there even be a dab of butter in there? She had to admit it was good.

"This guy Dean has a sailboat. And that's where they are right now. Somewhere off the Florida Keys, I'm guessing."

"Oh," said Mia. "Great." But her voice sounded flat, even to her. She took another sip, and then another; it felt so smooth going down.

"If it's any consolation, I haven't heard from her since she left town, either."

"Which was . . . ?"

"About a week ago."

"I still can't believe she didn't call me." Mia was almost finished with her cider; it would be so nice to have another one, but she knew it would be a bad idea.

"Maybe she got really busy."

"Too busy to call her best friend?"

"Look, she's in the head-over-heels phase. Completely smitten, gaga, whatever. Remember?"

"Huh," said Mia, looking down into the empty mug. She remembered. Remembered all too well.

Fred took the mug and, without asking, began preparing a refill.

Mia decided she would drink this next one very slowly, and make it her last.

"So what else is bothering you?" Fred asked, elbows on the bar, blue eyes staring into hers.

"Something else bothering me? What makes you think that?" asked Mia, mug suspended in the air.

"Oh I don't know. You just look kind of "—he stared some more, as if trying to nail it—"preoccupied. Tense."

"Well, I guess I am," she said. Drink number two was going down even more easily than drink number one.

"Is it money?" he asked.

"What else?" she said with a little smile, looking down into her mug. *What a nice little elixir,* she thought. Then: Elixir? Who was she kidding? Drink. It was an alcoholic drink.

"Oh, I don't know. Maybe love?" His blue eyes probed a bit.

"Nope. Not love. Not now, anyway."

"Well, that's a relief." He was still looking at her with that pool-blue gaze.

"Fred," Mia said, setting the mug down on the bar and glancing around to make sure there was no one else in earshot. "Can I ask you a question?"

"Sure."

Mia had the sense that she was taking a flying leap from a very, very high place. If the water below turned out to be rank and freezing, why that was just tough, wasn't it? Because once she'd stepped off the edge and taken the plunge, there were only two choices open to her: Swim. Or sink.

"Have you ever seen a ten-thousand-dollar bill?" she asked.

THREE DAYS LATER, Mia was sitting in the same bar, anxiously awaiting the arrival of a man Fred identified only as "Weed." Not a nickname that inspired confidence, but Fred assured her that he was an okay guy.

"How do you know him?" Mia asked.

"I'm a bartender, remember? Bartenders know people."

The logic of this escaped Mia, but she had certainly been willing to talk to Weed. After two long cell-phone conversations and another brief one, he had agreed to meet her at the bar, to inspect the bill himself. So here she sat, checking her watch and sipping the ginger ale Fred had thoughtfully poured for her. The bar was closed; it was after two a.m. Wild youth notwithstanding, Mia was no longer used to being out this late, and she knew she would pay for it the next day. At least she didn't have to worry about Eden, who was spending the night with Luisa upstairs; even though Luisa shared a room with her three sisters, Inez, her mother, had insisted that there was plenty of room, the girls would be fine.

Mia ardently hoped so. She had seen the grimy pink bedroom shared by four children: two sets of bunk beds flanking either wall, deflated Disney princess comforters covering each thin mattress, a scarred dresser like a deserted island marooned in between. There was no television set in this room, no computer, no DVDs, no iPod, though there was a single Sony Walkman that the girls took turns using. Eden told Mia about the dresser drawer filled only with white tube socks ("You just reach in and try to find a pair that fits," she explained), the suppers of bright yellow rice and ink-black beans ("Like a sunflower," said Eden), the underwear that was washed by hand in the bathtub and hung ("with those cool wooden clippy things") on a line outside the window to dry. To Eden, Luisa's life was picturesque, quaint, and slightly unreal, like something she would read about in a mold-speckled book found at some roadside yard sale. To Mia, Luisa's parents, Inez and Hector, neither one taller than five feet and looking uncannily like brother and sister in their matching McDonald's uniforms, were heroes.

Mia checked her watch again. Now it was two eleven. Weed had said two, but really, what was another eleven minutes when her whole night and next day were shot to hell anyway?

"He'll be here," Fred said for the third time. "Trust me." Clearly, he was nervous, too. Mia liked him for this, as well as for listening intently to her story about the bill and not pressing her for details about where she had gotten it.

EVEN THOUGH THE bar was closed, Fred acted like he was still on call, wiping down counters with a fat green sponge, rearranging bottles of imported gin.

"Hey, aren't you off duty?" Mia asked.

"Good bartenders are never off duty," said Fred.

"Couldn't you make an exception? Just for tonight?"

Before he could answer, there was a soft but distinct rattling of the metal gate covering the big plate-glass window. Weed. Mia watched as Fred let him in and the two men engaged in some ritual guy shake that involved pumping hand motions and gripping of forearms. When that was over, Fred nodded in Mia's direction, and Weed followed him across the room to where Mia was sitting. Everything about him was thin: lips, eyebrows, the pair of deep, curved lines incised around his mouth. His shoulder-length gray-blond hair was held by a silver clip at the nape of his neck, and the contrast between his puffy down jacket and his long, skinny legs made him seem unbalanced, like he might easily tip over.

"Can I see it?" he asked without preamble. His tone—soft, coaxing, intimate—made the request sound vaguely obscene.

Mia shrugged the Hello Kitty backpack from her shoulders, laid a sheet of clean white paper over the bar's surface, and pulled on a pair of latex gloves; she had to thank Solly Phelps for the idea. But before she could reach into the pack's zippered pocket, she dropped it on the floor. Her phone, wallet, and a tube of bronzer came skittering out. Mia grabbed for her things, but Weed was there first. He placed his hand on the wallet, which had flopped open. "Mia Saul," he read from her driver's license. "Nice." Mia hurriedly crammed everything into the backpack. *He knows my name,* she kept thinking. *He knows my name.* But the deal had already been set in motion; it was too late to pull out now.

Mia placed the bill down on the bar. Weed said nothing, but she could feel the hum of his interest growing steadier, louder, like the vibrations of a tuning fork. He leaned over, fingers hovering delicately above it.

"Here," Mia said, offering him a second pair of gloves.

"Thanks." He put them on and lifted the bill off the bar by its two upper corners. "Fred, can you turn up the lights a little?" Fred, who appeared to be transfixed by the sight of so much money in so little space, blinked and dropped the sponge. "Fred?" Weed said again, in a patient tone. "The lights?" Fred shook his head ever so slightly, as if he were clearing it. Then he picked up the sponge, set it near the sink, and fiddled with the lights.

Apparently satisfied, Weed brought his face so close to the bill that he and Salmon Chase were virtually eye to eye. He examined the front, the back, the edges. Then he put it back on the bar.

"I'll do fifty thou," he said, with the same detached calm he might have used to order a tuna on rye. He peeled off the gloves and set them neatly on the bar.

"It's worth over ninety thousand," Mia said.

"Then go to the guy who'll give you that."

Mia felt Fred staring at her, but she didn't return the look. What was the point? She knew what she had to do. *Use it well.* It was time to start.

"Deal," she said. She heard Fred exhale, big time.

"I have cash," Weed said, unsnapping his jacket to reveal a faded Grateful Dead T-shirt. It looked lumpy; she understood why when he reached up and under the shirt for what must have been a concealed pouch of some kind. He began extracting bills. One-thousand-dollar bills—in the now-bright light, Mia studied Grover Cleveland's heavy jowls and lip-obscuring mustache. When Weed had finished counting, he gestured for Mia to do so. Fifty bills, fifty thousand dollars. Again, she could feel Fred's stare, and this time, she looked back.

"Would you?" she asked. He took the stack, and she watched his lips move while he counted. When he was done, he gave them all back to her. The wad felt fat, almost alive, in her hands. Weed put on the gloves before picking up the bill and inserting it first between the cardboard sheets and then into the envelope. Mia wondered where he would put it now and resisted the impulse—ludicrous, she knew—to offer him her pink-and-red backpack. Then she saw he had one of his own, a frayed gray affair, one that would draw no attention to itself whatsoever. He zipped the thing up, and Fred accompanied him to the door, where they talked for a minute. Weed didn't say anything to her, but then again, he didn't need to. They had successfully transacted their business; what else was there to say?

FRED INSISTED ON taking her back to her apartment on his motor-cycle. Mia was surprised to see the thing—small, black, and glossy—parked at an oblique angle near the streetlight right out front. But then she was equally surprised to have a wad of thousand-dollar bills stuffed into her backpack, and two more wads each tucked into her boots; she could feel them shifting slightly with every step she took. It had been, all around, a night of surprises.

"I didn't know you had a motorcycle," she said.

"There are a lot of things about me you don't know," he said, hand-ing her a helmet.

It was scary, streaking down Fourth Avenue at three in the morn-ing; trucks roared by, and all the cars seemed to be speeding. And it was freezing, though at least her head was covered by the helmet, and the front of her, pressed tightly against Fred's back, was somewhat protected by the contact. When they reached her building, she felt obliged to ask him up. She willed herself to ignore—and certainly not apologize for—the state of the lobby, which this month was showcas-ing a partial set of wrecked dining room furniture, all chips, gouges, and missing legs.

The apartment was dark and still. Eden was upstairs with Luisa's family, and Mia never left a light on just for herself—she hated to waste electricity. Feeling the emptiness of the apartment made her wish she owned an animal. Cat, dog, parrot, pig. She had a sudden memory of the rabbit Lloyd had given her, its big rabbit self such a comforting weight in her arms when she'd held it, but then she banished the thought and turned to Fred.

"What a strange night," she said. "What a strange guy."

"No stranger than anyone else," Fred replied. "No stranger than a woman who has a ten-thousand-dollar bill in her possession and can't say where she got it."

"You promised not to ask about that," Mia said. "Remember?"

"I remember." Fred looked as if he wanted to do something—touch her shoulder, her face—but instead began unbuttoning his jacket. Mia took it from him and then dumped it on a chair along with her own jacket. She headed for the kitchen, Fred following along behind.

"I'd offer you a drink, but the strongest thing I have is grapefruit juice," she said, nervously peering into the refrigerator as he hovered behind her. "Of course, it's practically time for grapefruit juice anyway, so why don't I—" She stopped; he had put his arms around her and was kissing her softly on her open mouth. *Oh,* she thought. *Oh.* The kiss was warm, but not overly insistent; he was clearly waiting for a cue from her. She knew, of course, that this was coming. Was this payback? she wondered as she let herself kiss him in return. Quid pro quo?

Feeling her respond made him a little bolder; he used one hand to press her body closer to his; the other traveled from her face to her neck to the opening of her shirt, just below her collarbone. He brushed the gold locket briefly, and then moved on. But then he pulled his mouth away from hers and said, "Okay?" into her ear.

"Okay," she said back, wanting it to be true but not knowing for sure if it was. "Okay." Now he was lightly rubbing one nipple and then the other. It felt good, and she liked him, so why was she so skittish? It wasn't like she hadn't had sex with anyone else since Lloyd had left her. Though she had been slightly drunk the few times it happened. No, make that very drunk. So that was the difference. She was sober and was going to have to take full responsibility for what she was about to do.

"Maybe we could go somewhere and lie down," Fred said softly.

She led him into her tiny bedroom—astonishingly, the bed was made—and they both stretched out. She heard the clunk of Fred's shoes as they hit the floor, but her own boots still had the money in them, and even though they felt uncomfortable, she was afraid to take them off.

"Your hair," murmured Fred, touching it gently. "It's so pretty."

This is how it goes, she thought, all those first touches, first glimpses, the little revelations, the little discoveries. She knew that it was her turn now; she was supposed to say something to him. But she didn't have a thing to offer, so she closed her eyes, letting him unbutton her shirt and slip down the straps of her bra. The bra, at least, was sexy. It was this red lacy thing she had bought as a mental "fuck you" to Lloyd when he left her, and Mia was glad she was wearing it now, instead of one of the stretched-out, once-upon-a-time-was-pink-but-now-is-puddle-gray numbers in which she seemed to specialize. It was only when Fred pressed his lips to her skin that she started, without warning, to sob. She thought, uselessly, of Lloyd, both in the beginning, and at the sorry end. She thought of the first boy she'd ever kissed, at summer camp, his mouth, only recently emptied of spearmint gum, a cool, wet surprise. And of Josh, in high school. Her mind was crowded with too many people; there was no room for Fred.

"What?" he asked, moving his face up and away so he could look at her. "Is it something I did?"

This only made her cry harder.

"Jeez, Mia, I'm sorry. I'm so sorry. Please tell me what's wrong." He stopped when she put her open palm over his mouth.

"No, *I'm* the one who's sorry," she said. With effort, she got the sobbing under control, but her eyes were still leaking tears. "I like you, Fred. I really do. And what you did for me tonight was . . . amazing.

Simply amazing. I'm incredibly grateful, and I want you to know that.
But I guess I'm just not ready for—" She looked down at her partially
unclothed body, at his knee pressed between her parted legs. "For this."
As soon as she said the words, she felt a huge, visceral sense of relief,
like she'd set down a big sack of stones.

"That's all right," Fred said, clumsily attempting to pull the two
halves of her blouse back together. He didn't entirely succeed, and her
breasts, encased as they were in red lace and poking out of the blouse,
seemed faintly ridiculous.

"I can wait."

"You can?" she asked, rubbing at her wet face with her hands.
"Really?"

"Uh-huh." He put an arm around her shoulders and pulled her toward him. "Think maybe we should try to get a little rest? I could stay
here with you and we could sleep, okay? Just sleep."

"Just sleep," Mia echoed, into his chest. Suddenly she was so, so
tired. She shifted once, then twice, trying to find the most comfortable
position and wondering, through the fog of her fatigue, why it was
that the oblivion she craved was eluding her. Then she remembered—
she was still wearing her boots, the ones with the thousand-dollar bills
packed into their linings, tamped down like so many soft, silvery-green
feathers.

THIRTEEN

EVER SINCE THE automated teller had given her the ten-thousand-dollar bill, Mia had not been back to the bank. She hadn't dared. The words *Use it well* continued to turn up—in a television commercial, mouthed by a trim middle-aged woman with china-white veneers on her teeth; in a magazine article written by a financial expert; splashed across a billboard on the West Side Highway—with an eerie frequency. So Mia still believed herself to be in the thrall of something not quite normal, and she was afraid to tamper with whatever it was.

But the Monday after she met with Weed, she knew she had to set aside her apprehension and march herself up there. It was either that, or keep fifty grand in a shoe box at the top of her closet, an option that she was willing to concede was neither smart nor safe. So she placed three of the thousand-dollar bills in the zipped pocket of the Hello Kitty backpack and set off with Eden toward school. Eden did not appear to notice how nervous Mia was—what if the bills were numbered or marked in some suspicious way? what if the bank teller started asking her questions?—but she did eye the backpack with a mixture of mild curiosity and somewhat stronger disdain.

"So you really like that thing?" she asked.

Mia just smiled and said, "Uh-huh."

There was a line at the bank. Mia was actually grateful for this, because it gave her time to compose herself. Three people waited ahead of her; all of them looked irritated. Mia, however, was too freaked out to be irritated. *Inhale*, she instructed herself silently. *Now exhale.* There. Better.

Mia knew she could use one of the automated tellers, even *the* automated teller, but she was too scared. A machine that made money appear miraculously might be a machine that made it disappear, too. She was not taking any chances. So she reached up to give the backpack a little goodwill tap, trying to arrange her face in an expression of bored yet patient detachment.

The teller was a young man with a slim-fitting jacket and a major attitude. But she saw him snap to attention when he saw the bills. She felt like her breath was being vacuumed out of her as she watched him call over his supervisor, a matronly black woman wearing a fuzzy sweater and a pin in the shape of a Christmas wreath. After a careful inspection and some muted discussion, the bills were deemed acceptable and deposited to Mia's account.

The paper receipt she was handed felt dangerous; she had an impulse to pop it into her mouth, chew, and swallow. Instead, she managed to walk through the double doors, out into the street, without totally losing it. Now she just had to do this, oh, maybe ten or fifteen more times. Christ. She would have to find other branches of the bank, make some deposits in the Bronx. Or Queens. Otherwise, she didn't think she could pull this off again, at least not here.

The next day, Mia checked her bank balance at a Midtown branch of the bank. The deposit, all three thousand dollars of it, was there. This emboldened her to make another cash deposit on Twenty-third Street, as she was on her way into the office, and still another, at a branch on the Upper East Side. Each time, the bills were inspected, discussed, and ultimately accepted. Fred even offered to make a couple of the deposits for her, which she was just desperate—or crazy— enough to let him do. Within a week, forty-nine thousand dollars— almost the entire amount she scored from Weed—was safely socked away in her account. Forty-nine thousand was not the sum she had hoped for; it was most certainly not enough for a down payment on a piece of property in a place where she might actually want to live. But it could help pay the rent in a different and better apartment, an apartment that might convince her brother that she was on an incline, not skidding toward the bottom without any brakes. She started looking at the classifieds, checking out the options. Bay Ridge might have been an option, even though it was a long distance from Manhattan and any visible source of income she might generate. Bed Stuy would have been cheaper, but it was hardly an improvement in terms of neighborhood. Maybe she needed to think about leaving Brooklyn altogether, and striking out for the unfamiliar wilds of Queens or even Staten Island.

Yet there was one last thousand-dollar bill she didn't deposit. Fred didn't have to know about that one. No one did, except Mia and the person—or people—to whom she planned on giving it. She hadn't made up her mind about that part of the equation yet, but in some sense it didn't matter. The important thing was that a part of this gift, this windfall, passed from her hands to someone else's. The words *Use it well* were her mantra, her guide, her directive. When she remembered them, the decision suddenly became easy. She made another trip to the bank to break the bill, and then, late one night, slipped the hundreds—four for Mr. Ortiz, six for Inez and her family—under their respective apartment doors. She was just sorry she couldn't be there to witness the reactions.

The glow stayed with her all the next day. She woke early and prepared whole-grain waffles with syrup—okay, they were frozen, but still—for Eden's breakfast. At work, she was exceedingly cheerful, zipping through the text of *Power Pastry*—the newest addition to the series—as if her pencil were a newly honed knife slicing a ripe melon. Inspired by the glossy pictures of sugar-and-fat-laden desserts, she Xeroxed the recipe for apple pie, stopped in the store on her way home to buy the ingredients, and spent the better part of the evening with her forearms coated in flour, showing Eden how to roll out dough for a crust. She had forgotten that she didn't own a rolling pin, but an empty wine bottle was a handy substitute, and the pie, though a bit lopsided, was delicious. Eden ate two pieces, accompanied by a big glass of milk, before going off to bed, sated and happy.

Mia was in the kitchen cleaning up when she heard the buzzer sound. The intercom was only intermittently operational, and there were plenty of times when the front door to the building was not locked. Mia was well aware of the safety hazard this posed, but her complaints, like those about the elevator, were ignored. Going to the door, she expected to find one of Manny's clients, unaware of his present whereabouts. Well, she was not going to be the one to fill them in. Let them get that particular bit of information somewhere else.

But when she opened the door, she saw two police officers flanking a woman dressed in an overcoat and a plaid scarf. She was a bulky thing of about forty; her cropped gray-and-black coif was subdued into submission by a third of a can's worth of hair spray, and her shoulders were as wide as a linebacker's. Mia couldn't read her opaque expression, so she turned to the pair of officers. Their hats were perched on their heads with a kind of military authority, and their badges glinted, brittle and fake-looking as kids' plastic toys. Their names, Roy and Choi, were written below those badges. Roy and Choi? A joke? Not likely—they all looked dead serious. Roy was a baby-faced guy whose pink skin had the quality of something that had recently been boiled. His sidekick, Choi, was buff as a bodybuilder, with a neat scar just over the bridge of his nose.

Mia's first thought was to tell them that, hey, your work here is done. Someone had already come for Manny; hadn't they heard? But being snotty with police officers hardly seemed like a good idea. Especially not when the woman with them said, "Mia Saul?"

"Yes?" Mia said nervously. So they weren't looking for Manny. They were looking for her, and she could guess the reason why. She felt the trembling start, somewhere at the top of her spine and radiating out to encompass her whole upper body. This was what she had been dreading ever since that first encounter with the rogue machine: detection, inquisition, punishment.

"I'm Detective Costello. These"—she inclined her shellacked head—"are Officers Roy and Choi. Seventy-eighth Precinct."

Mia just stood there.

"Can we come in?" Costello continued. "We need to ask you a few questions. We've got a warrant to search the premises." The timbre of her voice was so deep that Mia had to wonder if she was not really a guy in drag. Now that would be something, wouldn't it? A cross-dressing police detective? Mia felt unhinged, slightly hysterical.

"Okay," she managed to croak out. She should have asked to see the warrant. But how could she even tell if it was the real thing? Better to seem cooperative. Like she had nothing to hide. "If you don't mind, though, can we keep it down? My daughter is asleep in the other room." Eden was a heavy sleeper, thank God. But still. She stepped back, and they followed her quietly into the apartment.

"Would you like to sit down?" Was this the right thing to say? Should she be offering them watercress sandwiches and lemonade, like they were guests at a garden party? Her social skills were not equal to this situation; she was completely, totally, at a loss.

"That's all right," Costello said. "We'll stand." She looked around, quickly checking out the books in their shelves, the mismatched pillows on the love seat, the small heap of clothing—Eden's, no doubt—on the floor, in front of the television. They hadn't even started their official search yet, and already Mia felt as if her panties had been yanked down in the middle of the school yard at recess and all her classmates had gathered around to jeer.

"We want to talk to you about the ten-thousand-dollar bill that was until recently in your possession," Costello said in that deep voice of hers.

"Right," said Mia. "The bill." Her own voice started doing that squeaky thing it did whenever she was nervous or uncomfortable, and she willed her vocal cords, her throat, to just *stop it*, right now.

"That's a very rare bill," said Roy. "Hardly ever seen in circulation anymore."

"But *hardly ever* is not the same as *never.*" Mia was desperate, but began to see a way she could play this.

"No," conceded Roy. "It isn't."

"Is there something illegal about the bill?" Mia asked. She noticed that Costello's overcoat actually had shoulder pads, a truly regrettable sartorial choice for someone with her body type. This observation gave Mia strength somehow, and she went on, "Aren't people allowed to own—and sell—them?"

"They are," said Roy.

"So then, what's the problem?" Was it really Mia who just said this, daring to challenge a police officer who had come into her home with a search warrant?

"There isn't a problem, per se," said Costello. She balled her fists and inserted them into her pockets; Mia could see them moving around in there, like a pair of agitated mice. "But when we picked up Phil Wedeen on a drug charge, he had this bill—a very large, very unusual, very suspicious bill—in his possession. And he said he'd gotten it from you."

"Phil Wedeen?" Mia didn't get it, and then she did. Weed.

"How long have you known him?" Roy asked.

"I don't know him actually," Mia said. "We spoke on the phone a couple of times. I met him only once—the night I sold him the bill." She prayed they wouldn't ask who introduced her, or where the transaction had taken place, because she didn't want Fred dragged into all of this.

"Uh-huh," said Roy. He touched his hand to his gun, wedged tightly in its black leather holster. His *gun*. The very fact of it was jarring,

painful even, like a poke in the eye. There were three strangers standing in her kitchen, and two of them had guns hanging off their belts.
They had a lot of other things, too: walkie-talkies, escape hooks, flash-
lights, summons books jammed into the pockets on the sides of their
regulation-blue pants. But the guns seemed bigger and weightier than
everything else, hyper-real, in the way things could seem when you're
stoned on pot, not that she had been stoned for at least a decade.

"So you'd never met him before?" Costello asked.

"Never," said Mia.

"And you haven't seen him since?"

"No. I haven't even spoken to him."

"Uh-huh," Roy said again. Was this a tic with him? Even through
her terror, Mia found it massively annoying. Choi, on the other hand,
had not said a word. Maybe he was mute.

"The bill," said Costello. "Where did you get it? And why did you
sell it to him? Were you conducting other business with him as well?"

"I can't tell you where I got it."

"Are you kidding?" Costello said, her opacity giving way to irrita-
tion. "You have to tell us. Otherwise you can go to jail. For obstruct-
ing justice."

"You wouldn't believe me anyway," Mia said. "It sounds too crazy."

But the word *jail*, even more than the word *search*, set up every pulsating, screaming alarm she had in her neural system. *Jail* was too terrible
to contemplate. Though even through her fear, Mia realized that it
might not have been true. Costello might have been trying to intimi-
date her.

"We've heard our share of crazy stories," Roy added. "Nothing
surprises us."

"I'll tell you," Mia said, boldly, on a hunch. "But not here. Not now.
I want a lawyer present. I'm entitled to have a lawyer, aren't I?"

Costello and Roy exchanged looks, and Mia knew she was right.
Thank Christ. Finally, she was reaping some benefit from all those

hours she and Stuart spent glued to the TV, glutting themselves on true-crime shows and courtroom dramas.

"You can have your lawyer," Costello said. "But we still have a warrant to search the place. It's just a question of where we'll start. Jim"— she turned to Roy—"what do you think?"

"Bedroom. Bedroom's good."

"No," said Costello, with what to Mia seemed like a sadistic kind of languor. "I think we should begin in the bathroom."

The bathroom was too small for all of them to fit in, so Mia stood outside the door, where she was only marginally removed from the indignity of having the contents of her medicine chest pawed and examined by strangers. Strangers who had threatened her with jail. She watched, silent with mortification, as Costello inspected her unopened package of Monistat cream, purchased in anticipation of the next wickedly persistent yeast infection, her tin of antifungal foot powder, her bottles of mouthwash, sad little trays of crumbling Maybelline eye shadow, and nearly spent pots of blush. Dandruff-fighting shampoo, volumizing cream rinse, extra-strength deodorant, boxes of CVS tampons and L'Oreal hair dye—every single thing was taken out or down, dutifully inspected, and put back again. The final indignity was when Choi lifted up the cover of the toilet seat to reveal a little bloom of paper bobbing in a pale yellow sea. Eden, of course. She believed it was a waste of water to flush every single time. Mia cringed as he peered into the bowl and, ever so slightly, drew his upper lip back in distaste.

From the bathroom, they moved into the living room and then the kitchen, their heavy black shoes—thick-soled, blunt-toed—making little squishy sounds as they walked. Costello's must have been a size eleven. No, make that a twelve. Mia wondered whether she had to have them special-ordered. She trailed behind as they made their way through the apartment, methodical, detached, impervious. Even the discovery of the glow-in-the-dark vibrator—a gag gift from Julie on her last birthday—failed to elicit the merest of smiles. When they had finally finished looking at the damn thing and put it back into its blue velvet case, Mia thought the worst might, just *might*, be over. But that was before Roy decided to tackle the closet, where he of course found the shoe box and its little stash of bills. Mia's small intestine coiled into a burning, merciless knot.

"Check this out," he said to Costello, handing her the box.

"How much is in here?" Costello wanted to know.

"I'm not sure," Mia said.

"I'll count it now," said Costello, thumbing through the stack. "Nineteen hundred and forty-five," she told Choi. "Make a note of that."

"Right," said Choi, scribbling down the figure on a small pad he produced from his breast pocket.

"So why is this money here?" Costello said.

"I just like to have a little around. For emergencies."

"Uh-huh," Roy said, and, scared as she was, Mia wanted to smack him. "And where did you get it?"

"I have a job," said Mia defensively. "I earn a living."

"Who do you work for?"

"I'd rather not answer that until my lawyer is present," said Mia. She most emphatically did not want Costello and her cohorts calling her present place of employment. She could just imagine how that would go down with her boss, the editorial director.

"All right." Costello handed the box back to Choi, who returned it to the shelf in the closet.

"What's in there?" Costello asked, thrusting her chin in the direction of Eden's room.

"That's my daughter's bedroom. But she's asleep." Mia was panicky; she would do anything, anything at all, to keep them from waking Eden and drawing her into this sordid little drama. In fact, it was a minor miracle that Eden had remained asleep all this time.

"I'm sorry, but we're going to have to go in."

"You are?" Mia appealed to Roy. "Really?"

"Really," said Roy, and Mia took some small consolation in the fact that for the first time since he had walked in here, he looked uncomfortable. He shifted his weight from one foot to the other. "But you can go in first if you want."

"Yes. I want. I mean, thank you." Mia hurried into the room and sat down on her daughter's bed. "Eden," she said, trying to be both gentle and forceful. "Eden, get up." Eden stirred, flung an arm over her face, and resettled into her pillow. Her breathing was deep and even. "Honey, you have to get up." Mia's tone assumed a hateful urgency.

"Not now, Mom," Eden said in the sleep-thick voice of the reluctantly roused. "It's still dark."

"I know, but you have to get up anyway. We have visitors." *Visitors?* She was back at that lawn party again, passing out the petit fours.

"I'm tired," Eden whined.

"I know . . ." said Mia. She looked up to see Costello and Choi standing there. She hadn't even heard them clomp over. "Come on," she said to Eden. "I'll carry you." She hoisted Eden into her arms—God, but she was heavy—and staggered across the room.

"Can I give you a hand?" asked Choi, who was right behind Costello.

"No, I'm okay."

"Who's *that?*" Eden asked, fully awake now. Awake and alarmed.

"We have company," Mia said.

"They're not company," Eden aptly pointed out. "They're the police." Her eyes got wider and rounder as her mouth got smaller and tighter. "Mom." She turned to Mia. "Why are the police here?" Mia couldn't meet her gaze and instead looked toward the open doorway, where Choi and Roy were busy opening and shutting, lifting and inspecting.

"Hey!" Eden cried. All at once she was off Mia's lap and streaking across the floor. "Don't touch Petunia!"

Roy ignored this and kept on at what he was doing, but Choi had the grace to stop and look slightly abashed, though he clearly had no idea of who or what Petunia might be. With great dignity, Eden took her balding stuffed cow from the bed and tenderly carried her back into the living room. Then she settled, cross-legged on the floor, to watch as the two in blue finished their job.

Mia could not bring herself to say a word about what was happening, and for once in her life, Eden seemed to have no more questions. They sat quietly for another few minutes, until Eden's eyelids began to flutter. Using Petunia as a pillow, she put her head down on the floor and was almost instantly asleep. Mia took the blanket from her own bed to cover her and then returned to Eden's room, where Choi and Roy finally seemed to be finished with their odious job.

"Thanks for your cooperation, Ms. Saul," said Roy. Mia saw him glance at Eden, tucked in her fetal curl on the floor, and in that second, she hated him just a shade less. "You'll be hearing from us soon."

"So don't go anywhere," added Costello.

"You mean I can't go to work? Or take my daughter to school?"

"I meant like out of state," Costello said, shaking her head slightly, as if she couldn't believe Mia was so naïve. Not a single hair moved with the motion.

Well fine, thought Mia. *Who's planning to go out of state? Not me.* Except the next minute she remembered that she had told her mother that she would be coming out west after Christmas. It was this new wrinkle that Mia was trying, mentally, to smooth as she walked the three of them to the door.

FOURTEEN

Mia, I'm really sorry," Fred said for about the tenth time in the five minutes they had been on the phone. "I've known Weed for years; I had no idea he was dealing. Using, yeah. But a lot of people use. And as for the police being on to him, I swear didn't have a clue."

"That's okay, Fred. I know you didn't know. You were only trying to help." Mia unbuttoned her coat and set down the bag of groceries she had toted home from Whole Foods. Eden was sitting in front of the television, and Mia had just started to consider the dinner options—pasta or eggs, eggs or pasta—when Fred called. She had called him earlier in the day, but a wine merchant from California had beeped in and they hadn't had a chance to finish.

"So there were three of them."

"Uh-huh." She peered into the bag and discovered that she hadn't bought eggs after all. How could she have forgotten?

"And they searched the entire apartment?"

"They did."

"You must have been pretty freaked out."

"I was." This was driving her nuts; didn't he get it? She was not free to discuss this, not with Eden sitting right there. While her daughter seemed to be engrossed by whatever twaddle she had on, Mia knew that if she so much as uttered the word *police*, the television program, in all its compelling inanity, would be instantly abandoned in favor of rehashing the real-live drama that had played out in their apartment last night.

"I guess you can't talk," Fred said.

Bingo! But she said, in the most offhand, conversational tone she could summon, "That's right."

"How about if I ask questions that only require a yes or no answer," offered Fred. "Here goes—do you have a lawyer lined up?"

"Not yet," said Mia. "I'm working on it."

"Guess you don't want a recommendation from me."

"No, Fred." She had to control herself, because this comment made her feel like shrieking or hurling the eggs she wished she had remembered to buy. "I really don't think that would be a good idea."

He was quiet for a moment; she could hear him breathing. "What are you doing?"

"Now?"

"Tonight."

"Not much. Making dinner, for a start."

"Let me take care of dinner. It's the least I can do."

"That's very sweet, but I don't feel up to going anywhere. And I don't want to ask Luisa's mother to watch Eden again."

"I'll get takeout and bring it over. You like Thai?"

"Sure, but—"

"Great. I'll be there in an hour. Kyra will be with me; is that okay?"

"That's fine," she said. Fred's daughter was what—sixteen? Seventeen? Eden would like hanging out with a teenager. "I really appreciate it. But Fred"—she marched into the bathroom with the phone and shut the door firmly—"I don't want to hear *one single thing* about last night in front of Eden. Not a *word*, okay?"

"Not a word," Fred repeated before clicking off.

He'd better be trustworthy, Mia thought. She had spent the entire day fixated on her one and only brush with the law, ducking into the ladies' room at the office to make furtive phone calls, completely unable to focus on the manuscript or any other aspect of her job. There was nothing more she could do about it tonight, and she needed, in a major way, to give it a rest. Plus, she was guilty about having told Eden an out-and-out lie: she had said that the police were in their apartment because of its proximity to Manny's; they were trying to find out more about him and mistakenly thought Mia might somehow be involved. Eden was not convinced and kept asking questions. But Mia was able to stave them off—barely, temporarily—and she most emphatically did not want the topic reopened again tonight.

FRED SHOWED UP forty-five minutes later; he had motorcycle helmets, plastic shopping bags filled with food, and his daughter. Kyra was tall—almost as tall as Fred, who must have been six feet. She wore her brown hair in two slightly goofy-looking pigtails that spurted out from either side of her head and was dressed in a confusing amalgam of layers: lace-trimmed baby-doll dress over jeans, two pairs of leg warmers bunched over the jeans, a long, tight sweater, and a cropped vest over that. Her bag, one of those canvas messenger affairs with all kinds of pockets and compartments, was bulging painfully with the essential contents of her young life. Mia imagined her lugging it everywhere with her, the teenage version of a security blanket. But she seemed sweet and not at all condescending toward Mia, Eden, or even, amazingly, Fred. After they had eaten—or, in Eden's case, nibbled—the glass noodles, spring rolls, and pad thai that Fred brought over, she asked Eden if she wanted to watch a DVD.

"We don't have a DVD player," Eden said, clearly disappointed.

"I do," Kyra said, opening up her bag and rooting around inside. Mia spied a bottle of hair gel, a makeup case, and a cell phone, and that was just the first layer. Sure enough, after a minute or so of digging, Kyra came up with a small portable player. "I just need a place to plug it in."

"If you want, we can go into my room," Eden said shyly.

"Sure. I want to see your room, anyway."

The two girls left the table, where Mia and Fred sat facing each other over a field of empty takeout containers.

"She's a nice girl," said Mia as she began to gather up the trash.

"About ninety-eight percent of the time, that's true," said Fred.

"And the other two percent?"

"Ah, you know. Typical teenage stuff. Plus, sometimes she gets mad at me because I split up with her mother. She blames me for the divorce even though it was my ex-wife's idea. *She* was the one who started sleeping with her Pilates instructor."

"Eden's the same way," Mia said. "Lloyd left, but she blames me."

"You said he's been traveling a lot lately?"

"In Asia. For a while, he was living with his girlfriend—the one he left me for—in Queens. But she's given up the apartment, and God only knows where he's going to land. Sometimes I wish it were far away; then I wouldn't have to see him."

Was this true? She didn't even know anymore. What she did know was that she was not up for exploring the nuances of her present feelings for Lloyd with Fred. "For Eden's sake, though, I hope it's somewhere close. This business of his swooping down and then disappearing is tearing her up."

A burst of laughter from the other room distracted Mia for a moment; she looked at Fred and smiled. If Eden was happy, how bad could anything be?

"She's good with younger kids," Fred said. "She wants to be a camp counselor this summer." He walked over to Mia, who was standing by the sink. "Hey, let me do that."

"I'll dry then," she said, stepping aside.

After the dishes were done, Mia suddenly felt awkward and unsure of what to offer next in the way of entertainment. Fred already knew she didn't have a DVD player, and her VCR had broken months ago. The reception on the television was erratic, but unless they wanted to join the girls in Eden's room, that was pretty much it.

"Do you want to see if there's a movie on?" she asked Fred.

"I've got a better idea." Fred searched the pocket of his jacket and held up his prize—a five-inch transistor radio with a titanium finish—so that Mia could see it. Then he turned it on and adjusted the frequency. In seconds, there was the sound of big-band music— shades of Tommy Dorsey and Duke Ellington—filling the room. "Care to dance?"

"You do think of everything, don't you?" Mia was actually charmed.

"I try," said Fred. "Though I mostly use it for listening to the game."

"Baseball?"

"Baseball, football, basketball, tennis, soccer—if there's a ball, I'm there. Oh, and hockey. I follow hockey, too."

"That's a puck, not a ball."

"Close enough," said Fred, and then he reached for her.

Fred was what once would have been called a smooth dancer. He knew how to lead, but he was not overbearing, and he had a nimble way of moving that made her feel graceful, even though she knew that she was only a mediocre dancer at best. She had taken a bunch of lessons once, while in college, because at the time it had seemed like a cool, retro thing to do. It *was* a cool, retro thing to do, Mia decided, as Fred spun her around. And it was fun, besides. Like sex, without all the attendant complications.

"You're good," she said, letting herself lean into him just a little bit more.

"You're not bad yourself."

"Liar."

"Well, okay. Maybe you are bad. But I don't care."

"Well, you should. I might step on your foot."

"Step, stomp, do anything you like," he said, dipping his head so that his lips tickled her ear. "I can take it."

She lifted her face and kissed him, quick and light, on the mouth. He didn't respond, so she tried again—a little harder, a little deeper.

This time he kissed her back, a long, juicy, Hollywood close-up kind of kiss. She ran the tip of her tongue over his chipped tooth, testing the sharpness, the delicately defined edge. It was only when they heard the cheering, a great swell of noise, that they pulled apart. Mia was momentarily confused until she realized it was the sound track from the DVD. "Maybe we should go and check on them," she said.

The door to Eden's room was closed. Mia knocked, but there was no answer, so she cautiously turned the knob and peered in.

"Everything okay?" asked Fred.

"Take a look." She stepped away so he could see. The two girls had fallen asleep on the bed, Petunia wedged in between them. Eden's face had been dabbed with color—sparkly blue on her eyelids, pink on her cheeks, a deeper shade of rose on her lips. The contents of Kyra's makeup bag—a jumble of brushes, pencils, wands, and tubes of shimmering pigment—were strewn around them. The DVD was still playing, and Fred turned it off.

"Kyra's down for the count," Fred said. "She's up by six for swim practice, and she tends to conk out pretty early."

"What time is it, anyway?" Mia asked.

"Ten past ten."

"Then Eden's probably out for the night, too. I guess we could just leave them there. Like they're at a slumber party."

"We could," said Fred. "We certainly could."

Mia didn't look at Fred until he was standing beside her again. "That leaves you and me . . ." he began. The music from the radio in the other room filled the silence. Mia didn't know what she wanted. She did kiss him after all. But a kiss was just a kiss, right? That was what the song said anyway.

"You okay?" Fred asked. When she didn't answer, he added, "I told you I'd wait. No pressure, all right?"

She looked at him then. He was so earnest it pained her. He had probably been a Boy Scout when he was a kid. So now he was a Boy Scout turned bartender. She giggled.

"Are you laughing at me?" he asked.

"No," she said. Actually, she had been, but immediately stopped. "I'm not." She touched his hair. His buzz cut was plush under her fingertips; it felt good. "You really think they'll stay asleep?"

"I do," Fred said. He pulled her closer and started to nuzzle her neck.

"I didn't make my bed today," she said.

"Do I look like I care?"

FRED WAS RIGHT: the girls remained asleep for so long that they got to do it twice. The first time was frenzied and awkward; in his haste to get Mia's panties off, he ripped them, which was actually kind of funny but annoying, too. He accidentally slammed her head against the wall, causing him to pull out so he could cover the nascent, just-blooming bump with kisses. And his hand caught in the braided chain that Mia wore all the time now; the chain snapped and the locket slithered deep into the bedclothes. Ruefully, Mia dug it out and set it aside to deal with later.

The second time was better—slower, less rushed. He had a nice smell to him, she decided. Still, when it was over, Mia had the powerful urge to cry. She didn't give in to it though; it would only hurt him, and she wouldn't feel any better.

"Hey," Fred said, tracing a finger down her spine. "Where'd you go?"

"Sorry," she said. "Everything's catching up with me, I guess." She raked her hands through her hair. "What a night."

"It must have been creepy to have them going over all your stuff."

"Don't ask," she said. "They found everything, and I do mean everything." Abruptly, she got up, pawed through a drawer, and handed Fred the blue velvet bag.

"What's this?"

"Go on, have a look."

When he pulled out the vibrator, he grinned. "This, too, huh?"

She nodded.

"You're funny, you know?"

"Funny ha-ha, or funny strange?"

"Both."

"Should I be insulted?"

"No," said Fred, and he leaned over to kiss her nose. "Not at all."

"Okay, then. I won't." She sat up. "We'd better get dressed." He pulled on his pants while she put on an oversized T-shirt and gathered the clothes she had been wearing earlier. The ruined panties went into the trash. Then she picked up the locket and let it dangle, momentarily, from the broken chain.

"I'm really sorry about that," Fred said. "Can it be repaired?"

"I'm not sure. I might have to get a new one."

"Would you let me take a look? Maybe I can fix it."

Mia placed it in his waiting palm. He examined the break and pulled out his Swiss army knife, the one with a hardware store's worth of tools concealed along with its blade. He tried several of the small, sharp implements, but none seemed to do the trick.

"Sorry," he said. "I'll spring for a replacement."

"It's all right," she said. "Maybe I can take it back to the store where I bought it." She popped it open, revealing the two blond children. "Maybe you could help me with this though; I've been meaning to take those pictures out."

"That should be easy." Fred used the knife's tip to pry the photos out. "Hey, there's an inscription in here."

"Really? Let me see."

"The writing is so tiny," Fred complained. "Do you have a magnifying glass?"

She did and she knew just where to find it. Together, they examined the engraved script that filled both sides of the locket's interior. *To FB from JK. A gift from one whose name is writ in water. Use it well.*

"Sounds sort of poetic," Fred said. "I wonder who FB and JK were."

"He called it *Keats's locket*," Mia said softly, disbelievingly, as she stared at the words through the lens. "But I didn't think he meant it."

"What are you talking about?"

"The man who sold it to me. He said that the locket could have belonged to Keats."

"I still don't get it," said Fred.

"JK would be John Keats. FB would be Fanny Brawne. The line about his name being writ in water—that's his epitaph. He wrote it before he died." But what about the words *Use it well?* They weren't part of the epitaph; she was sure of it.

"So you think the locket really did belong to this poet?"

"I really don't know," Mia said.

"If it did, it would be worth of lot of money, right?"

"A *lot* of money," Mia echoed. "But the inscription doesn't really prove anything. I'd have to find out more about it."

WHILE FRED WAS in the bathroom, Mia put the chain in the shoe box with the magic money. She ran her thumb over the circle of gold before closing the lid. John and Fanny? Could it be real? Not likely. But still . . .

"Maybe I should sleep on the love seat," said Fred when he came back into the room.

"It's pretty small; you won't be very comfortable." Then she remembered. "I still have Julie's air mattress. That'll work."

"'Night," she said when the bed was all made up. "See you in the morning."

"Good night."

She was on her way back to her room when he said, "So really, Mia, what are you going to do?"

She stopped and turned. "I'm not sure."

"I know you don't want any more recommendations from me, but you've really got to find yourself a lawyer. Soon."

"That's what I've been working on. All day long. While I was supposed to be focusing on my job."

"And?"

"Nothing yet. I don't want just anyone."

"Of course not. But you're going to have to tell a lawyer—any lawyer—the truth about where you got that bill," said Fred. "No more secrets."

"Fred!" She hurled a pillow in his general direction. "You promised you wouldn't badger me."

"That was before."

"Before what?"

"Before I made you mine."

Made you mine? Was he kidding? Insane? Mia had to stifle the sound— a cross between a snort and a yelp—that desperately wanted to pop, gremlinlike, out of her mouth. Did he really think that a roll in the hay, or even two, automatically entitled him to some sort of claim on her? She was ready to say all this, too, until she looked at that earnest Boy Scout face of his and realized, yes, that was *exactly* what he thought.

"I'll deal with that when I have to," was all she said. And then added, "I was even considering"—she paused—"calling my brother."

"He's a lawyer?"

"Not just a lawyer. A partner."

"You're on the outs with him, right?"

"Right," said Mia.

"Well, I just want you to find someone who can help you."

"I know, Fred," she said gently.

ALONE IN HER room, Mia spied the blue velvet bag still lying on her blanket, and she shoved it as far under the bed as she could.

Then she tried to settle down, but sleep just flat out refused to come. Fred's last remark reminded her of her fruitless, harried day and the dozen phone calls she made, each more dead-ended and frustrating than the last. So the final result was that she still had no lawyer *and* she was behind on the manuscript. And what to make of the inscription on the locket. A hoax? A joke of some kind? But Solly Phelps had been so interested in it; was that because he had guessed something about its provenance? When she went back to the shop to replace the chain, she would ask about it. Maybe Mofchum could tell her more.

The room was too hot, the pillow felt like it was filled with sawdust, her lower back was sore, and her head hurt where she had whacked it into the wall. She got up, cracked the window, and turned over once, twice, a third time. Then she gave the pillow a serious punch. It didn't change anything, but the gesture made her feel better, at least for a minute.

The sharp air from the open window was like a balm, and Mia turned her face toward it. Finally, *finally*, she felt herself starting to unwind. Closing her eyes, she remembered. Sixteen inches of snow, all the schools closed. She and Stuart wading through the thigh-high drifts to get to Central Park, the sled an inert and useless object dragging behind them. But once they arrived, positioned the stubborn thing at the crest of the hill, climbed on, and shot down like a comet, the sled, like the whole, wonderful, white world, came brilliantly alive, sprays of snow and ice-bright crystals rushing all around them. She could taste that ride, the stunning cold, the bite of the wind as it chapped her cheeks and lips and chin; she could taste it even now, thirty years later, and as she surrendered to sleep, she wished to God that she could have it back again.

FIFTEEN

THE JAIL CELL was a horrid little eight-by-eight cube, and the floor was filthy: obese dust bunnies under the metal beds that were bolted to the wall; a spreading gummy patch over by the stainless-steel toilet; grit crunching underfoot everywhere Mia stepped. It was also cold, a penetrating, invasive cold that seemed to travel up from her bare soles to her very core. Where were her shoes, anyway? How could she have lost them? All of her fear and disgust about actually being in jail were funneled into that question: Where, oh where were her shoes when she needed them most?

She picked her way over to the bottom bunk; the top one was occupied by a small woman whose face was turned away from her. She was talking to herself very quietly, and she seemed to have taken a bath in booze; even from down here, Mia thought she could be in danger of a contact high. But at least she could pull her feet up and under her, which she did.

How did she get here, anyway? She couldn't remember. Maybe she was drunk, too, but she hadn't been drinking—she was quite sure of that. Who brought her? The prizefighter, Costello? Her two boy toys with the rhyming names? Anyway, what about Mia's rights? Her one phone call? She wanted to get up, rattle the bars—if she could stand to touch them, that is—and get a guard's attention. But the floor. The floor! How was she going to navigate that?

Then she had a brilliant idea. She unzipped and then lowered her jeans so that their flared bottoms covered her feet; if she shuffled along slowly, she would be able to reach the bars without actually having to have contact with the floor. Fortunately, her jacket was long enough to cover her butt, or most of it anyway. Of course she would have to get rid of the jeans the second she got out of here; she would burn them, that's what she would do. Set them ablaze on the fire escape of her apartment and watch them turn to ash. This thought actually buoyed her a bit, and she accelerated her pace until she was almost at the bars when suddenly her left ankle was yanked out from under her and she fell, chin first, to the floor.

Mia tasted blood—she must have bitten her lip—and something else vile that might have been fecal for all she knew. She wanted to boil her tongue. Using her hands for support, she tried to pull herself up, but her ankle felt as if it were caught on or even in something. She struggled, but the, the, *thing* was stronger. Reaching down, she tried to pry it off. It constricted even more tightly. Her fingers grazed something covered in scales and strangely animate, like the limb or body of a reptile. And in that instant, she heard a low but terrible sibilant sound, a menacing little hiss. She screamed, jolting herself awake.

Awake! Thank the living God! She palpated the quilt, the mattress, her own face, filmed over by a slight coating of sweat. Her ankle was tingling, but that, she realized, was from a lack of circulation; she must have been sleeping in some weird position. What a dream. What a horrible dream.

"You okay?" Fred stood in the doorway to the room, scratching the back of his head. "I thought I heard you scream."

"You did," she said. "I was having a nightmare."

"Want to tell Uncle Fred about it?" He came over and sat at the foot of her bed.

"No," she said, closing her eyes again. "I don't."

"All right then," he said. "How about some breakfast? New College Inn? My treat."

Mia sat up and opened her eyes. Lloyd never would have taken no for an answer. He would have hounded her until she told him every last detail about what she'd dreamed, and then he'd have spent the next thirty minutes analyzing it. Fred's easy willingness to let it drop was positively liberating—imagine being with a man who didn't want to probe and pick through every single aspect of your existence. Who didn't live with a metaphoric microscope hanging from his neck. She scooted down along the bed and gently put her arms around his neck.

"Breakfast," she said, "sounds great."

They dressed, rounded up the girls, and headed for the diner on the corner of Union Street and Fourth Avenue. It was not crowded, and within a minute of their being seated, the waitress appeared with coffee. Mia drained her cup right away and then looked around, hoping to catch the waitress's eye so she could get a refill. Between sex with Fred, who was wrapped in some sort of honeymoon-like postcoital bliss this morning, and that god-awful dream, Mia was ready to go back to sleep.

"I'll have the pancakes, please," said Kyra, when the waitress appeared again to take their order.

"The same for me," said Eden, snapping the menu shut. Fred ordered what to Mia sounded like a massive quantity of manly type fare: fried eggs, hash browns, toast, and sausage. Mia, suddenly in sync with Eden's vegetarian stance, was revolted at the thought of it.

"Just the coffee will be fine for me," she said. Maybe she could avoid looking in his direction when the sausage arrived.

"You're not hungry?" Fred said, his tone threaded with worry.

"Yeah, what's up with that, Mom?" said Eden. "You should have something to eat." How ironic was that, Mia thought. *Eden* coaxing *her* to eat. The waitress waited, pen poised above her pad.

"All right. I'll have an English muffin. Lightly toasted." Could she take a nap? Right here at the table? But the food arrived quickly enough, and she was able to deflect the attention away from her eating—or rather not eating—and pretty soon they were done.

The four of them stood in front of Mia's building, saying goodbye; Fred had his motorcycle parked around the corner. The two girls gave each other big, dramatic hugs, while Mia and Fred confined themselves to chaste pecks on the cheek.

"Fred and Kyra are so-o-o awesome," Eden said as she accompanied Mia into their building. "Can we do that again sometime?"

"We'll see," said Mia as they mounted the stairs. As she climbed, she had to press her hands against her stomach. All that coffee—and lousy it was, too—was now sloshing and roiling around inside her.

"Mom, where did Fred sleep last night?" Eden asked abruptly.

"In the living room. On the air mattress."

"Oh."

"Why do you ask?"

"I wanted to know if he was your boyfriend."

"Well," stalled Mia. "He is a friend. A good friend." God, but she needed some Pepto Bismol. "Would you like it if he were my boyfriend?"

"Yes!" Eden answered without hesitation. "Daddy has a girlfriend, so it seems only fair."

Mia pondered the wisdom of that for a few seconds, and then Eden, apparently done with this topic, asked if she could run up and see if Luisa was home.

AS SOON AS she was gone, Mia heard the sound of a door opening, and there, facing her, was Mr. Ortiz with his dog.

"Hi," she said weakly, not wanting to stop and talk.

"Señora Saul," he said. "May I speak to you, please?"

"Of course," she said, trying to seem as friendly as she could, given the acid that was corroding her ileum. "What's up?"

"It's about the police." He stepped closer and lowered his voice to a whisper. The dog trembled.

"The police?" How did he know? Mia felt both exposed and shamed.

"I know that they came. Two nights ago." When Mia didn't say anything, he added, "I don't sleep well, and when I heard the noise in the hall..."

"Yes, they were here," Mia said tiredly. He already knew. What was the point of trying to pretend? "But everything's all right, Mr. Ortiz. You don't have to worry."

"Because if there is anything, anything at all I could do for you, Señora Saul"—he said, as if she had not spoken—"you have only to ask."

"Thank you, Mr. Ortiz," said Mia, his kindness momentarily overriding the pain in her stomach. "Thank you very much."

"If at any time you need a witness for your character, you call me, yes?"

He stroked the dog, which rested its dark snout against his chest.

"I really appreciate it, Mr. Ortiz. I hope it won't come to that."

"There's one more thing..."

"Yes?" She still needed that antacid, though the pain was definitely more manageable now.

"The money."

Jesus. Did he know about the bill, too? Did everyone know everything about her these days? She felt as if she were living in a glass house and had been too self-absorbed and preoccupied to notice.

"The night you slipped the bills under the door...I was awake then, too, so I heard the noise. When I went to look, I saw your door closing."

"You caught me," Mia said.

"I want to thank you for that, Señora Saul. You are a very special person. So special that I had to tell someone."

"You did?" she asked.

"Yes, I mentioned it to Señora Ovalle when I saw her the next day. She sometimes brings me food from the restaurant. So I now know that you gave her money, too."

Señora Ovalle? Restaurant? Then she understood: Luisa's mother.

The leftovers were from McDonald's, though Mia thought that calling the place a restaurant was a major stretch.

"It's okay," she told him. "I wanted to do it. My pleasure, in fact." Which was, Mia reflected, the truth. *Use it well.* She was trying. Mia went inside and headed straight for the medicine chest. Hadn't she seen Pepto Bismol when the police were here? Right behind the RID and the lice comb? She found it and guzzled the thick, pink liquid right from the bottle.

MONDAY MORNING MIA made sure she got to the office early. She had to hustle, what with her wasted day on Friday and all the work she now had piled up on her desk. But it turned out to be a day punctured by a half-dozen small and irritating distractions. A baby-shower breakfast for the very pregnant art director, some major screwup with the computer system, a meeting she had totally forgotten about.

The call came while she was at the meeting; Mia could see the editorial director glare at her when the phone beeped and Mia fumbled quickly to turn it off. But not before she saw the name and number on the tiny screen: Feinberg, Schrank, Liebowitz, and Saul. Stuart. Well, he was going to have to wait. She turned off the phone and stuffed it down, way down, into her bag. The meeting was mercifully brief, and Mia, sufficiently glutted by the bagel and sticky buns she had consumed at the shower, decided to spend lunch at her desk. She turned the phone back on to vibrate, and as soon as she did, she could feel it humming, like something set to explode. It was Stuart again, and this time she took his call.

"Are you stalking me?" she asked.

"Are you avoiding me?" he shot back.

"I'm not avoiding you."

"Mia, this is *me*, Stuart. I *know* you, remember? And I know when you're avoiding me."

"All right then. So I'm avoiding you. Can you blame me?"

"Look, I'm sorry about Thanksgiving. But I've been trying to call ever since; I can never get you."

Mia said nothing, but picked up a red editing pencil and began stabbing the point into a pad of Post-it notes.

"Mia? You there?"

"I'm here," she said. "I just felt really attacked. By everyone: you, Mom, Gail. But most of all by you."

"I'm sorry it seemed that way. We were worried. We're *still* worried. Lloyd told me he had another phone call from Frobisher. Did you know that Eden's refusing to do her math? She says math is useless so she's *boycotting*—her word—the subject. She's encouraging other kids in the class to do the same thing."

"No one told me!"

"That's my whole point. The teacher doesn't feel like she's getting the support from you that she needs; she's turning to Lloyd."

Mia silently continued her stabbing motions until the pencil snapped and she stared at it stupidly, like she couldn't figure out how *that* had happened.

"Listen, the welfare of your daughter is at stake, and you're in major denial."

"Denial? Me?"

"Yeah. You. Didn't you promise Mom that you'd bring her out there after Christmas?"

"Yes," she said, tossing the ruined pencil into a wastebasket under the desk.

"So? Have you made the reservation?"

"I will, Stu. I really will."

"So you say. But then you don't follow through." He made a loud, exasperated noise. "I know you can't see it, Mia, but I just want to help you."

"Really?"

"What do you mean 'really'? Of course I do."

"I need some legal advice then." There, she said it. If she was going to endure this conversation, she might as well get some useful information out of it.

"Advice? Maybe you should talk to Charlie Ellis."

"This isn't about the divorce," said Mia. Charlie Ellis, an old law-school buddy of Stuart's, had represented Mia when she and Lloyd split up.

"Oh? Is it a landlord-tenant kind of thing then? I could find you someone to talk to if that's what you need—"

"No, it's not the landlord," interrupted Mia.

"So then what is it?"

"Uh . . . it's . . . a criminal issue. Drug-related. But not for me. It's for a friend."

"Jesus, Mia, what have you gotten yourself into now?"

"I told you: it's not me. It's a friend."

"And I'm supposed to believe that? Don't kid a kidder, okay?" He sounded so superior that Mia wished he was standing in front of her so she could dig her hands into his hair and pull, hard, the way she used to when they were kids. "I'll find you someone, and it'll be someone good. But we're going to do a little exchange of goods and services here: I'm going to get you the phone number and not ask too many questions—*yet*—and you are going to book that flight. And I'm not asking you. I'm telling you."

"All right," she said, sullenly.

"Stop sounding so persecuted. I told you: I want to help. We all do. Even Gail, though God knows why, after the way you've treated her."

The way *she* treated *Gail?* There were no words, no words at all.

"I'll make that reservation," she said, suddenly desperate to end the conversation. "But I'm at work now. I've got to go."

When she got off the phone, she felt rattled, like she had taken a ride in a cement mixer. She checked her watch; it was not even one o'clock yet. She could still go for a quick walk outside, clear her mind, before tackling that stack on the desk. Grabbing her coat and bag, she was out of the building in minutes, glad she hadn't run into anyone on the elevator.

The street was crowded; Manhattan at lunchtime was always crowded. But the packed sidewalks felt good. That was one of the things she loved about New York, how you could lose yourself so easily, just slip into the stream and shove off. She began to walk, long strides, downtown, toward Union Square.

It was a cold, bright day, with a hard blue sky and no clouds. She stopped at a vendor's stall and bought a brown knitted hat flecked with tiny bits of red, burnt orange, and teal blue. Not her typical sort of purchase, but she was suddenly fed up with her overwhelmingly black wardrobe. The hat was warm and soft besides, and she felt better having it on. She wasn't hungry, but when she passed the greenmarket, in full swing, she stopped for a cup of hot cider.

It was nothing like the cider Fred had made, but it was warm in her hand, and for now that was enough.

She walked more slowly now because she didn't want to slosh the cider, so she had the time to notice a skinny black man with a luminous white Afro who stood on the corner of Eighteenth Street, singing. He had a clear, haunting falsetto, and Mia paused to listen.

So take a good look at my face
You'll see my smile looks out of place

His voice scaled up, up, and up again, hitting the highest notes with an astonishing sweetness. The small knot of people standing around him burst into applause when he had finished, and several put money in the pink plastic pail set up on the sidewalk.

Mia was too overcome to move for a second. Then she remembered that she had one of the bills, the special, not-to-be-mixed-with-the-other-bills one from the machine, squirreled away in the recesses of her bag. It was a hundred, too. Perfect. *Use it well,* she said to herself before depositing it in the pail. Most of the crowd had moved on now, so the man picked up the pail and began sifting through his haul. His fingers reached the hundred, and, after looking down, he looked up at Mia with a dazed, wonder-filled smile.

"Thanks, sister," he said, putting the bill in his pocket. "Thanks a lot." He grasped the pail under one arm and used his other hand to give her a thumbs-up. "*Much* appreciated."

Sister. He called her sister. The appellation suddenly seemed to take on great meaning, as if of all the things he had said today, this one word was unique, meant for her alone. She flashed to Stuart, whose sister she, in fact, was, and she suddenly wanted to call him back, to talk to him again, but really talk. She wanted to explain about why she hadn't made that plane reservation and why she couldn't possibly make it right now—

The phone began to vibrate, and she was sure it was Stuart, on her wavelength somehow, feeling a reciprocal urge to connect. She immediately clicked the Talk button without even glancing at the incoming number.

"Stuart, I was just thinking about you—" Mia began.

"It's not Stuart. It's Lloyd. I want to know why the police had to search your apartment, Mia." He sounded angry.

"Who told you that?" How did he even know about it? She almost dropped the phone.

"Eden called me. She was very upset. And I don't blame her. I want to know what's going on."

Eden! Called Lloyd to tell him about the police! Betrayal knifed through her, heedlessly slashing organs and arteries along the way. Her husband, her mother, her brother, her sister-in-law... betrayers all. Her so-called best friend, Julie, too, vanishing without a trace, not even calling to say where she was but letting Mia find out secondhand.

What kind of a friend *did* that? And now Eden. Eden, whom she loved more than all of them put together.

"I'm in the street," she said. "I cannot talk about this now."

"Well, we're going to have to talk about it soon." There was a momentary blankness, like the call had been dropped, but then Mia heard his cold, clipped voice again. "I'll be in New York on the twenty-first. That's the Friday before Christmas."

"Eden will be thrilled," Mia said. The sea of pedestrians eddied and flowed around her; no one was aware of her distress. Paradoxically, their very indifference gave her comfort, and even strength.

"I want her to spend Christmas with us." By "us" he meant his parents.

"But you had her for all the extra time over the summer; you said I could have Thanksgiving and Christmas this year."

"That was before."

"Before *what?*"

"Before the police came storming through your apartment and terrorizing my daughter."

"They hardly stormed!"

"Talk to Eden," Lloyd said. "I take my cues from her." There was a blank sound again, as if the call had been dropped, but then she heard Lloyd say, "Just make sure she's packed and ready when I get there."

When the call ended, Mia stared at the phone as if she expected it to offer some form of restitution. When nothing of the kind happened, she impulsively punched in Julie's number, and, to her amazement, her friend actually picked up.

"Where are you? Where have you been?" Mia blurted out. She hadn't expected Julie to answer, and her self-censoring mechanism wasn't fully in place.

"Didn't Fred tell you? I told him to tell you everything," said Julie. Then she added—to someone else, obviously—"No, not now; would you *stop?*" She giggled like a thirteen-year-old.

"Is this a bad time?" But Mia didn't care if it was; she thought Julie ought to contain her adolescent merriment and focus solely on her. They hadn't talked in so long.

"No, this is a great time. Great. How are you?"

Mia paused. How was she? Somehow, the parameters of this conversation did not seem sufficiently large enough for her to say. A truck roared by, and she ducked down a side street, hoping for a reprieve from the sound.

"All right . . ." she said after a few seconds. "There's been so much going on."

"I can imagine," Julie said. "And I'm sorry I've been so out of touch. But it's good to hear your voice!"

"Well, you could have heard it anytime you wanted," Mia said, unable to control herself. "It's not like you couldn't have called." Now who was acting like an adolescent? But she really was hurt.

"I know, and I've been meaning to—"

"What? It just slipped your mind?" Mia supplied.

"There's no need to be bitchy," Julie said.

"Takes one to know one," said Mia.

"I cannot believe how childish you're acting."

"I don't think I'm the one who's childish. I'm not the one who disappeared without a word, you know. I'm right here; I've always been here, remember?"

"Yes, I know," Julie said. "But this . . . this . . . negative *reaction* of yours is part of the reason I didn't want to call you, Mia."

"Oh, so now you're blaming your bad behavior on me?"

"Not blaming—explaining."

"Go ahead," Mia said. "I'm listening." Seething, too, but she didn't add that.

"I just thought you'd be . . . bitter . . . if you heard about Dean and me. That you wouldn't want to know."

"How can you say that? Didn't you think I'd be happy for you?"

"You don't sound like you're very happy for me now. I'm in love. For real."

Real? What was real? What Mia had had with Lloyd? What she was trying to build with Fred? She decided not to address that now.

"That's because you vanished," she said. "But if you'd bothered to tell me what was going on, I would have been happy." Mia had to raise her voice to be heard over a car alarm; side streets were only marginally less crowded than avenues, and certainly not any quieter.

"I just didn't think I could," Julie said. Then in another giggle-suppressed aside, "I said, not *now!*"

"You told Fred."

"Fred wasn't passing judgment."

"And I am?"

There was a pause, during which Mia heard some whispering. A delivery guy on a bicycle nearly collided into her, and she stepped aside at the last second. What was he doing on the sidewalk anyway? Idiot!

"Yes. And no one likes being judged. It's just not fun."

"Well, the fun seems to have gone out of my life at the moment," Mia said. "I'm about fresh out of fun." And with that, she clicked off.

MIA RETURNED TO the office in a fog and spent the rest of the afternoon shuffling the papers on her desk in an attempt to look purposeful. But it was all a sham. Her mind ping-ponged back and forth between Eden and Julie. *How could she,* Mia thought, the question applicable to either. She left as early as she dared, speeding back to Brooklyn and actually arriving at afterschool pickup on time for a change. *How could she, how could she,* the refrain that accompanied her over the Manhattan Bridge, past Dekalb and Atlantic avenues, up the subway steps at the Union Street station. And what about this business about Eden's boycotting math? How had Mia not even known this? She'd have to talk to her about this; she'd really have to lay down the law about what was and what was *not* appropriate to say and do in school. As for Julie, she just couldn't even deal with that now.

But when Mia arrived at the school and saw Eden—sitting by herself on a stack of torn gym mats, anxiously gnawing at a cuticle—her anger suddenly vanished, replaced by overwhelming sadness. Eden hadn't betrayed her the way the rest of them had; Eden was her baby, her daughter, her most darling of darling girls. Eden was the one who had been betrayed.

"Mom!" said Eden, hopping down from the mats when she caught sight of Mia. "You're early!"

No, thought Mia, as her heart crumbled quietly, *I'm late. Much, much too late.*

SIXTEEN

LLOYD'S PLAN WAS met with predictable elation on Eden's part. First, she was going to see her dad. Second, she was going to get to see her dad *and* spend Christmas with her grandparents Nana and Pops. The elder Prescotts no longer had the place in Maine that Mia remembered; they had sold it years ago, had since relocated to a tidy if lifeless subdivision not far from Chapel Hill, North Carolina. But Nana had reassured Eden that they would still put up a big Douglas fir, just like they had always done, and that Eden could still decorate it with all the fragile, paint-peeling-in-that-shabby-chic-sort-of-way glass ornaments that once belonged to Nana's own mother. They would bake pans of gingerbread and batches of sugar cookies and sing Christmas carols, accompanied by Pops on the very same upright black piano that had been in the family since the Prescotts got married.

The whole scene fairly oozed with a Norman Rockwell–inspired hominess, and thinking about it, Mia felt split right down the middle, like one of those black-and-white cookies that her father used to bring home from Grossman's bakery on Ninety-sixth Street. She had genuinely enjoyed those holidays spent in Maine with Lloyd's parents, gentle, reticent people, obviously in thrall to their only grandchild. On the other hand, the way they fawned over Lloyd made her sick. Virginia Prescott still called Lloyd Timmy and she served him tumblers filled with milk and mammoth slices of chocolate cake, fussing over him as if he were four years old. In that house, Lloyd, normally competent in the kitchen and willing to pitch in with domestic chores, wouldn't lift a plate from the table, hang up his coat, or replace a towel on the hook in the bathroom.

"Lloyd!" Mia had scolded. "Do the dishes, for Christ's sake. Chop some firewood. And stop leaving your clothes all over the floor."

"Relax, would you?" he'd said. "They hardly ever see me. It gives them a big kick to wait on me."

"Are you for real? And anyway, whether they like it or not, you shouldn't let them. They're getting old."

"Aren't we all?" he had said.

MIA DID NOT have the spirit to oppose Lloyd's plan, not when Eden herself was so excited by it. She decided to go along with it, and in so doing, reap the added benefit of not having to take Eden out west after all. As long as she was being given "a change of scene"—Betty's words—everyone seemed to feel that was sufficient. At least for the time being.

MIA TRIED NOT to feel bitter, but she did allow herself to wonder whether Lloyd was bringing Suim, and, if so, how the Prescotts would react to the woman who had supplanted her. The thought of Suim meeting Eden—sitting beside her at the Prescotts' walnut dining-room table, smiling at something she'd said or responding to a request to pass the mashed potatoes—filled Mia with a primitive, shameful fury. She wanted to curse Suim for stealing her husband, send her an elaborately wrapped and beribboned box containing a dead rat, fly to North Carolina and bitterly denounce her in front of Lloyd's parents.

While Mia was busy fantasizing revenge, and Eden with packing and unpacking the same suitcase a half dozen times, the Christmas season arrived in New York. Fragrant wreaths sprouted on doors; bushy trees, packed together as tightly as commuters at rush hour, lined the streets; holiday tunes, some smarmy, some poignant, were piped in everywhere Mia went. Hanukkah, that sad sack, second fiddle of a holiday, trailed behind, apologetic and self-deprecating.

Even though she was nominally Jewish, the season made Mia mo-rose, as if everyone else had been asked to attend a fabulous party from which she had most pointedly been excluded. So to compensate, she invited Fred and Kyra over for a preholiday dinner on a Saturday night before Eden was scheduled to leave town. Not that this deci-sion was without its attendant anxieties. She really liked Fred. But his ardent pursuit made her nervous. Maybe since Lloyd, the whole idea of romance had been permanently spoiled. Whatever the reason, she had to fight the urge to make fun of Fred, his boundless enthusiasm, his emoticon-filled e-mails, his late-night phone calls that featured such leading questions as "Do you miss me?" and "What are you wearing?" Then she felt guilty for being such a bitch, which in turn made her angry with him for making her feel guilty. It was altogether exhausting.

Despite her misgivings, though, the preparations for this dinner put her in a cautiously upbeat mood. She and Eden walked down to Ninth Street and Fourth Avenue, where a guy with a gold earring, bristling black beard ("Like a pirate," said Eden), and Buffalo plaid jacket sold them a small but shapely tree; he was especially happy with the extra twenty bucks that Mia slipped him after he had trussed the thing with twine and made sure it was not too heavy for her to carry home. Eden decided that all the decorations had to be eco-friendly and spent sev-eral hours patiently stringing cranberries, which she looped around and around the branches. And to think that those automatons at school were making noises about her having attention deficit disorder. Her attention span was just fine when she had something worth paying at-tention to, Mia decided.

Improvising slightly on recipes taken from *Power Pizza*, the two of them baked three pies—goat cheese and leek; olive and red pepper; fresh tomato, basil, and onion. Eden turned out to be quite good at slicing the vegetables, pounding and stretching the dough with the nec-essary vigor; Mia wished her teacher could see her now, brushing olive oil on the crust with a delicate, knowing touch. Maybe Eden would skip college altogether and go to culinary school. Mia could envision it all, her daughter a world-class chef, with her own restaurant, TV show, series of bestselling cookbooks—then the buzzer sounded, putting an end to her media-driven fantasies. Mia went to answer it.

"You're early," Mia said to Fred, aware that this was not the most gracious greeting in the world. But she had wanted to take a shower before they arrived; instead, here they were, and she was still in her oil-spotted T-shirt and her oldest, rattiest cords.

"Don't worry, we'll help," Fred said. He handed her a bag, which Mia saw was filled with several pints of Häagen-Dazs ice cream—she spied pistachio and rum raisin on top—and four glorious white roses, swathed in a dark green paper and tied with a dark red velvet ribbon.

"Thanks," she said, taking the flowers. They were real roses, too, fat and fragrant, not those hybrid things you got on every corner that had no smell and went from bud to dead without ever opening. "They're beautiful."

"Merry Christmas," Fred said, but Mia could see that his expression was clouded. Before she could ask him what was wrong, Eden appeared at her side.

"Hi, Kyra," said Eden. She started in with this little half-hopping, half-jumping routine, clearly unable to contain her excitement.

"Hi, yourself," Kyra said, tousling Eden's hair, which had started to grow out into appealingly soft, feathery wisps that framed her face. Mia tensed, knowing that Eden did not like to be touched, but evidently, Kyra—like Lloyd—proved to be the exception to this rule, because Eden grinned like she had been lit from within.

Fred took over in the kitchen, and the girls set the table while Mia showered. Then they all sat down to an extremely untraditional holiday meal of pizza, green salad, and ice cream in six flavors. Never mind that they were eating at the coffee table, which meant they all had to sit on cushions on the floor. The tree still looked pretty and smelled even better, and the white votive candles that Mia had set around the room softened the apartment's numerous deficiencies and gave everything a festive air. Or at least festive enough. Fred still seemed a little subdued; he praised the food but ate little. Eden, on the other hand, tried all three pies and had seconds of the goat cheese. Mia resolved to enlist her aid in cooking more often.

After dinner, Mia expected the girls to disappear to Eden's room, which they did, this time to anoint each other's face with skin-enhancing masks—mud, egg, apricot, and honey—squeezed from tubes that Kyra produced from her perennially swollen bag.

Fred settled down on the love seat, holding his transistor radio in his hand but not making any move to turn it on.

"We can dance," Mia prompted. "That was fun, remember?"

"Yeah, it was," he said. But he seemed glum.

"You okay?"

"I'm okay."

Mia was not convinced.

"I talked to a lawyer," she said, hoping to arouse his protective instincts; after all, he had been nagging her to do exactly that.

"And?"

"I liked the way he sounded." This was actually something of a lie. The guy talked at such a staccato, breakneck speed that he'd given Mia a major headache; she didn't know if she could keep pace with him. She'd even called her brother to complain. Stuart insisted the guy was an ace, and in the absence of any better alternatives, Mia had decided to go with him.

"Well, I'm glad for you." He sounded like she had just told him she had breast cancer. In both breasts.

"Come on, Fred. What's wrong?" she asked, sitting down next to him. "You seem so gloomy tonight."

"It's true. I am." He stared at her with those bluer-than-blue eyes. Maybe he stood in front of the mirror, practicing that puppy-dog look, because he certainly seemed to have perfected it. Then he looked down again, shifting his gaze to the radio in his hands.

"Well, come on. You can tell me," she said, giving him a playful little punch in the arm. When he didn't respond, she said, "I know—you're getting back together with your wife."

He shook his head.

"You've decided you're attracted to men?"

"This isn't funny." He glared at her.

"Sorry," she said, and she was. "I just get that way sometimes."

"It doesn't bother me. In fact, I kind of like it—the way I never know what's going to pop out of your mouth. Living with you would never be dull, that's for sure."

Living with me? she wanted to shout. *Who said anything about living with me?* But with great effort, she restrained herself and said only, "I really do want to know what's wrong. So please, whatever it is, just tell me."

"I had a little visit from the police," Fred said. "Detective Costello and a couple of officers."

"You're kidding."

"I wish." His thumb rubbed the surface of the radio. "They came to Juicy."

"That doesn't sound good."

"It isn't. Nothing puts a damper on a crowd like a couple of uniformed officers strolling up to the bar. It was like Moses parting the Red Sea."

"So what did you tell them?"

"The truth, Mia. Which is that Weed's dealing was total news to me, and I don't know where the hell you got that bill."

"So that should be it, right? They won't want you for anything else." Even as she said this, Mia knew how naïve she sounded.

"That all depends on what happens with Weed. The investigation's just started."

"Well, we're both in the same boat then, aren't we? We'll go down together."

"No, we're not," Fred said. "As long as you keep holding out on me, we're not in anything together. I thought we were," he said, putting the radio back in his pocket, "but I was wrong."

"It's not that I don't want to tell you—" Mia began.

"Save it," he said, standing up and reaching for his coat, "for your lawyer."

"You're leaving?" Mia asked. Though of course it was obvious; that was just what he was doing.

"Yeah, Kyra's got to be at her mother's first thing tomorrow morning. She wants to drive her to some mega-mall in Jersey and spend more of my money."

"Oh," said Mia. "I thought maybe you could stay over. Like last time. I still have Julie's air mattress."

"Let's take a rain check, okay?" Fred said, flashing her the puppy-dog look again. Then he started walking toward Eden's room. "Kyra, honey? We've got to be wrapping it up."

AFTER THEY LEFT, Mia was utterly deflated. But she tried to hide it from Eden, who was psyched enough about her upcoming trip not to mind. She helped Mia clean the kitchen, and then they found the perfect movie on TV—*It's a Wonderful Life*—and curled up together to watch it. Even the reception, so often spotty, cooperated. Eden brought in what remained of the vanilla ice cream, which they polished off right from the container. But Mia could not quite banish her sadness. She was sorry that Fred had gone. There, she had admitted it. And wasn't that a kick in the teeth? Still, Eden's fluffy hair was close to her face—she was in a touchy-feely mood tonight, which was unusual for her, but Mia wasn't complaining—and Fred's roses opened, their heady, dense odor mingling pleasantly with the sharper smell of the tree. Mia closed her eyes for a minute, inhaling. Then she must have dozed, because the sound of the buzzer startled her, and she nearly dumped Eden, who was also dozing, to the floor.

At first she thought it was Fred; he changed his mind and decided to come back. But it wasn't Fred at all. It was Detective Costello and her sidekicks, Choi and Roy. Roy nodded, the slightest dip of his chin, and Choi stomped lightly, wiping his feet on the doormat.

No, thought Mia, *no, no, no*. Still, she was hyperaware of Eden sitting just ten scant feet away. She had to remain calm for Eden.

"Can I help you?" She was aware of how stiff and uselessly formal this sounded, but it was better than shrieking at them to go away or bursting into tears.

"You're under arrest," said Costello. "You're going to need to come with us."

"Under arrest? What for?" Mia's voice scaled up in proportion to her panic and disbelief; Eden gaped.

"I think we should come in," said Costello, and Mia stepped aside to let them pass. Costello's hair and overcoat were dusted with glittering droplets; for a second, Mia was so frightened she couldn't process what she was seeing. Then the words *snow, it's snowing* came into her mind; she wanted to weep with relief.

"All right," she said. "Now can you tell me what this is all about?"

"Wedeen's been shot." Costello tugged the belt of her coat while Choi and Roy shifted, like a pair of restive ponies, beside her. "Once, right through the back of the head. His hands were bound and he was blindfolded. We think you may have been involved and we need to bring you in."

Mia vomited, a small and almost perfect milky circle on the floor. Shot in the head. Executed. How horrible. She took a deep breath and wiped her mouth with the back of her hand.

"Excuse me," she said to Costello. "I'd like to get some paper towels."

In the kitchen, she quickly rinsed her mouth at the sink and then darted around, trying to locate a fresh roll. While she was looking, Eden appeared.

"Why are they here again?"

"They need to ask me some more questions, sweetie." Mia stretched up to search the shelf above the fridge.

"About what? Manny?"

"In a way, yes," said Mia. This was not so far from the truth. Manny was a dealer; Weed was a dealer. Manny went, presumably, to jail; Weed was . . . but Mia couldn't think about that. There were no paper towels, so she grabbed a handful of napkins and returned to where Costello was waiting. Eden latched onto her hand—Mia didn't think her daughter had touched her so many times in one night in a year—and followed close behind.

Mia knelt to swab the floor. She had to remain calm. Calm and in charge. Bad as all this was for Eden, it would be even worse if Mia fell apart. The television was still on, and she could hear Donna Reed's cheery, can-do voice in the background.

"You can get your coat," Costello said. "We've got a squad car waiting downstairs."

"You're going somewhere?" Eden sounded panicky. "Where are you going?"

"Would you please go and turn that off?" Mia said. Her outburst had scared Eden; she was going to have to rein it. Eden stared at her like she was nuts but went to do it anyway.

"I want my lawyer present," Mia managed to say to Costello. She was still holding the wad of smeared napkins, but tried balling them up as tightly as she could. Maybe, like a wizard, she could make them disappear. And then she could follow.

"You can call your lawyer."

"And I'll need to find someone to watch my daughter."

"Go ahead." Costello looked at her watch. "We'll wait."

Mia nipped into the bathroom, where she scrubbed furiously at her teeth to get the sour taste out of her mouth. Then she splashed water on her face and lathered up her hands.

"Mom? Where are you going? Why do you have to go with them anyway?" asked Eden, who had followed her into the bathroom.

"Don't worry, everything's going to be fine," Mia said, depositing a kiss on Eden's forehead. "Go get your pajamas; I'll call Luisa's mom, and you can sleep over at her house tonight."

Mia moved through the next few minutes on autopilot. Inez, God bless her, said they would be happy to have Eden spend the night. She would even send Hector down to get her. Her lawyer, Chris Cox, said he would meet her at the station house in an hour. "The directions," he snapped, "give them to me." Mia said good night to Eden, who was trying valiantly not to cry, and watched as she followed Hector— Petunia clutched under one arm, grocery bag stuffed with pajamas and toothbrush in the other. Then she turned to Costello.

"I'm ready," she said. She had her coat, her bag, and her new knit hat. At least she wouldn't be cold. She had an urge to run through the apartment, making sure all the windows were closed, and that the taps and oven were off. As much as she had detested this place, leaving it to follow the trio of officers out into the night made her suddenly protective and even tender toward it, as if the rooms might vaporize in her absence. She double-locked the door and followed Costello, in her clumping black shoes, down the stairs; Choi and Roy brought up the rear. Outside, the snow was falling heavily. The police car, with its lazy Mars light circling, waited on Garfield Place. Costello got in up front, with the officer who was driving; Mia squeezed in back with Choi and Roy.

They drove in silence and when the car stopped, Mia got out and stood staring up at the wide limestone facade of the precinct. A pair of enormous green-globed sconces flanked the massive and ornately worked brass and copper doors.

Once she stepped through them, though, into the squat, battered vestibule, she knew that whatever grandeur this building might have once possessed, it had long since vanished. The building, like so many lost souls who had passed through its portals, was just another casualty of the slow, creeping rot brought on by ignorance, poverty, and plain old bad luck.

SEVENTEEN

ONCE PAST THE gun-toting guard, Costello and Choi disappeared. Roy escorted Mia to the front desk, where she had to contend with the avalanche of paperwork her mere presence seemed to generate. Forms, forms, and more forms. She listened to the rotelike recitation of her rights being read, and reluctantly surrendered her bag and coat. At least no one asked for her shoes. She tapped her still-shod foot on the bald linoleum, just to reassure herself.

Then Roy took her into a small room for fingerprinting. The printing was not done with ink but with a scanner, and Roy had her roll her index finger around on a flat glass plate; the digitalized image appeared on a large Sony screen in front of her. Then he asked her to stand still, while her photo was snapped with a digital camera that was mounted to the wall. It was over in seconds, and none of it felt quite real to Mia. Her dream of the dirty jail with its lurking reptile had been much more vivid; right now, it was as if everything had been swathed in bubble wrap, insulating her from its true impact. She had an impulse to bite the inside of her cheek, just to get herself to react.

"We're going to go upstairs now," Roy said. "Detective Costello's got some questions for you."

"But my lawyer isn't here yet." She looked down at her wrist to check the time, but of course her watch was temporarily gone, along with her handbag, keys, and cell phone. Cox, she thought frantically. When was Cox going to arrive?

Roy didn't answer, so Mia followed him upstairs and down a cramped, hot hallway. There was shouting coming from its far end, and Roy stopped abruptly, indicating with his hand that she should stop, too.

"...the fuck you are...!" said a loud, angry male voice. "I told him, 'Man, don't fuck with me, 'cause I can fuck you up bad, do you hear me? Fuck. You. Up.'"

"Keep it down," growled another voice.

"The fuck I will!" shouted the first voice. "Just fuckin' try and make me."

Even Mia, no stranger to four-letter words in all their permutations, was shocked by this outburst—the volume of it, the intensity. In the next second, a man charged into the hallway, his rippling, shoulder-length blond hair streaming behind him as he ran. Mia instinctively pinned herself against the wall as he streaked by; she could smell him, the pure, rank smell of adrenaline and high-octane fury.

"Stop right there!" bellowed the police officer who was right behind him. Another officer, even faster than the first, didn't say anything but managed to catch up with the fugitive; there was a short, fierce scuffle, and then the blond guy landed on the floor with a nasty thud.

"Fuck! You broke my face, you fuckin' pig!"

"Shut up," said the first officer. "Unless you want to be gagged."

"That's against the fucking law!" yelled the blond guy. "I'll have you arrested, you fuckface swine. You'll lose your badge, and I'll make sure it's shoved up your pig's ass—"

"Cuff him," said the officer who did the tackling; he was getting to his feet, rubbing an elbow that he must have slammed in the struggle. "And then get him out of here before I do something I'll be sorry about later." Another officer appeared from the room at the end of the hall, and Detective Costello—now divested of her coat and wearing the sort of wool jumper and white blouse worn by parochial-school girls all over the city—stepped outside as well. She watched as the blond guy, still struggling, was cuffed and led away. He continued to swear, though more softly now. No one seemed to pay him any attention. Costello gave him one last look before going back into her office.

"Come with me," Roy said. Mia was so shaken by the scene in the hallway that she had forgotten he was there. She blinked at him before following him through the door.

Costello was seated at her desk, an old oak thing with a broad, pitted surface. There were several small frames arranged along the back—one shaped like a heart, another an oval—but from her vantage point, Mia couldn't see the photos they held, and she felt that this put her at a disadvantage. If she could see whose picture was in there—the person or people Costello loved—she might have a better handle on how to deal with her. But it looked like even that slight edge would be denied her. The room was hot, even hotter than the hallway, and the window was open a tiny bit, allowing a layer of snow to pile up on the sill.

"Sit down," said Costello, indicating a wooden chair that looked as if it had been gnawed on by generations of police dogs.

Mia sat. Still thinking of the blond guy in the hallway, the rough hands that yanked and pulled him, she understood that her best defense was to appear cooperative and unthreatening. She repeated those words to herself, then realized, after only a few seconds, that Costello had been speaking to her and she had totally, but totally, tuned her out.

"We've got some more questions about your connection to Wedeen," said Costello. "And also to Fred Giordano. Is it true that Fred introduced you to Wedeen?" She held a chewed blue ballpoint poised over a yellow legal pad.

"My lawyer," said Mia, her tongue a fat, clumsy thing in her mouth. "I want my lawyer."

"Where's he coming from?"

"Scarsdale."

"Well, he's not going to be here anytime soon. It's still snowing out there. Have you looked?"

Mia followed her gaze out the window, where the snow continued to fall furiously, in swollen white flakes.

"I don't want to talk on record without my lawyer."

"Okay," Costello said, fiddling with her pen. "It's your choice. But then you'll have to stay until he gets here."

"Stay where?" Mia asked, fighting the panic that threatened to shoot up from her stomach and right out of her mouth. She had already tossed her cookies once in front of this woman, and she really, but really, did not want to do it again.

"There's a holding cell downstairs," Costello continued, as if mentioning the whereabouts of the ladies' room. "You can wait there."

"Cell?" said Mia. "You're going to put me in a cell?"

"What were you expecting?" Costello said. "A five-star room at the Ritz?"

Mia rose from the chair and followed Roy, who seemed to have become, in this place, her shadow. She was frantically trying to weigh the alternatives—talk to Costello now, or cool her heels in a holding cell. The mere thought of the cell made her want to heave again, no matter who was around to see it. On the other hand, how was she going to explain the bill—the crazy, heaven-sent or Satan-spawned bill? She hadn't even explained it to the lawyer yet; they had been planning to meet this week. So unless she was ready to spill the whole story here and now, she knew what she had to do. Meekly, she followed Roy out of the office and into the hallway. Mia sensed the echo of the blond guy's curses; they were still hovering somewhere in the airwaves. Downstairs, they met Choi again.

"Forget the holding cell," he said to Roy.

"Why?"

"There's a leak. In both of them."

"Leak?" said Mia.

"Yeah, from the roof or somewhere in the wall," said Roy, rubbing the back of his pink neck. "Happens every time it rains. Or snows."

"So you can't put me in there?" Mia felt relief, warm and sweet, flood through her.

"Nope. Against regulations to put anyone in a leaky cell. We'd have all kinds of negative shit to deal with if we did. Newspapers, TV, you name it."

"So you mean I can wait upstairs? In that office where we were?"

Roy looked at her almost pityingly.

"Hell, no," he said. "We're going to have to put you in one of the regular cells. You'll be more comfortable back there anyway."

"I will?" The relief she'd felt only seconds ago was now like a buzzer concealed in a palm or a phony snake that popped out of a can—a stupid, practical joke.

"Yeah, there's like a toilet and sink in the back. And the bench is bigger. You can sleep if you want to."

"Sleep?" Mia's voice was a squeak, and she thought of Mommy Mousie and her little mouse voice.

"Come on," said Roy, who clearly thought he had provided enough information for the moment. "Unless you want to go back upstairs and talk to the detective."

THE CELL WAS a cubicle at the back of the building, one in a long row whose end Mia could not see. Roy was right; there was a sink, a toilet—no seat though—and a wooden bench covered in brown, peeling paint. On her way, she and Roy passed the blond guy, who jumped up as they walked by.

"Hey you!" he said, hands on the bars. Mia was surprised to see that they were beautiful hands—well shaped, clean, and very white. "I'm talking to you!" For a second Mia thought he meant her, then realized that of course he was talking to Roy, who ignored him as he took Mia to another cell and ushered her inside. "You let me out, donkey dick! When my people hear what you've done to me, you're dead meat, you hear me? You're burned toast, you're scummy water down the drain. You've over, man, do you hear me? So fucking over." When Roy didn't answer, Mia heard him say "motherfucker" a few times, and then he was silent. Roy banged the cell door shut, and Mia was alone.

Alone in a jail cell. How had she let this happen? Mia wanted to scream, wanted to cry, wanted to do something, anything, but she didn't know what to do first. *Cox is coming,* she told herself, trying to calm down. *He's coming, and he'll get you out of here.*

She sat down, carefully, on the wooden bench. Sleep would be impossible in this place, but at least she didn't have to stand all night. She looked at the dirty toilet and was supremely grateful for her greater-than-average bladder control; there was no way she was going to sit or even crouch over *that.* She tried to focus on something concrete—the crabbed graffiti scratched into the wall, the pattern of the bench's peeling paint, which seemed to resemble a mountain range—when she heard a voice.

"College Girl," it said. "College Girl, you there?"

Mia actually felt herself flinch. Who was that? And who was "College Girl"? Then she put it together. The blond guy in the next cell. He was talking to her.

"I'm here," she said tentatively. What to do? She had heard this guy screaming and cursing; she had seen him scuffling with the police officers. That had been quite enough contact for her; she had no desire to talk to him now. But she also didn't want to anger him and spend the next God-knew-how-many hours listening to him scream at her. Maybe it would be better to placate him. "Why are you calling me College Girl?"

"You went to college, didn't you?"

"Well, yes, but that was quite a while ago."

"Still. It shows. The minute I saw you, I said to myself, 'She went to college. She's a college girl.' And I was right." Mia said nothing to this, and he added, "So what was it like?"

"College? I liked college. I had a lot of fun in college." *A lot of fun in college?* She was so nervous, and God, but she could babble like an idiot when she was nervous.

"Yeah? You party a lot? You had a boyfriend? A pretty lady like you, I bet you had lots of boyfriends."

This comment seemed like it was leading somewhere Mia did not want to go, so she didn't answer.

"What's the matter?" he asked; she heard the belligerence snaking into his tone. "Did I say something wrong?"

Mia remained silent, but her anxiety started to mount again. Why had she even started by talking to him in the first place? He was a psycho, he was deranged, and he was in jail, for Christ's sake. But then again, so was she.

"Hey, I'm sorry if I was out of line, College Girl." His tone was softer. When she still didn't answer, he said, "Come on. I said I was sorry. It's just that I'm so steamed over those asshole cops I don't know what I'm saying."

"It's okay," Mia said finally. Her butt hurt from the unyielding wood, and she shifted slightly, trying to get more comfortable. It didn't work.

"Good," he said. "That's good. You don't hold a grudge. I hate people who hold grudges, you know?"

"Uh-huh," she said. She hoped she wouldn't have to hear about what else he hated in people. Or what he did to the people who had aroused his hatred.

"So, like, what are you in for?"

Despite everything, Mia laughed—a great, surprised hoot. When had she ever in her life heard that line? Only in a movie, uttered by Jimmy Cagney. Or Edward G. Robinson. When she didn't reply, he added, "Nah. Let's not even go there. Forget I mentioned it. But let's keep talking, okay? You'll still talk to me, College Girl?"

"Sure," she said. "We can keep talking." He had made her laugh, here in a jail cell. She had to like him for that alone.

"I never went to college," he said. "Too fucked up by the system from way back. Those nuns I had for teachers . . . they were *fierce*. Whacking my knuckles or my open palms with a ruler; you ever been hit with a ruler? That metal edge may be thin, but let me tell you, it can really do damage. And when that didn't work, they hauled down my pants and whacked me raw. Man, it seemed like I was always getting whacked for something or other."

"They do sound fierce," she agreed. She had a sudden image of him as a little blond boy, hands outstretched and trembling as they waited for the stinging blows. The image hurt; why hadn't he been protected? "What about your parents? Didn't they do anything?" Her own parents would have demolished anyone who had actually dared to raise a hand against her.

"Hey, if I told my old man, he'd whack me again for getting in trouble." He snorted. "How about you? You like school when you were a kid?"

"Sometimes," Mia said truthfully. "But not always. My second-grade teacher was a horror." She hadn't thought about the teacher, Miss Cyril, with her pale, taffy-colored hair and narrow, pink-rimmed eyes, for years, but now here she was, risen from the past and practically breathing fire. "She used to yell a lot, and she made us tie her shoes for her—she wore orthopedic shoes that laced all the way up her foot, practically to her bony old ankle. She'd lean over you while you were tying them, to make sure you did it right." The details rushed back. "Spit collected at the corners of her mouth when she talked, and she used to tuck a tissue right down the front of her dress. Even after she used it, she'd put it back in there. I think I had a stomachache every day of second grade."

The blond guy made that snorting sound again; Mia realized it was laughter.

"Teachers really can suck, can't they? Almost as bad as cops." He paused, and Mia could hear his breathing, loud and labored. He suddenly sounded winded, even old.

"You okay?" she ventured.

"You want to know if I'm okay, College Girl?"

"It sounded like you were having trouble breathing."

"Nah. I'm all right. Those boys in blue get me tense, that's all. And when I'm tense, everything tightens up. But I'm fine." He waited a beat. "Thanks for asking."

"You're welcome."

"What's your name, anyway?"

"My name?" She hesitated. Should she tell him? What if he had some way to find her when they both got out of here? He could hunt her down, hurt her, hurt Eden.

"You don't have to tell me. But I'll tell you mine. It's Patrick. Patrick Fitzpatrick."

"I guess that's easy to remember," said Mia, trying to be diplomatic. Pity his parents had been so uninspired.

"I'm the youngest of seven. I guess they just ran out of steam by the time I came along. They couldn't come up with anything better."

"You must have gotten teased about that," she said.

"Hell, yeah," he said, almost with relish. "But I could give back as good as I got, you know? Fuck with me, and I would fuck with you. Only harder."

"Do you have a middle name?" asked Mia. It was time to redirect the conversation again; it was most definitely that time.

"Xavier. All the boys in my family got Xavier as a middle name. The girls all got Bernadette."

"I'm Mia," she said. She could have lied, made up something, but she didn't want to. And anyway, it was probably safe enough just to give him her first name. "No middle name though. Just Mia."

"Mia . . ." he said, as if road-testing it. "Mia-bia fo-fia, banana-fana-fo-fia. Mi-my-mo-mia. Mia." Then he made the snorting sound that for him was laughter. "So, Mia," he said. "You married?"

"I was."

"So you're, like, separated?"

"Divorced," she corrected.

"Ah, divorce sucks. Lose-lose proposition. Anyway, why'd you divorce him?"

"I didn't. He divorced me."

"Who," he said softly, almost caressingly, "would divorce you, College Girl? Was he a homo or something?"

"No," Mia said. "It wasn't a guy he was after. It was a girl. A different girl."

"Scumbag," said Patrick, as if that settled it. "Kids?"

"A daughter."

"Nice," he said. "Kids are good. Wish I had one. Maybe two. Not seven though—seven's too many."

"Seven would be a lot," Mia agreed. And then she asked, "What about you? Are you married?"

"Twice."

"And . . . ?"

"They both up and died on me."

"Really?" said Mia. He seemed very young to have had two dead wives. Then she had an appalling thought: maybe he had killed one—or both—of them. Maybe she had been talking to a murderer all this time. There was a sour churning in her stomach, and she had to bite the fleshy part of her thumb to keep from throwing up again.

"First one went in a car accident. Gory as World War Two; I'll spare you the details. But it was closed casket, if you get my drift. Second one died of an overdose. She was using, you know? I used to fight with her about it all the time. I told her to drink if she wanted to get wasted. Drinking is a nice, clean vice. A *safe* vice. A shot of bourbon is a shot of bourbon, no matter where you drink it: New York, L.A., Denver, Nashville, Anchorage, Honolulu. But that rat poison you snort or inject; who the fuck knows what's in it? And don't get me started on the cocksuckers who sell it."

"That's so sad." Mia abandoned the idea that he was a murderer. Not that he couldn't have been lying, but something told her that he wasn't, and she decided to believe that something, whatever it was.

"Yeah, ripped me in fucking pieces, that's for sure. But the guy who sold it to her is history now. Ancient history."

Mia found herself praying that Patrick had had nothing to do with the nameless dealer's untimely and possibly violent end. Drug dealers were frequently killed. Occupational hazard. Weed was a perfect case in point.

"Anyway, they say the third time's the charm. So I'm open, man; I'm wide open and ready. I'm going to find myself another wife. She's out there, I can feel it. I've got, like, a sixth sense about these things." He paused, drinking the air in that labored way Mia had heard earlier.

"What will she be like, your next wife?" Mia asked. She actually wanted to know.

"She'll be a looker, that's for sure. Eye candy is my candy. But there'll have to be something more than that."

"What would it be? The something more?"

"She'd have to be the kind of girl I'd feel comfortable with, you know? Like I could tell her anything. Loving her would be a great big mansion where I could visit all the rooms, every single one. There wouldn't be any locked doors in that mansion. Everything would be free and easy. And it would all be mine."

Mia let Patrick's description of love hover in her mind. She wouldn't have thought this man would have been capable of such a metaphor. But he had surprised her.

"How about you, College Girl? What's your dream date like?"

Before she could answer, Mia was distracted by the footsteps that were now coming down the hall. They were getting closer; they were almost here.

Patrick was instantly up and at the bars of the cell.

"Have you finally come back for me, you fat fuck?" he called loudly. "It's about fucking time."

Mia got up, too. Three officers approached Patrick's cell. Two were over six feet, and while the third one was substantially shorter, he was stocky and solid, with the kind of thick neck frequently seen on tomcats, the hulking, malevolent strays who had never been neutered. The hard gleam of the handcuffs dangled from one meaty paw.

"We're going to try it again," said the largest of the policemen. "And this time, you'd better behave."

"I'll behave all right," said Patrick challengingly. "But the question is, will you?"

"Come on," said the big one. "Let's go."

Mia watched as Patrick was yanked from the cell, snapped into the cuffs, and dragged away. She realized only then that he was wearing a white sweatshirt, torn white jeans, and white sneakers without laces. Everything about him was white or light. Everything but his voice, which seemed to break slightly as he called out to her, "Good night, College Girl. Good night and good luck." The sound of footsteps lingered for a few seconds, then it was quiet.

Being in the cell was even worse when Patrick had gone. She couldn't stop the frantic cycling of her own worry. How was Eden? Was she able to get to sleep? What time was it? Was it still snowing? Where was Cox, anyway? Would she ever get out of here?

To fight the anxiety, Mia recited every scrap of poetry she had ever memorized, tried to recall her childhood phone number and the names, first and last, of all the kids who had endured second grade along with her. When that began to pale, she resorted to counting the white subway tiles on the walls; over the decades, the grout had turned pitch-black, giving the cramped space a dizzying kind of op art look. She also had an urgent need to pee—what had happened to her usual camel-like control?—and thought she just might have to break down and use what passed for a toilet. Though maybe she could have used the sink; it was somewhat cleaner, and who would ever know? Before she had to make the choice, she heard footsteps again and, seconds later, was almost tipsy with relief to see Roy and Choi standing in front of her once more.

"Your lawyer's here," said Roy, as he unlocked the cell. "He's waiting for you upstairs."

EIGHTEEN

SPRUNG! THAT WAS the word that Mia kept repeating to herself, and each repetition gave her the same exhilarated little zing, as if a small silver pinball was ricocheting around in her head. *Sprung, sprung, sprung!*

She tramped through the quiet streets, scuffing her feet through the thick white blanket of snow. Chris Cox, the lawyer, said he would give her a lift back to her apartment, but she had refused. After the last several hours, the front seat of a car felt too confined. She told him she wanted to walk, though she did thank him, sincerely, for the offer. Chris, who was about five one in his shoes and bald as a cue ball, was definitely cool. Yes, he talked nonstop, but clearly, it was talk with a purpose. He handled the detective with the aplomb of a lion tamer flicking a long, well-oiled whip. And when she asked about his fee, he said that there would be no charge, professional courtesy.

"I can't tell her where I got that bill," Mia had told him when they were allowed, finally, to confer in an empty office adjacent to Costello's.

"Okay, we won't deal with the bill for now," said Cox. "Tell me about Wedeen. How you met him. What he said. What you said. Everything."

So Mia told him—there wasn't much to tell—and from her slim story, Cox was able to weave a web of words, convincing Costello that the possibility of Mia's involvement with Wedeen's death was virtually nonexistent.

"My client was nowhere near the deceased at the time of his death; you've got nothing on her—no prints, blood, nothing. Plus, she's got an airtight alibi, which I am positive would stand up in court—if we have to go to court, that is."

"Maybe she does," said Costello. "But what if she had taken out a contract on his life? Had him killed?"

"Have you actually *talked* to this client? Gotten a sense of who she is? If you had, you'd be fully aware of her financial circumstances, or, should I say, constraints? A single mother, raising a child all by herself. Ex-husband is God knows where—L.A., Korea, Vietnam. He sends her child support when he deigns to. Meanwhile she's working—two jobs sometimes—just to make ends meet. She's hardworking, she's devoted, and she's trying her level best. She sold that bill to Wedeen for far less than it was worth because she was desperate, don't you see? A woman in need. A woman with her back to the wall. And you mean to tell me that *this* woman, my *client*, is actually going to use one red cent of that money to have someone killed? I don't think so, Detective Costello. I don't think so at all."

Mia wanted to stand up and cheer when he'd finished. Costello looked less impressed, but she was willing to delay further questioning and release Mia on her own recognizance. But before she did, she handed Mia yet another form.

"DAT," said Cox succinctly as he ushered Mia from the room. Mia looked puzzled, so he continued. The DAT—desk appearance ticket—demanded her presence in court on January 4. In the intervening weeks, he said he would help her get her story spit-polished and ready to place before the judge. If she decided to bolt or not show, the police would take out a warrant for her arrest.

"But you won't do anything stupid, right?" asked Cox; he was seated behind the wheel of his silver Porsche, and talking to her through the open window. "You don't want any more trouble."

"Right," she had said, itchy to get out of there; she didn't even want to be on the same block as the station house. "No more trouble." Chris promised to call her in the next couple of days, and then, as the engine smoothly purred into life, he was gone.

* * *

MIA CHECKED HER cell phone as she walked; she had not checked it recently and there were messages up the wazoo. Her brother, her mother, her sister-in-law. Julie, calling from Key West, to say she would be back in New York after the holidays. Finally! Mia was simultaneously relieved and annoyed. Lloyd—twice. Lloyd's mother, the genteel and wispy-voiced Virginia. Eden, about twenty times. Someone from her present job, calling about a last-minute crisis with the *Power Pastry* manuscript, someone from her old beloved job, calling to talk about the abysmal state of publishing these days, the class mom calling to see if she would contribute money for the teacher's holiday gift. Teacher's gift? How about some coal for her stocking? Dried twigs, anyone? Mia gleefully deleted the message. Not one of these many calls, however, was from Fred. She was trying to decide whether to call him when the phone started vibrating, like a live thing, in her hand.

"Mom? Mom, are you there? It's me, Eden."

"I'm here, baby," Mia said.

"Mom! Where *are* you? I've been calling and calling! Why didn't you answer?"

"I'm coming home, Eden. I'm coming home right now." She decided to let the question about her failure to answer slide for the moment.

"You are? For real?" Eden's voice seemed to have slipped into a time warp; she sounded about five years old.

"For real," Mia said gently. She looked down at her watch; it was six twenty-five. "Is anyone else in Luisa's apartment awake?"

"Not yet. I went into the bathroom to call you. So I wouldn't wake them up."

"Well, just hold on. I'll be there as soon as I can."

"I love you, Mommy," Eden said. Mia couldn't remember the last time her daughter had used the word *Mommy.*

"Love you, too," Mia said before clicking off. The winter light, reflecting off the snow, was pale silver, whitening slowly as the sun rose higher in the sky. A bodega on Fifth Avenue was just opening its doors, so Mia bought a cup of coffee and a buttered bagel. The coffee—extra light, three sugars—was like nectar. She tore at the bagel with her teeth, buttering her chin in the process. God, but she was hungry. Three weeks. Three scant weeks to get herself out of this mess and her life back on track again. She walked faster, eager to be home. But when she came to the bank, she slowed so she could peer in the window.

There was the machine, looking perfectly ordinary in the morning light. She began walking away, and as she did, she caught what seemed like the aftermath of a pinkish glow. Mia whirled around. There! She *had* seen it—a rosy flickering on the screen that lent a brightness to the surrounding air before it faded away. She waited, ardently hoping to see it again. After her night in jail, she *needed* to see it. But after several minutes, it became clear that the glow would not reappear, and Mia, strangely bereft, moved on.

She was back in her apartment by seven. Although she had been in jail for less than a night, she had the sense that she had been away much longer and that everything had been somehow altered in her absence. The place seemed different to her. Unfamiliar. Had the light from the living room window always hit the wall like that? And what about the pattern of cracks in the ceiling? Hadn't they changed, realigned themselves? Even her most familiar possessions looked different. The spines of her books—and she had so many—were so vivid and various in their colors. A thick blue book that was next to a thin crimson one practically jumped off the shelf. She drank in the contrasts: deep green next to the brown, yellow alongside black. The rug, a relic from her parents' apartment on Ninety-ninth Street, was worn to a whisper; this rug had been present during her childhood, its warp and weft knew her father's tread.

Mia walked through the apartment slowly, marveling at her sense of dislocation. She thought about how she had been living her life, versus the way other people seemed to think she had been living it. Was she a good mother? Or was she guilty of having made poor and irresponsible choices? She stopped when she reached Eden's room. The bed, with its raucously patterned sheets, was rumpled, and Eden's clothes were scattered all over the place. But the tiny space was rich in color and pattern. Stacks of books—they had never gotten around to shelves—a puppet theater; an arcane selection of stuffed animals that included a walrus, a hippo, and the outsize giraffe Lloyd had bought; a toy castle; binoculars; a doll's house, with most of the furniture missing or broken.

Mia picked up the stuffed hippo—he had an endearing underbite—and stretched out on Eden's bed. Eden was having a hard time of it; that couldn't be denied. Yet in this strangely suspended moment, Mia didn't feel overwhelmed by the usual truckload of guilt. She was hardly a perfect parent. But she didn't yell—at least not often—and she never, ever hit. She talked to her, read to her, listened to her, loved her more than she had ever loved anyone. And she had always tried—oh, how she had tried!—to protect and cherish her. She would keep trying, too. That had to count for something. She got up, put the hippo back, made the bed, and folded the clothes. Then she went upstairs to fetch her daughter.

FOR THE REST of the weekend, Eden would not let Mia out of her sight. She declined all invitations, including one to go skating with Caitlin and another to a birthday party that featured a live DJ. She insisted on sleeping in Mia's bed and camped out by the bathroom door when Mia was inside. She wanted physical contact with Mia all the time, too—holding her hand, kissing her cheek, sitting in her lap. Mia understood, deeply, that she needed to indulge her. Eden was worried; Eden was frightened; Eden needed to be reassured. If sleeping in Mia's bed, liberal doses of candy—she refused to eat virtually anything else—and a brand-new stuffed animal, a reindeer made of luscious, deep brown velveteen, were what Eden needed, Mia wasn't going to argue. By Sunday afternoon, she had decided to buy Eden a cell phone of her own; otherwise, she didn't think she would be able to leave her at school the next morning.

Eden treated the new phone like a fetish, talking both into it and to it, nuzzling its sleek, metallic blue surface. "Can I call Daddy on it? Please?" Mia nodded, watching while Eden punched in the numbers with a light and practiced touch. Then she trotted off to the bathroom—door smartly closed behind her—to talk to Lloyd.

Mia didn't want the temptation of eavesdropping, so she went into the kitchen and started doing the dishes. There were always dishes in her sink. She was about halfway through this particular sinkful when Eden appeared, holding out the phone.

"Here," she said. "He says he wants to talk to you."

"Where have you been?" His voice was low but furious.

"I had to go over to the police station. To answer some questions." She would not let him rile her, especially not when Eden was standing right there. *Down girl. Down.*

"Your daughter has been out of her mind with worry. I don't know what you've gotten yourself into, Mia, and I really don't care. But when it affects Eden, then I have to step in."

"Really? It looks to me like you've stepped out." Her tone was reasonable, but she brought the bowl she was washing down hard in the sink. It cracked down the middle, and she was left holding the pieces, as cleanly broken as if they had been sliced. "You'll be here soon; you're taking her for Christmas. What else do you want?"

"I want some assurance that you still have control over your life."

"I do," Mia lied. "I absolutely do."

"Well, you'd better be prepared to prove it."

"Stop bullying me first." He was silent. "Lloyd? Are you there?" But he had clicked off, the conversation clearly over.

"Mom, you broke that bowl," Eden said, as if Mia didn't know this. "Now what are you going to do with it?"

"Dump it," Mia said grimly, depositing the two pieces in the trash. "What else?"

* * *

THE FRENZIED PREPARATION for Christmas continued to clobber the city with its shrill cheer. There were pseudo-Santas in cheap, fire-resistant costumes everywhere; the subways were packed; and the Empire State Building was lit in strident shades of red and green. Mia called her mother, ignored her brother, had a momentary urge to call Julie again but decided against it. She had a long conversation with Chris Cox and agreed to see him after the twenty-first, which was when Eden left town. She would be able to focus better then, she told him.

"We'll meet at your apartment." Cox didn't ask; he told. "I want to groom you."

"Groom me?" What did he mean, *groom*? Did he think she was a chimp?

"For your appearance in court. With the judge."

"Can't I just wear what I normally wear?"

"Sure," he said. "If you want to end up back in jail."

WORK WAS A madhouse; someone had screwed up, big time, with the raisin-oatmeal-date cookies in *Power Pastry.* The recipe, which as far as Mia knew had been tested a half dozen times, was now yielding cookies that had the texture and appeal of golf balls with little bits of melted eraser thrown in. So it had to be rewritten and retested; the new recipe threw all the subsequent page spreads out of whack. Usu-ally the managing editor would have dealt with a problem like this, but the managing editor had contracted viral pneumonia and so Mia had offered to step in. Three nights running, she worked until ten. Finally, the whole damn thing was corrected and ready to be shipped off to China, where it would be printed and bound. The editorial director was so grateful for her effort that she told Mia to take the day off— fully paid.

"Consider it a holiday bonus," she said. "You've earned it."

Mia decided she would do some shopping of her own. So far, she had treated the impending holiday like an enemy. But today she would try to make her peace with it. After dropping Eden at school, she headed for the same diner where she had gone with Fred the morning after he and his daughter had stayed over. She slid into a booth and ordered a hot chocolate, which arrived topped with ersatz whipped cream straight from a can. While she sipped, she composed a shopping list.

Eden
Julie
Stuart, Gail & the nieces (?)
Luisa's family
Caitlin & Suzy
Mr. Ortiz
Mom & Hank
Kyra & Fred???

Fred. Where had he been keeping himself these days anyway? She had thought he would have called by now. Did he know about the night she spent in jail? Unlikely. Who would have told him? Mia scrutinized the list; just looking at it made her tired. She folded the list in half and then in half again, before shoving it into her purse. Holiday shopping would have to wait. She had to do some errands of a wholly different nature.

Despite the chill, it was a sun-splashed morning, and the walk over to Juicy was invigorating. Snow, no longer pristine, was piled everywhere; Mia had to sidestep soiled mounds and ankle-deep slush at the curbs. The metal gate was still partially pulled down over the bar's plate-glass window, but Mia banged on it anyway. At first, there was no response, but she kept banging and soon one of the dishwashers appeared and raised the gate a little bit.

"Hey, Emilio," said Mia.

"Hey, yourself," Emilio said. "Kind of early for a drink, isn't it?"

"I was looking for Fred."

"You just missed him."

"Did I?"

"Yeah, he was here just a few minutes ago, but he had to leave."

"Did he say when he'd be back?"

Emilio shook his head. Mia stood there, feeling foolish. She should have called first. *How junior high school is this?* she thought.

"Can I give him a message for you?" Emilio asked.

"That's okay," Mia said. "Thanks just the same." She had the image of herself scuttling, like a bug, away from the bar. The wind had picked up, and she was cold, so she ducked into the first place she saw that was open: the Lonelyville Café. She had seen the place before but had never actually gone in. It was meant to resemble an old-fashioned sandwich shop in some small town of fifty years ago. The stools, rooted to the floor, were covered in red leatherette. Big glass jars that held pretzels and rock candy lined the worn marble counter; there were signs advertising eggs creams, lime rickeys, and root-beer floats. Hokey, but Mia didn't mind. She had had nothing to eat or drink apart from that hot chocolate, so she sat down at the counter and ordered a toasted corn muffin and a cup of tea.

There was only one other patron in the place, a grizzled guy tucked in the far corner, nursing a coffee in a thick white mug and reading the newspaper. Behind him were a jukebox and a phone booth. Now when had she last seen a phone booth in New York City? Phone booths were from an era when men wore hats, women wore gloves, and you addressed a stranger with the words *sir* or *ma'am*—not *dude* or *motherfucker.*

The phone booth looked like the real thing: sturdy glass walls, niftily folding door. Was there a little seat inside, too? Mia finished her muffin and ambled over to find out. Not only did there turn out to be a cunningly curved seat, there was also a phone book—scratch that, several phone books—all relatively intact. Yellow pages, white pages, Brooklyn, Manhattan. Mia felt like she had seen something rare and mysterious, like a red-tailed hawk soaring the Brooklyn skies.

She opened the folding door, and it glided back with satisfying ease. Then she sat down on the wooden seat and encased herself in the small glass booth. She liked the feeling of being inside, contained and safe, yet able to see out, too. She could sit there all day; maybe she would.

She pulled out the Brooklyn white pages and, on impulse, started flipping through the F's. Fa, Fe, here it was: Fi. She kept looking until she found it: Fitzpatrick, Patrick X. It was probably him. But why was she looking, anyway? What did she want to know?

Mia studied the address, somewhere out in Coney Island, a seedy neighborhood way out on Brooklyn's tip. She wrote down the address on the back of the shopping list and then got up to pay for her food. Suddenly, the day had a new shape and purpose to it. She knew, as surely as she knew anything, that what she was about to do was monumentally stupid. Stupid and dangerous. She could get herself killed, just like poor Weed, who, whatever he might have done, did not deserve a blindfold and a bullet in the brain.

But still. Something about her conversation with Patrick that night was haunting her, something that felt authentic, felt real. She was hungry for that feeling. Craving it. Plus, she knew that every single time she had given some of the miracle money away, she had felt so good, so light, so clean, as if her soul had been distilled and purified, refined to its most pellucid, least-contaminated essence. *Use it well*, right? Hadn't she been trying? She practically ran back to her apartment, moving so fast she actually broke a sweat. She took five hundreds from her shoe-box stash, then was off again, out in the street and down into the subway.

Mia emerged in what felt like a different city; there was a sharp, salt-infused smell of ocean in the air, and several gray-and-white gulls circled petulantly overhead. The wind was much stronger, too; she wished she had her hat, which she had already managed to lose. Instead, she pulled her collar up as high as it would go and hurried along. She stopped only once, to buy the least offensive holiday card she could find: a black-and-white image of a cottage, nearly covered in snow, with a plume of smoke coming from its stone chimney and an unobtrusive wreath on its wooden door. Inside, Mia wrote:

Happy holidays! All best, College Girl

THEN SHE TUCKED both cash and card into the plain white envelope and sealed it shut. She printed the name PATRICK X. FITZPATRICK on the front, and then was on her way again.

This part of Brooklyn was unfamiliar to her. She had been to the amusement park and the aquarium with Eden a couple of times, but the rest of the neighborhood was a blank that she began to fill in as she walked. The names of the avenues—Mermaid Avenue, Surf, Neptune—had the whiff of the sea, of fairy tales and legends, and bore no relation to the small low-rise buildings, mostly old and ugly or new and even uglier. A dental center with a four-foot neon tooth in the window, a Laundromat, a Kentucky Fried Chicken joint, two liquor stores, and a Chinese restaurant whose brilliantly colored, larger-than-life-size pictures of food had a lurid, almost pornographic glow.

Mia continued walking until the commercial strip gave way to a row of two-story houses, most with blistered or cracked siding and the occasional substitution of cinder blocks for a front step. She stopped at the one whose number corresponded with the address she had written down. This house was in no better or worse shape than its neighbors. The only distinguishing feature was the plaster cast of the Virgin Mary—paint flaking and the tip of her nose missing—which dominated the fenced-in concrete slab that passed for a yard. Mia approached the door, hesitated, and then rang the bell.

Almost immediately, the door opened and there stood a bulky woman in a pilled orchid-colored tracksuit and fuzzy slippers of a darker, soiled purple. She had long blond hair that was pulled back and fastened indifferently with a barrette. She took a long drag on her cigarette, and waited.

"I'm looking for Patrick," said Mia.

"Uh-huh," the woman said.

"Does he live here?"

"Who wants to know?" She took another drag, and then blew the smoke out, not exactly in Mia's face, but not exactly not in her face, either.

"I do," said Mia.

"What, did he knock you up or something?"

"No," said Mia. "We just met the other day."

"Really?" With her crossed arms and truculent expression, she looked ready for a brawl. "Where did you say you met him?"

"In jail," Mia said quietly. "A holding cell at the Seventy-eighth Precinct, to be exact."

"Oh," said the woman. "Oh." Her arms fell easily to her sides. The cigarette smoldered, and when it had nearly reached her stained finger-tips, she tossed it out the door. It made a small hiss as it hit a small patch of snow. "Do you want to come in?"

Did she? Who was this woman anyway? Could she trust her? Mia thought about the envelope, the card, the money. This was what she was here for, wasn't it? This was her mission.

Hesitating only slightly, Mia followed her past a cramped, dark living room with a large-screen TV—on, but muted—and an equally cramped dining room, whose table and chairs were nearly obscured by sheets of thick, yellowed plastic. The smell of smoke was everywhere, embedded in the fibers, the floorboards, the walls. Mia tried breathing just through her mouth—tiny, shallow breaths, like a puppy. They kept going until they got to the kitchen, which was at the back of the house. Lined with windows, it was filled with an unexpected, lemony light.

"Sit down." The woman gestured to a small round table and match-ing chairs; the table was covered by a vinyl cloth in a faded floral print. "Want me to take your coat?"

"That's okay, I'll hang on to it." Mia wanted to be able to make a quick escape. She lowered herself, perching uncomfortably on the edge of her seat.

"Cigarette?" the woman asked, extending the pack. When Mia shook her head, she took one for herself and lit up. "I'm his sister. Maureen," she said.

"Mia." She could see the family resemblance now.

"So," Maureen said. "So. You saw him, huh? How's he doing? He hasn't been home the last few days. He does that sometimes. Goes AWOL on me."

"He's okay," said Mia. "Though he was pretty angry. Cursed a lot."

"That's Patrick to a T," said Maureen, looking almost proud. "Always did have a temper on him. Like our dad."

"I left before he did," Mia said. "So I don't know what happened to him. But I had something I wanted to give him."

"You can leave it with me," said Maureen. "I've been living here since Trish died. Kind of taking care of him."

"Trish was his wife?"

"Trish was his world. He was pretty broken up when she went," Maureen said. "I thought we were going to lose him, too."

"I'm so sorry," said Mia.

"Yeah, well, it's all over and done with now. Water under the bridge, and all that. Or at least that's what I keep telling him." She stubbed the cigarette out in an ashtray shaped like a frog—its open mouth swallowed the butts—and immediately lit another one. "See, he thinks it was his fault."

"His fault? How?"

"He should have gotten her into rehab sooner; he shouldn't have believed her when she said she was clean; he shouldn't have left her on her own. But that girl wanted to get high, and there was nothing anyone, not even Patrick, could do to stop her. That's just how people are. They do what they do. The rest is just luck."

Mia said nothing, but pulled out the envelope and laid it on the table. *Maureen could open it herself,* she thought. *Open it and keep the money.* But this did not deter her. The important thing was that she gave it. What happened after that was not in her control.

"Hey, I didn't even offer you nothing," said Maureen, grinding out another cigarette. "Want some coffee? Or cake? I've got a Sara Lee banana cake in the freezer; I can stick it in the microwave."

"That's all right," Mia said. Her lungs were whimpering for relief. "I'm not hungry. I just wanted to be sure Patrick got this." She slid the envelope over toward Maureen, who picked it up and pressed it to her chest.

"You're nice," she said, as if she had just decided. "I'll give it to him when he comes home."

"Send him my regards, too, okay?" Mia stood. "I hope things start to go better for him."

"Like I said before: it's all a matter of luck," said Maureen, standing up along with Mia. "Good, bad, and everything in between." The barrette holding her hair suddenly popped open, and rippling blond waves poured down around her shoulders. Maureen's hair, like Patrick's, was beautiful; it seemed to belong to some other woman in some other life. Maureen didn't appear to notice though; she just gathered it back into the barrette as she walked Mia to the front door. Mia heard the lock turn behind her.

MIA TOOK THE N train from Stillwell Avenue into Manhattan. Usually, the N made good time, but today there was a delay due to "an incident on the tracks," an MTA euphemism for God knew what sort of mayhem, and she was forced to sit and fume for almost thirty minutes. Finally the train started moving again, and when it reached Fifty-seventh Street, she hurried out. She didn't have much time before she had to be back in Brooklyn to pick up Eden. But she missed the weight and feel of the locket around her neck and was intent on going to Mofchum's. Either he could fix the chain or sell her a new one. Not that she couldn't have picked up a gold chain elsewhere, but she wanted it to come from him. Besides, she was burning to ask about the inscription. She had not put Eden's picture in the locket after all; she hadn't wanted to cover up the writing.

Mofchum's business card was in her pocket, but Mia didn't need it; she knew the address by heart. She walked quickly along the street, scouting for the numbers: 335, 337, 339—here it was. Or rather, should have been. She stopped short in front of the window, which was as dirty as she remembered. But now it was empty. The shop was dark, and she pressed her face against the glass door, trying to see in. The interior was as empty as the window; there was no sign of the clutter she remembered, no sign of the affable Mofchum. Mia stepped back and looked up. The sign was obscured by some complicated arrangement of scaffolding; for all she knew, it might have disappeared, too. She reached inside her coat to feel for the locket and the ruined chain; they, at least, were still there.

Mia glanced at her watch. It would be tight, but she decided to walk to the diamond district on Forty-seventh Street. Store after store held stalls of dealers hawking gold, diamonds, and precious stones. Mia ducked into the first place she saw, purchased the plainest, least expensive chain she could find, and fastened the locket around her neck. It felt good to have it back. She raced to the subway and managed to slip into the arriving D train only seconds before the doors shut. Though she had to stand the entire way, she was only five minutes late for pickup; and in Mia's book, five minutes didn't count at all.

"Do you have a lot of homework?" she asked Eden when they were on their way home.

"I did it all in afterschool," reported Eden. "Every little smidgen."

"Yay for you," Mia said. And yay for her, too. Tonight there would be no pitched homework battle, and that alone was a huge relief. "How about a game of Scrabble to celebrate?"

"Only if I get a seven-letter word," said Eden. The last time they had played, she had been ecstatic after having made the word *grunted*; she now expected a repeat performance every time.

"Eden, you know it's just a matter of luck," she said, echoing Maureen's words. "You can't predict which letters you're going to pick."

"I can," said Eden confidently. "Don't you know I have superpowers, Mom? I can read your mind, too. Like I know you're going to let me stay up late tonight, aren't you?"

Eden turned out to be right about that one, and even though she didn't make a seven-letter word, she played a very respectable game and lost to Mia by only three points. Mia never intentionally let her daughter win; she thought it would be an insult to Eden's intelligence, but she was glad that the margin of loss was so small.

When Eden was down for the night—Mia had agreed to let her sleep in her bed until after she was back from visiting her grandparents—Mia went into the living room with the newspaper, a *New Yorker* magazine, and a new novel by a friend-of-a-friend that she had been meaning to start. Proust was for another decade, she decided. But she couldn't sit still; she had no *sitzfleisch*, as her mother would have said. She was exhausted, but at the same time revved up, and she badly needed to unwind. Every time she thought about the money she had just given away, she got a little rush, intoxicating and sweet. She imagined Patrick holding the envelope, opening it, and finding her card and the bills inside. Not that she wanted to see him again. She had done what she needed to do; the money was the piece of her that she freely gave. Now she was through. But she couldn't stop thinking about it, and thinking about it made her more, not less, stoked. And then there was Mofchum, whose business phone had been disconnected and name she had been unable to locate through directory assistance, at least not in the five boroughs, New Jersey, or Connecticut. There had been a moment of hope when she discovered a Sylvia Mofchum on Staten Island, but the woman knew nothing of Gerald and could not help her.

A drink, that was what Mia needed. Something mellow and smooth. But a quick search of her cabinets revealed that she was almost out of options: there was barely a finger's worth of gin, and the bottle of vodka turned out to be empty. No wine, no beer. Maybe she could run out to the deli for a six-pack, but what if Eden woke up? Mia didn't want to risk it.

She contented herself with the gin, stirring it into some cranberry juice and adding a desiccated bit of lime. She sipped it as slowly as she could, trying to make it last. What she really wanted was one of Fred's who-knew-what-he-would-come-up-with-next concoctions, something truly surprising. She salivated, just thinking about it.

So what was going on with Fred anyway? He must still be annoyed at her. But the splash of gin had done its work: Mia felt all soft around the edges, soft and slightly blurred. She was going to call Fred at Juicy. Right now, in fact. But she must have misplaced her phone. She checked her purse, her pockets, under the cushions on the love seat. It was not in any of those places. She felt confident it would turn up, though; for the moment, she used Eden's phone. The keypad was so tiny it might as well have been designed for a doll. Mia had to squint to see the numbers.

"Hey, sailor," she quipped when Fred answered. "Looking for a good time?"

"Very funny," he said. "Are you wasted?"

"Hardly. I had one drink. One teeny-tiny drink."

"Sounds like it wasn't so teeny."

"Scout's honor."

"You were never a scout."

"No. But you were."

"How did you know that?"

"I know things," Mia said. "I just do."

"You're making fun of me," Fred said, with a distinct chill to his voice. "Again."

"I thought you liked it when I teased you."

"I changed my mind."

"I'm sorry, Fred," said Mia. Whatever ebullience of spirit had been brought on by the liquor was now completely and totally dissipated. "I really am."

"It's okay. Sort of," he said stiffly. Clearly he was still angry. "Anyway, what's up? I heard from Emilio that you stopped by this morning."

"I just wanted to know if you'd had any more visits from the police," she said, rubbing a worn spot on the love seat, as if the action of her fingers might somehow repair it.

"I haven't," he said. "How about you?"

"Actually, I did."

"No shit? Did they search your place again?"

"They arrested me."

"Jesus, Mia. You must have been scared."

"You don't know the half of it."

"And I guess you're not going to tell me, either." Now he was angry again. Damn, just when she thought he was thawing.

There was a long, uncomfortable silence.

"I spent the night in jail," Mia confessed in a small voice.

"Really?" He sounded incredulous.

"I didn't want to talk to the detective without the lawyer there, and that big snowfall delayed him. So I had to wait in a cell until he showed up."

"Snow? You mean, this all happened the night Kyra and I were over, and you waited until now to tell me?"

"I would have told you sooner, but you didn't call." Mia kept rubbing that worn spot on the love seat—rubbing, rubbing, rubbing—until she ended up tearing the fabric even more. Stuffing sprouted from the quarter-sized hole.

"I wanted to," Fred said. "But I wouldn't let myself."

"Why?"

"I already told you: I just don't think things are going to work be-tween us if you keep holding out on me."

"I haven't even told the lawyer everything yet."

"You haven't slept with the lawyer," he retorted. "Or at least, I don't *think* you have." Mia decided to let that one slide.

"Okay," she said, sitting up straighter now. "Okay. If it's so impor-tant to you, I'm going to tell you where I got that bill."

"I'm listening," said Fred.

"I know this will sound unbelievable, and I know that it *is* unbeliev-able, except that it also happens to be true. There is a cash machine at my bank that has been giving me money without debiting my account. Extra money. First, it was just a hundred, then a thousand, and finally it gave me a ten-thousand-dollar bill. The one you saw. The one I sold to Weed."

Mia waited for a response, but Fred didn't seem to have one.

"Are you still there?" she asked.

"If this is your idea of a joke, Mia," he said finally, "you'll have to play it on someone else. Because I'm not laughing."

"I'm serious," Mia said. "Completely serious. I've never been more serious in my life."

"You really think this is funny, don't you? Getting your kicks at my expense?"

"Fred, you're taking this all wrong—"

"No, it's you I was wrong about. Dead wrong," he said, and with that, he hung up.

NINETEEN

THE NIGHT BEFORE Lloyd was scheduled to come to New York to pick up Eden, Mia hardly slept at all. Eden snored lightly beside her, bracketed by both Petunia and the new reindeer, whom she had named, inexplicably, Sparrow. Just when Mia finally drifted into a light, dream-splattered doze, Eden popped up like a jack-in-the-box, ready for her big trip.

"I've got my suitcase all packed," she said, giving the overstuffed valise an affectionate little pat. "And guess what? I even folded everything."

"That's great, but we're not seeing Daddy until later this afternoon, remember?" said Mia, stumbling into the kitchen in a quietly desperate quest for caffeine.

"I know," said Eden serenely. "I just want to be ready."

"Ready," echoed Mia. Who was ready? Not her. Not a chance.

It was a light day at the office, so with the help of more coffee and liberal infusions of Tylenol, Mia was able to coast through the morning. In the afternoon, there was a holiday party—she steered clear of the spiked punch—and she was out of there by four, beating the rush back to Brooklyn. She picked up Eden first, then the suitcase, and maneuvered them both back onto the subway train to Manhattan. They were meeting Lloyd at Balthazar, a restaurant in Soho, and while Eden was a veritable glass of champagne—all bubbles and pop—Mia was filled with a lead-weighted sense of dread. She didn't want to see Lloyd, much less have dinner with him. She had already had a lengthy, exhausting conversation in which they had chewed over the details of her two encounters with the police; that was more than enough Lloyd for Mia. But she was doing it for Eden.

They walked along Spring Street, suitcase bumping the sides of Mia's legs. She wished Eden would have let her buy a new one. This one was well past its prime, all stained and torn in one corner, but Eden would not part with it; it was the suitcase she had always used for her weekends with Lloyd, and her attachment was strong. She called it "The Little Suitcase That Could," which made Mia smile. Though right now, with its frayed, ready-to-snap handle, it looked more like "The Little Suitcase That Can't Anymore." *Oh well*, she thought. *Lloyd will just have to deal with it.*

Lloyd. She spotted him as soon as they arrived. He was wearing a bright red cashmere scarf and stood a good half a head taller than anyone in his immediate vicinity. The red was like a traffic light, a fire truck, a brand-new lipstick. It was the pure, primary red of a St. Valentine's Day die-cut heart, *her* heart, the one that Lloyd stomped, trampled, and ground into the dirt when he left. Even though he had his back to her, Mia knew that he was flirting with the pretty blond hostess in the lacy, low-cut top. The girl tipped back her head and laughed at something he said, exposing her smooth white throat. Then Eden scooted over and he turned to wrap her in a huge hug while delivering a cool, offhand hello to Mia. It was only when they were led to a prime piece of restaurant real estate—center table, right by the window—that Mia realized there was one more in their party. She was a tiny woman in a paisley coatdress and black ballet flats. Suim. He had brought Suim along to dinner. Mia felt her face flame. He hadn't told her about Suim. He hadn't dared.

Lloyd made the introductions. Mia forced herself to extend her hand; the hand Suim extended in return was no bigger than Eden's. Eden was momentarily shy in the presence of her father's diminutive girlfriend, but she quickly recovered. Of course, it didn't hurt that Lloyd was pouring on the charm as if it were maple syrup over a short stack. Mia tried to focus on the menu so she could avoid looking into his sneaky, conniving eyes. She quickly decided on the grilled chicken over wilted lettuce, and then set the menu aside. It was noisy, making conversation difficult, which was fine with her. She had nothing to say to anyone anyway; though for Eden's sake, she tried to look interested and even offered a comment or two. But mostly she looked around at the gilt-framed mirrors, the heavy chandeliers, the pattern of maroon-and-white honeycomb tiles on the floor, the rosy-colored marble bar at the far end of the room. Balthazar was one of those places modeled after a nineteenth-century French brasserie, and while Mia had to admit the simulation was good, at the same time, there was something precious about it. Precious and pretentious, too. Just Lloyd's kind of place.

Right now, he was studying the menu, asking the waitress all sorts of questions that, coming from anyone else, would have seemed obnoxious but which he somehow fashioned into a kind of seduction. It was the voice, Mia decided, as she watched the waitress flutter and flush in response to Lloyd's queries. The voice and the eye contact, the little gestures with the head and hands. Was the salmon wild or farm-raised? Were the nuts in the salad chopped or whole? And when he started to tackle the whole topic of wine, Mia was ready to take her fork and stab him in the thigh. Had he always been like this and she had just failed to notice? Or had she been so in love that she hadn't cared? Finally, the order was placed. Mia asked for her grilled chicken, and Eden ordered ratatouille. At least Lloyd had offered to treat them; her entrée cost twenty-three dollars; Eden's, eighteen.

"Good choice," Lloyd said to Eden, like he was giving her a grade. Eden beamed. Then he ordered a salad and the scallops for himself, and salmon for Suim, who had not yet uttered a single word to anyone beyond the "Hello, it's nice to meet you," which Mia knew to be a bald-faced lie anyway. The waitress, still giddy from Lloyd's verbal foreplay, toddled off to reapply her lip gloss and perhaps convey their choices to the kitchen.

Suim helped herself to a slice of baguette. She started to butter it, but Lloyd gently took the knife from her tiny hand.

"In Paris, they don't butter their bread at dinner," he said, stopping her small hand with his huge one.

What if she doesn't care what they do in Paris? Mia fumed. But she was not here to quarrel, so she kept quiet. This, however, set the tone of the meal. Lloyd took a stance on everything: how the chicken should have been grilled, which variety of potatoes made the best side dish, exactly how much fresh pepper should be ground on the salmon, when to take the next bite, when to make the next swallow. Suim ducked and bobbed her sleek, dark head in acquiescence, not seeming to mind. Nor did Eden, who gobbled her food and took Lloyd's every word as gospel.

Mia, however, was beside herself, and she moved from annoyance to rage to finally, amazingly, something like relief. How had she put up with Lloyd for all those years? And more important, why? Realization came like a flood.

This is what life with Lloyd had always been like. He was forever directing, managing, fine-tuning. There was no subject on which he did not have an opinion and no opinion he failed to share. Maybe it was her fledgling romance with laid-back Fred, or maybe it was the night in jail, but somehow, Mia felt pushed into some new place, one that allowed her to reevaluate all the relationships in her life. For the first time, she felt *relieved* to be done with Lloyd. It was a strange, almost giddy sensation, as if she had been filled with helium, or bouncing weightlessly on the moon. By the time she tucked into her berry-strewn Pavlova—of course Lloyd had to explain the derivation of the dessert's name—she was actually smiling. Smiling! When she said good night to Suim, she thought, *You've got him, you can keep him. Oh and by the way—good luck!* She felt drunk, the happy, bouncy kind of drunk, though this was clearly not the case. She had accepted only a single glass of wine, and, not wanting to give Lloyd any further ammunition against her, she hadn't even finished it. She knew, of course, that this feeling wouldn't last. She was not about to get over Lloyd in the time it took to order and eat dinner at a phony French brasserie. But if she could feel this way for one night, then surely there would be other such nights—and days—that followed.

THE REALLY HARD moment was saying good-bye to Eden, whom she wanted to kiss about a hundred times. Since the no-touch rule was back in effect, she had to content herself with a quick peck and a hug. "Have a good time, baby. See you next year," she said. Lloyd grasped the suitcase by its nearly ruined handle, Eden waved frantically, and Suim nodded politely a final time. Then they turned a corner and were gone.

Mia was not prepared for the hollowness she suddenly felt inside— gutted, like a fish—and she stood there for several minutes staring at the place on the sidewalk where they had stood. People streamed by her, but she didn't yield until a fat guy in a tight, shiny baseball jacket bumped her shoulder hard. He scowled like it was her fault. She said nothing but slowly started walking back to the subway train. The next morning she felt no better. The prospect of being without Eden until the beginning of January seemed to demolish her. January seemed so far off it might as well have been June.

Mia remained in bed, not sleeping, not reading, just staring up at the ceiling, whose pattern of cracks she turned into pictures—a long, knobby flamingo here, a unicorn there—the way you would with clouds. But doing it inside, and alone, was less than satisfying, and she forced herself to get up and face the Eden-less day ahead. She drank a cup of coffee and spooned down some granola while flipping through yesterday's paper, and then devoted the rest of the morning to the sort of penitential, obsessive cleaning that she had not undertaken since Lloyd's last visit. With an old toothbrush, she attacked the hinges that held the toilet seat in place, poured a small lake of bleach on the bath-room floor and let it sit for an hour, attached a soft cloth to the broom handle and swabbed under the stove and fridge. The sound of the phone interrupted her manic activity. Mia dropped the rag she'd been using and tripped over the mop. Could it be Eden? No. It was Julie. But Mia didn't answer and didn't even listen to the message. She wasn't ready to speak to Julie yet.

There was, however, only so much cleaning she could tolerate, and at around one, she decided to resurrect her abandoned shopping excursion. She still had money in the shoe box, and she extracted two hundred-dollar bills for holiday gifts. She was in no mood to brave the Manhattan crowds today, the last Saturday before Christmas, so she decided to keep her shopping local. That would have pleased the author of *All That Trash,* whose recent phone call she needed to return.

There was a flea market in the school yard of P.S. 321 every weekend, and Mia found a woman with an impressive selection of used books. Wouldn't Stu's horse-crazy daughter love a gorgeously illustrated copy of *Black Beauty*? For Stuart, she bought a cloth-bound edition of Auden's collected works—he had been an Auden lover since college—and, for her mother, a gardening tome devoted entirely to the propagation of cacti. Just because Mia privately suspected the plants were flesh-eating was no reason not to purchase the book.

The rest of what she bought was entirely consumable. Bars of oatmeal and carrot soap, jars of locally produced jam and honey. Orange-scented body butter for Eden, who would, she knew, be tempted to eat it. When she was through, she could barely carry it all, and she decided to buy a shiny black shopping cart at the hardware store to wheel everything back home. It would come in handy for schlepping the laundry, too.

It was dark by the time she got back to her apartment, the winter night filling rapidly with swollen, sooty-gray clouds. Mia's brief good mood disappeared with the light. She stowed the shopping cart in the kitchen and dumped everything else in the middle of the living room floor, intending to deal with it all tomorrow. But then she noticed the cache of upscale chocolate bars—infused with exotic flavors like green tea and chili pepper—that she'd bought for Fred, who happened to mention that he ate chocolate three times a day. Fred was not speaking to her at the moment, but what if she were to deliver these chocolate bars, all six of them, to him personally? It was Saturday, and he would be at Juicy.

Suddenly, this seemed like a very good idea. But first, she would take a long, hot shower. Wash her hair. Slather body butter—okay, she bought some for herself, too—all over. Curl her eyelashes. Swipe on some blush.

It was not like she didn't know what she was doing; she was on to herself. The question was whether it would work. She had been thinking about Fred steadily over the last few days. Regretting that she hadn't taken him more seriously. And hoping she could mend things between them. Of course he didn't buy her story about the cash machine; who would? But it was the truth, and somehow, she had to get him to believe her.

Mia stood in front of her minuscule closet, wrestling with hangers to yank out clothes, and then stuffing them back inside. No to the stretchy black velvet dress—it was sexy, but it was trying too hard. No to the black cords, black jeans, countless black sweaters and shirts. None of them struck just the right note, the one that chimed festive yet abashed, casual but caring. Briefly, she considered a plum mohair miniskirt that belonged to Julie, but she decided that the shaggy wool made her look like a llama. A closet full of clothes, and nothing, but nothing, to wear.

Nothing to wear. Wear nothing? Now *that* would get his attention. It would also get her arrested. Or pneumonia. Maybe both. But what if she were to pull one of those crazy stunts, the kind she had seen touted in women's magazines about how to rev up your sex life? She wouldn't actually wear nothing, but close to it. How about a push-up leopard-printed bra and matching panties—another good-bye-to-Lloyd present she'd bought herself—and a coat over it? Eagerly, she pawed through her closet again, unearthing a bona fide Burberry trench, replete with epaulets, plaid lining, and preppy charm. It was a castoff from Gail, who had the annoyingly patronizing habit of giving Mia her old clothes, as if she were the cleaning lady. Actually, Mia happened to know that Gail gave her cleaning lady her better rejects, such as a pair of worn-not-at-all Manolo Blahnik raw-silk mules and a Jil Sander jacket with the price tag still on it. Mia was given the second-tier stuff. But the coat, the Burberry coat, all buttoned to the neck and belted around the waist, worn over the animal-print underwear might, just might, do the trick.

Mia stepped into the panties, fastened the bra, and started hunting for appropriate footwear. She found a pair of thigh-high brown suede boots, also from Julie (just because they weren't speaking was no reason to forgo her footwear), that would surely add that je ne sais quoi to Mia's happy-hooker ensemble. For it was a hooker look; Mia knew that. But tonight, she would be a hooker with a heart of gold. Or at least, of chocolate. She gave her hair a volume-enhancing tousle and anointed her wrists with a few drops of perfume; those sample bottles she got at Barneys were still going strong. Then, after stuffing the chocolate into her purse, she was off.

It was cold, with the wind whistling up her coat; there must have been goose flesh aplenty on her thighs and her butt. But as she walked—no, strode—she began to generate her own body heat. A regular little furnace, that was what she was. Hot and filled with glowing coals.

Juicy was jammed. There were people crammed three deep at the bar, and more little clusters spilling off from that central crush. Strings of white twinkling lights ran along the walls and the window; a three-foot wreath decorated with silver ornaments hung over the bar. It was Christmas, all right. Christmas with a vengeance.

It took Mia a few minutes to make her way through the crowd. By the time she had, she wished she could take off her coat—the press of bodies was making the room uncomfortably warm. But taking off the coat was not an option. Fred was down at one end of the bar. He didn't see her right away, but when he did, he smiled, then frowned. It was the smile she chose to honor. The smile and the sky-blue shirt that he was wearing, the one that turned his eyes into two tiny lagoons. He finished with the drink he was making before walking over to Mia.

"Hi, Fred," she said. She was really warm now; her cheeks were red and her neck was slightly damp.

"Hi," he said. And nothing more.

"You're still mad at me." The noise was so loud she had to raise her voice to be heard.

"I guess I am, but this isn't the time to talk about it." Someone called his name, and he turned.

"I know. I just wanted to give you something. A little present."

"You bought me a present?" Fred turned back and studied her face. "Why?"

"It's Christmas, right? Or it will be in a few days."

"I don't get you, Mia. I don't get you at all."

"Yo, Fred!" Now someone else was hailing him, demanding his time, his attention, his expertise in pouring libations.

"Can you come outside with me? Just for a minute?" Mia wheedled.

"What for? You have another crazy story for me? How about a taxi with wings? That'd be a good one."

"Please?" she asked. She was not begging, no, not her.

He ignored her for a second and then called out, "Hey, Chuck, cover for me, will you?" And to Mia: "I'm giving you five minutes. Come this way." He gestured for her to walk behind the bar, and they went through the kitchen—she waved to Emilio, who was standing at the sink—and outside. The cold air felt good on her hot face. She remembered now that there was a little garden, with slate paving stones and lilac or wisteria all along the wall at the far end. Back in the spring, it had been lovely; a fragrant, verdant surprise where she would have least expected it.

"Here," she said, taking the chocolate bars from her bag. "These are for you."

He peeled back the tissue paper and looked at them. "Chocolate." He continued to stare at the wrappers. "Thanks. Thanks a lot."

"I hope the flavors aren't too way out for you," she said.

"It's you. You're too way out for me."

"Am I?" She stepped closer.

"I just can't figure you out." But he didn't move away.

"That story I told you? About the cash machine? It's true."

"Are you crazy?"

"No. Not crazy. And I can prove it, too. Just give me a chance."

"You're serious, aren't you?"

"That's what I told you. Now I'm here to show you."

"Show me what?" He sounded suspicious.

"Look," she said, and started to unbutton the coat.

"What the—" He stopped when she reached the bra. "What are you doing?"

"Isn't it obvious?" she said. She began to untie the belt.

"I think you really *are* crazy," he said, but he stepped closer and encircled her bare waist with one hand; in the other, he gripped the chocolate bars.

"Oh, I am," she said. "Crazy for you." Were these words even true? She wanted them to be.

He had his lips an inch from hers when Emilio poked his head out the door. "Hey, Fred, they need you inside." Fred dropped the chocolate bars with a small clatter while Mia quickly started buttoning her coat.

"I'm coming," he said. And then to Mia, "I'll try to get off early, okay? Go back to your place and wait for me?" He knelt, gathering the chocolate.

"Okay," she said, thinking, *Yes, yes, yes.* "I'll wait."

"But first we have to talk."

"Talk. Of course." She retied the belt and followed Fred back inside, once again through the kitchen. She didn't know what Emilio had seen, but she studiously stared down at the floor; the black rubber mats with their raised black dots stared back at her.

BACK IN HER apartment, Mia shed the coat but left on the underwear and boots. Fred would enjoy it. Buzzing with happy anticipation, she made her bed and brushed her teeth—again. She was grateful to be getting another chance; she would try not to ruin things this time around. Spying the still-folded copy of *The New York Times,* she decided to tackle the crossword puzzle. She and Stuart had gone through an intense period of working the puzzles. Sometimes they'd get two copies of the paper and make it a contest; on Sundays, they did it together, yanking the pen out of each other's hand. But somehow they had lost the habit. She only vaguely recalled those arcane little words: *en,* a printer's measure; *joe,* coffee. When the door buzzed, she was so flustered that she knocked the paper off the table; it fluttered down and fanned out on the floor.

He's here already, she thought, hurrying to answer it. *He's here.* She yanked the door open, and there, in the open rectangle, stood Patrick. Not Fred. Patrick! He had come to kill her. Of course. He had come to kill her, and it was just a question of how—a bullet, a blade, the brute force of his bare white hands as they closed tightly around her throat. Her mouth fell open, as if her jaw had been unhinged.

"Hey, College Girl." He barged right past her and into her apartment. "Love the look." He rubbed his chin, with its three-day growth, thoughtfully, as if he'd had to consider the idea.

"I thought you were in jail." Her voice was a strangled thing. Should she scream? Hit him with something? Run down the fire escape? All of these things tumbled through her mind, like clothes in the dryer. But first she had to get dressed. She grabbed the trench coat, draped over a chair, and pulled it on. Her fingers were shaking as she fumbled with the buttons.

"Hell, no!" he said, with that snorting laugh of his. "They try to pin all sorts of shit on me, but shit doesn't stick to Patrick X. Fitzpatrick. I'm like rubber; everything just bounces right off."

"How did you find me?" She was squeaking. Mia Mouse. *Squeak, squeak, squeak.*

"It wasn't so hard." He was wearing the same zip-up white sweatshirt she'd seen him in last time—it was a dazzling white now—and he dug around in the pocket. Did he have a gun? Was that what he was searching for? "After you left that night, I overheard someone at the station saying your last name. Saul. Mia Saul. So of course I remembered it; I've got an amazing memory, have I told you that? Anyway, once I knew your name, finding you was easy. Easy as pie."

"Oh," she said, but she was mesmerized by the movement of his hand. When he finally took it out, she involuntarily sucked in her stomach, as if she had been hit. But then she saw that he was not holding a gun or weapon; he was holding a cell phone. Her cell phone.

"You left this behind." He extended his hand.

"My phone," she croaked, taking it. "How did you get my phone?" But she knew the answer to this already; the phone had been missing since the day she had gone to his house in Coney Island.

"Maureen found it. You must have dropped it, so I wanted to bring it back." He smoothed down his hair. "It seemed like the least I could do."

"Thank you," she whispered. "Thank you very much." She should have been screaming now, screaming her head off. But something stopped her. If she screamed, she would make him angry. She remembered quite well what he was like when he was angry. And she also remembered what he was like when he was not, when she talked to him like he was human. That was what she had to do now—appeal to his human side. She knew it was in there. She had seen it.

"I actually came to thank *you*, College Girl. For that money."

"The money," she repeated. Fear was making her into an idiot, a mindlessly parroting idiot. *Think*, she told herself. *Think for your life.*

"Yeah, the money. Maureen gave it to me and told me how you'd come looking for me. Not many people would do that, College Girl. Nah—that's not right. Not *any*."

"Well, I thought you might be able to use it," she said, trying to control her trembling. "Since it's almost Christmas."

"Cash is good in any season. Christmas, Easter, Veterans Day—you name it."

"Cash is handy, all right," Mia agreed. She had lost the struggle and was shivering violently.

"You cold?" Patrick asked, staring at her more closely. "You look cold."

"Yes, I guess I am."

"Well, seeing as you're not wearing very much under that coat, no wonder." She must have looked terrified because he continued, "Hey, you don't have to worry about me. You could parade around here buck-naked and I wouldn't do a thing to you. Not unless you asked me to, anyway." His grin was lewd yet charming.

"I didn't think you were that kind of person," Mia said. *Find the human side*, she reminded herself, though the shivering did not stop.

"And you'd be damn straight, too. I've always had a soft spot for the ladies; I'm not ashamed to admit it, either. I'm a leg man myself. Know many leg men? We're a special breed; a breed apart. And seeing as I'm a leg man, I can tell you that yours are choice, Grade A specimens. Not that the rest of you is bad, either. Not bad at all. But I don't stick my finger in the frosting without an invitation. Anyone, and I mean *anyone*, I ever laid a hand on has wanted it as bad as me or more. I never forced myself, you know? Never had to."

"No, I'm sure you didn't."

Mia was desperate to get him out of there.

"Hey, do you have anything to drink?" he asked.

Drink! Jesus, the last thing she wanted to do was offer him a drink! But she was too afraid to say no.

"I don't have anything alcoholic, if that's what you mean—"

"How about a Coke? You got a Coke?"

"I'll check," Mia said, hurrying to the kitchen with Patrick close behind. She never bought Coke. But maybe there was a carton of orange juice. All she found was a nearly empty bottle of organic apricot nectar. She hadn't shopped for food this week, and her fridge, like her cupboards, was bare.

"No Coke," she said. She held the bottle aloft. "Will this be okay?"

"Sure thing, College Girl," he said, accepting the small glass she offered. He sniffed it and then raised it to his lips. "Cheers."

"Cheers," she repeated, though she didn't have a glass. She adjusted the belt more tightly around herself.

"Looks like you're pretty low on provisions, College Girl."

"I just haven't gotten around to going to the supermarket."

"Yeah? Is that it? Or are you short on money?"

"No, I'm okay."

"Doesn't look like it."

"No?"

"No. Looks like you coulda used that five hundred as much as me."

"That's what you think?"

"Uh-huh. When I first saw those bills come spilling out of the card, I thought, 'Well, fuck me stupid, she's loaded, she's rich, she's got one silver spoon coming out her mouth, another out her ear, and a third one out her ass.' But then I found out where you lived, and I thought, 'This does not compute.' And now that I'm here, I'm even more confused. I mean, this building is a shit hole, College Girl. A regular shit hole. No offense, of course."

"Of course," Mia squeaked.

"Now you've seen where I live—that's a shit hole, too. It's the house I grew up in though. All seven of us lived there, plus my parents. But my dad was a garbageman. Broke his back hauling other people's crap. How about your dad? I bet he didn't have much to do with garbage."

"Uh, no, he didn't."

"What'd he do?"

"He was an astronomer."

"No shit? Did he, like, name stars and stuff?"

"He taught astronomy. At Columbia University."

"See, that's what I mean. If your dad was strolling the halls of a big-time, high-class place like that, then you shouldn't be living here. And since you *are* living here, in a shit hole with an empty fridge, how do you come off giving me, a stranger, five hundred bucks? Are you some kind of saint or something? A holy person?"

"Holy? Me?" Mia actually found it in her to smile. It was a weak, thin smile, but a smile all the same. "I don't think so." She looked down at the coat that was now covering her leopard-clad body, the va-va-voom boots.

"You must be," Patrick insisted. "There's no other explanation for it. Someone like you, who needs scratch, is giving it away? Like I said, it doesn't compute."

The buzzer sounded, imperious and loud. This time it *was* Fred; she was sure of it. She looked at Patrick, who looked at the door.

"Aren't you going to answer it?" he asked.

Mia teetered to the door and asked, still in that maddening, mousy squeak, "Who is it?"

"It's me. Fred."

"Your boyfriend?" Patrick asked.

Mia nodded dumbly.

"Well, let him in."

She opened the door and there stood Fred, his brain working hard to process what he was seeing.

"So you're the boyfriend," Patrick said, looking Fred up and down.

"Who are *you*?" Fred spit out.

"Patrick Fitzpatrick," he said, and thrust out his hand. Fred stared at the hand for a second before taking it.

"College Girl over here'll tell you all about me. But you don't have to worry. I was just leaving anyhow." He set the empty glass down on the table.

"Okay," said Fred. *"Okay."*

"Thanks for the juice. Nectar. Whatever," said Patrick. He burped softly.

"You're welcome."

"Take care of yourself, College Girl," Patrick said. "Stay safe. Don't let those men in blue—or anyone else—fuck you over, okay?"

"I won't," Mia said. "I promise."

"And you." Patrick turned to Fred. "Boyfriend. You're a lucky son of a bitch, and I hope you know it. You got yourself a special girl here. Very special. You better treat her right. Otherwise you'll have me to fuck with, and let me tell you, it won't be pretty. I can be one mean cocksucker when I'm mad."

Fred didn't say anything, so Patrick turned back to Mia.

"You hear that, College Girl? He gives you any trouble, you know who to call. Patrick's your man, so you don't have to worry." He hiked up his white pants, which had begun a slow descent past the waistband of his boxers, and zipped up his white sweatshirt. Then, with unexpected dignity, he walked through the door and disappeared.

TWENTY

PACK A BAG," ordered Fred. "Now." He looked at her, standing in the kitchen, shaking so hard she couldn't move.

"O-o-kay," she said, her voice as quavery as the rest of her. "But where am I going?"

"Home with me. You can't stay here anymore. Not when that guy knows where you live." He breathed out savagely. "You're lucky he didn't slit your throat from ear to ear. After he had raped you."

Mia's response to that was to burst into tears.

"Hey," said Fred, at her side in an instant. "Hey. Fred's here now. It's all right." He held her while she cried. Mia knew he thought this was about Patrick, and, of course, in a way it was. But there was more to it than that. It was everything, really—Eden's being gone, the damn DAT with its toxic glow, her belated realization that maybe Lloyd had always been an opinionated, controlling egomaniac and she'd never really understood that until now. She felt totally unmoored, lines cut and vessel spinning wildly out to sea.

"Come on," Fred said. "Let's get your stuff, okay?"

FRED LIVED IN a narrow row house in Kensington, a neighborhood deeper into the borough than Park Slope. Outside, the place looked suitable for midgets, or at least for the anorexically inclined; it was only sixteen feet wide and seemed squashed by the houses on either side. But inside, the place felt surprisingly open and flowing. He had knocked down several interior walls and installed a new flight of stairs with spaces between the treads; the new staircase, made of pale, pickled wood, looked as if it were floating, suspended between the two floors it connected. The back wall of the house was mostly glass, in the form of sliding doors, and beyond that Mia could see what looked like a garden, now blanketed with snow. She thought of the garden at Juicy, which she knew was Fred's work. The man was certainly handy with a spade.

"When you say you 'knocked them down,' do you mean you, personally?" she asked.

"Uh-huh."

"That must have been some job."

"Yeah, well, it was right after my divorce. It was a good outlet. Kept me from thinking too much. Or killing someone."

Mia nodded as she glanced around the front room. It was tidy and comfortable, with a low, streamlined sofa in a pewter-colored velvet, a tweed-covered armchair, and a round braided rug. There was a small mantel, on which stood a crudely fashioned vase with a bilious green glaze dripping down its sides. Mia picked it up to inspect it.

"Pretty hideous, huh?"

"Now that you mention it, yes." Mia put the vase down.

"Kyra made it. It's from her green period." He smiled.

"Got it." She smiled back.

"You know how it is when you're divorced—you've got to work extra hard to make your kid feel like she still has a home with you. Living with an ugly vase is nothing compared with what I've done. Or what I'd do."

"So where should I put my bag?" Mia asked, shrugging off her jacket.

"In my room," Fred said, reaching for it. "Want to go up?"

"Can we wait a little bit?" Mia asked. She was all right, on the way over here, pressed like a strip of masking tape to Fred's back as they sped along on his motorcycle. But all of a sudden she was feeling something like aftershock, and she badly needed to sit down. "Actually, I was hoping for a drink."

"Not tonight, Josephine," Fred said, mock sternly. Then, relenting slightly, he added, "How about a cup of steamed milk with a little splash of pixie juice to give it bite?"

"Perfect," she said, sinking into the chair. She remained there while Fred puttered around in the kitchen. He had a nifty Italian espresso maker with a steamer attached; it made a ferocious huffing sound, like it was ready to blast off. Fred returned with a mug of something white and frothy. A dusting of brown hovered on the surface of the foam. She sipped, tasting cinnamon, vanilla, and a hint of something stronger that she thought was cognac.

"Just what the doctor ordered," she said. "You're not having one?"

"I'm okay," Fred said, looking serious as she sipped. "But you're not."

"No?" She tried to keep her voice light.

"No. You're coming apart at the seams, Mia. I'm worried about you."

"Join the club," she said. The cognac-laced milk was making her joints all loose and limber; God, but she had been wound up tonight. Tight as a spring. It was good to let go, relax a little.

"Well, maybe they're right to worry."

"Why, Fred?" she burst out. "Why? I'm doing my best here. Can't you see that?"

"I know you are, baby," Fred soothed. "But you've got to admit that some of your choices are a little . . . questionable." Mia waited, knowing what was coming next. "This Patrick person, for instance. You just happen to get a little visit from a guy you met in jail? You're lucky he didn't kill you."

"I know," she said, looking down into her cup and watching the tiny white bubbles burst.

"And what if Eden had been there when he showed up? Huh?"

"I said I *know.*" She drained her mug.

"When are you meeting with that lawyer?"

"Next Tuesday."

"After work?"

"The office is closed for the holidays. I'm a free agent until January."

"Well, I'm glad you're going to meet with him." He waited, studying her. "Are you going to tell him about the cash machine?"

"Only if he asks," said Mia. "So far, he's said he doesn't want to know where I got that bill. He just wants to focus on Weed—the where, when, and how. He says he wants to prove beyond a reasonable doubt that I had nothing to do with his death."

"And how about me? You said you would show me," Fred said in a low voice.

"Is it really so important to you?"

"Yes," he said, "it is."

"Then I will."

"When?"

"Give me a couple of days, okay? After Christmas?"

Fred said nothing, so Mia added, "Come on. I'm scared even to go back to that neighborhood right now. You can understand that." This was not, strictly speaking, true. Still, she didn't have to tell that to Fred, did she?

"Okay," he said finally. "You do love to stall though."

"I'm not stalling," she said, standing up and walking over to where he sat. "Not really."

He looked like he didn't believe her; why should he? She was lying. Again. Suddenly, she felt very, very tired. What was the point of being with Fred, of being with anyone, if she had to lie about everything, especially what was most essential to her? It occurred to her that she'd had to do plenty of lying—to herself, mostly—when she'd been married to Lloyd. Not at first, of course. But as his overbearing ways began to stifle and then anger her, she had had to pretend that he was brilliant, he was strong; that he took over because he deserved to. There had been a price for her self-deception, one she hadn't even realized she'd been paying. And now here she was, doing it again.

"All right," she said, settling onto the couch next to him. "I guess I am stalling. Even though I said I would show you, I don't want to."

"Why, Mia?" he asked, lifting his thumb to trace the line of her jaw. "Don't you trust me?"

"You'll think I'm crazy."

"Oh, that," Fred said with that smile of his, the one that was all chipped tooth and sparkling. "I already know you're crazy; what else is new?"

"Stop!" She slapped his arm lightly, but with intent. "I'm trying to tell you something."

"Sorry," he said. "I'm listening."

"It's just that ever since that machine started giving me money, money that I didn't ask for, money that I didn't expect, I've felt, oh, I don't know, charmed, somehow. Like I'd been chosen for something special. Not that you'd think it from looking at my life, especially lately. But to me, do you see? It felt like that to me."

Fred said nothing, but he was looking at her with the sort of slack-mouthed attention men usually reserved for the World Series or the Super Bowl.

"This machine has been my secret, my private jackpot, maybe even my private hell, but it's been mine. All mine. And I haven't wanted to tell anyone about it."

"Not even me," said Fred. It was not a question; it was an answer.

"Not even you." There, she had just come out and said it. She waited for something, anything to happen—skies to fall, lightning to flash, bolts of thunder to be hurled from on high—but nothing did. Fred sat quietly; he didn't press, didn't ask, and didn't say anything more. His silence was not golden, thought Mia; it was like a prism, scattering rainbows all over the place.

"Maybe we could go upstairs now…" she said, placing first one arm, and then the other, around his neck.

"Maybe we could," he agreed.

But they didn't go upstairs; they did it right there on the sofa, and this time it was especially tender and sweet. Mia didn't think of Lloyd, not even once. She wanted to tell this to Fred but then decided no, better not. The omission didn't feel like a lie; it felt like a different kind of truth.

MIA WAS VERY grateful for the distraction of being at Fred's; it kept her from missing Eden too much. She had been tempted to call her several times, but each time, she held off. Let Eden call her if she needed to. Instead, Mia puttered around Fred's place, looking for things to do, like polishing a pair of candlesticks she found tucked away in a cupboard and then buying long white tapers that she lit when they sat down together for dinner.

"Nice touch," Fred said, touching the rim of his wineglass to hers, "very nice." One of the perks of dating a bartender was that he always served excellent wine. And unlike Lloyd, he didn't analyze it endlessly. He just handed her a glass of whatever he had poured and said, "Try this. I think you'll like it."

She also made the acquaintance of Fred's three cats, a pair of ginger-colored females and a seventeen-pound long-haired gray male. The male was rather repulsive, with a squashed-in face and a slow, almost waddling gait, but he had taken a shine to Mia, plopping himself down on her feet or lap when she least expected it. The first time, he parked himself on her face when she was sleeping, causing her to emit a small, strangled scream.

"What?" said Fred sleepily, as he moved out of the orbit of her thrashing. "Did you have a bad dream?"

"I … I don't know," Mia said, panting a little. "It felt like something furry and hot was stretched out over my mouth. I couldn't breathe."

"Oh, that was Dudley," Fred said affectionately, looking around for the cat. "Hey, boy." Fred stroked the animal on its abysmally low forehead.

"Does he always do that?"

"Only when he likes someone. He must have a thing for you."

"How nice," Mia said, shuddering as she pulled the covers up around her neck.

But the force of the animal's affection—patient, unwavering, asking so little in return—began to eat away at her reserve. When she tentatively patted his head, she was rewarded with his purr, a rich, vibrato hum. A gentle scratch under his chin yielded a look of slitty-eyed adoration. Soon, she was mincing shrimp scraps to add to his dinner, and combing out mats in his silky gray fur.

"I've never seen him take to someone new so quickly," said Fred. "It's like he's decided you're his person."

"Maybe I have a secret power that he senses," Mia said. "Something mysterious and compelling."

"That's you all right," Fred said without a trace of irony. "Mysterious and compelling."

FRED INVITED MIA out to Bensonhurst, where he would be spending Christmas Day. Since Mia had no other plans, Bensonhurst seemed as good a place to be as any. Well, perhaps not as good as Capri or Gstaad. But since she hadn't been asked to any of those places, Bensonhurst would have to suffice. With its detached single-stories, its driveways, and its lawns, it reminded Mia of the burbs. Fred led her to a brick house, on top of which blinked a trio of stars and a lone angel with outstretched wings. Down below were a full-scale crèche and about twenty-five cars parked around it. *Adoration of the automobiles,* thought Mia.

"I have a big family," Fred said. He shifted the bag of presents he was carrying from one hand to the other. "You're not shy, are you?"

There were easily forty people in the house, which was all gussied up for the holiday with artificial wreaths in every window, artificial garlands wound around the banister and door frames, and a light-studded, tinsel-clotted artificial tree that grazed the ceiling. Fred steered her through the crowd, stopping to kiss, hug, or pump the hand of everyone he saw.

"There's my mother," Fred said, gesturing to a sixtyish woman across the room. She was solid rather than fat, squeezed into a black sequined top and black pants. Her hair was a cascade of dark waves; Mia thought she might have colored it with shoe polish. Even at this distance, it was impossible not to notice her inch-long fingernails, painted a dark, frosted scarlet.

"I call her the Babe of Bensonhurst," added Fred. Mia hung back for a second, but Fred took her hand and gently led her along. "Come on, I'll introduce you."

"Freddie!" the woman said, and grabbed Fred in a hug; she caught him somewhere between his waist and his chest. Fred hugged her back, grinning at Mia over his mother's inky head. Mia felt a little knot of discomfort begin to tighten inside, the diminutive form of his name a little warning bell pinging in her head. Lloyd's mother was prone to this kind of thing, too, with her *Timmy this* and *Timmy that.* But then Mia reminded herself of all the ways in which Fred was nothing at all like Lloyd.

The woman broke away from Fred and extended her hand with its vivid nails in Mia's direction.

"I'm Bev," she said. "Glad you could join us. Any friend of Freddie's is a friend of mine. What's your name?"

"Mia."

"Well, Mia, I hope you brought your appetite. The food's in there. Freddie, take her inside and fix her a plate."

Which he did: roast turkey, sweet potato puree, glazed ham, pickled beets, green beans, lasagna, garlic bread. Mia was suddenly ravenous and took seconds of mostly everything. The beets. The beets were delicious. So tangy. She had never had better beets. And the sweet potatoes—so light and fluffy. Finally, she put her fork down.

"I hope you saved room for dessert," said Fred.

After everyone had eaten, the group splintered off in several directions. The kids went into the bedroom to watch a DVD; a bunch of guys turned on ESPN. Bev organized a card game in the kitchen—all turquoise Formica, circa 1974—and began to shuffle.

"Mia, can I deal you in?" called Bev.

"I'll sit this one out," Mia said. She disliked most card games, but in the interest of being sociable, she would sit and watch.

"Okay, if you change your mind, just let me know," said Bev. Her hands on the deck were practiced and light; the cards skittered across the table.

"What's the game?" whispered Mia.

"It's called Fuck Your Neighbor," said Fred.

Loud, fast, and explosive, it was not a game with which Mia was familiar. Even though she couldn't quite catch the rules, she still found herself enjoying it.

Bev yelped with delight when she made a good play and cursed with impressive brio when she lost. Finally, she gathered the cards into a neat stack and shooed everyone away from the table.

"Game's over," she announced, hoisting her tubby little body up. Encased in the tight black clothes, she reminded Mia of a seal. "Freddie's making a fresh batch of coffee."

"I am?" said Fred.

"Would you please?" asked Bev. "The coffeemaker's all set up and ready to roll."

"All right," said Fred. "If you want."

"Thanks, Freddie," Bev said. "You're a good boy." She leaned over Fred, who was still sitting, and planted a crimson kiss on his forehead.

"In the meantime, I want to talk to your new lady friend here. I'd like to get to know her." Bev pulled up a chair next to Mia. "So you're a Brooklyn girl?" she asked.

"Only for the last dozen or so years. I was brought up in Manhattan."

"I love Manhattan," Bev said. "Broadway—I could see a different show every night. And that Metropolitan Museum uptown; it's a palace, I swear. No, not a palace. A temple. A temple of God."

"So you like the Met?"

"Like it? I love it, just love it. The costume gallery's my favorite," Bev said. "I was just there with my friends Selma and Glowie—see, that's Glowie over there, in the red-and-green sweater with the Scotties on it—and we saw all these fabulous wedding dresses. I wanted to get married again, just so I could fantasize about wearing one. And how about that Christmas tree they put up? The one with all the angels . . ." Bev was off and running: Impressionists, Greek and Roman statuary—"Those naked young boys are hot, hot, hot"—the American Wing, Renaissance Madonnas. She didn't stop until Fred handed her a cup of steaming coffee. She took a sip and nodded. "You done good," she told her son. Then, to Mia, "How about you? You like the museums, too?"

"I do," said Mia. "But I hardly go anymore. I'm afraid I'm stuck in the same old groove—working and taking care of my daughter. That's about all I have time for. Or energy."

"I think you have a lot of energy," said Bev. "I can kind of feel it coming from you. In waves, you know? Like heat or light."

"Really?" asked Mia, intrigued in spite of herself. "You do?"

"Definitely," said Bev. The imprint of her lower lip on the white cup was a bright red semicircle. "I know these things. Didn't Freddie tell you? I can sense things about people. I read the cards, too."

"Cards?" Mia sipped her own coffee, which had already started to cool. Was she referring to the game?

"Tarot cards. I know . . . I'll read yours." Bev put her cup down hard enough so that coffee splashed over the rim and dripped down the side. She didn't appear to notice.

"Now?" asked Mia, looking over at Fred. But he was talking to a man with a head of curly white hair and his back was turned, so he didn't see her.

"Sure, why not? You have something to hide?"

BEV'S BEDROOM WAS an ode to the color pink. Mia could tell that Fred's dad had died years ago; no straight man alive could endure a room this aggressively femme. The walls were pale blush pink, the satin coverlet was rose, and the tufted headboard was a still darker shade of the same color. The windows were covered in balloon shades with a pattern of pink-and-green cabbage roses, and there was a matching overstuffed armchair with about a half-dozen fringed pillows piled on its seat. There was also a mirrored vanity that hosted an army of perfume bottles and a glass-fronted cabinet crammed with a dolls, teddy bears, and a six-inch plastic bride and groom that Mia guessed was from Bev's own wedding cake.

"Come sit," Bev said, patting the pink bed. Her black-clad thighs rubbing together made a soothing *swish-swish* sound.

Mia sat down as Bev bustled around, first finding the cards and then laying them out on the slippery pink surface of the bed.

"Turn over three cards," she instructed.

Mia picked the cards, revealing the brightly colored pictures on the reverse sides.

"The Hanged Man, the Three of Swords, the Seven of Wands," said Bev. "Interesting."

"The Hangman is interesting? I'd say gruesome or morbid is more like it."

"No, you can't take it literally," said Bev. "You have to interpret it."

"How?" Mia knew very little about tarot cards, though she found their old-fashioned imagery and symbolism kind of quaint. Like a do-it-yourself fairy tale; the cards provide the nouns, and you added all the verbs and adjectives.

"Well, the Hanged Man could mean letting go, surrendering to experience. Or it could mean putting your own interests aside in favor of someone else's. Or being vulnerable and open."

"Sounds like it could mean a lot of things."

"Of course," said Bev confidently. "It's all got to be taken in context." She gathered the cards, shuffled them thoughtfully. "That was just a warm-up. Just to get the juices flowing. Now I want to do a universal reading. This time, pick six cards."

Mia hesitated before making her choices. This was silly, wasn't it? She was just humoring Bev, whom she was starting to like.

"The Hanged Man again," said Bev.

"Uh-oh."

"No, it's like I told you: don't be so literal about it. The Hanged Man is one of the most mysterious figures in the deck. He's simple, but complex. He attracts us, but also disturbs. He's a constant contradiction. And then when you have him next to the Magician . . ." Her lacquered nail tapped another of the cards Mia had turned over. "This is good. Very good."

"Is it?" Mia couldn't believe she was taking any of this seriously.

"Oh, yes. The Magician is all about action, awareness, concentration, and power. It's about creating miracles." Something in Mia's face must have changed, because Bev added, "I can tell that you've had the experience of some kind of magic recently. Something strange and compelling that you can't explain."

"Actually, I have . . ." Mia said, thinking, *It's just a coincidence; she can't know.* She felt a little uneasy though. Uneasy, yet curious, too. What else might those cards be able to tell her?

"Of course you have," said Bev. "The cards never lie. Now, look at this card, the Lovers—"

"Ma," said Fred, who had walked into the room. Both women turned to look at him. "Enough."

"Oh, you're a party pooper," she said, giving Mia a conspiratorial wink. Her thick, had-to-be-false eyelashes were like a black centipede against her cheek. "We were having fun until you came in."

"I'm sure you were. But people are looking for you. Peg and Mike want to say good-bye."

"They're leaving? Already?" Bev looked regretfully down at the cards on their field of shining pink. "To be continued," she told Mia, gathering the cards. "I'm not done with you yet." She rose, with some effort, and stopped in front of the mirror to adjust her sequined top and perform a little series of taps under her chin, as if she were trying to tighten the loose flesh there.

"Okeydokey," she said to her reflection. "Duty calls." But on her way out of the room she stopped and put a hand on Mia's wrist. "There's good things ahead for you. I can tell."

"I like your mom," Mia told Fred when Bev had gone.

"She likes you, too," Fred said.

"How can you tell?"

"What do you mean how can I tell? She's my mother. Haven't I spent a lifetime learning how to read her signals?" He smiled. "But those tarot cards of hers—I gotta rein her in sometimes, you know what I mean?"

"Oh, I didn't mind the cards," said Mia. And she hadn't, either.

They stayed until the dessert table—three kinds of pie, chocolate cake in the shape of a Yule log, platters of cookies—had been successfully depleted. As they hovered by the door, saying their good-byes, Bev gave Mia a hug instead of a handshake.

"Freddie, you bring her back here, okay?"

"Okay, Ma," Fred said, managing to sound dutiful and ironic at the same time. "Can do."

The traffic was extremely light on the way home and the motorcycle—which Fred had insisted on driving—seemed to fly over the highway. Despite all the layers he had made her wear, Mia was freezing; the wind sliced through her jacket as if it were paper. Still, when she looked up, she could see the weak but steady glow of the stars overhead, a pale reiteration of the thousands upon thousands of dazzling lights that shone brightly from almost every doorway, every roof, every fence, and every tree that they were passing.

TWENTY-ONE

CHRIS COX WAS a dandy. The lawyer appeared at Mia's apartment wearing a three-piece suit and molasses-colored wing tips that radiated a muted, costs-a-fortune glow. His tie was an exquisite, lushly patterned silk, and the French cuffs of his impeccably tailored shirt were secured by two opulent hunks of hammered gold. On his wrist was a complicated, expensive-looking watch, the sort that indicated all the time zones, even those on Mars, and there was a diamond stud winking in one earlobe. But he wore his finery lightly, as if it were running or boxing gear, and, in fact, he reminded Mia of a boxer, darting and jabbing his way around the room, his small hands clenched in tight, emphatic fists.

"The coroner put the time of Wedeen's death at between eight and eleven on the morning of December sixteenth. Now can you tell me exactly, and I mean *exactly*, where you were that morning? Because I want to make sure your alibi is airtight."

"The morning of the sixteenth..." Mia tried to remember. "I would have been taking Eden to school; I must have seen a few people I know at drop-off. I know—I ran into her friend Caitlin's mom, Suzy. We even talked for a few minutes. I'm sure I can get her to verify that."

"Good, good," said Cox. "Now what else? What about after you dropped her off?"

"I took the subway into work. So there are at least a half dozen people, maybe more, who saw me at the office. Though I wish I didn't have to get them involved in any of this."

"Get over it," Cox said. "You don't have a choice. But so far, so good. I'm liking what I'm hearing. We've got several reliable witnesses to say that you were nowhere near Wedeen at the time he was killed. Now, I'm going to want their names, addresses, and phone numbers from you; can you get me all that information by tomorrow at the latest?"

"I guess so," said Mia. He gave her a look, and she added, "All right. I will."

"Better," he said. "Remember, I can't help you if you don't want to be helped." He straightened his already straight tie. "Show me your clothes; appearances are very important with the judge."

Mia led Cox into the bedroom and watched with mild amazement as he ruthlessly sorted through the contents of her closet. He made two piles—maybe and no. Most of the clothes fell into the no category, which was growing bigger by the minute, though Mia could not see why her black ribbed sweaters, turtlenecks, and black pants of all materials were so summarily rejected.

"No pants," said Cox. "And, unless you're in mourning, no black either. Black reads as too cool, too cynical."

"Oh," said Mia. Who knew?

"We want you to project a look that's open and sincere. I could see you in a crisp white blouse and a string of pearls, maybe. Or a sweater, but in a soft, light shade: beige or ivory. I want you to look responsible and mature. Yet innocent, too. Innocence is a crucial theme here."

Mia said nothing. This was all feeling very familiar, the digging through of the closet; the feeling that nothing she owned would project the right image, the right message, and the right self. But the stakes, she knew, were high, so she tried to cooperate. Then she thought of the night she got dressed for Fred's visit, the night Patrick showed up.

"How about this?" she asked, digging through the crowded rack for the Burberry coat. After all, it had worked before.

"I like it," Cox said. "I like it a lot." He nodded, taking the coat from her. "Now we just have to find you something to go underneath."

Mia didn't mention the outfit she had chosen the last time she'd worn this coat, but allowed Cox to keep looking until he found a weird brown corduroy dress with buttons down the front—another of Julie's fashion experiments gone awry—and a brown faux-croc belt.

"Send the coat and the dress to the dry cleaner's before you wear them," he instructed, rolling the belt into a neat circle before handing it back to her.

"But why? They're not dirty."

"I thought I made this clear already: I'm the expert here. And if I say *cleaner's*, then I mean *cleaner's*."

"Cleaner's," she said. "Right." Mia began putting all the rejects back in the closet.

"Now, the next thing we need to deal with is that bill you sold him."

"The bill . . ." Mia, who was holding a pair of pants in one hand and a hanger in the other, paused.

"Yes. The bill. Costello is going to bring it up, and the judge is going to want to know where it came from. I haven't pressed you about it before because you didn't want to talk about it. But I have to address the things people don't want to discuss—that's my job."

"I'll tell you," Mia said, "even though you won't believe it." She left the pants on the bed; they could wait.

"Try me and see."

So Mia told him the story about the cash machine gone haywire, the money that came, unbidden, from its brushed-steel slot. When she was through, Cox was, for the first time since he walked through her door, quiet, though his bald pate seemed to pulsate from all the activity taking place within.

"Mia, there's an option we haven't discussed yet," he said.

"What's that?"

"We tell the judge that you can't answer because you were not in your right mind at the time. You don't know where you got the bill; you had been having hallucinations, hearing voices—that kind of thing."

"That's a lie."

"I know. But it's more plausible than the truth." He sighed. "*Way* more plausible."

"Sorry," she said. "I won't say it."

"No one is going to believe your story," he said.

"I can't help that, can I?"

He studied her, as if trying to get a sense of who she might be, what she would—and wouldn't—do.

"All right," he said finally. "Maybe it's better that I don't know where you got it. Our main focus is Weed, and clearing you from any possible involvement in his death."

"We're in good shape with that, right? I have an alibi; I can provide the corroboration you wanted; you vetted the outfit. What else do we need?"

"There is one more thing I haven't brought up yet."

"What's that?"

"Costello mentioned something about a gold locket. She thinks it's in your possession."

"Do you mean this?" Mia dug it out from under her dress; she had taken to wearing it concealed.

"That fits the description, yes."

"Why is she asking?" Mia asked.

"She contacted a few local currency dealers. One of them said that you had approached him with the bill."

"Solomon Phelps," said Mia, remembering with distaste that cool, blue gaze.

"Right. He said that when he asked you where you got it, you lied. And that you had a very unusual piece of jewelry, one that he thought might have significant value."

"So what if it does?" asked Mia defensively. "It's mine; I bought it."

"From whom? Can you provide a receipt?"

Mia thought of the empty, darkened shop, the disconnected number.

"No," she said. "I can't."

"I somehow figured that would be the case." His fingers moved to his tie again, as if seeking its reassurance.

"Is there a problem with my having it? It's not like it's been reported stolen or missing. Or has it?" That Gerald Mofchum might have sold her a piece of stolen jewelry was too disheartening to contemplate.

"That's what Costello and her crew are working on now. So far, there's no evidence that it was acquired unlawfully. But paired with the bill, it doesn't look good for you."

"What can I do about it?"

Cox looked at her steadily. "Not much," he said at last. "We'll just have to see how far Costello wants to take it."

AFTER COX LEFT, Mia decided she would stay in the apartment, despite Fred's loudly voiced concern about her safety. But once the shock of Patrick's visit had worn off a bit, Mia was not worried, at least not about that. She replayed the entire scene, several times, in her mind. Not once did she catch a glimmer of violence, brewing or actual. Crazy as it might have seemed to Fred, she was certain that Patrick would not harm her.

The mailbox downstairs had been stuffed, and she now sorted through its contents, discarding the junk, saving any real correspondence for last. In this category was another postcard from Julie that read, *I don't care if I get skin cancer; my tan is amazing. I'll fill you in on the details when we speak, but I really think Dean is The One. XOXOXOX*

The postmark was weeks ago; clearly, Julie *had* been trying to stay in touch. Mia felt a pang when she thought of their last conversation but squelched it. There was also a two-page, single-spaced letter from the

author of *All That Trash,* in which he thanked her profusely for her editing. *You really saw to the heart of this story, and helped me bring it to life,* he wrote.
If the book does well—and it certainly seems poised to—I owe it to you. Mia read
the letter three times before putting it aside. What a sweet man. And
what a thrill it was to think that her work could help give birth to this
larger, more significant work.

But the distraction of the mail lasted only so long, and soon Mia
was thinking of Eden. Again. She had not spoken with her in days,
and she suddenly felt like she couldn't bear one more second without
hearing from her. She called, waiting impatiently as the number rang
and rang. No answer. Finally, she heard Eden's breathless message and
then the ubiquitous beep. Mia wasn't sure whether she wanted to talk
to her daughter badly enough to call Lloyd's parents, but, after about a
minute, she decided that she did.

Lloyd's mother, Virginia, answered.

"Mia dear, how *are* you?" she asked. She sounded so worried. God
only knew what Lloyd had been telling her. Mia fought the bitterness
that seemed to flood her mouth. *It doesn't matter,* she told herself. *It doesn't
matter what they think. I love Eden. And Eden loves me.*

"I'm fine, Virginia; how are you?"

"Oh, getting along, getting along. We had a lovely holiday with
Eden, just lovely..." She trailed off, clearly embarrassed. "But we
missed you, dear. We really did."

"Well, um, I missed you, too." This, actually, was true.

"Well, I suppose you're calling to talk with Eden," Virginia said
brightly. Clearly, that was sufficient soul-baring for one conversation.

"I am actually. Is she there?"

"No, Lloyd took her to see a play over at the college; they're doing
A Christmas Carol. I would have gone, but my arthritis was acting up so
I had to stay behind."

"That's too bad," said Mia, wanting to get off the phone now.

"Aging and its discontents," said Virginia. It sounded like she was striving for lightness. "I'll have Eden call you when she gets back, all right?"

"I'd appreciate that," Mia said. "Thanks so much."

"Not at all, dear," said Virginia. There was a pause. "I do hope everything will be all right . . ." she said, sounding tentative again.

"Everything is fine. Really."

"Oh, I'm glad to hear it," Virginia said. "You know how much we love Eden . . ."

"Happy New Year," said Mia, just wanting to end this.

"Happy New Year to you, too." Virginia's voice sounded thin, as if it were stretched on a rack and was ready to snap.

AFTER THAT HIGHLY uncomfortable exchange, Mia went back into her bedroom to attack the piles of clothing once more. When the phone rang, she was sure it was Eden, and she made a lunge for it.

But it was Lloyd.

"I heard you talked to my mother," he said by way of greeting.

"I'm sorry her arthritis is bothering her."

"Thanks for the sentiment. I'm sure she appreciates it."

Was he being sarcastic? Did she care?

"How was the play?" she asked, stuffing a hanger back into the closet.

"Not bad for a piece of provincial theater. Eden loved it, though. She's ready for Dickens now. I'm going to get her the book."

"Is she right there? Can I talk to her?"

"She's actually not here now."

"Where is she?"

"She's out with my father."

"Well, would you make sure she calls me when she gets back? I want to talk to her."

There was a major pause, enough time for Mia to start feeling anxious. Was he trying to *prevent* her from talking to Eden? Because that was what it felt like.

"Actually, I think you and I need to talk first."

"Okay," she said, abandoning the strewn clothes once more. "I'm listening." She nudged the clothes aside and made a place for herself on the bed.

"I've been thinking that maybe Eden shouldn't come back to New York in January."

"What?" Mia experienced this last comment as a physical attack.

"You heard me: she needs a change of environment."

"Did Eden suggest this, Lloyd? Or is this your idea?"

"It's my idea, of course," said Lloyd at his most lofty. "I'm still the parent. The one in charge."

"Like I'm not?"

"Not exactly."

"That's a crock, and you know it," she spat.

"Is it?" he asked. "Look, I told you that I didn't know what you were doing, but that whatever it was, it had to stop. Eden's told me everything—about the visits from the police, the fact that you spent the night in jail. She's freaked out, Mia. Totally freaked out. You're in some kind of trouble. I can see that and I'm even sympathetic, I really am. Still, sympathy has its limits. I can't let you or whatever crazy mess you're in hurt Eden. So I think it would be better if she didn't go back to New York, at least not right away."

"You can't do that! It violates the terms of the divorce agreement!"

"Under the circumstances, those terms are no longer . . . operative. And I know that any family court judge *you* might care to petition will back me up."

"I'm calling my brother; that's what I'm doing. I'm hanging up on you right now and calling my brother. He'll know what to do to get her back home where she belongs—"

"I've already spoken to your brother. And he agrees with me that, at the moment, it might not be in Eden's best interests to be living with you."

"Stuart. Said. That?" The enormity of this betrayal was like having her head dunked suddenly into black water, cold and churning. She had to struggle for breath.

"Yes, he did. He said that he agreed you were volatile, unstable, and—"

Mia put the phone on the bed, under a mound of clothes. Lloyd continued to talk, enumerating her many failings as a mother and as everything else, too, but his voice, his deep, rich, mellow voice, was rendered inaudible by the mounds of fabric. She didn't care about what he was saying. The only thing she cared about was Eden: how to get to her, how to get her back. She sank to the floor, allowing herself to howl, to wail like the wounded thing that she was; she remained there until her breathing was less ragged and the howls had subsided to whimpers. When she reached for the phone again, Lloyd was gone. She called Stuart's office, and someone answered on the second ring.

"Is Mr. Saul in the office today?" she asked.

"Yes, he is; would you like me to transfer you to his secretary?"

But Mia had already hung up. He was there. Good.

Mia endured the subway ride into Manhattan in a kind of rage-steeped fugue. Everyone in the car infuriated her: the man seated to her left, with his open-legged sprawl, squeezing against her thighs and hogging her space; the young woman across the aisle tweezing her eyebrows with the kind of narcissistic abandon that should have been reserved for her own bloody bathroom; the kid whose iPod was cranked up so loud Mia could discern all the lyrics of the rap tune he was grooving to; the overweight mom who barked at her toddler while impatiently yanking on his hand.

By the time she reached Fifty-ninth Street and Lexington Avenue she was ready to pop. She marched the few blocks to Stuart's office on

Park Avenue, signed in at the security desk, and zoomed to the twenty-first floor in a sleek, empty elevator. Fortunately, she knew Stuart's secretary, Anita, well enough to ask her to keep the visit a surprise until she was actually upstairs.

"Is it his birthday or something?" asked Anita.

"Something," said Mia darkly.

Stuart's office was posher than posh. There was heavy mahogany paneling everywhere, thick carpeting that soaked up the sound of any human footfall, hulking leather-covered chairs in the reception area, and enough floral arrangements to stock a funeral parlor. She waited outside the door while Anita knocked discreetly, and then, in response to Stuart's "Yes?" Mia walked into the office.

"Hey, Mia!" said Stuart, getting up from his desk. "Anita didn't tell me you were here." He crossed the room, reaching out his arms to give her a hug.

"Fuck you," she said, nimbly sidestepping the embrace. "Fuck you and your phony good cheer."

He stopped, looking stunned. "What's with you anyway?" he said.

"What's with me? What's with *you*?" She was so angry she had to hold on to her own wrists; otherwise, she would start hurling things: the crystal paperweight, the stapler, weighty law tomes, or the brass clock that squatted on the gloomy, ostentatious credenza.

"Would you please keep your voice down? You're in my office, for Christ's sake." His eyes glanced nervously toward the door, which Anita had tactfully closed behind her.

"I know where we are."

"I don't even know what's bugging you; care to clue me in?"

"Lloyd," she said, his name pure bile in her throat. "Lloyd is bugging me."

"Did you talk to him?"

"Did *you*?"

He fingered the collar of his shirt, looking uncomfortable. "Well, yes, I did, but—"

"No *buts*, Stuart! I'm not interested in your *buts.* Lloyd just told me that he's not bringing Eden home in January. And that you said you'd back him up!"

"That's not exactly what I said."

"That's what you meant, though! And that's what he heard. Eden. He's taken Eden away from me, and you're just going to stand there and let him do it." She started to cry then, not as loud or hard as before, but with an even deeper, more piercing kind of sorrow.

"Come on," he said, grabbing her by the arm. "We're going to take a walk."

Once outside, she and Stuart headed west and north, past the hot-dog vendors and the T-shirt hawkers, past the gorgeous old Plaza Hotel, past the flocks of fat, jaded pigeons that could scarcely be bothered to move out of their way, until they reached Central Park. Mia hardly minded the sharp wind biting her ears; it was an almost blessed distraction from her fury with her brother, her grief about Eden.

She was still crying, albeit more softly now, and Stuart handed her his crisply pressed linen handkerchief. She took mild pleasure in filling the snowy square with mucus, tears, and the cloudy black remnants of her mascara. When she was done with it, she balled it up and let it fall from her hand. He could pick it up if he wanted to, but he seemed oblivious.

"I understand how hard this is for you," Stuart said after they had been walking in silence for a few minutes.

"No, you don't," she said. "You don't understand at all. Everything's always gone your way: school, marriage, work, kids. Well, I haven't been so lucky. And instead of understanding me and supporting me, I feel like you're punishing me."

"Punishing you? For what?"

"For not being rich enough, or successful enough. For not staying married. For being a loser," she said, kicking the sidewalk with the toe of her boot, in precisely the way, she realized, that Eden did.

"This is your script, Mia. Every word of it." He shoved his hands deep into his pockets.

"Maybe it is," she said. She was tearing up again and wished she had not dumped his handkerchief. "But that's how I feel. I miss you, Stuart. No, I miss the person you *used* to be." There, she had gone ahead and said it; she hadn't realized just how hurt she was until the words were out.

"I miss you, too."

"I'm not the one who's changed."

"Yes, you have."

"How?" she demanded. "Tell me."

"It's the bitterness. You're letting it eat you up so that there's nothing else left. You resent my success, you detest my wife, you scorn my kids. I constantly feel judged by you: I'm a sellout, I have no scruples, I'm a shit."

Bitter. There was that word again. Hadn't Julie called her bitter? But with Stuart, she felt she had just cause.

"You broke bread with the enemy!" she burst out. "You talked to Lloyd; you listened to Lloyd. You think Lloyd is more trustworthy than I am. Even after everything he's done."

"Not true," Stuart said. "Not true and not fair. You're so reductive: black, white, good, bad. I know Lloyd gave you a raw deal. Believe me, I know, and I'd like to punch the guy out. But how will that help you? Or Eden? She still loves him, you know. She still loves him, and she always will."

Mia was silent, hating him for being right. However she felt about Lloyd, she would have to find a way to endure him because of Eden. Expunging Lloyd was a luxury she couldn't permit herself. But she wasn't ready to give up her grievance against Stuart.

"And then there's Gail. She's despised me from the start."

"Only because she thinks you despise her."

"Well, I do."

"I love her, Mia."

"I can't imagine why."

"Then you need to enlarge your imagination."

"But she's so condescending! Snobbish! Empty, calculating, and dishonest—let's see, have I missed anything?"

"Are you through yet?" Stuart asked.

"Not really," Mia replied. "In fact, I was just getting started."

"I'm willing to concede that you two got off on the wrong foot. And I'm sorry for that; maybe I should have stepped in earlier on. Then things might not have gotten to this point."

"That," said Mia with mild astonishment, "is the first time I've heard you apologize for anything connected to her. You're always so defensive where she's concerned."

"I guess I am," he said. "And maybe she hasn't always been the most sensitive. She's tough because she's had to be." When Mia didn't say anything, he added, "Look, I'll talk to her, if you want. That is, if you're willing to meet her halfway." Mia still didn't answer. But she ceased ranting about Gail, at least for the moment.

They came to Bethesda Fountain, which was silent and dry. The Angel of the Waters, with outstretched wings, stood at the center of the fountain. Her bronze gaze was downcast, as if she were ashamed of something. A sparrow landed lightly on the top of her head and then fluttered away.

"So where does that leave us?" Stuart asked. "A shit and a loser. Except you're not a loser, Mia. Never to me."

"Is this my cue to say you're not a shit?"

"In a word, yes," said Stuart.

"Okay, so you're not a shit," she said. "At least not a *total* shit." She smiled, the first smile of the day.

"Do you remember the last time we were here together?" Stuart asked, looking at the statue. "It was the night I graduated from high school."

"I remember," she said.

"Aimee Polansky and Gretchen Dineen were with us. And Tobin Wheeler." He paused. "Oh—and Josh Horowitz, too."

"My first love," she said.

"We all got so wasted," Stuart said. "I brought a couple of six-packs, and so did Josh. Didn't we take off our shoes and wade in the fountain?"

"I did," she said. "You were too chicken." She could see herself at seventeen, tucking her long, gauzy skirt into the elastic band of her panties, singing what even then were old Beatles tunes in varying off-key harmonies, wishing she could have slipped off somewhere to make out with Tobin, whom she hardly knew but found wildly sexy, instead of Josh, her ostensible boyfriend at the time.

"You always had a lot of spirit," he said, looking at her with admiration. "You still do."

"Is that what you think? God, judging from that inquisition—excuse me, intervention—at your house, I'd never have known."

"Okay, so we were too harsh," Stuart said. "And I was clumsy. But it's because I love you, you dope. Love and am worried sick about you. Don't you get it?"

"Jesus, don't get all smarmy on me," she said. "Otherwise, I'll have to throw up, and I dropped your handkerchief back there, so I won't even be able to wipe my mouth." But it was good hearing Stuart say that he loved her, especially when he sounded like he meant it.

"I have another one," Stuart said. "Do you need it?" He produced a second white folded square from the depths of his coat.

"Do you buy them by the caseload or something?" She took the handkerchief anyway, and this time, she stuffed it deeply into her own pocket.

"Mia, I'm not going to support Lloyd in a bid for full custody, or anything even approximating it. What I am going to suggest, though, is that you let Eden stay with him for a while, at least until after your court date."

"How do you know about that? Have you been talking to Chris Cox?"

"Of course I've been talking to him; I found the guy for you, didn't I? And it's as a professional courtesy to me that he's not charging you a cent. Do you have any clue about what his hourly rate is?"

"Big deal. So he costs a lot," she bristled. "That doesn't give you the right to pump him for confidential information about me."

"Mia," Stuart said, putting a hand on her arm. "I haven't even asked why you had to spend a night in jail. So just stop, okay?"

She looked at the hand on her arm, as if trying to decide exactly what she should do about it.

"Oh, all right," she said finally. "Pump away."

Stuart walked her to the Fifth Avenue subway station. Before she descended the subway stairs, Stuart once again put his hand on her arm.

"I didn't even buy you lunch," he said.

"Next time."

"Okay. But that means there has to be a next time. Will you call me? Or at least take my calls when I call you?"

"I guess."

"Come on, Mia. I thought we were past that."

"Let me get through this court date, okay?"

"Fair enough." He stood there fiddling with a loose button on his coat. "I'm going to be there, you know."

"You are? Why?" How could perfect, perfectly in-charge Stuart have a loose button? She wished that he would pull it off, throw it away. Go buttonless, live a little.

"It's open to the public. Didn't Cox tell you?"

"Yes, but you're not exactly the public."

"No. I'm your brother."

To Mia's surprise, he did yank the button off, though perhaps not intentionally. It went scooting along the curb, then veered into the sewer grating at the corner. There must have been a plop, but it was too small and far away to be heard.

"You lost your button," she said.

"Yeah, well. I've lost things before."

"Haven't we all?" She grasped him tightly, enfolding him in the hug that she wouldn't give him earlier in the day.

ON THE SUBWAY platform, Mia thought briefly about the heaps of clothing still on her bed, but the prospect of returning to the apartment to deal with them was too daunting. Instead, she transferred to an F train and took it out to Fred's house. Fred was not home; he was at the bar already, but she had the set of keys he had loaned her.

Once inside, she flopped down onto the couch and tilted her head back. *Eden,* she thought. *Eden, Eden, Eden.* Maybe Stuart was right about letting her remain with Lloyd for the time being. But *only* for the time being. After the court date, she was going to get her back, no matter what it took. She would go down to North Carolina herself, she would camp out on the Prescotts' doorstep, she would—a rasping, wheezy sound distracted her, and then Dudley flung himself into her shins with the force of a bowling ball headed for a strike. She gathered all seventeen sloppy pounds of him onto her lap and pressed her face into his magnificent, misshapen skull.

TWENTY-TWO

MIA SPENT THE following day on the couch. She sat on the couch, and she reclined on the couch. She shifted from her stomach to her back, and then curled up on her side, like a shrimp. For variety, she relocated to the floor next to the couch, stroking Dudley whenever he waddled by. The other two cats studiously ignored her, but Dudley, well, Dudley was her *man*. Fred was tender and solicitous, bringing her coffee, a scone, freshly squeezed tangerine juice while she was parked there, but eventually he had to go. It was New Year's Eve day, and he needed to be at the bar early.

"I'll call you later on, okay?" he asked, standing by the door. "To check in on you?"

"That's fine," she said without any enthusiasm. She had tried reaching Eden at least six more times, but none of those times had she picked up. Mia was sure that Lloyd had found some pretext for which to take her phone; what else could have kept her from answering? Mia's inability to make contact with Eden had left her hobbled and in pain, as if her ankles had been broken.

"And you'll come to the bar tonight?"

"I guess."

"You've got to come, Mia. You need to get out."

"Okay," she said. "I'll be there. You don't have to worry about me. I'm all right."

"If you say so," he said dubiously. "Anyway, I wish I could hang out longer, but I really have to go."

Once she was alone, Mia considered her options. TV, but that meant she actually had to get off the couch and climb the stairs. A book would be good, but she had just finished the novel she'd been reading and didn't have anything new with her. She tried Eden for the seventh, eighth, and ninth times, and, of course, there was still no answer. She was about ready to pour herself a drink—it was almost New Year's Eve after all—when the cell phone bleated. Eden!

"Hi, baby," she said, holding the phone tightly pressed to her ear, as if she could touch her child by proxy.

"I like it when you call me 'baby,' College Girl," said a male voice. "In fact, you just made my day."

"Patrick." Mia's mood plummeted.

"Guilty as charged." When Mia didn't answer, he continued, "You all right there, College Girl? You don't sound all right."

"No," said Mia. "I'm not." And with that, she was crying again, crying as if she could not stop.

"Is it the boyfriend? He been smacking you around? 'Cause if he has, I'll have to come over there and kick his fucking ass. I'll take him apart, limb by fucking limb. Just say the word."

"Fred's not the problem," said Mia, hiccupping through the tears. "It's my daughter, Eden." That was all she could say before the sobbing started again.

"Hey, this is not good. Not good at all."

"No, it isn't," she agreed. "It's terrible."

"How about I come and see you, College Girl? I was calling to wish you a happy New Year. But I could do it in person."

"See me?" said Mia. "See me where?" He couldn't come here; it was out of the question.

"Anyplace you want. You name it, I'm there."

"Well, I don't know . . ." Mia said, but then thought, *Why not?* She was going to go crazy, sitting around here all day, brooding about Eden. But she would not invite Patrick here, nor would she let him into her apartment. She would meet him somewhere else. Somewhere public.

"You can cry on my shoulder," Patrick was saying. "Might make you feel better."

"Okay," she said, sitting up straighter and dislodging Dudley from her lap. He gave her an insulted look and huffed off. "There's a coffee shop on the corner of Union Street and Fourth Avenue. Can you meet me there in about an hour?"

"On my way," he said.

PATRICK WAS ALREADY seated and waiting for her by the time she arrived. He had exchanged the white sweatshirt for a white parka—maybe he was channeling Emily Dickinson?—and his long blond hair had been smoothed back into a ponytail. He was freshly shaven, too—the line of his jaw, newly visible, was crisp and well defined. When he spotted her, he smiled and scooted a menu across the table in her direction.

"The New College Inn," he said, referring to the name printed in bold letters across the menu. "Figures you'd pick this place. Tailor-made for you."

"I guess," she said, peeling off her coat and hanging it over the back of her chair.

"So why all the waterworks?" he asked. He put his white hands palms down on the table and waited.

"My ex-husband took my daughter to see his parents for Christmas. And now he says he's not going to bring her back."

"No wonder you're freaked out," said Patrick. "But why? What's his beef?"

"He says I'm not a fit parent. Because I spent a night in jail." Mia suddenly felt self-conscious. She still had no idea what Patrick was in for that night, and she was not sure she wanted to find out.

"So? Plenty of innocent people end up in jail. Doesn't he know that?"

"Evidently not," she said, staring down into her water glass.

"What'll it be?" asked the waitress, who had appeared with her pad.

Mia hadn't even looked at the menu but that didn't matter; all coffee shops in New York had the same food.

"Rice pudding," she said. "And a cup of coffee. No, make that tea." The last time she'd had coffee here she had rued it for hours.

"I'll have a spinach omelet, rye toast, and home fries," said Patrick.

"Bacon or sausage with that?" the waitress wanted to know.

"No bacon." He handed her the menu and leaned over. "I'm a vegetarian. No leather either." He stuck his foot out in the aisle to display one white canvas sneaker.

"So is my daughter," said Mia.

"You miss her a lot."

"Yes," she said, eyes pooling again. "I really do."

"Of course you do," he said soothingly. "She's your kid. Your only kid, right? So all your eggs are in that basket." Mia nodded, grateful. "You've got a lot invested in that, haven't you? Like, just about everything."

"That's right," she said. "Everything."

"That ex of yours really sucks," Patrick said. "First, because he dumped you. And now, because he's stolen your kid. 'Cause that's what he's done, you know—stolen her."

"I'm not sure a judge would see it that way."

"Judges," Patrick said. "Bunch of thimble-dicked shit suckers."

Mia didn't say anything, but opened a packet of sugar to empty into the tea when it appeared.

"So he doesn't like that you were in jail. What was it, anyway? One night? Big fucking deal."

"One night," said Mia. The tea, which had arrived along with their food, was good, hot, and sweet. "What about you? Have you ever been in jail?"

"You mean, like, done time?"

Mia just nodded, wide-eyed.

"Nah. I've spent a night or two here and there. But I've never gone behind the wall." He seemed quite calm as he said this, and he began to eat his eggs. "What'd you do, anyway? I mean, I know we weren't going to bring it up, but . . ."

"It's a long story," said Mia.

"Aren't they all?" asked Patrick, and raised his golden eyebrows with such contained eloquence, such understated compassion, that she found herself telling him everything, but everything, the words bubbling up and pouring out of her mouth like foam from a shaken bottle of beer.

"You mean to tell me that there's a machine that's just handing out money? Money that it doesn't record?"

"I know it's hard to believe, but it's true."

"I believe it," said Patrick.

"You do? Why? No one else has."

"I do because you told it to me, College Girl. And I believe in you." Delicately, he took a bite of his omelet.

Mia wanted to cry all over again.

"Hey, don't look so weepy," he said, reaching across the table for her hand. She let him take it. "Maybe you should eat something. You haven't touched your rice pudding." He looked at the glutinous mound and then pushed it aside. "Here—have some of my toast."

"No, that's okay."

"I insist." He raised the toast to her lips. The surface was lightly browned and gleamed with butter; she could smell the yeasty odor of the bread. Patrick's hand remained where it was until she finally opened her mouth for a bite, just a small one. Oh, it was good. So good. She didn't know she was this hungry, and she kept taking bites until the entire piece was gone. He was still holding her other hand in his, and she withdrew it slowly, even reluctantly, so that she could pat her mouth with a paper napkin.

"So I've got another question for you, College Girl," he said. "How come a girl like you is so hard up for a buck? Don't you have a family who could help you? Friends?"

"I do," she said. "But there's a little tension in my family right now. More than a little. And my best friend, well, she and I had a kind of falling-out."

"How about the boyfriend? Couldn't you touch him for a loan?" She shook her head, and he didn't press any more. Mia took another sip of her tea. There was no doubt that Patrick was a strange guy, but in that moment, she decided she liked him. He was the first person who had heard her story and not implied that she was crazy—or a criminal.

"So tell me more about this machine. It sounds pretty wild," he prompted.

"Do you want to see it?" she asked.

"The machine?"

"Yes. I haven't shown it to anyone, but I want to show it to you." Mia felt as if she had crossed some boundary, stepped neatly outside her life and into some other, parallel zone, in which Patrick was not an alien to be feared and reviled, but a kindred spirit, or even, God help her, an alter ego.

"Okay," he said. "I'll just finish my eggs." He continued to eat, with no particular haste or impatience. When the check came, he wouldn't let Mia anywhere near it. "I called you, remember? Besides, I owe you."

"No, you don't," said Mia. "Not a thing."

ONCE THEY WERE actually on their way, Mia was nervous. She hadn't tried the machine since it gave her that ten-thousand-dollar bill. She hadn't even gone near it. Now, the bank was almost empty, and no one was using the cash machines at all. Still, she felt like she was being watched.

"It's that one, on the left," she told Patrick in a low voice. She approached it warily. He stayed close, but averted his eyes while she tapped in the code, asking for one hundred dollars. The machine emitted its customary whirrs and hums; no lights, and certainly no music. Mia grabbed the bills as they were ejected from the slot.

Twenties, just twenties. And there were only five of them.

"Shit," she said, raising her face to look at Patrick. "Shit, shit, shit."

"It's not what you thought?"

"No!" she exploded, thinking of Chris Cox, of her brother, of the judge who would, in a matter of days, have to sift through and weigh every word she uttered. "No, it's not." She stuffed the money in her bag and charged out the door, nearly colliding with a woman on her way in. Patrick hurried to follow.

"Slow down," he called when she was halfway up Garfield Place. "You're going to bust a gut."

Mia slowed, but only a little.

"I can't believe it," she said when he had caught up to her. "I have to appear in court on January fourth, and what am I going to say to that judge? Can you tell me that? Can you?" She was yelling now, yelling right in the middle of the street. An old man with a cane glanced in her direction and edged away, giving her a wide berth.

"Just calm down. You're going to kill yourself, give yourself a heart attack or something."

"You're right: if I lose my daughter, I will kill myself." Her head throbbed, and she felt like the energy was pouring right out of her, glugging away into the gutter like so much dirty water.

"Don't say that, College Girl," Patrick said with unexpected tenderness. "You can't say that." He leaned close, his face hovering near hers for a second. Then he kissed her.

At first, Mia was too surprised to pull away, and by the time it occurred to her to do this, it was too late. His kiss was galvanic, electrifying, brain-sizzling, crotch-drenching—every single hackneyed, porn-derived cliché she could think of. She kissed him back like she was drowning and he was the rope, like she was choking and he was the open window, like she had waited her whole life to do it, which, she thought giddily, maybe she had. It was Patrick who pulled away first, and when he did, he looked as dazed as she felt.

"Well, fuck me stupid," he said softly, gripping her tightly by both shoulders. "Who knew a College Girl would be like this?"

"Now what?" she asked, breathing heavily, a bitch in radiant heat.

"I don't know. I don't have a fucking clue."

"The machine," she moaned, as the rank reality of her situation settled itself back down in her, obliterating her options, canceling out her choices. "What am I going to do about that machine?"

"Listen, tell me again about all the times it worked. Every single time you tried, every single time it happened." He looped an arm around her shoulders, and slowly, they started to walk back down the block.

"Well, the first time was in September. I had bought groceries and ended up leaving them in the street. So I needed to get some food for Eden. For supper." Her voice caught a little when she said Eden's name, but she went on, recounting all the times she had gone to the machine and received something more than she had asked for.

"So what was different about today? Anything?"

"Only that someone—you—were with me."

"I have an idea. We're going back to the bank."

"What for?"

"To try it again."

"It won't work. You saw; you were there."

"You didn't let me finish, College Girl. We're going to try it again, but this time, I'm not going to stand so close. I'm going to be off to one side, see? I'll be able to watch what's happening. But I won't be right in front of the machine."

"Like that will make a difference?"

"You never know, do you? I mean, maybe they don't teach you everything in college." Mia had to smile at that.

Together, they walked back into the bank and neared the machine. But before Mia touched the keypad, Patrick moved off to the right. He could see her, could see everything she was doing. Just from a slight re-move. She inserted her card and punched in the request. One hundred dollars, just like every other time. There was a rapid flickering of the screen from dark to light to dark again. She waited, lungs flattened by anxiety, for the machine's whirring to stop. Then she reached for the bills, and, as she did, her mouth opened into a perfect O.

The bills, all ten of them, were hundreds. The receipt, when it emerged, was for one hundred dollars. But in her shaking hands, she was holding a thousand.

Before Patrick could say a word, a woman in a knit poncho walked into the bank to use the machine. Mia quickly stepped aside, and silently handed him the receipt. She saw his eyes grow larger and rounder, a dumb show of recognition, as he compared it to what was in her hands. It was only when the woman finished her transaction and walked out again that Patrick spoke.

"It worked," he whispered. "Just like you said it would."

"I told you it was amazing." She was clutching the money tightly, watching his face.

"No, it isn't," Patrick said.

"What are you talking about?"

"It's you. You did it."

"No, I had nothing to do with it—"

"You're the amazing one," he interrupted. "Not the machine. You. It was always you. I knew it right away." And then, with the bills still a leafy green salad crumpled between them, he kissed her again.

"Get a room," said a man who had to sidestep them on his way out of the bank.

Patrick turned to confront him while Mia shrank back, anticipating an ugly scene. But Patrick only nodded in a formal and even dignified way. "Thanks for the advice," he said. "I think I'll take it." Mia hastily stuffed the money away, and the disapproving onlooker gave them one last disgusted look before he left.

284 | YONA ZELDIS McDONOUGH

* * *

MIA DIDN'T QUESTION the wisdom or even the sanity of what was about to happen. She simply brought Patrick back to her apartment, where they proceeded to have sex without any sign of tiring for the next sixty minutes. To say it had never been like this was not very original, but it happened to be true. Not even in her earliest, headiest days with Lloyd had she felt this exposed, this exhilarated, this known, this freed. He was beautiful, Patrick was, with a well-proportioned body and marble-white skin. His chest was surprisingly smooth and hairless, but the thick hair on his legs and between them was gold and silky. When they finally rolled away from each other, she was quite literally speechless. She didn't have the words to tell him what this was like for her, but then, he didn't require any because he already seemed to know.

Carefully, she got up from the bed. The clothes that were still on it from yesterday were now on the floor, and Mia picked her way through them on her way to the bathroom. Every orifice in her body was tingling and raw, and when she looked in the mirror, she saw that her lips were swollen. She turned on the water to wash her face and heard her phone ringing in the other room.

Jesus, she had completely forgotten about the time. She raced for the phone, clicking on just as Patrick, still naked, walked into the room.

"Hey," Fred said. "Sorry I didn't call you sooner. It's been crazy. Just crazy. First, I found out that not one but *two* of the waitresses aren't going to be here tonight. Can you believe the timing of that? Then that shipment of vodka I was counting on never showed . . ."

The boyfriend? Patrick mouthed. Mia nodded. None other.

"So anyway, I've just been racing around all day, putting out fires. How about you?"

"I've been okay," she said, unable to meet Patrick's gaze.

"Did you reach Eden?"

"No," she said. "I didn't."

"I'm sorry. I know you wanted to talk to her."

"I think Lloyd's behind all this."

"You're probably right—" He paused, and she heard him saying, "Not yet. I'm still waiting. They swore up and down that it's coming."

"You sound busy."

"Sorry about that. Yeah, I *am* busy. So I'm going to go now. But you'll be here later, right?"

"Later. Of course."

"One more thing," said Fred.

"Sure." Would this conversation ever end?

"Could you feed the cats before you go? I forgot to do it this morning."

"The cats," Mia said. "Right."

"Not that it would kill Dudley to do without dinner. But I just can't bring myself to starve the guy, you know?"

"I know, Fred," said Mia, desperate to get off the phone. Patrick was staring laser beams into her breasts, and, believe it or not, he was getting hard again.

"Besides, when he's mad at me, he goes and shits in one of my shoes. Damn cat." Fred chuckled affectionately.

"I'll feed them. You can count on me." Oh, she hated herself for this, she really did.

"Thanks. Food's in the cupboard to the left of the sink."

"Got it."

She said good-bye and stared at Patrick, who was now standing beside her. He took her hand and placed it on his erection. She may have hated herself, but that wasn't about to stop her.

"You got time for a quickie before you have to meet the boyfriend?" he asked, and, with that, gently tugged her back into the bedroom.

TWENTY-THREE

EVEN THOUGH MIA had already showered once today, she didn't want to walk into Juicy reeking of infidelity and sex, so she stood under the hot spray for a long time, lathering her body and sudsing her hair. Patrick appeared while she was toweling off; the bathroom was a tight fit for two, so he waited just outside the open door. He was wearing his white jeans but no shirt, and she could see the blue-tinged veins under his milky skin.

"You want to shower?"

"Nah," he said, bringing his fingers to his nose and inhaling deeply. "In fact, I don't think I'm going to shower ever again."

Mia said nothing but felt herself getting red.

"Oh, come on," he said, tilting her chin up with his hand. She could smell herself on his fingers; it was both arousing and terrifying. "After what we've done to each other today, you're suddenly going to get all coy on me?"

"No," she said, meeting his eyes. "I'm not." She knotted the towel around her body, just above her breasts, and began combing her hair.

"So you're meeting him?"

"Uh-huh."

"You going to let him fuck you tonight?"

"That's not fair," she said, comb poised above her head.

"Sorry. Let me rephrase that. When he fucks you, is it like it is with me?"

"No," she said. "It isn't." That seemed to satisfy him, and she resumed the combing.

"What's this?" he asked, touching the locket she had not taken off from around her neck.

"Something I bought for myself. Though maybe I shouldn't have."

"Why not? I liked that you kept it on; it's sexy."

"My lawyer told me that the police are interested in it."

"Is it hot?"

It took Mia a second to realize he meant stolen.

"I'm not sure." She told him, then, about Gerald Mofchum and the shop that had just vanished.

"Maybe I can help," he said.

"You? How?"

"I told you: I know people, and those people know other people. You want to find out what happened to your jeweler? I'm your man. Now, where did you say his shop was again?" Mia gave him the information, and Patrick nodded slowly, as if the motion of his head would imprint the information into his brain.

MIA DRESSED QUICKLY. She had to get over to Fred's place to feed the cats; she would try Eden again while she was there. From Fred's, she could walk over to Juicy, ring in the New Year, though she hardly felt like ringing in anything.

"I'll be going now, College Girl," Patrick said. Mia looked up to see that his parka was on and zipped.

"I don't know what to say . . ."

"Try saying good-bye."

"Not good-bye forever, is it?"

"I think that's up to you."

"I don't want it to be forever." She came close, and inhaled the scent—both infinitely familiar and infinitely new—that was uniquely his. He kissed her lightly on the forehead, and then walked to the door while she trailed behind. She watched him lope down the hall and disappear when he turned into the stairwell. Mia closed the door and stood against it for a minute. Bringing him back here was one of the most ill-considered, impulsive things she had ever done—and she had done many ill-considered and impulsive things in her life—yet she didn't regret it at all. But she couldn't stop to think about any of that now; she had to get into gear. She called a car service, applied her lipstick in the backseat, handed the coal-skinned driver a lavish tip.

"Thank you, miss," he said, the island cadence of his voice following her as she hurried into Fred's house. "Thank you very, very much."

DUDLEY WAS DELIRIOUS when he saw her, pressing his face against her feet and rolling over to expose his wide, soft cat's belly.

"Who's my boy?" she asked as she stroked him. Who, indeed.

Mia was only about three steps from Juicy when her phone rang and there was Eden, her beloved Eden, on the other end. Mia promised herself that she would not break down, would not let Eden know just how much she had missed her. Upbeat, that was what she was determined to be. *Think Donna Reed, Betty Hutton, Jane Wyman,* she told herself. *Think of all those spunky Hollywood gals, emanating good cheer and a positive outlook from every pore of their apple-cheeked, squeaky-clean faces.*

"Hi, Mom," Eden said. Her voice had a tremulous sound, as if she might be ready to cry.

"Hi, Baby Cakes," Mia said. "Have you been having fun?"

"Lots of fun," Eden said. The quivery moment passed, and she seemed to regain her self-possession. "Daddy took me to a play and shopping and to this really neat vegetarian restaurant, where all the furniture is made by hand, and they get the milk and eggs and stuff from animals they raise themselves."

"I'm so glad that you're having a good time."

"And we had a really great Christmas; Nana and Pops got a huge tree, and we used real candles on it and it was so, so pretty. I wish you could have been here to see it."

"I know, darling. I know."

"But Mom—" Her voice changed again; Mia could tell she was moving into emotionally charged territory. "Daddy's been saying that he doesn't want me to come back home in January. He thinks I should stay with Nana and Pops for a while. He said there's a school down here that he can enroll me in, and that I'll have a really nice new teacher."

"Would you like that?" Could Eden hear the sound of her heart breaking, being sawed in two, over the phone? Because to Mia, the noise was deafening.

"Well, sort of. I love hanging out with Nana and Pops. And their new house is very cool. There's like this forest out back, a real one, you know? I've seen all these great birds, and a deer walked right up to me and took a piece of bread right from my hand."

"That *is* cool," Mia agreed. She should be getting an Oscar for this performance, she really should.

"I know. But I miss you. A lot." She took a breath, let it out. Mia swore she could feel the faint puff of the exhalation on her own cheek. "Why can't we all be together, anyway? Why did you and Daddy have to get divorced?"

Desperately, Mia looked around. Great lurching buses, the whales of the avenues, glided along; buildings and cars, fire hydrants and street signs were the urban backdrop for the bands of revelers, many drunk already, stumbling in and out of Juicy's door.

"Eden," she said slowly, as if everything depended on these next words, getting them right. "Eden, you know I have to go to court in a few days, get some things straightened out, right?"

"Right," said Eden in a tiny voice.

"I'm going to be very busy with that until it happens, and I think maybe Daddy is right: it would be a good idea for you to stay with Nana and Pops until it's all over."

"You mean you don't want me to come home?"

"No, that's not it at all. I love you, and I miss you like crazy. But I want to respect Daddy's wishes." God, how was she even *uttering* such words? "So if he says he wants you to stay there, well then, maybe you'd better stay. And when it's all over and settled, he can bring you back."

"Promise?" asked Eden. She was crying now; Mia could tell.

"Just ask Daddy, okay?" she said, not wanting to promise what was not in her power to deliver.

"Okay," Eden said.

"And you can call me anytime you want to, all right? Anytime at all."

"Okay," repeated Eden. There was a resignation in her tone that was almost worse than the crying. "Happy New Year, Mom."

"Happy New Year to you, too." They talked for another minute before she said good-bye and tucked the phone back into her bag. Then she blew her nose—luckily, Stuart's handkerchief was still jammed in her pocket—and walked into Juicy. She caught sight of Fred right away, but he didn't see her—a short reprieve. Guilt was a dead thing around her neck, but there was no shaking it off.

"Hey, aren't you Eden's mom?" Mia turned to see a guy with a goatee and wire-rimmed, John Lennon–type glasses standing next to her.

"Yes," she said, not placing him right away.

"I'm Kyle—Caitlin's dad," he said, transferring his wineglass to his left hand and extending his right for her to shake.

"Oh, of course," said Mia. "I knew you looked familiar."

"Suzy will be here in a little while. Can I get you a drink in the meantime?"

"A drink would be great."

"What are you having?"

"How about a shot of bourbon? Straight up?" She didn't even know why she asked for that; she never drank bourbon. Maybe it had something to do with Eden's being in North Carolina.

BREAKING THE BANK | 291

"Whoa, you're serious, aren't you?" said Kyle. Mia just smiled. "Well, why not? It's New Year's Eve, right? I say, go for it."

Kyle ordered her bourbon, and presented it to her with a flourish. Then he looked toward the door. "There's Suzy," he said. "I'll bring her over." But he and Suzy were waylaid, so Mia was left alone with her bourbon. That was all right; she wasn't really up for socializing and was here only because she'd said she would come.

"You look great." Fred's voice made her glance up from the drink.

"Thanks," she said. She had made an effort: the stretchy black velour dress; strappy, black shoes; dangly rhinestone earrings. But she could barely face him. "I fed the cats."

"You're a doll," he said. Then someone next to her wanted a drink, and he turned. "Later?"

"Sure, later."

Mia allowed herself to get drunk. It was a calculated campaign, her drunkenness, and she pursued it single-mindedly throughout the evening. She had another shot of bourbon, then switched to sangria when a rowdy group of guys on her left invited her to partake of their sloshing pitcher. Later, she ran into Kyle and Suzy, and the three of them broke out a bottle of champagne near midnight. Mia and Fred didn't get back to his place until after four in the morning, at which point she was fit only to kneel, a humble supplicant, on the bathroom floor, while yielding the booze-soaked contents of her stomach to the stoic patience of the white bowl.

"You've got to learn to hold it better," chided Fred, putting her to bed with a cool washcloth, an empty ice bucket—so she wouldn't have to get up—and an extra pillow. "Mixing bourbon and sangria—jeez, what were you thinking?" But he was not at all angry. Mia drifted off to sleep, though not before she had the realization that her physical wretchedness was a small price to pay for getting to avoid, entirely, the whole issue of sex with Fred. Somewhere around dawn, Dudley wandered in and, with a world-weary heave, deposited himself on top of Mia's aching head.

The next day she was massively hungover—of course—and played that for all it was worth. Fred gave her the newspaper and her space. He was disgustingly clear-eyed and chipper this morning; when he tended bar, he never touched a drop. She heard him puttering around downstairs and began to fret. What was she going to do? She liked Fred; she may even have been on the road to loving Fred. He was a sweet guy, a decent guy, the right sort of guy to make a life with. But that was before Patrick. Screwing Patrick was like that stunning moment in *The Wizard of Oz* when the movie switched from black-and-white to full, glorious Technicolor. Now that the scales had dropped and she had seen the light, how was she ever going to go back? She thought about Patrick and she burned; her whole body was hot and feverish. She was tempted to take her temperature, just to check. She wished she could call him, but she didn't dare, not with Fred downstairs—too slutty, too low.

But she also had other problems and conceded that Patrick might be the least of them. Her court date loomed, and she had no idea how her crazy tale would play itself out before a judge. And then there was Eden, miles away from her in North Carolina, forced to listen to— and maybe absorb—all the unalloyed venom that Lloyd was no doubt spewing. It made her sick to think of it. Sick and scared that if things didn't go well in court, she would never get her daughter back. So given all that, Patrick, Fred, and the sudden triangle that was her love life, would just have to wait.

Mia dozed fitfully, sipped some tea, skimmed the paper. She hadn't planned to get up at all until Fred appeared in the doorway of the room late in the afternoon.

"I forgot to tell you—I invited my mom for dinner."

"Tonight?"

"I can call her and say you're not feeling well," said Fred. "Make it another night." But it was obvious he didn't want to do that.

"No, it's fine. I'll be okay," she said, determined to make the effort.

"Thanks," he said, flashing that chipped-tooth smile. "You're a trouper."

In deference to her unsettled stomach, Fred prepared chicken soup with rice, dill, and lots of baby carrots. Along with a salad and the bread Bev brought, it was a soothing meal, and Mia felt better once she had consumed it. After dinner, Bev shooed Fred away and pulled out her deck of tarot cards.

"I told you I wasn't done with you," she said to Mia. Her glittering blue beads—a triple strand that was a few shades darker than her filmy, blue chiffon blouse—caught the light as she shuffled.

Mia looked at the cards, facedown and in a line, and suddenly she was afraid to choose.

"Go on; don't be nervous," urged Bev. "The future is your friend, if you're strong enough to face it."

Reluctantly, Mia picked the cards and waited for Bev's interpretation.

"Oh, look—the Lovers again. Didn't you pick that one last time?"

"I'm not sure," Mia said, but she knew that she had.

"This is a fascinating combination. See, here you've got two reinforcing cards." She pointed to the images; tonight her long nails were painted cotton-candy pink. "The Empress and the Nine of Cups both represent sexual and sensual pleasure; turning over all three together is a powerful triad. Very powerful. Too hot to handle, you could say. But then you've got three opposing cards—the Three of Swords and the Five of Cups; they spell rejection and separation. And then there's the Hermit; he's a loner who doesn't relate sexually at all."

"So what does it mean?"

"Just your garden-variety ambivalence. Wanting love but fearing it, too."

"Fearing what?" asked Fred.

"Oh, you—you're always interrupting us," said Bev. But she gathered the cards and tucked them back in her bag.

"You ladies about ready for dessert?"

"I'm always ready for dessert," said Bev.

IN BED THAT night, Fred brushed his fingers along the nape of Mia's neck. When she didn't respond, he moved them slowly down her back, as if he were polishing the vertebrae, one at a time. She tried to will herself into the mood. *You like him,* she reminded herself. *He's a sweetie, and you like him.* Still, she felt inert; her skin might as well have been made of plastic. Fred deserved better. Even *she* deserved better.

"Something wrong?" he asked.

"I'm sorry. I just don't seem to be in the mood tonight."

"Everything okay?"

"I'm just worried about the court date." This was not untrue.

"Oh," said Fred. "Got it." He removed his hand from her back and leaned over to kiss her cheek. "Night then."

"Good night," said Mia. The guilt she felt was like a case of poison ivy: she itched all over. But when she closed her eyes, all she saw was Patrick.

In the morning, Fred took one of the female cats to the vet while Mia got ready to return to her apartment. Kyra was due back that night, and it seemed like the perfect moment to segue out of their improvised ménage. Mia was ready; she was grateful to Fred for offering her the refuge when she needed it, but by now she was feeling restless and wanted to be home.

She had just finished gathering her makeup and toothbrush from the bathroom when the bell rang. A package? Meter reader? She went to answer it and found Fred's mother, dressed in a regally purple fur-trimmed coat.

"Bev," Mia said, leaning over to kiss her cheek. The scent of perfume that wafted up from her small, solid body was dizzying. "Fred's not home, but he'll be back soon."

"I know," Bev said, stamping snow from her high-heeled boots. "I spoke to him this morning. I came to see you; he told me you'd be here."

Mia made coffee, and Bev sliced the red-and-white string on a bakery box with a knife. Mia looked inside—biscotti dipped in chocolate, cookies covered in sprinkles and studded with colored sugar crystals. Mia took a cookie and bit into it. Then she waited.

"I'm sure you're wondering what this is all about," Bev said. She blew on her coffee but didn't drink it. "So I might as well be up front with you. I like you, Mia. I like you a lot, and I think you're good for my son. Better than that coldhearted tramp he married—but we won't go there, at least not today."

"I like you, too, Bev," Mia said. "And I like Fred."

"But you don't love him."

"No," said Mia simply. "I don't."

"And there's someone else you do love. Or think you do."

"Why do you say that?"

"I saw it in the cards. And I told you, the cards don't lie."

"I don't want to hurt him," Mia said.

"You will anyway."

"Not intentionally," said Mia. "I can't help how I feel though. Or how I don't."

"Why not give it some time? You may not love Fred now. But in three months, six months . . . who knows? Sometimes love is like a thunderbolt; believe me, I've been there. Other times, it can start slowly, just a trickle at first." She popped a cookie, whole, into her mouth.

"You could be right," Mia said, although she didn't think so.

"That wasn't the only reason I wanted to see you. There's something else."

"Is it about Fred?"

"No. Not directly anyway. I saw something else in the cards—something I could sense but couldn't understand. Something I've never encountered before. You're in the middle of something, Mia. Something big and strange."

Anxiety made Mia silent. What had Bev seen?

"You don't know what it is," Bev continued. "And you're afraid."

"I'm not afraid." Mia looked straight into her eyes. "I'm terrified."

Bev reached over and took Mia's hands in her own. "Of course you are, baby." Her nails had the color and gleam of an eggplant. "Who in her right mind wouldn't be?"

Bev stayed for another cup of coffee and several more cookies. When she left, she crushed Mia in a sweet-smelling hug. "You can come to me, you know," she said. "Anytime."

After Bev had left, Mia sat on the sofa, awash in equal parts gratitude and shame. If she lost Fred, she would lose Bev, too. The realization made her sadder than she would have expected.

WHEN FRED GOT home, Mia said nothing about the visit. She was sure Fred wouldn't be happy to learn about his mother's meddling. So instead, she asked about the cat's health and got all her things together in the living room. Then she asked Fred if he would call the car service.

"I'm still worried about you going back there," he said, phone in hand.

"I'm okay, I really am."

"Maybe you could stay at Julie's place; it's empty."

Mia had not told Fred about her last conversation with Julie. "It'll be okay," she repeated, and Fred was quiet.

"How about the locks?" he asked after a moment. "Are you going to get them changed?"

"Maybe." She fiddled with her bag so she didn't have to look at him. "Actually, I hadn't thought about it."

"I know a locksmith on Court Street. Want me to call him for you? I'll bet he could be there today."

"Fred," she said. "I'm not Kyra, okay? So please, switch out of daddy mode. I'll call him when I want to. *If* I want to."

"Fine," said Fred, clearly stung. Dudley lumbered into the room and, sensing the ambient discord, uttered an aggrieved mew. "But is it such a crime to be concerned about your safety?"

"It's not a crime, it's just a pain." Then she saw how wounded he looked, and she softened. "Look, I appreciate your concern, I really do. But I'm a big girl now. I can take care of myself."

When Mia got home, she fairly panted with relief at finding herself alone again. She sat on the love seat and thought about all the things she needed to do. Then she picked up her cell phone to do the only thing she wanted to do—call Patrick. But it was Maureen, not Patrick, who answered.

"Sure, I remember you," she said. "Patrick's not here right now, but I'll tell him you called."

Mia was disappointed. She forced herself to return to the tedious—and endless, for she couldn't ever seem to finish it—task of putting her clothes away. When the phone rang, she grabbed for it, not even checking the number. It was not Patrick though; it was her mother.

"Hi, darling," said Betty. "Happy New Year."

"Happy New Year, Mom," said Mia.

"I know it's a little after the fact, but I haven't been able to reach you."

"Sorry, sorry, sorry," Mia said. Ever since Thanksgiving, she had been avoiding contact with her mother. First, it had been because she was still angry about how her mother had just handed her over to Stuart and Gail on the proverbial silver platter. Then, because she had not wanted her mother to find out about her night in jail. But the price for her avoidance was guilt, and she was clearly going to have to pay for it now.

"I spoke to Stuart," Betty said, "and he told me that Eden is with Lloyd's parents."

"For Christmas," Mia reminded her. "She wanted to go."

"I'm sure she did," Betty said. "But Stuart said that she's going to stay a little longer. Possibly a lot longer . . . she may enroll in school down there."

"That was Lloyd's idea," said Mia. "I never agreed to it."

"I do wish you had called me to talk about this, honey. I know you're probably very upset, but right now, things are so unsettled with you. It may be the best thing for her. Best thing in the world."

Best thing in the world? Was she kidding? Mia wanted to crumple the word *honey* like it was a dirty sock, ready for the hamper. But then she remembered how hurt Betty had been when she'd snapped at her before for this very transgression. Betty was who she was. A good enough, if imperfect, parent. Like Mia herself.

"Mom, what happened to all of your paintings?"

"My paintings?" Betty asked, obviously thrown by this sudden detour in the conversation. "Why are you asking about my paintings?"

"I've been thinking about the old apartment lately and wondering what happened to everything we used to have."

"You took some things," Betty pointed out.

"Yes, I know. But what about the rest?"

"I gave a lot away," Betty said. "I found this wonderful charity, New Beginnings, that helps people set up apartments after they've been homeless. I gave a lot to them—furniture, bedding, dishes . . ."

"And your paintings? You donated them too?" Mia remembered a massive canvas, streaked and blobbed with red, yellow, burnt orange. She and Stuart had called it *Towering Inferno.*

"Some. Yes. But I still have most of them. Why?"

"I thought I might take one. If you wanted to give it to me, that is."

"You," said Betty, clearly incredulous, "want a painting of mine?"

"Yes," said Mia, not realizing that she did until this moment. "Is that all right?"

"Of course it's all right. I just never thought you liked them. I know you and Stuart used to say things—"

"We were young," Mia said, ashamed now of their hazing. "What did we know?"

"I have a small one I could send you," Betty said. "I don't know if you remember it—pinks, a sort of baby blue, lilac . . ."

"Vaguely floral, right?" Mia did remember; it had hung in the hallway that led to the bathroom. The colors were very delicately applied, almost a glaze or wash, and there was something springlike and tender about their effect.

"Yes, that's the one."

"I'd love to have it. I could hang it in my bedroom."

"Then I'll send it," Betty said, sounding very pleased. "Hank will help me wrap it up, and we'll ship it off."

Something in her mother's tone—surprised, delighted, almost shy—wrenched Mia's heart, and she suddenly wanted to weep. But they were interrupted by a small beep. Mia saw the number she had just tried—Patrick's number—flash onto the phone's tiny screen.

"Mom," she said, "I'm sorry, but I've got to take this call."

"You go ahead, sweetie," Betty said. "I'll send that painting right away."

"I HEARD YOU called, College Girl," said Patrick when Mia clicked over.

"I did." Her heart was like a basketball slam-dunking in her chest.

"What's up? The boyfriend's out of town?"

"Sort of." She paused, then jumped right in. "Want to come over?"

"When?"

"How soon can you be here?"

He was there in a little over an hour, same white parka, same white sweatshirt, same smooth white body. They didn't even make it to the bedroom; instead, they went at it on the floor, on the love seat, in the kitchen, with Mia leaning over and supported by the sink. They used the bed only to rest, afterward—Mia lying with her head on Patrick's chest, while he smoothed her hair—tangled and a bit sweaty now—away from her forehead.

"If I hadn't called you, would you have called me?" Mia asked. She sounded—and felt—like a teenager. That was what lust did—wakened the dormant fifteen-year-old.

"Dunno."

"That's hardly flattering."

"It's not that I didn't want to call you, College Girl. I've had a non-stop hard-on just thinking about you ever since I walked out of here last time. I just didn't know how it was going to go down with us."

"What do you mean?"

"We're good like this"—he waved his hand over their prone, naked bodies—"but the rest of it . . . it's not gonna work. First problem is the boyfriend; something tells me he's not the kind who likes to share. Not that I blame the son of a bitch; who would?"

"I'm not married to him," said Mia. But she knew she was betraying him all the same.

"I know," said Patrick. "If you were, I wouldn't be here. I have a theory about fucking married women; it's a surefire way to get yourself killed. Anyway, that's not the only problem."

When she didn't respond, he continued.

"I mean, can you picture introducing me to your family and friends? Trotting me out at the office cocktail party? How about your brother—you think Mr. Hotshot Lawyer is going to appreciate his sister getting banged by a guy like me?"

"A guy like you. What kind of guy are you anyway? You haven't told me." She shifted away from him slightly so she could look at him better.

"Told you what? I've got no secrets from you, College Girl. I'm an open book. *Your* open book." He took her hand, put it between his legs.

"You know what I mean. How do you make a living? Do you have a job? Why were you locked up that night?" She felt him throb under her touch, but she wanted to keep talking.

"No nine-to-five prison sentence for me; I couldn't stand any fucking boss telling me what the fuck I can and can't do. Time clocks, rules and regs, pensions and paychecks—they're all bullshit, see? Pure bullshit. Me? I'm a dabbler. I know a lot of people, go a lot of places, do a lot of things."

"Sounds . . . complicated."

"Not really. It's a little of this, a little of that. I'm a broker type. Sometimes I buy; sometimes I sell."

"Buy what? Sell what?"

"Whatever people want. Whatever they need. Only no drugs, and no weapons. Fucking drugs killed my wife, Trish, and I wouldn't touch them for a million fucking bucks. Not for two million, not for ten million. And weapons are for wimps who've got gun barrels where their dicks ought to be. If I have to fight someone, I use my hands. You know what I mean? I fight like a man, not a pussy with an automatic."

"Do you get in a lot of fights?" Mia asked.

"As many as I have to, College Girl."

"You could go to college, too, you know." She sat up, excited. "You're certainly smart enough. You could go to Brooklyn College, or one of the other city schools. I'd help you with the applications."

"I'll bet you would," he said. "And I appreciate the offer. But college for me? I don't think so."

"Why not?"

"Let's just say I did take you up on it—let you help me with filling out those papers, stick me in a suit and parade me in front of those admissions guys. They ask me a lot of questions, and I give all the right answers. Let's say I even get in. It wouldn't change a thing. I'm thirty-three, and the clay's already set. Yeah, I might go to college all right. But I'd never be a college boy." Something like pain flickered—fleetingly—across his face, and then it was gone.

"That's okay," she said, touching his cheek. "Maybe I've had enough college boys in my life anyway. Maybe you should stay just the way you are."

"That's pretty much all most of us do." He took her face in his hands and kissed her. "Anyway, I'm getting a little tired of you asking all these questions. Now it's my turn."

"Okay, what do you want to ask?"

"What's better, you on top or me? Do you like it from behind? How about when I do you with my tongue? Those are the questions that really count." He put his hand between her thighs and started stroking. He was right; this was really all she needed—or wanted—to know about him. Who cared about the rest of it? Not her, not now.

LATER, MIA GOT up and climbed on a chair to get to the shoe box in the closet.

"What are you doing?"

"Here," she said, taking five hundred-dollar bills from the box. "This is for you."

"Hey, I know I'm good, but—"

"It's the money from the other day. From the cash machine. I want you to have it."

"No way."

"Yes way. You take it; you can use it."

"So can you."

"That's why we're splitting it," she said, pressing it into his hand.

"You're something else, College Girl," he said. "I'll take it, but then you have to let me buy you dinner."

"Deal. Where do you want to go?"

"Right here," he said. "Can you call in for Chinese?"

THEY ATE FRIED vegetable dumplings, bok choy, noodles with peanut sauce, and Buddhist Delight sprawling on Mia's bed. Patrick had put on his pants, in deference to the delivery guy; Mia, a robe that had been a gift from Betty.

"Could you wear that coat instead?" he asked. "That one you put on the first time I came over here?"

"The Burberry coat? You liked that?"

"Liked it?" He snorted. "It was all I could do to keep from jumping your bones that night—seeing you in that leopard number, and then the coat over it, knowing what you looked like underneath." He ran a hand inside her robe. "Man that was *tough*. But it's like I told you: I don't take what isn't being offered. Works out much better that way."

"I'll say," she murmured.

"So the coat? You'll put it on for me?"

"I would but it's at the cleaner's. I have to wear it for the court appearance."

"Hey, that's in a couple of days, right?"

She nodded.

"So are you ready?"

"I guess. My lawyer will be there. He's coached me on what to say and how to say it. He's acting as a wardrobe consultant, too—he's the one who picked out the coat."

"Are you going to tell the judge about the cash machine?"

"I have to," Mia said. "What choice do I have?"

AFTER THE FOOD had been eaten and the empty containers rinsed and readied for the recycling bin, Patrick got up to leave.

"Don't go," Mia said.

"It's late."

"I know. Stay here tonight."

"You sure, College Girl?" He had his parka half on, one empty sleeve still dangling. "Maybe it's not such a good idea."

"It's not," she said. "It's a terrible idea. But I want you to do it anyway."

"Well, it's a-okay by me," he said. "Though I gotta warn you: I may snore."

"I'll take my chances," she said, and went into the bathroom. When Fred called—as she knew he would—she took the call while standing at the sink. Kyra was there, so they didn't talk long.

"Call me tomorrow, okay?" asked Fred.

"Promise," she said, relieved to end the conversation. Lying to Fred the other night had felt bad enough; now, it was even worse. She wasn't going to lie to him anymore. She would tell him, she decided. The question was no longer if, only when and how. It had to be at the right time, and it had to be gentle. She wanted to be real with him—real, but not cruel.

Mia finished brushing her teeth, washing a froth of blue foam cleanly down the drain. Then she called Eden; though she didn't expect her to answer, she savored the opportunity to hear her daughter's recorded voice. "Love you, baby," she said into the phone before clicking off. "Love you lots."

Patrick had a turn in the bathroom when she was through, and then he came back to bed, almost shyly.

"What do you usually do before going to sleep?" he asked. "I mean, besides fucking."

"I like to read," she said. "When I'm not too tired, that is."

"Figures," he said, settling in beside her. "You being a college girl and all."

"But I don't have to read tonight," she added. "We could watch TV, if you want."

"Maybe you could read to me," he said.

"Read to you? What should I read?" She was charmed by the notion.

"One of those books you read in college. I don't care which one. You pick."

"Okay," she said, looking at him and beginning to smile. "Okay." She hopped out of bed and went to the bookshelf; her hardcovers were in the other room, but in here, she kept some old, disintegrating paperbacks she had had since Oberlin. *The Picture of Dorian Gray*? Too mannered. *Ethan Frome*? No, sex led to a bad end in that one. *Anna Karenina*? No, sex led to an even worse end in that.

"I know," she said out loud, plucking a book from the shelf. Then she got back into bed and positioned herself next to Patrick, who was waiting, with a touching eagerness, for her to begin. "I think you're going to like this," she said, cracking open the book she had chosen and looking down at the first page. "But feel free to stop me if you don't."

In my younger and more vulnerable years, my father gave me some advice that I've been turning over in my mind ever since.

"Whenever you feel like criticizing anyone," he told me, "just remember that all the people in the world haven't had the advantages you've had."

"*The Great Gatsby*. F. Scott Fitzgerald," said Patrick, reading the cover. "Hey—he's a mick. Like me."

"Yes," Mia said softly. "Like you."

"Well, go on," said Patrick. "Keep reading. It sounds good."

TWENTY-FOUR

Mia left Patrick sleeping when she went out to pick up her clothes at the dry cleaner's. Chris Cox was due by later for a run-through of tomorrow's events, and he asked that she wear the outfit she planned to wear in court.

"Think of this as the dress rehearsal," he said to her on the phone.

"Does that make the court date a performance?"

"Absolutely. A courtroom drama is a performance of the highest order—it can be stripped down and minimal or baroque and over the top; it all depends on who's in the cast that day. But everyone has a part to play—you, me, the judge. So I just want to be sure that you've got yours down pat."

On her way back, she picked up a couple of jelly doughnuts and two coffees; Chris would be at the apartment soon and there was no time to linger over breakfast. She had just reached her floor when she saw Inez, Luisa's mother, going down the stairs. The hem of her McDonald's uniform peeked out from under her coat. She stopped when she saw Mia.

"How are you?" she asked. "I haven't seen you in a while."

"Keeping my head above water." *But barely,* she thought.

"Luisa's been asking for Eden," Inez said. "She said she missed her."

"Eden's not here." Inez didn't say anything. "She's with her father and his parents. In North Carolina."

"Ah . . ." said Inez, but it was enough.

"I'll tell her Luisa was asking about her," Mia said. "She'll come up as soon as she's back." Inez nodded, and Mia heard her footsteps as she continued to descend the stairs. The heavy glass door in the lobby wheezed open and then shut with a disconsolate sound.

PATRICK WAS UP and finished showering by the time Mia let herself into the apartment. He was wearing one of her towels and nothing else. But as good as he looked, she had to feed him and hustle him out.

"Hungry?"

"Starved." He tore into the doughnut and took a deep swig of the coffee. "Thanks, College Girl."

Mia hung the bags from the dry cleaner's from a hook on her bedroom door.

"Hey, that's the coat," said Patrick, licking powdered sugar from his fingers.

"All ready for its close-up."

"How about you? Are you ready?"

"Ready as I'll ever be," she said.

RIGHT BEFORE PATRICK was ready to walk out the door, he handed her a small piece of pink paper, folded in half.

"What's this?"

"Open it," he said.

Mia unfolded the piece of paper. *One gold locket, $200, tax included.* The address and phone number of Mofchum's shop was stamped, in blurred blue ink, at the top; his scrawled signature and a date graced the bottom.

"A receipt for the locket!" she said. "Where did you get this? How did you even find him?"

"Does a magician reveal his secrets?" Patrick asked. He kissed her, leaving traces of powdered sugar on her lips.

* * *

LESS THAN AN hour later, Chris Cox, stripped down to his vest and Egyptian cotton shirt, was pacing the floor in Mia's apartment, jabbing at the walls with his fists. His navy-blue topcoat and tweed suit jacket were carefully folded over a chair; Mia offered to hang both in the closet, but she could actually see him wince at the suggestion. He was so energetic that he had worked up a sweat, a fine sheen that coated his head like oil.

"Now, the courtroom is going to be crowded. Very crowded," Cox told her. "You'll see perps of all sizes, shapes, and colors in there."

"You mean other criminals?" Mia could feel her eyes widening.

"Not serious ones," said Cox. "No murderers or rapists, if that's what you're worried about. DATs are only given for misdemeanors, not felonies. So you might get check forgers, drunk and disorderlies, shop-lifters with no prior record—small stuff."

"Great," she muttered. "Just great."

"I don't want you to look at those other people in the room or even think about them, okay?"

"Okay . . ." she said. But that was ridiculous. How could she not look? Or not think?

"I want you to focus on the judge, and only the judge. Everyone else is invisible."

"Except you, right?"

"Right," said Cox, pumping his fist in a small, controlled gesture. "Except me."

They went over Mia's story, several times. Cox told her which words to stress, when to pause, the optimal angle at which to tilt her head, the right time to deflect her glance downward, toward her folded hands in her lap.

"Act innocent," he instructed. "Innocent and contrite."

"I am innocent," she reminded him. "Remember?"

AFTER COX LEFT, Mia didn't know what to do with herself. Activity on the cooking series she was editing had wound down; now there was a new series in the planning stages—Kids' Krazy Krafts—but she hadn't been asked to work on it. She had said nothing to any of her colleagues about her court date, though she knew that Cox had been in touch with at least a few of them. So she had to accept the fact that there might not be a job for her when all this played out. At the moment, though, there was nothing she could do about it.

She sat down to read another chapter of *The Great Gatsby*, picking up where she had left off reading the night before. No use. She read the same passage over three times, thinking not of the words or unfolding of the story, but of Patrick, how much he had liked the novel. What had Bev said? That there was someone else she loved? Or thought she did?

She put the book down and decided to do something really useful, like file and polish her nails. Even better—she would go out and have a professional manicure, which Cox had suggested. "But stick to light, neutral colors," he said. "Clear, peach, beige. Save the reds and purples for your boyfriend."

Which one?

She got her coat and headed down the stairs. There were a couple of nail places on Fifth Avenue, but they were owned and staffed by Korean women. Lloyd had filmed at those places; it was at one of them that he had met Suim. Mia decided to walk up to Sixth Avenue, where there was a salon owned and staffed by two Russians.

Once she was outside, sidestepping the moms with their strollers, the professional dog walkers with their clusters of poodles and Jack Russell terriers, the kids giddy on their winter break, she couldn't resist the urge to pass by the bank, just to check on her machine. It would be tempting fate to use it today; she had no intention of trying. Still, it couldn't hurt just to walk by. Just to give it a little nod. A friendly wave.

As she neared the bank, she felt an adrenaline surge, and she was tempted to break into a run. She controlled herself, with some effort, and refrained from actually trotting, though she did pick up the pace.

Okay, here was the corner, here was the bank, the doors swung open easily and . . . she stopped, not wanting to believe what she was seeing. The machine—*her* machine, the one that had set her life on its wild, off-kilter spin—was cordoned off by a dark red velvet rope. Behind the rope, she could see the blue screen filled by big white letters. TEMPORARILY OUT OF ORDER. Out of order? In what way? Mia felt pulled down by the hateful undertow of dread that had been dogging her ever since she had had her first encounter with the bank's crazy magic. Someone had found out about the machine, its unprecedented bounty, its pouring forth of riches. Someone had found out, and that was why the machine was not operational. Had they traced it to her though? Was someone looking for her, even now, standing in front of her apartment door, impatiently sounding the buzzer?

The two other machines seemed to be functioning. A young couple stood at one of them, quietly arguing about something; Mia couldn't hear what they were saying but could decipher the girl's tight expression, the guy's exasperated sighs. A fiftyish woman in a dyed shearling jacket was at the other. Mia waited, uncertain of what to do. She wanted to ask someone inside the bank about the machine, if it would be fixed anytime soon. But that would be stupid; she might arouse suspicion. If she hadn't already aroused it. No, better to leave, immediately, and to act like none of this had anything to do with her.

She backed out of the bank and started walking, but not toward home—what if she were being followed? In her present state of mind, this seemed not only possible but likely. Rather, she walked toward Fred's house, in Windsor Terrace. It was a good twenty-five minutes away, but she was moving so fast she did it in a little over fifteen. She was out of breath when she rang the bell.

"Hey!" Fred pulled open the door. "I've been calling you, but you haven't been picking up."

"Sorry," she said. "I've been with the lawyer most of the day." This was not entirely true; she had seen Fred's number flash on the phone and decided not to answer because she was just too guilty to talk to him.

"Well, it's good to see you. You look spooked though. What's wrong? Are you nervous about tomorrow?"

"You could say that," she said. "Can I come in?"

"Actually, I was just heading out."

Mia noticed, then, that he was wearing his leather jacket and had his helmet cradled in his arm.

"You're on your way to Juicy?"

"Uh-huh. Tell you what," he said, stepping outside and locking the door. "Take a ride over there with me now. I'll pour you a drink"—he stopped, taking note of her expression—"just one. It's something new I'm trying out. Blue Zen."

"Sounds like I could use one of those . . ." she said. "Zen of any color."

"It's got Bacardi, Blue Curaçao, and pineapple juice; come on. You have one, take the edge off, and I'll put you in a car service home."

She looked up at his open, smiling face, and, suddenly, she was dying to unburden herself, to tell Fred all about Patrick. She would hurt him, she knew. No doubt lose him, too. Still, it was better than deceiving him. Only she couldn't do it tonight. It would have to wait until after the court date. After tomorrow, she promised herself. After tomorrow, she would come clean.

The Blue Zen turned out to be smooth and potent; by the time she had finished it, the razored edge of anxiety she had been feeling was blunted, and she was no longer afraid to go home. Fred took the empty glass from her and made sure she was safely in a car.

"I'll see you tomorrow," he said as she was fumbling with the seat belt.

"Okay," Mia said. "If you're sure you want to come. Chris says the place is a zoo."

"I can handle a zoo," said Fred. "I tend bar, remember?"

* * *

THERE WAS HARDLY any traffic on Eighth Avenue, and she was back at her apartment in minutes. She dug into her wallet for a few seconds before locating what she wanted; then she handed the driver a ten-dollar tip for a five-dollar ride. It had become almost a reflex by now, tipping big. The driver took the money and peered at her in the rearview mirror.

"Hey, I know you," he said, turning around to look at her directly. His teeth flashed white in his dark face. "You gave me big tip last time I drove you, too."

"Did I?" she asked. She wasn't sure she remembered.

"Yeah, you did. You the same lady."

"I guess I am." She opened the door, ready to get out.

"Here," he said, writing something quickly on a card. "My cell. You call me anytime you need a ride, okay? I be there for you."

MIA FULLY EXPECTED to be up most, if not all, of the night. She was armed with several books and an array of junky, self-indulgent snacks—potato chips, chocolate-covered raisins, and two bags of gummi bears. But after reading only a few pages, she felt sleepy enough to close her eyes, and suddenly, there was gray light filling the bedroom window, and the hopeful, hysterical sounds of sparrows. Morning.

While Mia was showering, the phone rang. She turned off the water and grabbed a towel, but she was too late—the call had already gone to voice mail.

"Mom?" asked Eden when Mia played the message. "Mom, I just wanted to say good luck. Daddy told me that today is the day for that court thing you have to do. I miss you, Mom. Miss you lots."

"Miss you too," Mia said to nobody. She tried Eden right away, but she didn't pick up. Mia pressed a key to bypass the recording and leave a message. At least Eden would know she tried.

Then she dressed. The outfit so carefully handpicked by Cox made her look ridiculous and phony, she decided, so she took off the dress, abandoning it in a sorry little heap on the floor. There was another struggle at the closet—for a woman living on a shoestring, she had certainly managed to amass a lot of clothing—before she settled on a gray flannel skirt that had somehow slipped by her radar before, and an ivory blouse of some silky, patterned material. The high neck hid her locket; though she was afraid to call attention to it, she didn't want to take it off, either. Digging around in an old box of junk jewelry that Eden used to like for playing dress-up, Mia found a strand of imitation pearls. Perfect. She put the whole outfit together and scrutinized the result: pure Republican. Cox would approve.

Her plan was to meet him in the lobby of the courthouse on Adams Street; they would go upstairs to the courtroom together. Fred said he would be there, and so would Stuart. She wondered, with some alarm, whether Lloyd would show up. He hadn't said anything about it, but it was a distinct possibility.

Mia took the subway to Court Street and walked over to Adams. The sidewalks were filled with people headed in the same direction. Many of them were off to jury duty; she knew, because she had been one of them, just a few months ago. The summons, always a nuisance when it showed up, had come during the summer, and since she had postponed twice already, she had *had* to show up. But it felt quite different to face the massive, block-long building from the other side of the equation. Now, she was not going to sit in judgment of someone else; the law's long arm was going to be pointing at her.

Under her coat, she started to sweat. The blouse, clearly made of some infernal synthetic material, stuck to her armpits like Saran Wrap. She stopped outside the courthouse to adjust her skirt, which had twisted uncomfortably on her waist, and noticed there was a run in her panty hose. No spare pair and no time to go buy one either; there was nothing to do but submit her bag and her person to the security guards at the entrance and, once inside, scan the space for Cox.

He was there, of course, topcoat draped neatly over his arm, brief-case clasped firmly in one small hand. His suit today was also gray flannel—she fervently hoped no one would think they planned it—and his shirt was the palest shade of lilac. His hammered gold cuff links looked heavy enough to bruise.

"You've got a run," he observed.

"It just happened on the way here," she said. "Sorry."

"I've got a fresh pair. Hang on." He set down the briefcase and snapped open its heavy clasps. Inside, on top of the neatly arranged papers, were several pairs of panty hose in unopened packages. There was also a necktie, a box of Band-Aids, a bottle of mouthwash, and a comb.

"You carry these around with you?" He certainly thought of every-thing.

"You think you're the first client to spring a leak on court day?" He handed her one of the packages. "Go to the ladies' room and put them on."

When she emerged, she saw Stuart deep in conversation with Cox. Lloyd was nowhere in sight, which was a relief. The expression on Stuart's face—so intense, so absorbed, so focused—reminded her of how he looked at eight, at ten, at fourteen, at seventeen. He was her brother. No one else knew what it was like to be the children of those particular parents, in that particular family; Stuart was a witness, *the* witness, to their shared past, a touchstone for everything that had ever happened to her and everything that ever would. She was glad he was there.

"Hey, Stu," she said, touching his sleeve.

"Hey, yourself." He hugged her. "I was just grilling Chris on your prospects. I think you're in good hands." *Good, though small,* thought Mia.

"There's something I just found out," Cox said. "Costello isn't going to press you on the locket. At least not today."

"Not any day," said Mia. "Look what I have." She pulled out the receipt.

"I thought you said you couldn't produce one," Cox said, narrowing his eyes as he read.

"I was wrong."

"Well, that takes care of one headache," he said, folding the receipt and tucking it into his briefcase. "Now we just have to deal with the bill. But you know what to do in there, right? You've been coached."

"Coached by the best," she said. He nodded. They rode up in the elevator and followed the small stream of people headed toward the courtroom.

Cox had been right when he said that the joint would be jumping. The rows of wooden benches—pewlike, Mia thought—were almost completely filled. There were twenty-year-olds and seventy-year-olds, blacks and whites, Asians and Latinos. Here was a big burly guy wearing wraparound sunglasses; he was accompanied by a woman in a black vinyl coat, open to reveal her plunging neckline and a complicated array of gold necklaces. Next to her sat a young woman with badly bitten-down nails; she was with an older woman who was furiously winding a skein of yarn around one wrist.

Mia saw Costello up near the front. And there was Fred, seated on one side. Mia waggled her fingers at him, a tentative wave. He waggled back. Since he had told her he would be here, she was not surprised. What did surprise her, though, was the sight of Patrick, sitting in the last row. What was he doing here? Suddenly, it seemed like there was a small grenade in the room. The blouse felt as if it were glued to her underarms; she had better not take off the coat. Patrick caught her looking at him, and he mouthed something; she was not sure what he was trying to say, but it seemed to contain the words *College Girl*.

"Come on," Cox whispered, as he steered them toward a bench near the front. "We have to find a seat." Stuart worked his way in first, then Cox, and finally Mia, who awkwardly pressed past all the people in the

row, murmuring, "Sorry" and "Excuse me" as she went; she accidentally stepped on the foot of a grossly overweight woman whose perox-
ided hair revealed a stripe of rich, dark brown at the scalp.

"Ow!" wailed the woman, and several people turned to glare at
Mia.

"I'm so sorry," Mia said, as the woman struggled to bend over so
she could massage her instep. "I didn't mean to—"

"Why don't you sit down?" said Cox gently, taking Mia's arm.

Stuart looked over to see what was the matter. Giving the woman
a last, apologetic look, Mia sat down. Knowing that Patrick was here
threw her off balance. She willed herself not to look at him, though
she was sure she could feel him looking at her.

"Milosz Karnov," called out a policeman standing at the front of
the courtroom. "Milosz Karnov, please approach the bench."

The man with the sunglasses got to his feet and walked up to
where the judge was seated. The judge. Mia had not really looked at
him before, but she looked now. He was in his sixties, with a long,
sorrowful-looking face and the big, down-turned eyes of a basset
hound. His dark robe and wooden gavel seemed like props—not
entirely real yet still menacing. He spoke quietly so she couldn't hear
him, but his authority was clear; Mr. Wraparound seemed to lose
his swagger and nodded his head meekly in response to something
the judge said. A suited man with slicked-back hair—his lawyer?—
interrupted, and the judge swiveled slightly so that he could turn his
full, accusatory gaze in the man's direction. The man fell silent. More
words were exchanged between the judge and Mr. Wraparound. Then
the judge rapped his gavel—Mia could hear its implosive sound
even from where she sat—and Mr. Wraparound left the courtroom,
escorted by his lawyer and the woman in vinyl, who tottered behind
on her spiky heels.

Mia sat riveted as versions of this drama unfolded once, twice, three
times. The young woman with the ragged nails approached the bench.

The woman with the yarn began tugging on the strand with both hands; Mia waited for it to snap.

Then the officer at the front of the room called out her name: "Mia Saul." It sounded as if she were being summoned by God. Mia stood, inched her way back across the row of bodies—the overweight woman recoiled visibly—and approached the bench. As she moved forward, Mia felt like everyone in the room was staring at her; she imagined that Patrick's smoldering gaze might have the power to burn through cloth, leaving two singed, round holes where it penetrated the back of her coat.

Then she felt a hand at her elbow, and she looked up. Cox. It was Cox, escorting her to the bench. Her breath released slightly. Cox was here; he would know what to say. And indeed he did. His delivery was even smoother, more mellifluous than it had been the first time she had heard it, in Costello's dreary office. He had clearly been practicing, and he glided through the whole song and dance—her heroic plight as a single mom, her seamless alibis—as if he really were onstage. Costello was scribbling madly on a legal pad while he spoke, and even Stuart looked deeply impressed.

"And so I think you'll have to agree, Your Honor, that my client had nothing whatsoever to do with Mr. Wedeen's unfortunate death."

"Thank you, Mr. Cox, for your stirring presentation," said the judge. His voice had a thick, almost clotted quality, as if he badly needed to clear his throat. "But there's still the matter of the mysterious ten-thousand-dollar bill, which, so far, no one has been able to explain. And I have to say that the presence of this bill—its origins, its history—fascinates me."

"Well, Your Honor, that bill—"

"I'd like to hear from Ms. Saul directly, Mr. Cox. I've heard everything you've had to say, and now I think it's time for Ms. Saul to offer her version of events." The judge turned those big canine eyes in Mia's direction, and for a few seconds, she couldn't say anything.

"Ms. Saul?" He sounded impatient. "We're all waiting." He gestured to the district attorney on his left and the court officers standing nearby.

Still nothing. Cox was discreetly pumping his clenched fist, in pre-victory mode, and the judge's eyes continued to bore into her. Then she thought of Eden, and she found the words that had been eluding her.

"I do want to explain about that bill, Your Honor," Mia said. "Even though the story seems to defy explanation." She launched into the story of the cash machine, its escalating offerings, culminating in the ten-thousand-dollar bill that she sold to Weed shortly before his death. She abandoned the script that Cox had dictated, all the coy little glances, the girlish shrugs, and instead told the story openly and forthrightly, just the way it had happened. She didn't look at Cox as she spoke; she didn't dare.

When she was through, she could feel the judge's silent attention had intensified, like sunlight through a magnifying glass.

"Mr. Cox," he said at last. "You didn't mention before that your client was delusional—"

"But I'm not," said Mia firmly. "Not at all. And I can prove it, too." Had she really said that, out loud, to the judge and everyone else within earshot? Had she just offered to expose her magic, not only to Patrick, who was some kind of weird, kindred soul, but to the world? The judge stared at her silently and she stared back. The last time she had gone by the bank, the machine had been out of order. So her offer was a huge gamble. But hadn't it all been a gamble? A horse race, the Kentucky Derby, waiting for that dark horse to hug the rail in the last lap and burst on through to the finish line?

"Prove it?" the judge asked at last. He looked over at the D.A., who tapped the side of his head, as if he were testing a melon for ripeness, and shrugged. "How?"

"Well, I know this would be unorthodox—"

"Your Honor, you've got to believe this woman. She's telling the truth." Patrick's voice rang out from the back of the courtroom, and everyone, but everyone, turned around to stare. "That machine she's talking about? It's for real. I know, 'cause I've seen it." He was standing now, arms outstretched beseechingly. The hood of his white parka framed the back of his blond head, a fallen halo.

"Who is that?" growled the judge.

"I have no idea," Cox said.

Fortunately, no one looked at Mia, who was shaking her head and silently saying, *No, no, no.*

"Get him out of here," said the judge. "Now." Even before he was finished speaking, police officers stationed at opposite corners of the room began to converge.

"You can haul me away, but you can't shut me up," Patrick said. "Because I'm telling the truth, and so is she. She's not like everyone else, see? The machine gave her that money because it *knew* she wasn't, and then she started giving it away, to people she didn't even know, people like me—"

"Clear the aisle, clear the aisle," barked an officer. At first, the people in Patrick's row appeared frozen; there was no movement in any direction. Then, as if everyone had been given the cue simultaneously, they all started shoving and jostling in an effort to get out of the way. Patrick remained where he was, calmly watching the exodus. Two officers approached him from either side; one had a hand on his gun. But Patrick offered no resistance to the silver bracelets that were snapped onto his wrists.

"That's right, go ahead and cuff me," he said, almost tenderly, to the officer. "They cuffed Jesus, too, didn't they? Cuffed him good and nailed him to that cross. But they couldn't shut him up, either, even when those motherfuckers crucified him." He looked down at his shackled wrists. "That's 'cause the truth will out, even if you pigs in blue try to stifle it. You can't. You just can't." He allowed himself to be pushed along the aisle and toward the door. Just before he had been

pushed through it, he suddenly halted, colliding with one of the officers, who grabbed him by the shoulder.

"Keep the faith, College Girl," he sang out. "I love you!"

No, she thought again, *no, no, no, no.* But there was another voice, soft
and clear, urgently whispering beneath it, and that voice breathed *yes.*
If Patrick said anything else, Mia didn't hear it because he was out of
earshot now, dragged out the door and along the corridor.

The room erupted in a frantic buzzing.

"Did you hear—?"

"Did you see—?"

"Who the hell—?"

"What the fuck—?"

"College Girl? Who's College Girl?"

"Order in the court!" roared the judge. He slammed the gavel down
hard, and his long jowls shivered from the impact. "Order in the court!"

"Everyone can sit down now," said one of the remaining officers.
"Show's over." He began shepherding all the displaced occupants of
Patrick's row back to their seats. It took a few minutes, but eventually,
people filed back in and settled down. The buzzing and whispering
continued.

"Ms. Saul, do you know that man?" asked the judge. He looked to
Mia as if he had aged perceptibly in these last few minutes.

"Actually, I do, Your Honor."

"Then would you please tell me how you know him? And what
possible relevance that outburst of his had on what we've been discussing?"

"He's seen the machine in action," said Mia. "So he knows I'm telling the truth."

"Ms. Saul," said the judge, setting down his gavel and leaning over
the high podium behind which he sat. He brought his face disturbingly
close to hers; she could see the pores on his nose, the tiny black dots
on his chin that would, if unshaven, have turned into a beard. "You

seem like a reasonable woman. An educated woman. Do you really expect me to believe that there is a cash machine in New York City that's been dispensing money it does not debit or record in any way, shape, or form?"

"Yes, Your Honor."

"And that the bank has had no inkling that it's handing out money in this fashion?"

"No, I don't think so," she said, remembering the cordoned-off machine.

"Let me ask you this then. Did it ever occur to you to *tell* the bank about their error?"

"No, Your Honor." She felt her whole body heating miserably and wished she could have taken off the coat.

"Why not?"

"It's hard to explain . . ."

"That's what we're here for, Ms. Saul. Explanations." His face was still closer to hers than she would have liked, but something in his expression had changed. He seemed kinder somehow, almost avuncular. He even reminded her of her own uncle Bernie, with those long, velvety-looking earlobes of his.

"I thought that the money was some kind of signal."

"A signal? What kind of a signal?"

"Something telling me to hang on. Things weren't going well for me. My husband had left me, my daughter was getting in trouble in school. I lost my job and had to move. The money seemed like it was a gift. Like it was meant just for me." She paused, steeling herself before she uttered the next, most outlandish revelation of all. "And then, when the machine gave me the ten-thousand-dollar bill, I found out that I was right—it *was* a gift for me. The machine said so."

"The machine said so?" His voice scaled up in disbelief. "You are standing here and telling me that an *automated teller machine* communicated with you?"

"Yes, Your Honor."

"How?"

"Words appeared on the screen. *A gift. For you, Mia. Use it well.* So I really did think the money was intended for me."

The two bushy caterpillars of the judge's eyebrows arched high in surprise.

"I didn't know why I was chosen to receive it, but I didn't ask. And then when I started giving it away, I thought, well, this seems fair. I'd been given something; it was only right to give something back."

"So you gave away the money you received?"

"Not all of it. But some of it, yes. To homeless people, cabdrivers, a couple of my neighbors who looked like they could use some help."

"And you gave money to that man who was here earlier? The one who had to be removed from the courtroom?"

"Yes," Mia said, "I did."

"Well, this is all most interesting," said the judge. Costello was still scribbling away. "But it's very difficult to believe."

"Come and see for yourself," said Mia, thinking of that dark horse again, only this time he was going for the Triple Crown. "Come to the bank, and I'll show you."

The judge looked at her for a long moment, and then he turned to the district attorney. "Do it," he said. The D.A. looked back at him with a "what the hell?" look, but the judge didn't falter. "Send two of your men over there with her. Tomorrow morning. First thing." He banged the gavel again. "Court's adjourned for fifteen minutes." He stood, black robe bunching around his ankles, and disappeared through a door just to the right of the podium. Costello jumped up, dropping her pad on the floor.

There was more furious hissing, but Cox was hustling Mia down the aisle and out of the room.

"What men?" said Mia, trying to match his pace. "What's he talking about?"

"The D.A. squad. They'll go with you to the bank tomorrow morning to see this alleged money machine of yours." He stopped. "I don't know what you were doing in there, but all I can say is that I really hope it works."

"That makes two of us," Mia said. What had she been doing in there? Did she think that the judge would just believe her without proof? The door opened again, and there were Fred and Stuart. She could feel their questions, rising up like steam from boiling water. But Mia shut her eyes, shut them out. They would have to wait. Right now, close enough to smell, was the dark horse, *her* dark horse, his bright eyes bulging, his great column of a neck in a lather, as he came thundering around the track.

TWENTY-FIVE

"ALL RIGHT," SAID Cox. "Tomorrow morning I'll be at your place at eight forty-five; the D.A. squad should be there by nine. Then we're all going to take a little stroll to the bank and watch the machine perform its hocus-pocus." He drained the last dark drops from his thick white mug and made a face. "Swill," he added. "How can this place stay in business?"

Cox, Fred, Stuart, and Mia were sitting in a coffee shop across the street from the courthouse. Fred and her brother both deferred to Cox, who was clearly eager to offer his game plan for tomorrow and then get the hell out of there.

"I have to admit, I'm as curious as the judge to see how this thing is going to play out," Cox said now. "I'm sure the D.A.'s guys are going to want to speak to someone at the bank."

"You don't believe me," said Mia, holding a sugar packet but not opening it. Cox was right; the coffee was undrinkable, no matter what you did to it.

"Come on, Mia. Who in their right mind would believe you?" Stuart said before Cox could answer. "I mean, I'm used to coming up with some pretty wild stories, but this—"

"Can I get youse some more coffee?"

Youse. The waitress—frumpy, short-skirted, thick-ankled—had just said *youse.* Mia kicked Stuart, gently, under the Formica-topped table. In the past, this was the sort of thing that they would have jumped on and run with; they would have been making *youse* jokes all day long.

"We're okay, thanks," said Cox. The waitress placed the check on the table and drifted off.

Stuart's eyes remained averted. Mia stared at him, willing him to laugh or at least smile. *Come on*, she thought, *you can do it.* His refusal to acknowledge her was frustrating, even painful. She wanted to kick him again, harder.

Cox reached for the check, but Stuart got there first.

"It's on me," he said. "I'm treating all of youse." He looked at Mia, and she burst out laughing. Cox and Fred just looked at each other, not sure what was so funny. Mia and Stuart laughed harder. When it was clear no one was going to explain, Cox stood, gathering his coat and briefcase.

"Tomorrow," he said, giving Mia a small salute. A signet ring glinted on one finger; it was even bigger than the cuff links.

"Tomorrow."

"Can I give you a lift uptown?" Cox asked Stuart.

"Sure." But he hesitated, looking over at Mia.

"We can talk later," she said, silently urging him to please leave already. Poor Fred had been mute ever since they had left the courthouse, and she really did need to talk to him.

"All right." He looked at Fred, and then at Mia again. "I'll be in my office. You can call me."

Then Mia and Fred were alone. The waitress appeared again, clearing the mugs and wiping down the table. But since the place was nearly empty—no great surprise there—she didn't rush them out.

"You slept with him," said Fred as soon as the woman had gone. "You slept with that guy. He's a criminal, and you slept with him."

"He's not a criminal. He's never actually done time."

"Done time?" Fred repeated. "Listen to yourself. You're even talking like him." He stared down at the table.

"It's just an expression, Fred."

"Yeah. *His* expression."

"I'm sorry," she said. "Very sorry."

"Why should I believe that?"

"Because it's true. And I was going to tell you, too."

"When? On the Fourth of July?"

"Today. I would have told you today. I had no idea he'd show up in court. That was a total surprise to me, too."

"I thought we had something. I thought maybe—" He stopped, reached for her hand, but didn't take it.

"You thought what?"

"That you were falling in love with me."

"Maybe I was," she said, thinking of what Bev had said. "Maybe I was."

"So then why did you screw him?"

"I don't know. It's something that just . . . happened."

"Screwing someone doesn't just happen. *When* did it happen? How many times?"

"Does it matter?"

His blue gaze was clouded and angry, but Mia didn't lose purchase.

"No," he said after a moment. "You're right. It doesn't. Once, twice, five times. It's all the same. You slept with him. But it was me who got screwed."

"I'm sorry," she said again. "I really am."

"Sorry doesn't cut it," he said bitterly. "I've got to know where you are with this. Do you actually want this guy? Or do you want me? Because you can't have both of us."

"I don't know what I want." Mia put her fingers against her temples, feeling the slight throb beneath their tips.

"Well, if you figure it out, you can call me." He stood, groping for his jacket.

"You're leaving?"

"Bright girl." He turned. She could still call him back, get him to stay. But would that be fair? She was being truthful before: she really didn't know what she wanted, other than to dig her way out of this courtroom mess and bring her daughter home again. She saw Eden's small face in her mind; she conjured the smell of her skin, her hair, and felt an emptiness that was as ravishing as it was total. Then she looked across the table. Fred was gone.

AT HOME, MIA changed out of her Laura Bush drag and began making phone calls. There was a driven, desperate quality to the effort, as if she were marooned on some ice floe, frantically sending out distress signals. She tried Stuart, who was in a meeting and could not be disturbed. She tried Eden but got only her recorded message. She tried Lloyd, who didn't pick up. She even tried Lloyd's mother, Virginia, who said that neither Lloyd nor Eden was there at the moment.

"He didn't say when he'd be back," she said. "Can I give him a message?"

"No, that's all right," said Mia. "I'll try his cell again." Why did Virginia sound so uncomfortable, as if she were covering up something? Mia fretted over this as she said good-bye; but she continued making calls. She considered calling Julie, but something kept her from it. She tried Patrick—she never had asked for his cell number, or found out if he even had one—but the phone in the house in Coney Island just rang and rang. She called her mother in New Mexico, only to hear from Hank that she was on her way to New York.

"New York? Are you sure?"

"That's what she told me," Hank said.

"Well, she didn't tell me." She was puzzled; why would her mother keep a visit to New York a secret? She tried Stuart again; now he was on a conference call. *Jesus,* she thought, *where* is *everybody today?* Enough. She had to get out of here. Now.

She pulled on a big sweater and a tired old parka with a drawstring hood—she still hadn't gotten herself a new hat—before locking the door behind her and heading for the stairs. As she passed Mr. Ortiz's apartment, it occurred to her that she hadn't seen her neighbor in a while; was he all right? She stopped, wondering whether she ought to ring the buzzer.

There was a sound, a small but distinct *yip* from the other side of the door. Was that Mariposa, the dog she helped rescue? Then she heard the sound repeated: *yip, yip, yip.* That was not a dog. That was a puppy.

Curiosity won out. She rang the buzzer, and when the door opened, there was Mr. Ortiz, with the black Pom at his feet and a tiny black-and-brown creature in his arms.

"Señora Saul! I am so glad to see you." He stepped aside so she could come in. "I have stopped at your door, but I do not find you at home."

"I've been busy," she said, eyeing the puppy. "But it looks like you have, too." The animal Mr. Ortiz held was a strange-looking thing with a stubby snout, pointed ears, and a kind of chewed-up-looking ruff of fur around its tiny neck; it couldn't have weighed more than three pounds.

"Mariposa is a mama," he said proudly. Mariposa dipped her black head downward and pawed the floor, as if aware she was being discussed.

"A mama!" echoed Mia, incredulous. The girl at the shelter had assured her the dog was spayed.

"I was also . . . surprised," said Mr. Ortiz. "My cousin came to visit with her Pepe; he's a Yorkshire terrier. They must have gone in the other room. We didn't see it happen."

"Well, congratulations," Mia said. She offered her hand to the puppy to sniff. The puppy wriggled in Mr. Ortiz's grasp and unspooled its pink tongue. Eden would love this. *If* Eden ever came home again.

"His name is Tiki," said Mr. Ortiz. "And he has a brother. But my cousin kept him."

"Does he use the litter box, too?"

"He is learning," Mr. Ortiz said, looking fondly at the puppy. "Aren't you, papi?"

"He's adorable," Mia said as she moved toward the door.

"Thank you, Señora Saul," said Mr. Ortiz. "For everything." Mia was nodding and smiling, ready to go, but she sensed there was something else he wanted to say. She was not wrong. "I am hoping your troubles are over."

"I'm all right," she said stiffly. Mr. Ortiz was a very sweet man, but she didn't want to be discussing her private life with him.

"I don't see your little girl anymore," he continued.

"She's with her father now," Mia said. *Maybe forever.*

"I see," he said, and she thought he probably did.

"When you speak with her, tell her about Tiki. Tell her to come visit him when she gets back."

"I'll tell her," says Mia. "I'll tell her as soon as I can."

OUTSIDE IT WAS cold, and a few snow flurries had begun to sift gently down. Mia walked quickly up the hill, toward Prospect Park. The winter light was weak and fading, but she thought she could do a quick loop around the park before it grew dark. She entered at Third Street and stayed on the main road, just to be safe. Most people were heading out, toward home, but there were still a handful of joggers and a couple of die-hard cyclists. She walked quickly, hands in her pockets, hood pulled tight around her head. The park offered a vision of spare winter beauty—black, ice-bright branches against a Wedgwood sky; the flat silver expanse of the lake, ringed by flecked gray stones—but she didn't really take it in.

She was thinking instead about Lloyd and Eden, and of her mother's mysterious visit to New York. Stuart never called her back. And Patrick—what had happened to Patrick after they hauled him away? Mia couldn't believe that he was nutty enough to come into the courtroom and pull a stunt like that. Was she the teensiest, tiniest bit happy to see him, crazy as his behavior was? Because he was crazy, all right—as crazy as she sometimes thought she was. Or maybe not crazy. Impulsive, emotion-driven, spontaneous. Like her.

She kept her pace swift, slowing only when she came to the entrance of the zoo. She hadn't been here in ages. She and Lloyd used to come with Eden when she was younger, but since the divorce, Lloyd had switched his allegiance to the Bronx Zoo. Mia stood, weighing her options, and then walked up to the ticket booth. If she couldn't find any human company today, she could still consort with animals.

"One adult, please," she said, taking out a bill.

"Zoo'll be closing soon," said the young woman who took her money.

"I'll be quick," said Mia.

The sky was turning a deep jewel blue, and harried parents were leading tired children along the paths, toward the exits. There was a little boy crying, being comforted by his father, and a pair of twins—cheeks reddened from the cold—asleep in their double-wide stroller.

Where to go? Chimps? Penguins? Lions or tigers or bears? Most of the cages seem uninhabited; the animals must be hunkered down, unseen, for the night. It was only when she came to the habitat of the great horned owl that she was rewarded by the startling swoop of the creature; she could actually feel the draft from his sudden flight on her face. His appearance was so silent that she hadn't heard him approach. Mia's first—okay, her only—Newbery-winning book had been about an owl. She had known that book would be a winner from the moment she had found it in the slush pile, winking up at her like a gold coin in the gutter. *Owls rock*, she imagined herself telling Eden if she were here. *Owls rule.*

The owl flexed his wings and then settled on a roost very close to where she stood. Mia remained as still as she could, and they looked at each other across the great, yet somehow meaningless divide between species. Meaningless because she could feel, suddenly, what it might be like to be him, the ancient-looking talons gripping the roost, the lemon-lime eyes studying her so closely. His thick feathers were so glossy they might have been oiled. She had a sudden longing to press her face into them. What would they feel like? Soft or bristly? How would he smell? The owl continued to look at her, his unblinking eyes as bright as headlights. Mia didn't blink, either; it seemed imperative to keep her own eyes open and her gaze steady.

"The zoo is closed now," said a uniformed guard walking past. "This way out, please."

Reluctantly, Mia took leave of the owl. He continued to stare at her. *I'll be back,* she silently told him. *I promise I'll be back.*

The light was gone now, and she still had a fair distance to go before she got home. She cut across Long Meadow instead of completing her circuit, and she walked back down the hill, melding with the commuters pouring out of the subway at Grand Army Plaza. She was tired by the time she reached her apartment, and she lay down with all her clothes still on, just, she told herself, for a few minutes. But she fell asleep and didn't get up until the sky was light. Her neck ached and her shoulder was sore; in sleep, she must have been twisted like a pretzel. What time was it anyway? Anxiously, she checked her watch. Only six thirty. Plenty of time to shower and change, to look alive before Cox arrived and the curtain went up again. She was just toweling off when the phone started ringing.

"Sorry I didn't call you yesterday," said Stuart. "I had a lot of fires to put out."

"That's okay." She surveyed her sartorial options. She had no directive from Cox but that was fine; today she was going to wear what *she* wanted to wear.

"So are you ready?"

"I think so," she said.

"I'm going to try to make it out there."

"You don't have to."

"I know," he said. "I want to, though."

"Well, I appreciate it."

"And what about Fred?"

"I doubt it," Mia said.

"I could tell there was a storm brewing when I left. What's up with him? He your new boyfriend?"

"He was. But not anymore."

"Too bad."

There was a pause that Mia knew she was supposed to fill.

"I'll tell you all about it, Stu. Just not now, okay?"

"Okay."

"I should go," Mia said. "But I have to ask you one more thing. I called Mom yesterday, and Hank said she was on her way to New York. Do you know anything about this?"

"Yeah." He waited a beat. "Actually, I told her to come."

"You did? Jesus."

"Don't get all hissy. She has a right to be here, you know."

"I suppose," Mia conceded grudgingly. "Anyone else you've invited without telling me?"

"Well, Lloyd is coming, too."

"No!"

"It was his idea. And he's bringing Eden."

"He is? Why?"

"Hey, I thought you'd be happy."

"I am. Only I don't trust him. He's been so adamant about shielding her from my so-called bad influence. Why is he bringing her back here all of a sudden?"

"Well, the thing is, she stopped eating."

I knew it, Mia thought. *I knew it would come to this.* To Stuart, she said tensely, "Since when? Has she lost weight? What is he doing about it?"

"She's okay, I swear she is. It was only for a couple of days."

"A couple of days? Stuart, that's a long time for a kid of her age to go without eating. Why didn't he call me? Why didn't he let me talk to her?" Mia felt slightly hysterical; Eden didn't need to lose a single ounce.

"At first he just thought she had a stomach flu. But then she told him she wouldn't eat unless he brought her to New York with him."

"And so he said yes?"

"She ate two grilled cheese sandwiches and a bowl of soup as soon as he agreed."

"This is serious, Stuart. She can't afford to fast."

"I know, I know," he soothed. "But it's over now. She's eating again, okay? So you can calm down."

"Where are they staying?"

"He didn't say."

"I want her here with me," Mia said firmly. "I want her to come home."

"You've got to work that out with Lloyd," Stuart said.

"Oh I will, believe me."

AS SOON AS she got off the phone with her brother, the phone rang again. Julie. Mia hesitated, but this time she took the call.

"Are you still speaking to me?" Julie asked, without saying hello.

"I answered the phone, didn't I?"

"Mia, I am so sorry," Julie said. "Whatever I thought, whatever I expected, I still shouldn't have disappeared like that. I should have tried harder to keep you in the loop."

"Harder! You didn't try at all."

"True," Julie said. "I can't argue when you're right."

"I felt like everyone was against me, and I wanted to talk to you. But I couldn't," Mia said. "It made me feel so shut out."

"I was a fool," Julie said. "A fool in love."

"That's not an excuse," Mia said.

"No," said Julie. "It isn't. But I hope we can get past this. I really want to try."

"I don't know," said Mia. "I really don't know."

"Can I come over?"

"When?" said Mia. She wasn't even dressed yet.

"How about now?"

"Now? I don't think so, Julie. I'm waiting for the D.A. squad to arrive and—"

"I know all about it," Julie said. "That's why I want to be there. I thought you'd need some moral support."

"Who told you?" Mia asked. But of course she knew the answer to that: Fred. She felt the lash of guilt even thinking about him. "It was Fred, right?"

"He's feeling pretty terrible," Julie said. "You know, he really did love you. No, I take that back. He still loves you."

"I didn't mean to hurt him," Mia said, and looked at the clock. "But I really can't go into all that now. I've got to get ready." She yanked up a pair of black patterned tights. She inspected them carefully for runs. There weren't any—yet.

"Why don't you let me come over?" Julie said. "I'll bring breakfast."

Mia knew that Julie's idea of breakfast was a box of Krispy Kremes. Suddenly, she craved one of the sticky, calorie-laden confections. And she wanted Julie to bring her one. Or several.

JULIE HADN'T LIED about her tan; it may have spelled a future studded with basal cell carcinomas, but Jesus, did she look terrific. They hugged tightly, stood back, and looked at each other, and then hugged again.

"Here," said Julie, handing her the box of doughnuts. "All the trans fat, sugar, and cholesterol you need for the week."

"There's so much to say I don't even know where to begin." Mia plucked a doughnut from the box. But before she could take a bite, she saw that Julie's attention had been diverted by something out the window. "What?" she asked. "What are you staring at?"

"There's a TV crew in front of the building," said Julie.

"Let me see." Mia joined Julie at the window. There was a van parked out front; it had the emblem of a local news station emblazoned across the side, and the back doors were wide open. She watched as a couple of guys emerged, hauling cameras and other equipment out

onto the sidewalk. What was going on? Mia hurriedly ate her doughnut and opened the window. She saw a young woman with a massive
amount of shiny red hair and an alarmingly green suit—she looked
kind of like a leprechaun, only prettier—standing patiently in front of
the building while her face was anointed with a long wandlike makeup
brush.

The phone rang again. Eden—at last!

"Eden!" said Mia, so happy to hear her voice. "Where are you?"

"In Queens, staying with some friends of Daddy's girlfriend. We
went to a Korean restaurant last night."

"You did? Was it fun?" She refused to let herself ask, *Did you eat? Are
you eating now? Please don't stop eating.* There would be time for all that later,
when she actually saw Eden, wrapped her tightly in her arms.

"Yeah, except they brought over a pile of raw meat and cooked it on
this big grill right at the table; my finger got burnt. Also, the smell of
the meat was so gross. It made me sick."

"Mia, there's another TV van outside," said Julie, who was still at
the window. "This one's from ABC."

"Eden, why are you in New York now? Did Daddy bring you here
to see me?" She was trying to have this conversation and pay attention
to Julie at the same time.

"He says that something important is happening with your court
thing today, and that we have to be there to see how it turns out."

"So you're on your way to Brooklyn?"

"We're leaving in a few minutes. Daddy said I could call you to let
you know."

"I can't wait to see you," Mia said. The doughnut, while delicious
going down, had been a big mistake; it was now lodged, a hot, immo-
bile mass, in her stomach.

"And I can't wait to see you. But I don't want you to go to jail again,
okay?"

"Okay, baby. No jail for me."

"Oh, and Mom? Grandma's coming, too."

"Did you talk to her?"

"No. She's with Uncle Stuart. He called Daddy."

"Mia, I really think you should take a look at this," said Julie. The remaining doughnuts were ignored while Julie surveyed the drama unfolding in the street below. "It's a media circus out there."

"Eden, honey, I've got to go now," said Mia. "I'll see you soon, okay?"

"Love you, Mommy," said Eden.

"Love you, too." But Eden was already gone.

Mia returned to the window. There were two vans, more camera and sound equipment, and another pert young thing—this one in an orange pantsuit—submitting to a touch-up. Mia was ready to pull her head back inside when she spied Cox on the sidewalk, talking to the newscaster in green. Mia saw him shake his head and try to pass her. Green Girl stepped in front of him, and he started moving in another direction. But she placed herself in his path again; from up above, it looked like they were doing a dance.

Although the intercom had not yet been fixed, Hector, Luisa's dad, had gone ahead and installed a lock on the front door. Now Mia's guests had to yell up and wait for her to toss down the small Ziploc bag in which she kept the key. She was just about to toss it to Cox now, but something told her to wait. She saw him pull out his phone, and, a second later, her own phone was ringing.

"I don't want to alarm you or anything," Cox said. "But there are a couple of camera crews down here that want to talk to you. And there's a guy from the *Daily News,* too."

"Talk to me?"

"About the cash machine. Someone seems to have tipped them off that there might be something very unusual about to take place."

"Chris, that's impossible."

"Are you looking out the window?"

"Uh-huh."

"Then you'll know it's not only possible, it's happening. Now."

"So what should I do?"

"Come on down. It's showtime, remember?" Cox clicked off, and Mia walked slowly away from the window.

"You okay?" Julie asked.

"I don't know," said Mia. "All those TV people down there? They're waiting to talk to me."

"Who were you talking to just now? One of them?"

"No, that was my lawyer. He's outside."

Julie peered out the window again.

"The bald one in the fancy coat?"

"That's him."

"How are you paying for him, anyway?"

"Stuart."

"Mia, I think I see Stuart out there. Talking to the lawyer. Did he say he'd be coming?"

"Let me see."

Stuart was standing next to Cox, intently listening to whatever he had to say. Then she saw Lloyd, towering over everyone, red scarf fluttering in the wind. And to top it off, he was wearing a beret. A beret! Who did he think he was—François Truffaut? Next to him, hopping lightly from foot to foot, was Eden. She was looking straight up at the window, and when she saw Mia, she started waving frantically.

"There's Eden," Mia said to Julie. "I've got to go."

IT WAS CROWDED outside the building, and in Mia's effort to move toward Eden, she and Julie were separated. But at that moment, the only thing that mattered was her daughter. She called to her, and Eden came charging in her direction, not stopping until she was in Mia's arms.

"Eden," Mia crooned. "I missed you so much." Was she thinner or was that Mia's worry-fueled imagination? Under the coat, it was hard to tell. She looked up and saw Lloyd, hovering on the periphery of their embrace. He just stood there, looking big, and for once he didn't say a thing.

"That's her," said a guy with a camera. "She's the one."

"Ms. Saul, over here, over here," called someone else.

"Is it true that there's a cash machine just handing out money?" asked still another voice. "Or is this just some kind of publicity hoax?" Several of the TV guys started moving in on her; Mia stepped back. Their proximity was mildly alarming, and she was just about to say so when Cox came barreling up.

"Coming through," he said in a loud voice. "She's not saying anything right now. You'll just have to wait." Then to Mia, he added, "These are the detectives from the D.A.'s office." Two men nodded. The taller one, who was black, said, "I'm Smyth, from the Seventy-eighth Precinct. And this is Blauner." They both wore dun-colored raincoats and drab scarves; maybe it was some kind of detective uniform.

"What's going on?" asked Smyth.

"I'm not sure," said Mia. She had her arm around Eden's shoulders and scanned the crowd for Julie. After a minute, she saw her, standing next to Fred. Why was he here? And look at that—Bev was with him. Bev caught Mia's eye and waved.

"Ms. Saul, what did you think when you saw a ten-thousand-dollar bill? Did you know right away it was real?"

"Did you try to sell it through legitimate sources at first?"

"What about Solly Phelps? Why wouldn't he buy it? Did he suspect it was a fake?"

Solly Phelps! How did he know anything about her visit to Solly Phelps?

"I told you—no questions," Cox snapped. He was small, all right, but he could snarl with the best of them.

"I think we're ready," said Smyth. He looked at his watch. "We've got other dog-and-pony shows to see this morning."

Mia finally let go of Eden as they began to make their way up Garfield Place, toward the bank on Fifth Avenue. It was a cold, bright day with a strong wind blowing; the red-and-yellow McDonald's wrappers whirling in the breeze had an almost festive quality.

THE TV VANS remained parked where they were, but several crew members walked along with them. The reporters were a noisy bunch, tossing questions in the air like confetti. The group advancing on the bank seemed to swell by the minute.

"Mom, there are so many people here!" said Eden.

"I know."

"Look, there's Luisa's mom. And Mr. Ortiz. And look over there!" She pointed, though Mia had told her a thousand times that pointing was rude. "There's Grandma!"

Mia turned to see her mother, wearing a colorful cape—a cape!—made out of some patchwork material, and walking beside Stuart. Behind them was Mr. Ortiz, holding tightly on to Inez's arm. He moved slowly, with great deliberation. There *were* a lot of people. Who had told them to come? What did they want? She scanned the crowd again and realized that she knew more than a few of the faces in it. Caitlin and Suzy. Wasn't that the driver from the car service? And wasn't that a guy she'd given money to once, when he was standing outside of the bank? This couldn't all be a coincidence. It just couldn't.

"Mom!" she called out, but there was too much noise, and Betty didn't hear.

"Hey, College Girl," called a familiar voice. "College Girl, over here." Mia whipped around, and there was Patrick, long blond hair spilling out over the top of his parka. A gust of wind lifted a lock of it, momentarily obscuring his expression. When the hair fell back into place, she could read his mile-wide smile, even from here. Was she smiling like that, too? She must be. Patrick. This crowd was all Patrick's doing; she was certain of it. But how? "A magician never reveals his secrets," he had said. Well, he certainly didn't.

"Patrick," she called back, but she was blocked by the throng and couldn't move any closer.

"Who's that?" Eden wanted to know.

"That? That's just a friend," said Mia, trying to keep him within view as she walked.

"I've called the bank to let them know we would be coming," said Smyth, more to Cox than to Mia. "So you can expect a decent amount of security. Though I don't think they're going to be expecting this." He used his hand to indicate the group of people walking up the hill.

"No one was," said Cox. "They'll have to deal."

The group began to resemble a parade. Patrick was in his element working the crowd—he might as well have been campaigning for mayor—shaking hands, chatting up the women, nodding emphatically. She almost expected him to start handing out balloons, playing the kazoo, kissing babies. But he also kept her in his line of sight; every so often, she could see him looking over at her.

Mia, however, was too jittery to be enjoying any of this, strange and antic though it may have been. She was the one who had to worry about what would happen when they actually reached the bank. For most everyone else, it was just entertainment.

Cox reached the bank's doorway first. He looked at the detective and nodded.

"Everyone stand outside," said Smyth. One of the camera guys tried to slip by while his back was turned to the door. "Hey, that means you, too. What part of *outside* don't you understand?" The camera guy stepped back into the crowd.

"Okay, Mia," said Cox. "Let's go in."

Mia took a last look at the group assembled outside. She saw Patrick and Lloyd right up front. Reluctantly, she surrendered Eden's hand and urged her to go stand with her father. Eden gave Patrick a curious look before taking Lloyd's hand. Just behind them stood her mother, her brother, and, lo and behold, Gail. Julie. Fred. Bev. People she had worked with at various publishing houses. Mr. Ortiz and Inez. Solly Phelps, in a fedora. Reporters and photographers.

She turned and walked through the doors. There was the machine, just where it had always been. The velvet rope was gone; she saw no impediment now. Blauner stood alongside her while Smyth went into the bank. He brought over two uniformed security guards, along with a nervous-looking guy in an ill-fitting suit who must have been the manager.

"All right, Ms. Saul," said Blauner. "You can go ahead now."

Mia groped under her coat for the locket. She felt it at the hollow of her throat, right where it belonged. She took a step toward the machine. But before she could do anything, she heard a voice—Patrick's voice—rising up and over the assembled crowd.

"There she goes, folks. Just watch and see what she can do. She's amazing—a real live magician, only the magic's not make-believe, it's in her. I know, 'cause I've seen it. Watch and believe," he said. "You won't be disappointed."

Mia turned sharply around. Two of the cameramen had their lenses trained on Patrick; the redhead in green began talking rapidly into a cell phone.

"That guy." Cox rolled his eyes. "That's the nut who was in the courtroom yesterday."

"Go ahead, College Girl," Patrick called out, his gaze locking with Mia's. "Don't be afraid."

"What's going on?" asked the bank manager. He was shrinking inside the voluminous jacket. "Who is that man? Can you get him to shut up?"

"He's not doing anything wrong," said Mia. "He's just talking. He's allowed to talk, isn't he?" She felt sorry for the bank manager; the worry pulled his features, as if by magnetic force, to the center of his face, leaving the periphery bare and vulnerable.

"I don't want this getting out of hand," Blauner said. "There are a lot of people out there. We don't want a situation."

"You know him," Cox said to Mia. "Can't you get him to be quiet?"

"I'll try," Mia said, going to the door. "Patrick," she called out. "Patrick, these guys want you to chill, okay? They don't want any trouble."

"There won't be any trouble, College Girl. I'll make sure of that. I just want everyone to know who you are, what you've done."

"Let's just get on with it," said Smyth, who walked over to where they were standing. "The bank's got their security in place, and I've already called for some backup. They should be pulling up now." The door closed again; the group outside seemed eager, not hostile or violent.

"All right," said Mia, quietly. "All *right*." She walked resolutely up to the machine, inserted her card, and pressed the familiar commands. She had not a clue about what would happen. One hundred dollars, that was all she had ever asked for. Everything else had been a windfall—unearned, unexpected. For an awful moment, the machine was still. Was it out of order again? Or angry, in some inexplicable way, that she had drawn this crowd and was about to expose its secrets?

Then the screen changed color, the blue warming to periwinkle, violet, and, finally, a pale, celestial pink. The whirring started, followed by the strains, once again, of a harp. Words, this time in black, appeared on the screen:

You used it well.

Mia felt the hum and throb of the crowd behind her, but she didn't dare turn away. The words faded, leaving a rectangle as pink and glowing as the dawn. And then came the bills, thousands this time, all so crisp and fresh and new.

"Did you do it, College Girl? Did you?" Patrick somehow managed to yank open the door, outmaneuvering the policemen who stood in front of it.

"Yes!" she cried, spinning around and holding up the bills to show him. "Look, just look——" A sudden gust of wind blasted through the open door, and the bills were snatched from Mia's hand. They swirled around the bank's lobby, and a few of them flew out and into the street.

"Money!" cried someone in the crowd. "They're giving away free money!" Everyone surged forward, drawn by the bills.

"I've got a thousand!"

"Me, too!"

"I've got two—no, three!"

The police started moving forward, but they were not fast enough. The door was wide open now, and people flooded in: Patrick, Stuart, Gail, Betty, Lloyd. Fred hesitated, but when Bev charged ahead, he followed. Eden wriggled through the press of bodies.

"Let me see!" she crowed. "I want to see, too!"

The machine kept churning out bills—thousand after thousand— that were caught up by the billowing wind, blown and scattered to the amazed, delighted crowd. The police and the security officers vainly tried to catch them, but there were too many.

"Where are they coming from?" asked someone.

"Who cares?" was the reply. "Just make sure you get some!"

"You did it, College Girl!" Patrick laughed, grabbing her in his arms. "You fucking did it!" Mia looked at him, and at the two bills still clutched in her own hands. Then suddenly, she tossed her arms up and let the wind take the bills, blowing them around with all the others.

Cameras started rolling, and the news dolls began talking into their microphones. "We're live here in Brooklyn today to witness a most amazing occurrence . . ." began the one in orange.

"Coming to you live from Park Slope . . ." said the one in green.

"How can this be happening?" moaned the bank manager; he looked a little green, too, as if he might be sick. "What does it mean?"

But no one really heard him. Instead, they were all caught up in the thick, impossible swirl of bills, bills that were, to Mia's astonished gaze, like leaves, like seeds, like manna from heaven, raining down upon the waiting soil of the world.

EPILOGUE

THE STORY MADE the nightly news on NY1, Fox 5, and ABC. It ran in the three New York newspapers—the *Times*, the *Post*, and the *Daily News*—as well as in a smattering of papers across the country: Akron, Chicago, Fort Lauderdale, San Francisco, and Boston. There was a flurry of calls from TV and radio shows, the most memorable of which came from that most hallowed of all television goddesses, Oprah herself. In the end, though, Mia's appearance on the show was bumped by the story of a transgendered "man" who had given birth to twins. But Oprah's interest acted like blood in the water, and several TV executives eagerly came sniffing around. Mia sold the rights to her story to a twenty-six-year-old hotshot producer at HBO who planned to turn it into a movie. Plus, all the media attention gave her another edge: she was able to shine some unwelcome light on her slimeball landlord, forcing him, quite literally, to clean up his act. The junk was hauled out of the lobby; the hallways were washed and waxed; and, praise the Lord, the elevator was finally fixed. Lloyd got his act together, too—he started sending checks at regular intervals, and, since he was now back in the States, he set up a regular schedule for seeing Eden. Mia could tell he was impressed about the HBO offer; he even hinted about being introduced to her contacts there. How typically, totally Lloyd, Mia thought. Maybe she would actually introduce him to some of those HBO people. Then again, maybe not.

The court eventually decided that since the money had absolutely no explicable source and could not be traced, Mia was allowed to keep whatever she received from the machine. The branch of the bank near Mia's apartment closed down—temporarily, the sign said—but there was no indication of when, if ever, it would reopen. The ten-thousand-dollar bill, however, remained in police possession, still part of the on-going investigation into Weed's death. Then there was the locket, which Mia had taken to Sotheby's for appraisal. It was, in fact, a documented piece, missing for decades, and now rapturously welcomed back into the public eye. Mia put it up for auction, where it was purchased by a major museum for a substantial sum; she kept a small portion of the money and donated the rest to a nonprofit organization whose mission it was to kindle interest in poetry in the public schools. She was truly sorry to see it go. But when she learned of its history, she knew she was doing the right thing; truly, it belonged to the Keats lovers of the world, not around her neck.

Mia was sitting pretty now. Between the money she had socked away from the machine, the money from HBO, and the money from the sale of the locket, she was able to set up a college fund for Eden and buy a house on East Fifth Street, just off Caton Avenue. It was a small, lop-sided affair, with below-code wiring and floors so pitched you could roll marbles down them. But there was a slate mantelpiece where the (nonworking) fireplace sat, parquet floors under the buckled linoleum, and a backyard that was home to both a fig tree and a crab apple. There was also a separate apartment on the top floor, perfect for a tenant, once Mia got the place into some kind of decent shape. Which she did, hiring a dreadlocked Rastafarian contractor and spending every free minute she had trolling the aisles of Home Depot and Lowe's. After too many months of plaster- and Sheetrock-infused dust, she and Eden were ready to kiss Fourth Avenue a not-so-fond farewell and settle into their new home. There was even enough money for Mia to buy a used Prius, which was handy since she planned to invite both Luisa and Mr. Ortiz to visit, and she wanted to be able to ferry them back and forth.

It was early June by this point. The crab apple tree out back had al-ready bloomed, exquisitely, and its soft, candy-pink petals still carpeted the ground. Mia knew she ought to clean them up but really, they gave the place such an enchanted look—perfect for the engagement party she threw for Julie. The fig tree produced exactly two figs, both green and small and nearly juiceless, but there was always next year, right? Who knew just what fruit she might reap? She and Eden planted geraniums in the window boxes and started a compost pile in the yard. Her brother brought Gail and the girls for a visit; when she and Stu were briefly alone together in the kitchen, he handed her a large white box.

"What's this?" she asked.

"House-warming present," he said.

"The house is warm enough as it is," Mia said, strangely flustered. "I didn't put in central AC."

"Just open it, would you?"

Beneath the white tissue Mia found the painting of the birds' eggs she had spied—and loved—in Stuart's house, as well as an envelope containing a very generous check.

"You didn't have to," Mia said; she didn't know what meant more, the fact that he knew she would want the painting, or the amount of the check.

"I know. But I wanted to."

"That's a lot of money," she murmured.

"Use it well," Stuart said. His tone was light but his look, intense. "Isn't that your mantra these days?"

All That Trash won a coveted award for best nonfiction of the year; at the ceremony, to which both she and Eden were invited, the author, Howard Shapiro, kissed her on both cheeks and thanked her publicly for her role in his success. After that, she was offered not one but two plum editorial jobs, and had the unprecedented luxury of choosing between them.

EVERY NOW AND then, she ran into Fred, whose house was not far from hers. At first they kept each other at a palpable distance—only the briefest of nods, the curtest of hellos were exchanged. But one night, Mia got a frantic call from him saying that Dudley had been having seizures, and Fred was taking him to the emergency veterinary clinic on Warren Street; would she meet him there? Mia thought of Dudley, his heavy tread, his squashed face. Of course she would.

It turned out that the cat was in end-stage bladder cancer, and Mia remained in the room with Fred while the vet administered the injections that would quiet, and then still, his great feline heart. Afterward, Mia accepted Fred's offer of a ride home on his motorcycle, though she didn't invite him in. Instead, they sat on the front stoop together, Fred sobbing quietly and Mia gently rubbing small, concentric circles on his back until eventually the sobs subsided.

"Let me get you something to drink," she said, when she saw he had calmed down. "I made lemonade. Freshly squeezed. I could pour a splash of vodka in it, too."

"So now you're making drinks for me?"

"Why not?" she asked, trying to keep her tone light. "I'll be right back."

She returned to the stoop with two tall glasses and a wad of napkins on a tray. Fred accepted the drink and took a sip.

"Pretty good for an amateur," he said. She smiled, but didn't reply. "So," he began again. "Do you still see that guy? The one with all that hair?"

"Patrick," she said, though she was quite sure Fred knew his name. "Not really," she said. "Not anymore."

"Huh," he said. He didn't say anything else. But he let his shoulder lean against hers, and Mia did not move away. She found herself wanting to comfort Fred and, even more than that, heal him. What she felt might not have been love, but, as Bev had told her, who knew what the feeling might one day become?

MIA HAD SEEN Patrick exactly once since the media frenzy back in the winter. They'd had a wild night of it, too. But shortly after that, he'd disappeared. Calls went unreturned; his sister, Maureen, could offer little information.

"He just vanishes from time to time," was the only explanation she could offer.

"What do you do if you want to get in touch with him?" Mia had asked.

"You wait," said Maureen.

So Mia waited. And waited some more. Nothing. After a couple of months, she stopped thinking about him, at least on a daily basis. Instead, she thought about Fred. Wondered how he was, and if he were dating anyone new. Somehow, the thought did not please her. She found herself hoping she'd run into him in the neighborhood, and when she didn't, she circled closer and closer to his house, until finally, early one Saturday evening when Eden was off with Lloyd and the sky had turned that rich, blood-orange color that presaged a spectacular sunset, she saw him, coming down the stoop of his house, his motorcycle helmet tucked under his arm.

"You," he said, surprised but clearly not unhappy to see her. "What are you doing here?"

"It's a glorious night for a ride," she said. "Don't you think?" So he took her for a ride that night, and for one the following week, too. Still, they were slow with each other—slow and cautious, as if one of them might easily break. That was all right with Mia, though. More than all right, in fact.

Her heart, she discovered, was resilient in ways she would not have guessed. It was stretched, it was sore, but despite Patrick's silence, it was far from shattered. And it wasn't like she wasn't busy; what with supervising the renovation, finding tenants for the upstairs apartment, following the ins and outs of the movie deal, and settling into her new job, she had plenty to occupy her.

Then the card arrived. A bright glossy rectangle of palm trees and a sky as blue as a Renaissance painting. The postmark said Mexico.

I haven't forgotten you, College Girl. I never will. Don't know when or even if I'll be back. But the future is a wide and mighty place. Maybe I'll see you there.

Love from your Patrick

Patrick's handwriting was neat and even; dividend, no doubt, of all those years with the ruler-wielding nuns. Mia traced her finger over the careful loops and dips as she secured the card to the front of the refrigerator with a magnet. "A wide and mighty place," she said out loud, thinking not only of Patrick but of Fred, too. Who was she to say that it wasn't?

BREAKING
THE
BANK

YONA ZELDIS McDONOUGH

BOOK SUMMARY

Harried single mom Mia Saul tries to juggle her career, personal life, and raising her ten-year-old daughter, Eden, with not-so-great results. After her husband, Lloyd, leaves her for a manicurist, Mia struggles to regain some semblance of a normal life, but when her ex conveniently leaves the country and forgets to send child support, she finds herself scrambling to make ends meet. When she discovers a bank machine that bestows free money, Mia decides that she will share the wealth with those who need it as badly as she does.

QUESTIONS FOR DISCUSSION

1. Mia finds a magical ATM that dispenses free money. Do you think Mia made good decisions about dispersing the money? What would you do if you ever found such a machine?

2. The author opens the novel with the following epigraphs: "Money doesn't talk, it swears," a line from Bob Dylan;

and "Money talks, all right. It says good-bye," from author Richard Russo. Why do you think she chose those particular quotes?

3. Do you think Mia's family was justified in staging an intervention? How might they have handled it differently? Was her outrage appropriate?

4. Both Fred, the sweet, mild-mannered bartender, and Patrick, the unpredictable free spirit, intrigue Mia. Who do you think is better for her, and why?

5. What did you think about Gerald Mofchum, the enigmatic jeweler, and his mysterious disappearance after selling Mia the locket? Was obtaining the Keats locket just part of Mia's "magic"?

6. How would you describe Mia's parenting style? Do you think she is a good parent? Can you relate to her struggles as a single mom? How is her relationship with her own mother?

7. How does Mia's ex, Lloyd, undermine her relationship with Eden? How might she have handled Lloyd's visit differently?

8. In *Breaking the Bank*, Mia is editing a book about recycling and America's growing trash problem. How does she try to incorporate "green living" into her own life?

9. Mia seems to mourn the loss of her relationship with Stuart, her only brother. Why do you think they're not as close as they used to be? Why does she feel especially betrayed when she learns Stuart has been talking to Lloyd?

10. When Mia and Eden meet up with Lloyd and his new girl-friend, Suim, for dinner, Mia is surprised at her reaction to her ex: "And when he started to tackle the whole topic of wine, Mia was ready to take her fork and stab him in the thigh. Had he always been like this and she had just failed to notice? Or had she been so in love that she hadn't cared? . . . Mia, however, was beside herself, and she moved from annoyance to rage to finally, amazingly, something like relief." Why do you think her opinion of Lloyd changed?

11. Do you agree or disagree with Lloyd's decision to take Eden to his parents' place in North Carolina indefinitely? Is it a better environment for Eden?

12. When Mia finally breaks down and confesses where she's actually getting her money, Patrick believes her but Fred doesn't. Why do they respond differently? What do their reactions say about their characters?

13. After her ordeal is over, Mia discovers "her heart . . . was resilient in ways she would not have guessed. It was stretched, it was sore, but despite Patrick's silence, it was far from shattered." Were you surprised by Patrick's departure in the end? What lessons do you think Mia learned from her experience with the magical ATM?

A Conversation with Yona Zeldis McDonough

Q. Where did the inspiration for a magical ATM come from? What sort of research process did you undergo for this novel?

A. *I was having a conversation with my brother and he asked why whenever the bank made an error, it was always in their favor. I agreed, but was then reminded of an incident that happened years earlier (before the advent of ATMs) when a young teller gave me four hundred dollars more than I was supposed to get. I admit I got a little rush when I saw all that "found" money; it was thrilling and I had a few seconds of imagining what I might do with it. But I knew I couldn't keep it and so I returned to the window and pointed out the mistake to her. She was enormously grateful; it turned out she had only been on the job for a week or so, and her error would have gotten her fired. I told all this to my brother and it prompted me to think about what might have happened if the "giver" had not been a person but instead one of the by-now-ubiquitous ATMs. Would that have changed my feelings? Those musings were the first stirrings of this story.*

In order to research certain aspects of the novel, I consulted with the community outreach office at my local police precinct; they were able to show me around the building (my first time seeing an actual jail cell and a holding pen) and outline certain aspects of police procedure. I also did some research into U.S. paper currencies, and the ten-thousand-dollar bill, to find out if such a large denomination had ever existed, and if so, when.

Q. When beginning a new novel, do you have a set outline that you follow, or do you go where the narrative takes you?

A. *In writing fiction, I never work from an outline. Instead, I work from a voice that starts whispering, with varying degrees of intensity and urgency, in my ear. I wait to hear that voice and when I do, I am led by it. I feel like the writing, when it is going well, is less about invention and more about faithful transcription.*

Q. In your earlier works, such as *In Dahlia's Name* and *The Four Temperaments,* and also in *Breaking the Bank,* a central theme seems to be a strong sense of family. How important is family to you? How much inspiration do you draw from your real life?

A. *I think family is the primal narrative; it's the first cast of characters for every single person on earth. When I was younger and writing only short stories, my work was more concretely autobiographical, but in my novels, this has been less true. Instead, I've attempted to weave bits and pieces of my own experience into a larger fictional context. Sometimes the connections between the work and the life are apparent to me at the outset; other times, those connections are forged in a less conscious way and I become aware of them only after the fact.*

Q. You've written adult novels and a great many children's titles. How is writing for an adult reader different from writing for a young one? What made you decide to write in both genres?

A. *I wrote my first children's book because my mother, a painter and illustrator, came to me with a contract in hand. At the time, I wasn't sure if I wanted to write for children or if I even could. Now I find that I enjoy it very much; it offers an interesting and useful balance to the other work I do. The books that are most satisfying to me are the chapter books (I've written three), which are in effect novels for children.*

Q. Mia is a modern woman faced with all the agonies and ecstasies that go along with that. Did you set out to address the struggles that single working mothers face today?

A. *Not in any deliberate way, but once the character took hold, I realized that I could articulate the concerns, frustrations, and hopes of so many women who find themselves in this position.*

Q. You were the editor and a contributor to *The Barbie Chronicles: A Living Doll Turns Forty*. How did you come to be involved in this project?

A. *In 1998, I wrote an essay about how much I continued to love Barbie despite the backlash against her; the essay appeared in the Lives section of* The New York Times Magazine *and it generated sufficient interest for me to put together a book.*

Q. You wrote an article about thrift stores for *The New York Times* (December 5, 2008). Is thrift-store shopping a passion of yours?

A. *A deep and abiding passion. I've always been drawn to the lure of the old. The more worn, used, discarded, and abandoned it is, the better I love it. The smell of mildew gets my heart racing. I feel like I am rescuing these objects, finding meaning and value in what has been left behind.*

Q. What are you working on next?

A. *A novel about a fortyish former ballet dancer, somewhat bitter, somewhat dissatisfied, living in New York City. At the outset of the book, her younger sister dies suddenly, and the protagonist moves in with her brother-in-law to help out with her three young nieces and nephews.*

Q. If you were to find a magical ATM like Mia, what would you do with the money?

A. *Aha! The 64,000-dollar question! I think I'd splurge a little (redoing the kitchen, taking my daughter to Paris) and then make sure I had money tucked away for my children's education, my retirement, etc. And I hope I'd follow Mia's example and give a good bit of it away.*

ENHANCE YOUR BOOK CLUB

1. Mia has her tarot cards read by Fred's mother, Bev. Bring a set of tarot cards and do readings for your members. (You can use the book *Tarot Made Easy* by Nancy Garen, to help beginners interpret the cards.)

2. Mia, the lead character in *Breaking the Bank*, works on a book about environmental awareness. Discuss ways your book group can make a difference and adopt one "green" habit. Many websites can provide suggestions, such as www.campaignearth.org.

3. To find out more about author Yona Zeldis McDonough, check out her official site, www.yonazeldismcdonough.com, which includes information about her other titles as well as biographical information.